TRACELESS

Debra Webb

St. Martin's Paperbacks

This is a work of fiction. All of the characters, organizations and events portrayed in this novel are either products of the author's imagination or are used fictitiously.

TRACELESS

Copyright © 2007 by Debra Webb.
Excerpt from *Nameless* copyright © 2007 by Debra Webb.

Cover photo of woman © Herman Estevez.
Cover photo of town © John Halpern.

ISBN: 0-312-94222-2
EAN: 9780312-94222-9

Printed in the United States of America

St. Martin's Paperbacks edition / September 2007

St. Martin's Paperbacks are published by St. Martin's Press, 175 Fifth Avenue, New York, NY 10010.

10 9 8 7 6 5 4 3 2 1

DEDICATION

This book is dedicated to my family.

Nonie, my husband, without whom I would be lost. I would not have wanted to take this journey with anyone else. You truly are the reason I live and breathe.

My daughters. Erica, who has given my life depth and meaning and whose unfaltering determination inspires me to carry on no matter how insurmountable the task before me. Erica's soul mate, Ashley, a man who makes her happy and to whom I will always be grateful for doing so. My baby girl, Melissa, who has infused excitement and possibility into my very soul, and whose dreams remind me that our dreams are an open window to our futures where anything is possible if we only believe.

My niece, Tanya, who is like my daughter and who is always there when I need a backup plan, and who will forevermore be my traveling partner and partner in crime far and wide. Ray, Tanya's husband, for being the man of her dreams and whose dedication and genuineness is so rare in this life.

My brother, John, whose resiliency and resolve have my

undying respect, and for loving his big sister even when, at age nine, she satisfied her curiosity about flying by talking him into jumping off the roof with only a towel for a Superman cape. Our childhood adventures will always live in my heart.

My nephews, Robby and Chad, two totally handsome guys whose love and respect and compassion give me hope for the world's future. Chris, my youngest nephew and the "baby" of the family, who is as smart as a whip and who never fails to keep life interesting.

To my extended families, the Wrights and the Allens. You are special people in our lives . . . true friends which are so very rare. Thank you for taking Missy into your families like one of your own. A special thanks to Jimmy and KarenSue Allen for giving this story an early nod of encouragement.

Last, but never in a million years least, to my dearest friend, Donna. We are as different as night and day and yet the same somehow. My life would not be complete without you in it.

ACKNOWLEDGMENTS

First, I must thank Stephanie Kip Rostan, my agent, for her relentless faith in my ability to make this leap. Her expert guidance, keen eye for detail, endless patience and outstanding grasp on the industry amaze me. She is simply incredible. I will forever be in her debt.

Jennifer Weis, wow! It is an honor to have her as an editor. Her enthusiasm and vision are remarkable. The sheer excitement she generates inspires me to reach deeper, to push the limits of the creative process. Working with Jennifer and the team at St. Martin's is truly a privilege.

I sincerely want to thank teachers across America. As a dedicated parent volunteer for a number of years in the public school system, I am keenly aware of the hard work and dedication required to be a teacher. You are the people who shape our future, you have the most important job of all: teaching our children. I am ashamed of those who pretend to be one of you and who dare to harm a child.

Small-town law enforcement is another group of sometimes overlooked heroes. Not often in the limelight, the village chief or sheriff carries an awesome burden: keeping the citizens safe. More often than not, this burden is carried with insufficient resources. I salute all who take on that burden. Though we rarely say so, we need you, we thank you.

I have a few friends in the business I must thank. Vicki Hinze, for being so much more than a critique partner. You are an extraordinary woman. You reminded me that I could. Rita Herron and Julie Miller, for being wonderful friends who listen without judging and who never fail to make me feel better no matter what is going on. Stephanie Hauck Bond, for being an endless supply of encouragement and knowledge. You are an inspiration to us all. Beverly Beaver Barton, for being you. Your work ethic and love of the craft and willingness to share is a pattern by which all should follow. Don't ever stop being you. Linda Howard, for forging the way. We all owe you.

This lady has to have her own paragraph. Rhonda Nelson. We began this journey together. You have always believed in me and cheered me on. Thank you. The trip would have been so boring without you.

Lastly, to my readers, thank you. You have given me this opportunity. You make the stories come to life.

CHAPTER ONE

Holman Prison
South Alabama
Monday, July 15, 8:05 A.M.

The gray prison walls loomed behind Clint as he moved forward, his steps hindered by the manacles connecting his wrists and ankles with lengths of chain designed to impede movement. The shackles had been one last humiliation. *For old times' sake,* the warden had said. The guards on either side of Clint had snickered and snorted as they carried out that final order. Clint had simply stood there and allowed the bastards to do what they would.

For more than ten years his choices had not been his own. Accepting that reality had equated to survival.

No more.

The early-morning sun drew his gaze to the sky. Clint closed his eyes a moment to relish the welcome warmth. He couldn't remember the last time he'd been allowed to come outside. It had been months, at least.

The law said he got one hour a day in the fresh air, but that privilege had been cut long ago with a sham of an excuse. The guards liked putting pressure on inmates, amping up their anxiety level. They especially liked doing it to Clint. Just another attempt at causing him to fuck up.

Clint hadn't let the bastards get to him. He'd taken the punishments, the beatings for no apparent reason, the forgotten meals, all of it . . . without so much as a word in argument or the slightest effort in retaliation.

He'd played by every single rule. Now his freedom was so close he could taste it . . . smell it. There was nothing anyone could do to stop him from walking away.

As if to deny that certainty, fear, bone cold and irrational, trickled inside him.

A muscle in his jaw jerked with the pressure of holding back the questions about what happened next that he suddenly wanted to ask. The parole board had made its decision. He was free. The guards, the warden, no one here could prevent Clint from leaving. The affirmation rang hollowly inside him.

The command was given and the twelve-foot-high gate topped with its concertina wire yawned open, creaking and groaning as if it, too, was reluctant to permit his long-awaited departure. The *boddom,* the pits of hell called Holman Prison, didn't like vomiting back up the men it devoured. At least not until they were properly punished as God and the warden saw fit.

That trickle of fear widened into a stream of pure panic, knotting Clint's gut, clamping around his chest like unyielding arms. He'd waited for this moment for so long. The blood rushed to his brain and exploded there in a burst of sheer terror, urging him to go back . . . to seek the security and sanctuary of that five-by-eight cell—the only place he'd felt the least bit safe for so damned long.

Fighting the impulse, he aimed his attention on the hope that open gate presented. His hands clenched into fists as the muscles in his legs cramped with the compulsion to run, but the shackles and the fear kept him paralyzed. Sweat squeezed from his pores as the air sawed in and out of his lungs. He ordered himself to be still. To focus. No sudden moves. The remembered pain from far too many reminders of that hard-earned lesson stung through his body.

The guard on Clint's right unlocked the cuffs around his wrists, then gave him the key. He bent down, his hands shaking, and released the steel bands circling his ankles. As he straightened, he handed the key back; then he froze.

What now? He'd been given no specific exodus orders, no directions on how to proceed. Reason had deserted him, leaving his already raw senses cluttered with confusion and doubt.

"What the hell you waitin' for, Austin?" The guard on Clint's left nudged him in the spleen with his baton. "Get the fuck outta here before we decide to keep your sorry ass."

Clint's heart rammed against his chest, urging him to act. Another prod from the baton ignited his long-slumbering fury, fueling the courage that had betrayed him this morning. He stepped away from the impotent shackles, resisted the temptation to break loose and run without ever looking back.

The guards would be watching, hoping he would make a move of aggression . . . itching to use the weapons stationed at their hips. The snipers in the towers would be clocking his every move through the scopes of their high-powered rifles, praying for the opportunity to rid the planet of one more worthless piece of shit. It didn't matter that he was unarmed; they would have a story to cover up whatever played out this morning.

Not going to happen. He was out of here.

Clint took the four paces necessary to put him beyond the boundary of the fence that surrounded what had been his home for an eternity; then he stopped stone still. He turned around slowly, his hands hanging loosely at his sides in the expected submissive stance. His gaze met the warden's where he stood shielded by the guards, and Clint felt himself smile for the first time in over a decade.

He didn't say a word, didn't bother with any dramatic offensive gestures, no matter how deserving; he simply stared at the man, forced him to face the cold, hard truth . . . he had lost this battle. Those three or four brief seconds almost made the years of pain and suffering worth it.

Almost.

Turning his back, Clint walked, his steps measured and deliberate, toward the visitor's entrance where his ride out of here waited.

The feel of unwashed denim and stiff polyester chafed his skin. His toes were stuffed into the cheap shoes that had no doubt been ordered a size or two too small for the sole purpose of ensuring his discomfort. It was one of the perks of surviving an Alabama prison. When and if you were released, you left wearing new clothes and in possession of whatever personal items you'd surrendered upon arrival. In Clint's case it wasn't much. His wallet that contained an expired driver's license and twenty bucks.

There wouldn't be much in the way of financial assets waiting for him back home. But he would have full access to the one thing that he wanted nearly more than his next breath . . . .

The people who had stolen his life.

Samford Medical Research Facility
Birmingham, Alabama
9:15 A.M.

Your concerns were duly noted, but the decision has been reached and executed.

Emily Wallace sat at her desk, her fingers clenched on the arms of her chair, as the words reverberated inside her.

How could the parole board let this happen?

A convicted killer was being allowed to walk after only ten years—half his sentence.

Unwillingly, she filled her lungs, the repetitive action suddenly a burden. Medical records and reports that needed to be filed stood in mounds on her cluttered desk, vying unsuccessfully for her attention. She hadn't been able to concentrate on work for the past week. Hadn't been able to think of anything but the results of the hearing.

And now it was over.

She thought of the somber faces on that board as she'd offered all the reasons for Clint Austin's continued incarceration. Not so much as a flicker of emotion had slipped past those unfeeling masks as Heather's father had echoed those same pleas. They didn't care. It wasn't their daughter or friend who had died. One board member had gone so far as to say that she had read the trial transcript and felt the preponderance of evidence had been insufficient for a conviction in the first place. She'd gone on to toss out scenarios suggesting Clint Austin's innocence, each one a slap in the face to those who had loved Heather Baker.

Only moments ago the district attorney's office had called to confirm Emily's worst fears. She hadn't been able to move since dropping the receiver back into its cradle.

It was official now.

He was free.

The wail of Emily's own remembered screams filled her head, drowning out all other thought. She told her mind to quiet, but it refused. Like a faulty fluorescent light, images from that night flickered one after the other. Her old room in the house on Ivy Lane with the retro sixties stripes and the posters of her rock star idols plastered on the walls. The tiedyed comforter on her bed . . . and Heather lying there in a pool of blood. Gaping wounds marring her beautiful face . . . her slender arms.

He was there. His hands on Heather's throat, blood all

over him. Emily had tried to pull him off, but he was too strong. Beyond the horror in her room she had heard the sirens in the distance . . . so damned far away. Finally she'd managed to push Clint Austin aside and then she'd seen the other wound on her friend's throat. Nothing Emily had attempted had stanched the flow pulsing from that fatal gash . . . all that blood had just kept seeping out around her fingers.

And then the police were everywhere . . . the paramedics had urged Emily out of the way. Everything had happened so fast and yet it was all too, too late.

Heather was dead.

The room tilted and Emily's stomach churned violently. Moving with extreme caution, she stood, her legs trembling, then walked stiffly, slowly, to the ladies' room.

Fortunately, all three stalls were empty. Having anyone bear witness to her breakdown would only lead to questions. Questions she couldn't bear to answer. She went into the first stall, closed the door, and dropped to her knees in the nick of time. Her stomach heaved viciously. She vomited until there was nothing left before wiping her mouth with the back of her hand and collapsing on the cold tile floor.

She couldn't be sure how much time passed, but she cried until no more tears would come, until pain had gathered in a fierce band around her skull. Each breath proved a monumental task with the weight of guilt crushing against her chest.

She had failed.

Her friend was dead. Emily hadn't been able to save her all those years ago and now hadn't been strong enough to keep her killer behind bars.

Emily had failed her friend twice.

A decade's worth of rage lashed so abruptly inside Emily that she twitched with the force of it. The fury obliterated the weaker emotions in an instant. She sat up straighter and leaned her throbbing head against the wall of the stall.

He was out.

How the hell could she sit here wallowing in self-pity like this? There was more she could do. More she had to do.

The law could set him free, but that didn't mean she had to give up for one second on proving what she knew in her heart.

He was guilty.

He would pay for what he'd done. A mere ten years wasn't nearly compensation enough. There had always been the possibility that this day might come. All she had to do was be strong. It wasn't over until she said it was over.

Emily braced a hand on the toilet seat and levered herself to her feet. Still feeling a little unsteady, she flushed the toilet and pushed out of the stall. She washed up and headed back to her office, mentally ticking off the list of things she would need to do before leaving: clear her desk, transfer her calls to the switchboard, and divide up her workload between two of the file clerks in her department.

In a few hours she could be on her way to Pine Bluff to do what had to be done.

Clint Austin would not be free for long.

CHAPTER TWO

Jackson County
11:18 A.M.

Clint took in the familiar passing landscape like a starving man introduced to an all-you-can-eat buffet for the first time. A hell of a lot had changed in ten years, but the closer they got to Pine Bluff the more things looked the same, as if the hole-in-the-wall that was his hometown had been frozen in time. Equal parts dread and anticipation coagulated low in his belly.

"You listening to me, Clint?"

Clint aimed one of those cold stares that had backed down more trouble than he cared to recall at the driver. "Yeah, sure."

Three hours on the road and Chief of Police Ray Hale had tried initiating a conversation several times, but Clint had no desire to talk or even to make the effort. The idea that Ray was likely the only friend Clint had should have but didn't arouse the necessary motivation.

He and Ray hadn't actually ever been friends, just acquaintances. Ray had graduated from high school the year before Clint. He'd been a green recruit on the Pine Bluff police force a decade ago, but now he was the chief and, truth told, he was probably the main reason Clint was free.

He was free.

He inhaled deeply. Even the air smelled different outside those damned prison walls. Gone was the heavy stench of days-old sweat and perpetual fear. A shudder rocked through him before he could stop it. He was never going back there.

"I know it isn't fair, Clint," Ray went on in spite of the lack of interest from his captive audience, "but the folks around here are going to expect a man filled with remorse and humility. Do you think you can handle that for a little while?"

Like Clint gave one shit what people in this damned town expected. Ray should give it a rest. No way was he going to make Clint feel what he wanted him to feel. . . . Ray couldn't make Clint say what he wanted him to say.

"Mr. Higgins is offering you a job at his repair shop, and your mama's place is ready to move into."

Guilt broadsided Clint and he flinched. His mama was dead. Six years now. His request to attend her funeral had been denied by the warden. Clint's fingers fisted into tight balls of contempt. That was one son of a bitch if given the opportunity Clint was pretty sure he could kill and never feel the slightest guilt.

But he couldn't let anger rule him. He'd done that at first and he'd paid the price. Prison wasn't the place to go with a chip on your shoulder, especially if you didn't possess the necessary skills to back it up. What the hell did a nineteen-year-old kid who'd thought he was a tough guy back home know about surviving prison life with hard-core criminals?

Not a damned thing.

"Everything's pretty much set," Ray went on, determined not to let the one-sided conversation lull. "Be sure to keep in mind that a job is one of the conditions of your parole."

Clint surprised himself and said, "I'll talk to Higgins about the job." His voice sounded rough and unfamiliar, even to his own ears, but then there hadn't been a lot of need to talk where he'd been.

Ray made the final turn that would take Clint home. The house, weathered barn, and plot of land his mama had owned sat five or so miles outside Pine Bluff proper, surrounded by nothing but woods and mountains and dusty dirt roads going nowhere.

"You've paid your debt to society," Ray added, as if he hadn't said enough already. "Start clean from here, Clint. Don't be looking back." His gaze shifted to Clint's as he came to a stop in the driveway. "Looking back will only create problems you'll regret."

The naïve police chief had no idea. Regret was something Clint had learned not to feel, along with a host of other emotions. As if to contradict him, his heart started that fierce pounding that made him feel out of control. He had to concentrate hard to make it slow. That was the thing about prison; there wasn't much a man could regulate outside his own emotions. Getting real good at that kind of control had been Clint's only escape.

But he was home now and with that came baggage he couldn't hope to dismiss with the usual techniques. Adjustments would need to be made to ensure no one got too close. He couldn't afford to let that happen.

His gaze settled on the place he'd called home before his life had gone to hell. The aged, peeling paint left the small frame house a ghostly shade of silvery white. The yard was freshly mown, probably Ray's doing. Even the perennial plants Clint's mother had cultivated year after year were in bloom. He felt his chest expand with air. He hadn't realized until then that he'd stopped breathing.

He was back.

"Power's on," Ray said. "Well's working fine. The ladies from church came over and did a little cleaning. I stocked the kitchen so you wouldn't have to worry about that for a few days." He propped his elbow in the open window of the driver's side door. "You'll need to go into town to meet with Lee Brady, your parole officer. Be best if you did that today. Other than that, you might want to take some time before running into any unnecessary . . . situations." He shrugged. "I know it'll be tough for a while."

Situations. Ray meant before showing his face around town any more than necessary. Before coming into contact with the folks who'd stolen a major portion of his life for a crime he hadn't committed.

Clint shifted his attention from the house to the man sitting behind the wheel. Anger whipped through Clint before he could stop it. "I don't need your pity or your advice, Ray." He knew he should have simply said, *Thanks,* but he didn't.

Ray let go another of those heavy, exasperated sighs. "That attitude won't help," he offered in response to Clint's edict. "Most folks don't want you back here. But, with time and patience, it'll all blow over."

Clint stared at the house he hadn't set foot inside in over ten years. "I don't give a damn what they think."

"That may be," Ray countered, "but your anger won't keep you from feeling the shame. You might think it will, but it won't."

Clint didn't remember the last time he'd laughed at something anyone else said, but the words prompted the strained sound from his throat. "That's where you're wrong, Ray. There isn't a damned thing these people can do that will make me feel anything at all."

Clint opened the truck's door and Ray put a hand on his arm, making him hesitate before getting out and sending a new surge of tension through him. He didn't like being touched, but he let it go this once.

"You have every right to be bitter, Clint. But what the hell good is your freedom if all you're going to do is wrestle with a past you can't change?"

Clint didn't answer. He got out of the truck, didn't look back or say good-bye as he strode forward. Ray's well-meaning counsel was something he didn't need. He didn't need anything or anyone. He wasn't wasting the effort pretending. He had his own agenda, and nothing or no one was going to get in his way.

He walked up the steps and across the front porch to the door; his hand shook as he unlocked it. Gravel crunched as Ray drove away. The silence settled around Clint and still he hesitated before going in, waited for permission the way he'd been trained—like a dog—to do. That automatic reaction renewed the anger simmering deep inside him. He didn't need anyone's permission to enter his own goddamned house.

He crossed the threshold, elbowed the door closed behind him, and trembled as a flood of memories washed over him. The house still smelled like her. Felt like her. His chest ached. Same old worn-out furnishings. Same framed photos scattered about, glimpses of his history. Such as it was. He'd graduated from high school by the skin of his teeth, but he hadn't cared. His future had been all mapped out. He'd owned a fast car, had a slick job, women begging for a date with him, and was the envy of the town's male population. Life had been full of promise.

But that happy-go-lucky arrogance had deserted him hard and fast as he lay facedown on a cold concrete floor his first night in prison.

Pushing aside the memories, he walked to the fireplace and picked up the porcelain music box that sat amid the other cheap knickknacks on the mantel. At seventeen he'd gotten his first decent-paying job. Sylvester Fairgate had paid Clint fifty bucks to deliver a message to a scumbag who owed him money. That had been the beginning of Clint's tough-guy reputation and his barely legal career. No one could believe he'd driven to Decatur and waltzed into Frank Dennison's TV repair shop that fronted a small-time bookie operation and passed along the warning issued by Fairgate.

Lots of balls, not nearly enough brains.

Afterward Clint had gone straight to Treasures Gift Shop and bought the music box. He'd seen his mama stop many times at the big trinket-filled window to admire the porcelain image of a red-haired beauty in a flowing gown playing a baby grand piano. When he'd given his mama the present, she'd cried and insisted he take it back. He'd refused. She'd cried some more before finally accepting his gift and thanking him again and again. That silly music box had meant the world to her.

The mistakes he'd made had hurt her. Maybe even worse than those of his no-good, low-down daddy. That bastard had taken off when Clint was four years old. Just another bad-luck chapter in the life and times of Clint Austin.

He wandered through the house, feeling restless and wary. If he'd been smart, he would have headed anywhere but here. But no one had ever accused him of being a rocket scientist.

He pushed open the door to his room and felt a ripple of surprise. His mother had painstakingly put everything back just exactly as it had been before the police had ripped it apart looking for evidence. Evidence they hadn't found.

Hatred seared him. He'd been at the wrong place at the wrong time. They'd had nothing on him, except bad timing, stupidity, and the testimony of one person.

Emily Wallace.

Jaw clenched, he picked up his senior yearbook, still prominently displayed atop the dresser. He wondered how many times his mother had thumbed through it wishing for happier days. He paused on the page showcasing the varsity cheerleaders. There she was, all smiles alongside her best friend, Heather Baker.

He had thought Emily was the prettiest girl he'd ever seen. No matter how many girls he dated, she was the one he fantasized about in bed each night during those final minutes before drifting off to sleep. But she'd been out of his league, a good girl from a well-to-do family.

Long dark hair, big brown eyes. He'd wanted her so badly.

That desire had served as the primary motive behind his actions, according to the district attorney. Clint had been obsessed with Emily and had decided that if he couldn't have her, no one could. Only it wasn't Emily who'd been sleeping in her bed that night, and when he had realized his mistake it had been too late; Heather was mortally wounded. That was the State's version of what happened, and they had stuck to it, all the way to closing arguments. The jury had unanimously agreed.

Clint slammed the yearbook closed and walked out of the room full of pointless memories.

Emily Wallace was the main reason he'd spent the past ten years in hell. She was the reason his mother's heart had given out far sooner than it should have, ensuring that he lost the last thing in this world that he cared about.

The whole damned town had been on Emily's side.

The bitterness twisted like barbed wire in his gut. Someone else had killed Heather Baker. Clint might not be able to prove it, but he knew it . . . because it sure as hell hadn't been him. And maybe, just maybe, if he dug around long and hard enough, stirred the pot until folks got riled up, the real killer would get nervous and bob to the surface.

It didn't matter how long it took. Clint had nothing but time. He would focus primarily on the one other person who had been in the room that night.

She was the reason he was back.

Pine Bluff
3:15 P.M.

Preparation was essential. In order for Emily's effort to be of any benefit, she needed to familiarize herself with any and all infractions that translated into parole violations. Austin's slightest mistake could work to her advantage. She wanted him back in prison. The sooner the better.

As long as she lived and breathed, *he* would not get away with what he'd done. The only way to make sure that happened was to come back to Pine Bluff and get it done.

She owed it to Heather.

Emily rarely visited her hometown, and when she did she conscientiously avoided other people. Yet here she stood, hesitating at the corner of the block where the streets and the sidewalks crisscrossed on the western end of Pine Bluff's Courthouse Square. The very heart of town. Once she rounded that corner the pedestrian traffic would be heavier and the likelihood of running into someone who recognized her would be much greater. She'd spent her entire senior year in high school the object of the whole town's morbid curiosity, and then there had been the breakdown she still hadn't lived down in her parents' eyes. The painful memories whispered through Emily, reminded her of just how bad it had been. She'd been running away from it ever since.

No more running. She squared her shoulders and strode determinedly around the corner. The sidewalk wasn't as busy as she'd anticipated, allowing her to relax marginally. She picked up her pace, trying not to linger too long in front of any one particular storefront. Most looked the same other than a little new paint or decorating. Cochran's Shoes, Half Moon Café, she'd loved both places as a kid. And Hodges's Drugstore. She'd spent part of one summer working behind the old-fashioned soda fountain counter there. An eternity ago.

As she neared the middle of the block, the crowd of people gathered at the eastern corner caused her to falter. The shouting reminded her of a rally she'd accidentally gotten caught up in back in college. She couldn't make out the words being chanted. Hand-painted signs that displayed threatening slogans such as "The Wages of Sin Is Death" and "Prison Was Too Good for You" jogged above the sea of faces.

A demonstration against Austin's return, she realized slowly. The idea that all these people were protesting at this particular spot because Austin's parole officer had an office on that corner of the square suddenly sank in.

That could mean Austin was in there.

Her palms started to sweat and her heart began that pointless race against disaster. She should just go back to her car and go home. She could talk to Mr. Brady tomorrow. She could ask the necessary questions by phone and avoid a face-to-face meeting altogether.

The shouting grew more frantic as the crowd grudgingly parted for someone to pass. Emily's lungs refused to take in any air.

It was *him*.

She recognized the way he moved. Long, confident strides that had once made her heart stop, then thump wildly. Fluid grace combined with the bad-boy good looks that had made her pray that this time, just maybe, she would be the girl he was coming to talk to.

He came closer. Her mouth felt as if she'd gone days without water. She couldn't move. Couldn't run away. He would walk right past her. Would he recognize her? Would he stop?

She fell back a step, flattened against the brick facade in a futile attempt to become invisible. She should go back to her car . . . slip into a store . . . run like hell . . . anything to get out of his path.

A dozen or so yards away he abruptly darted across the street before continuing westward—toward her but with the width of the too-narrow street between them. Relief made her knees weak, allowed her to breathe again.

He reached for the door of a car . . . his car. The red vintage Firebird he'd driven all those years ago. When he would have gotten into the driver's seat, he stopped as if someone said his name . . . or as if he felt her watching him.

Emily's heart lurched when his gaze locked with hers. Even from thirty feet away she felt the focused intensity of those gray eyes. She tried to look away but couldn't master the necessary motion.

Every horrifying detail of that night flashed in vivid 3-D color. The blood . . . the struggle. The pain of knowing that nothing Emily had done had been enough . . . that her mistake was the reason her best friend was dead.

Austin broke eye contact first, then got into his car.

Time and place returned with jarring force as he backed out of the parking slot and sped away. Utter clarity washed over Emily for the first time since that night. She had tried to pull Austin away from her friend. She'd hit at him with her fists, screamed at him to stop. All to no avail. It would have been so easy. No one would have blamed her for actions that certainly would have amounted to self-defense. The knife he'd used on Heather had been lying right there on the floor . . . within easy reach. That was where Emily had made her second mistake.

She should have killed him when she had the chance.

CHAPTER THREE

Probation and Parole Office
3:25 P.M.

The trouble had already begun, not a block from City Hall. Police Chief Ray Hale had no intention of allowing this first wave of community reaction to trigger a domino effect. It was his job to ensure this kind of thing didn't happen.

For ten years his town and the people he served had gone on with their lives, allowing old wounds to heal and a painful tragedy to fade into memory. Now the worst of Pine Bluff's past had been resurrected and there appeared to be nothing he could do to stop the gathering momentum. He felt the shift in the air like the accumulating charge of an electrical storm.

Ray had thought the weight of responsibility he felt would lessen once Clint Austin was a free man again. But that hadn't happened. If anything, the reverse was true considering the reality Ray had had to face this morning. The man he'd brought home from prison wore a hard mask of chilling indifference. Strict regulations had required that Clint keep his black hair shorter than before. The pallor that spoke of little or no exposure to the sunlight had stolen the glow of youth and vigor he'd once radiated. Sometime during his incarceration a nasty laceration had left a prominent scar just beneath his left cheekbone. His lean, wiry frame had morphed into a more heavily muscled build. But the most telling change was in his eyes. Dull, lifeless gray reflecting an unnerving emptiness.

No, Clint was not the same man Ray had known back in high school or even in those final days before the trial had ended. For that he felt deep regret.

To top off this crappy day, only steps from the courthouse Troy Baker and his friends had orchestrated a protest to publicly lodge their complaints regarding Clint's release. Ray heaved a lungful of frustration. Troy was a good man, under normal circumstances very levelheaded. But this situation was anything but normal. Troy's sister had been the victim. His family had tried everything within their power to stop Clint's bid for parole to no avail, ultimately accepting the decision the parole board had made. Troy's intentions, however, had not changed and were as obvious as if he'd thrown down a gauntlet. He would not rest until he was satisfied with the price Clint had paid. If Ray could talk some sense into Troy, that one step would go a long way in keeping down the trouble. Others would be taking their cues from his actions.

To escape the crowd still loitering outside, Deputy Mike Caruthers herded the ringleaders of the disturbance into Lee Brady's office, giving the whole lot a good chewing out along the way. Mike's red hair and multitude of freckles gave him the look of a rather large Opie Taylor from Mayberry, but he was no pushover small-town deputy. Ray counted on him more than anyone else in the department. They'd been best friends since first grade, had graduated from high school together and gone onto the police academy to serve the town they loved. Mike had no patience for this business, either. He was just as pissed off at these guys as Ray and was making no bones about it.

For the most part, Pine Bluff was a picturesque southern town filled with law-abiding citizens where life was generally peaceful and uncomplicated. A place where folks supported one another through the good times as well as the bad. The problem was Clint Austin's release didn't fit neatly into either of those categories. As God-fearing folks, the citizens of Pine Bluff would want to support a man's bid for a second chance at living righteously. But anyone who offered a hand to Austin was, in effect, turning a hand against the Bakers. In their eyes he would always be a killer. Only time would make a difference, and only if folks would let it.

Lee Brady sidled up next to Ray. "Chief, I hope this isn't any indication of what's to come."

Ray wanted to reassure the man who had been saddled with the job of serving as the parole officer on this case, but he couldn't make any real guarantees, especially in light of Clint's own attitude. "I'll do all I can, Lee."

Troy Baker ambled into the office last, with Mike's prodding, and aimed his considerable fury at Ray. "Did you drive all the way to Holman to pick up that murdering sonofabitch?"

Ray steeled for the full brunt of the storm. Telling Troy to take a breath would be pointless. "Yes, I did. I felt it was my duty as chief of police to escort Austin back to town and to ensure he understood what I'd be expecting of him now that he's served his time."

"I can't believe you'd take his side," Troy roared. His hands planted on his hips, he turned to his accomplices. "My sister is dead and our chief is seeing after the needs of her killer."

The flash from Grady Lassiter's camera signaled that he'd captured the moment on film. Lassiter was co-owner of the *Pine Bluff Sentinel* and was undoubtedly only too happy to be on hand to document the whole drama for the local paper. By tomorrow morning even those folks who'd moved to

Pine Bluff since the trial would know all about Clint Austin and the gruesome singular murder in the town's history. Sides would be taken and the community would be torn apart all over again.

Larry Medford, Perry Woods, and Keith Turner, the same Turner whose daddy had donated to the department an entire fleet of brand-new official vehicles, including two four-wheel-drive Jeeps, stood in the background. All except Keith worked at the aluminum plant with Troy, and unlike the others, Keith appeared to have kept his cool. Seemed a little ironic to Ray, considering Keith had more reason than most to be out of sorts. But he'd learned to maintain his composure from the man who wrote the book on perception and power—Granville Turner. Keith's dear old daddy owned half the county and was another citizen who wouldn't be happy about Clint's release. Ray knew he'd be hearing from Granville any time now. Just something else to look forward to.

"Ray," Keith said with all the calm self-assurance he'd learned from his old man, "we don't want Austin back here. All he'll do is remind us of what we've lost. We just want to protect our wives and children, and our community. That's what this protest was really about."

"Don't waste your breath," Troy snarled, still glaring at Ray. "He's been helping Austin all along. I heard he visited that bastard nearly every month the whole time he was in prison. Even gave the parole board a favorable recommendation on Austin's behalf. Didn't you, *Chief*?"

Ray tamped down his irritation. Somebody had to think rationally in this situation, no matter that Troy's blatant disrespect made Ray want to kick him square in the ass.

"Yes, I did," Ray confirmed. "Clint Austin has served his time. He's a free man and he has every right to return to his home if he wishes. I represent all the citizens of this town, Troy, not just a chosen few. I intend to see that Austin is treated fairly and that he doesn't do anything to violate his parole. You'd be doing the whole town a favor if you settled down and tried to act like the Christian son I know your mama and daddy raised."

The words did not have the desired effect. "You go right ahead and do your duty," Troy threatened, "but don't think for a second I'll ignore mine. She was my sister, damn you, and I won't let her killer roam the streets a free man without trying to make his life the living hell it should be. That's *my* duty."

The challenge was on the table, but Ray wasn't going there with all Troy's buddies chomping at the bit for a fight.

"This public spectacle was not only uncalled for; it was conducted without a permit." Ray made eye contact with each man in turn. "You'd all be well advised to remember that Austin has rights the same as you. We may not always agree with the law, but we all have an innate responsibility to abide by that law. I don't want to hear of any of you letting emotion cause you to cross that line."

"That line," Troy butted in with a dramatic slam of his fist against Ray's desk, "has already been crossed."

Troy Baker did an about-face and exited with the same arrogant fury with which he'd entered. His supporters filed out right behind him.

"Damn, Ray," Mike said with a shake of his head. "They aren't going to make this easy. I don't think there's a man in the department who would want to be in your shoes right now."

Ray doubted there was a soul on earth who'd willingly take his place just now. But the truly disturbing part was that this was only the beginning. "We'll just have to do what we have to do." Certainly none of the players, Clint and Troy in particular, seemed inclined to play nice. That left the full burden of acting as mediator and keeping down the risk of unnecessary trouble squarely on Ray's back.

Mike hitched a thumb toward the door. "I'll make sure they go on home."

Ray nodded. "Don't forget to drive by the Austin place."

"Will do," his deputy and friend called on his way out.

Technically the Austin place was just outside Pine Bluff city limits and fell under the county's jurisdiction. But Ray had briefed the sheriff on the situation and they had worked out an agreement on how any trouble would be handled. Ray and his deputies would take care of whatever came up unless they needed backup, and then the sheriff's department would step in. This was the city of Pine Bluff's mess, and Ray wanted to handle it personally. He knew these folks; they knew him. The last thing he wanted was for someone who wasn't familiar with the situation to make a rash decision.

If Troy had a lick of sense he would stay away from Clint. The man Ray brought home today gave the subtle but undeniable impression of danger. Clint Austin had paid his debt to society in one of the harshest prisons in the country. No one walked away without scars. Some thought the killers and rapists behind those bars deserved no better. Ray didn't exactly disagree. Unless they were . . .

He stopped himself. Why the hell was he going down that road? There was no changing the past, no righting old wrongs or chances for doing over stupid mistakes. There was only here and now and the choices to be made from this moment forward. Everything else was pretty much a waste of time. That was the point he needed to get across to everyone, including Clint.

As hard as life in prison had been, what Clint was about to face might be worse. Running interference on his behalf was imperative. Ray owed him that.

Truth was, Ray owed him a hell of a lot more. But the truth was something that wouldn't help anyone now. Not poor dead Heather Baker. And not the angry, bitter Clint Austin.

Some things were better left in the past where they belonged.

"*Oh, my God!* Did you see all that?"

Justine Mallory refused to react, even as most of the ladies in the shop hovered at the front window to gawk at the unpleasant scene breaking up on the street. You would think the Almighty himself had appeared on the courthouse steps.

They had all wanted to get a final glimpse of *him*. Clint Austin, the resident convicted killer.

"I can't believe they let him out after only ten years," Jean Cook, the shop's manager, declared indignantly.

Justine bit her tongue rather than say what was on her mind. Clint Austin didn't deserve their avid curiosity, much less all the fanfare that had gone on outside.

"Well, personally I don't think we'll ever know the whole story on that one." Cathy Caruthers, perm rods still dripping, strolled back to her chair. "Mike and I discussed the issue just last night. All the deputies are talking about it."

Cathy liked reminding everyone that she was almost an attorney about as frequently as she liked cheating on the husband she crowed over. That was the trouble with a man in uniform; it seemed he never had time to pay proper attention. Such a travesty.

"Didn't look like he's been wasting away in a cell all this time," Violet Manning-Turner commented, one professionally waxed eyebrow arched in distaste. Violet had always thought herself a cut above the rest. A concept perpetuated by the idea that she'd married far better than she deserved.

Truth was, Clint Austin had always been good-looking. Justine doubted prison had changed that. She would, however, keep that assessment to herself.

Megan Lassiter glanced up from her magazine. Like Justine, she'd ignored the brouhaha and remained seated. "The way I hear it, there's more fighting and killing in that place than in any other prison in the country. Austin probably had to stay in shape to survive." Her expression hovered somewhere between distressed and sympathetic. She never had been able to think badly of anyone, even when they deserved it. Unlike her husband, Grady, who made his living seeking out news, by hook or by crook, to sell newspapers.

Misty Briggs, Justine's teaching colleague and friend, adjusted her glasses repeatedly as she lingered at the window. Just went to show how boring small-town life could be. Justine's idea of real excitement involved two things: a special gift and a more intimate setting with the bearer of said gift. She turned the magnificent gold bracelet on her right wrist around and around. She did love pretty things.

"Does that look okay? I didn't take much off the length."

Justine turned her attention back to the here and now, accepted the mirror Jean offered, and surveyed her long blonde locks. "Perfect." She smiled appreciatively. "As always." Jean wasn't a lifetime resident of Pine Bluff. Not many of the local women liked her, but she was a damned good colorist and stylist, so most tolerated her—at least to her face.

Misty finally shuffled back to her chair. "I remember there was gossip," she said, her hazel eyes huge behind those Coke-bottle lenses as she covertly glanced around the shop, "that Austin was actually innocent."

Tension trickled through Justine. She turned and stared at her friend in utter disbelief. Excited or not, that remark was going too far. "Emily Wallace said he was guilty." Justine's voice reflected her offense. The very idea that Misty would say such nonsense out loud and in the beauty shop, of all places.

Misty put a hand to her throat. "Oh, Justine, I didn't mean that the way it sounded. Of course he was guilty." She reached over and squeezed Justine's hand, her face a study in regret, but the hint of satisfaction in her eyes ruined the effect. She loved manipulating a moment like this. It was the only time she managed to draw any real attention to herself.

Megan piped up, "Heather was my friend. Emily, too. If she said he was guilty, then he was guilty." That was about as close as Megan came to dissing anyone, even a convicted killer.

The others punctuated her pronouncement with a litany of agreeable sounds and pacifying remarks.

As the high school's cheerleading coach, Justine had known both Heather and Emily well, as she did the rest of those present, excluding Jean of course. Might as well have her say. "Clint Austin killed Heather Baker in cold blood," Justine said, with a stern glance at Misty. Absolute silence fell over the shop as all waited in anticipation of what came next. "Emily was the one who sealed his fate at the trial." Justine looked from one expectant face to the other. "You all know she hasn't been the same since. Considering the lack of real evidence, without her testimony I imagine he would've gotten off scot-free."

Megan's eyes rounded with fear. "You don't think that's why he's back, do you? To hurt Emily?"

"No," Cathy rebutted. "Mike and Ray are all over this. Every cop on the force has orders to keep a close eye on Clint Austin. He's not going to get a chance to hurt anyone."

All eyes shifted back to Justine for her take on Cathy's argument. Justine turned her palms heavenward and offered a simple truth: "I don't know why Clint Austin is back. *But* if I were Emily Wallace, I'd be scared to death."

CHAPTER FOUR

Cedar Hill Cemetery
6:00 P.M.

Emily followed him.

Tomorrow would be soon enough to get the information on parole violations and the consequences. But keeping up with Austin's every move had to start now. He'd driven around for over an hour. She was pretty sure he'd recognized that he was being followed, but he made no attempt to lose her or to confront her. He just kept driving. Eventually he returned to town, visited Donna's Floral Shop, and then came here.

To the cemetery.

Emily hadn't anticipated that move. Only people who had hearts cared enough to visit the graves of their lost loved ones. Austin had no heart.

Still, he'd tracked down his mother's grave, laid the flowers he'd purchased on the headstone, and been standing there ever since. For about half an hour now.

Emily had eventually gotten out of her car. After wandering aimlessly, keeping one eye on him, she'd ended up at Heather's grave. The shiny black granite headstone displayed an inset cameo of Heather's senior picture. They'd gone for their portrait sittings just one week before the murder.

Emily dropped down to her knees and traced the picture of her friend. She missed her so much. There were so many things they were supposed to have done together. Like go off to Auburn for college as roommates. When wedding days came they would have been each other's maid and matron of honor. Godmothers to each other's children. Maybe even neighbors. Their whole lives had been plotted out with years of late-night talks and afternoons spent daydreaming.

Heather hadn't gotten to do any of those things, and neither had Emily. She had managed to muddle through two years at a small business school in Birmingham between lapses into depression, one major breakdown, and a couple of trial drug therapies. Eventually she'd gotten a job and ended up in charge of the files department at a research facility.

Things pretty much began and ended there.

Nothing had turned out anything like she'd planned. For all intents and purposes her life had ended that night almost as surely as Heather's had. The only difference was that Emily was still breathing. Few nights passed that she didn't lie in bed and wonder why that continued to be. Or what it was that Heather was supposed to have told her that night. *There's something we have to talk about when you get back . . . something really important.*

Emily glanced across the expanse of bleak headstones. The man who had robbed her of so much hadn't moved. He still stood like a statue next to his mother's grave. He hadn't knelt down for a closer inspection or checked for errant weeds. Just stared at the headstone as if waiting for some news flash or epiphany.

His mother had been a soft-spoken woman with the same dark hair and intense gray eyes as her son. She'd insisted time and again at the trial that her son would never harm anyone. That he was a good boy. But no one had believed her. Even Austin's court-appointed attorney hadn't believed her.

He'd just done what the court forced him to do, represent a man who couldn't afford legal representation otherwise.

The judge and the jury had all sympathized with the Baker family . . . with Emily.

Emily pushed to her feet. Thought about returning to her car just in case Austin decided to leave, but he still hadn't moved, so she didn't bother. Instead, she watched him.

His profile could have been chiseled from the same stone as any of those marking these final resting places. Lean, angular features that tugged at long-banished memories. She had loved looking at him . . . before. Square jaw softened by full lips that had spent most of their time stretched in a cocky grin. Eyes that twinkled with wicked invitation. The way he'd smelled . . . the way he'd said her name in that teasing lilt had beckoned to her on every level.

"There isn't a day goes by that I don't miss her."

Emily spun toward the voice, her heart in her throat. Troy Baker, Heather's brother, moved to her side. Guilt and shame scalded her as if Troy might see that she'd allowed *those* thoughts for even a second.

"Troy, Jesus, you scared the hell out of me."

He threw his arms around her. Emily ignored her jangling nerves and hugged him back just as fiercely.

"Sorry, Em." He pulled away as if he'd rather not let go and stared down at his sister's grave. "My folks told me what you did at the parole hearing." His gaze met hers once more. "I appreciate that more than you can know. I couldn't be there. . . . I knew what those bastards were going to do."

She cleared her throat of the emotion lodged there. "It was the least I could do, Troy. Heather would have done the same for me."

He nodded. "She would've. She loved you like a sister, Em." He laughed softly, the sound painful to hear. "She'd have given me up for you any day of the week."

Emotion flooded Emily's eyes and she couldn't hope to contain it. "No, she wouldn't have, silly. She loved you, too, even if you were a pain in the butt. Fifteen-year-old guys can't be counted on for much else."

He smiled, his eyes bright as well. "I don't want him to get away with this, Em, and it feels exactly like he has."

Emily's gaze moved across the cemetery and settled on Clint Austin once more. It was hard to believe they were all standing in the same place like this. Austin appeared completely oblivious to their presence, but he couldn't be.

"He's not going to get away with anything," she said out loud. That was a promise. And until she could make that promise a reality her presence would remind him every day that he wasn't wanted here . . . that he was a murderer.

"You're right," Troy agreed. "He's not, because I'm going to do whatever it takes to see that he doesn't."

Emily hadn't seen Troy often since the trial, but she recognized the same resolve in him that she felt.

"If we watch him closely enough," she proposed, wondering if Troy had a similar plan, "he's bound to make a mistake. All we have to do is catch him. I don't know all the rules related to his parole just yet, but I know Austin never was very good at following rules. He won't be able to toe the line."

"Maybe," Troy contended, seeming to reflect on something a moment before he went on, "but, personally, I don't think he'll live long enough for us to have to worry about whether or not he makes a mistake."

The sheer hatred in Troy's voice scattered a cold spray of goose bumps across her skin. She couldn't deny that the thought of killing Austin had crossed her mind. It had. But a part of her always recognized that the notion was wrong.

Somehow she didn't sense that same comprehension in Troy. She had to be overreacting. She'd known Troy Baker his whole life. As much as he loved his sister, he wasn't a killer.

Movement in Emily's peripheral vision dragged her attention back to Austin. He was finally leaving.

"I should go," she said to Troy, though she felt reluctant to leave him. She hoped he wasn't going to do anything rash. Her need to keep an eye on Austin won out.

Troy wrapped his fingers around her arm and held on when she would have moved away. "Don't go, Em. Stay and talk to me. We can visit Heather a while longer."

She started to argue when he tagged on, "Don't worry about him. He's not going to get into anything tonight. Trust me."

County Road 18
6:45 P.M.

The sun had started to sink into the treetops as Clint drove the last couple of miles toward home. He'd put off going back there for as long as he could.

He was damned exhausted. The day had lasted a lifetime.

The visit to the parole officer had gone as expected. Lee Brady had laid down the rules and the ramifications of failing to follow those rules. Like most of the folks in town, Brady didn't agree with Clint's release, saying it hadn't been necessary. Clint had felt Brady's antipathy.

The scene outside had made leaving a nuisance. Thirty or so people, their frenzy tuned to a fever pitch by Troy Baker and Keith Turner, had gathered to make their opinions known. Like Clint told Ray, he didn't give a damn what people thought. They had a right to do and say whatever was on their minds. Didn't change a damned thing. They'd just have to get over the fact that Clint was here, because he wasn't going anywhere.

None of it had really bothered him until he'd seen *her*. She'd been headed to join the crowd of demonstrators. He hadn't expected to run into her one-on-one. Actually, he hadn't expected her to let him run into her. He'd figured she would avoid him by staying insulated by the crowd. But he'd seen her *twice* today, both times with nothing more than a meager span of asphalt or grass between them.

Emily had followed him, then hung around the cemetery watching. Then Troy Baker had appeared. Clint had been aware that Troy or one of his cronies had been close by all afternoon. After everything Clint had been through, he'd still tensed when Troy hugged her. It made Clint want to kick himself. Talk about fucked up.

He'd watched her when she hadn't been watching him. She hadn't changed at all. Still wore her dark brown hair long. The skirt and blouse were a little more conservative, but she was as pretty as ever, thinner maybe. Too bad she'd been like poison to him. She had single-handedly destroyed his life. If she kept following him around, maybe he should invite her over and tell her about a few of his jailhouse experiences. She'd change her mind in a flash about whether or not he'd gotten the full extent of what he deserved.

Or maybe she wouldn't.

Either way, he had to stay focused, to watch his step or Miss Emily Wallace would be reporting him to Brady. Clint figured she hadn't shown up back here in Pine Bluff the same day he had for nothing. Ray had mentioned that she'd moved away years ago and rarely visited. Given her obvious agenda, Clint damned sure shouldn't be attracted to her. But considering he hadn't been with a woman in over a decade, it wasn't a major shock. Still, she was his enemy and he had to keep that in front of him.

He checked his mirrors again. He was surprised she hadn't followed him from the cemetery, but she'd been too busy chatting with Baker. Maybe the two of them had been planning the next phase of their surveillance strategy.

Well, Clint had plans of his own. Plans that included not only Emily Wallace but also his former boss's son, Sid Fairgate. The man who'd hired Clint to take that car that night was dead, but the son would know whatever secrets the father had carried to the grave. Clint was sure of that. Just as he was sure that Emily, if given the proper motivation, would recall that night with a little more clarity. All he had to do was manipulate a reaction that would reverberate through the whole damned town.

Movement in the rearview mirror snagged Clint's attention. A truck, an older-model Chevy, had topped the hill behind him moving way too fast. Clint edged nearer the shoulder of the road to allow plenty of room for the driver to get on by. But he didn't do that. He roared up behind Clint.

"What the hell?" He braced just in time for the impact.

The truck pushed against his rear bumper.

Clint tightened his grip on the steering wheel and floored the accelerator in an attempt to put some distance between them. The truck responded likewise, nudging him again before he could get his momentum going.

Clint topped the next hill. A slow-moving car on the road in front of him forced him to brake hard. The truck didn't.

A sharp cut to the right avoided the crash and sent him bucking across the shallow ditch and into the cornfield, clearing a wide path of stalks.

He swerved left, came down hard on the brake.

The Firebird skidded to a jarring stop.

CHAPTER FIVE

212 Cedar Street
7:10 P.M.

"How long will you be staying, honey?"

Emily pushed the peas around on her plate and considered how best to answer her father's question. Silence had started pressing in on the family dining room as soon as she'd arrived late for dinner. This moment had been coming ever since.

Despite his affable tone, her father wore his *seriously concerned* face.

Since the breakdown her parents had used alternating zones for dealing with her: curiously indulgent, surprisingly relieved, seriously concerned, or deeply troubled. Tonight, apparently, was seriously concerned.

"A week or so. I haven't decided." Emily stuffed a forkful of potatoes into her mouth to avoid further elaboration. She'd asked for two weeks' vacation, but she would take as long as necessary. That she was a grown woman and could make her own decision on the matter wouldn't be relevant to her parents.

Stevie Wonder couldn't have missed the look that passed between them. They weren't anywhere near finished yet.

Edward Wallace set his fork aside and peered down the length of the table with sympathy in his brown eyes, the same brown eyes that stared back at Emily every morning from the bathroom mirror. Only sans the emptiness.

"You're welcome to stay as long as you like, Em."

There was a *but* coming and then the event she dreaded with every fiber of her being each time she visited. Emily settled her hands atop the linen napkin in her lap and braced for the *talk*. They were about to enter the *deeply troubled* zone.

"But your mother and I are worried about your reasons for taking this abrupt vacation." He searched her eyes as if he hoped to see the answer he sought there. Evidently he didn't find it, so he went on. "We know how you feel, honey."

Impossible. The word resounded inside her, but she didn't allow it to cross her lips. Any argument from her would only accelerate the disintegration of the already unstable climate. What she felt was dead. When she didn't feel dead inside, she felt angry. Like now. They couldn't know.

"What your father is trying to say, dear," Carol Wallace jumped in, as if they had assigned parts and had carefully rehearsed, "is that it's a crying shame that boy's not still in prison, but nothing you do is going to change the facts. Em, you're twenty-eight years old; it's time you paid attention to yourself . . . to your future. We don't want you going backward."

Carol was a lovely woman no matter that she shopped in the plus-size departments these days and wore the gray invading her black hair like a badge of honor. Despite a nursing degree, she'd spent her life serving her family, her church, and her community—in that order. The same could be said for Ed Wallace. Long hours at his investment firm had never once prevented him from being a loving, devoted father.

As much as Emily's parents loved her and wanted to believe they felt just as she did, they didn't. Holding that against them wouldn't be fair. It wasn't their fault.

It was hers.

They waited expectantly for some revelation that would show progress on her part. A mere smidgen of hope that she intended to divert her life toward some more conventional course could close this argument right now. Tension would recede and the parental scrutiny zone would drop back down to *curiously indulgent.*

But Emily couldn't give them what they wanted.

"I have to do this." Emily placed her napkin on the table next to her scarcely touched plate. Inside she was shaking, but outside she held on to her calm to avoid inciting their suspicions further. She'd gotten really good at that kind of deception over the past few years. "If I don't do what I know in my heart is right, I'm not sure I'll ever be able to move on. I realize you can't understand that, but that's the way it is."

Another visual exchange in that unspoken language gained through thirty-five years of marriage transpired before her father took the next turn at battle. "Dr. Brown would really like you to come back to counseling. He believes that's the best way, Em. Your mother and I agree."

Counseling. It was like a bad penny; it showed up every time. She'd tried therapy. It hadn't worked. Once Dr. Brown had released her, a whole year after her four-week stay at the Calhoun Treatment Center, she'd never gone back to him. She didn't intend to now. Wouldn't that be doing exactly what her parents feared? Going backward?

"You'll have to excuse me." Emily stood. "Thank you for dinner," she said to her mother, then managed a tight smile for her father before walking away from the table.

Deeply troubled. She didn't have to look back to know,

Emily could feel the weight of their troubled gazes on her back as she left the room. The telephone rang, but she didn't slow her retreat. It wouldn't be for her. She hadn't been here long enough in the last decade for anyone to associate her with the address or the number.

She no longer belonged in Pine Bluff.

She didn't actually belong anywhere.

Her mother's voice drifted down the hall behind Emily. The caller was obviously Emily's brother, James. The change from troubled to elated in her mother's tone related the identity of the caller without the mention of a name.

James was in medical school, was on the dean's list. James hadn't prematurely self-destructed. Too bad his success couldn't be enough for Emily's parents.

Emily went into her room and closed the door. She leaned against it and surveyed the space she barely recognized. It felt more like a hotel. She'd spent her senior year in this room, but there was no connection . . . nothing. She'd slept here and dressed here and that was about it.

Her mom had gone out of her way to try to make this new house home . . . this new room *Emily's* room. Some of her stuff was carefully arranged on shelves or pieces of furniture. Cheerleading trophies. A neatly framed picture of Bon Jovi, another of Mel Gibson. Stuff. Junk. Nothing that mattered. The items that were important had been hidden away. Packing away all those mementos of the past had been her mother's idea of moving on. Unfortunately, nothing new had filled the emptiness. No diplomas matted and framed for bragging rights. No wedding pictures or snapshots of grandchildren to show off to visitors.

Just a room. With beige carpet. And beige walls.

There was nothing that stood out or defined the space or . . . Emily. She was beige . . . almost invisible.

The panic started its dreaded creep beneath her skin. Her heart reacted, bouncing into a faster rhythm only to flail helplessly like a fish dropped on the bank right next to the river's edge. Relief was in sight, but you couldn't quite reach it no matter how hard you tried.

The overwhelming sense of doom would descend next, and then there would be no stopping a full-blown anxiety attack. She'd had her first one six months after the murder. She'd taken several different types of antianxiety medications until she'd gotten fed up with the futile efforts and/or dependency and she'd stopped.

She couldn't be here right now.

Her purse and keys were in her hand before second thoughts could slow her. A drive would help. Give her a chance to think without any interference or static, no matter how well-meaning. Her mother was still on the phone with Emily's brother. Her father had settled into his recliner with the day's paper.

They wouldn't even know she'd gone.

Outside, the suffocating July heat and humidity still hung in the air even at quarter of eight. Emily wrenched the car door open and dropped behind the steering wheel. She closed her eyes, leaned her head back, and struggled to regulate her respiration, to slow her heart's frenzied pounding.

When she could breathe normally again she opened her eyes and stared out at the street where her parents lived . . . in a house that had never been home to her. They'd sold the house on Ivy Lane right after Heather's death. No place had felt like home since. Regret closed around Emily's chest in ever-tightening bands triggering another rush of adrenaline.

Just go. She shoved the key into the ignition and started the engine, then pulled out onto the street with no particular destination. The streets of Pine Bluff were pretty much rolled up for the night and it wasn't even dark yet. A couple of fast-food restaurants were still open. The neon glow from the Sack&Go reminded passersby of the dozens of brands of beer available most any time of the day or night.

Emily wound past a row of newly built houses in an

upscale subdivision on the edge of town. Ten years ago the location had been just another field. As a child she'd felt certain that real life didn't exist outside Pine Bluff's city limits. Beyond those borders there had been only two things: cotton fields and sweeping pastures where cattle dozed in the Alabama sun.

Pine Bluff was nestled amid the mountains and lakes of northern Alabama. A place brimming with old-fashioned values, where folks shunned urban sprawl and big-city troubles.

Until one of those would-never-happen-here problems had found its way to her hometown.

Drive; don't think. Breathe, slow and deep.

The cotton fields on either side of the road gave way to fields of tall corn, some partially harvested already. The change prodded a vague recognition.

County Road 18.

She slowed at the turn that would lead to *his* house. Not that she'd actually intended to show up at his place at this time of the evening. But why not? She wasn't afraid of him.

What more could he do to her? Kill her? How did you kill someone who was dead already?

After making that final turn, she parked on the side of the dirt road next to a cluster of shady maples. The narrow, curvy road wound through the woods at the base of the mountain, finally reconnecting with 18. There wasn't another house for as far as she could see. The red Firebird was parked in front. He was home. His first night outside those prison walls.

She thought about those seconds this afternoon outside the courthouse when he'd stared right at her from across the street. He didn't look that different. There were small changes; his hair was shorter, his skin paler. He looked heavier or maybe just more muscled. There was a scar that hadn't been there before. On his left cheek.

But the eyes were exactly the same.

Her fingers clutched the steering wheel as she recalled

the way that silvery gaze could reach right inside her and make her feel totally lost. He'd been very good at making her feel vulnerable and helpless . . . and needy.

She'd fallen in lust with him at sixteen. No one in the world had known except Heather. Emily's best friend's crushes had fluctuated between Keith Turner and Marvin Cook, both football players, with their lettermen jackets and massive egos.

Not Emily. Nope, she'd picked a guy who'd barely managed to survive his senior year. He'd missed nearly as many days as he'd attended. Austin had had a bit of an ego himself, but his vast charm had rendered most females blind to its presence. Emily's father had called him a thug.

Em, you stay away from that boy. He's trouble.

She'd known it was true, but that hadn't kept her from fantasizing about him. After all, fantasies were supposed to be about the forbidden.

A detail as simple as the way his clothes had fit made her heart beat wildly and her foolish adolescent hormones surge. The T-shirts that had molded to his body, the faded, tattered jeans that had wrapped his lower anatomy, were nothing short of sinful. Everything about him, the way he talked, the way he moved, all of it, had been designed for sex appeal.

He would slide those dark sunglasses into place and spin out of a parking lot in that racy red Firebird and she would long to go with him. To have the wind rushing through her hair . . . to have him put his hand on her bare thigh and foster all those forbidden sensations that just breathing in the same airspace as him had the power to ignite.

She remembered the way his lips would tilt when he smiled. That sexy curl that no mere woman, much less a teenage girl, could hope to resist. He'd teased her, flirted with her ruthlessly. Each time, she'd turned her back on him. Pretended not to notice. She'd been a good girl; she hadn't associated with boys like him outside her fantasies.

At first he'd laughed at the way she ignored him. Then it became a sort of challenge to him. See just how far he could go before she turned tail and ran.

Once they'd even kissed.

At the movie theater he'd sneaked up behind her and put his hands over her eyes. She'd whirled around to face the culprit. He was the last person she'd expected to see. He'd never gotten quite that close before, never once touched her. Shock had frozen her to the spot when their gazes collided and his fingers lingered against her hair. Something had shifted in her small world as he'd stared into her eyes. She had known in the deepest recesses of her soul that she was about to be kissed.

It was her first.

His lips had met hers and she'd leaned into the incredible sensations . . . had reached her arms around his neck and let her trembling body rest against his strong, lean one. He'd kissed her long and deep, used his tongue in ways she'd only read about. His palms had cupped her face, those long fingers threaded into her hair. A kind of heat she'd never before experienced had flowed through her, settling between her thighs.

As if the voice of reason had suddenly kicked in, he'd drawn away, winked, then walked off without so much as a word. She'd been humiliated. Even that infuriating episode hadn't made her stop wanting him.

A deep shadow fell across the driver's side window and jolted her back to the present. She looked up, blinked. He stood right outside her open car window.

Fear exploded in her veins.

How could she have not heard his approach?

Her brain issued all the appropriate flight commands, but her hands . . . her fingers refused to act.

With her heart clanging and the blood funneling like a hurricane in her ears, she couldn't think. She couldn't piece together what to do next.

He didn't move, just stood there and waited for her to do or say something.

She reached for the ignition, but Heather's face, frozen in cameo on her gravestone, suddenly flashed in Emily's mind. *No.*

This was a public road. It was a free country. She could park here if she damn well wanted to. He couldn't touch her, not without risking a violation of his parole.

Daring him, she wrenched open the door. He backed up a step to avoid being hit by it as she got out.

She grabbed on to her fledgling courage with both hands and pretended not to be scared to death. "Is there a problem?" she demanded, staring directly into those seething gray eyes, her hands planted on her hips in challenge. He was bigger than she remembered, taller . . . his shoulders broader. And then there was the scar, marring the angle of his jaw and the hollow beneath that lean cheek. She shivered at the idea of how he may have gotten it before she could stifle the reaction.

He looked away a moment, as if he didn't trust himself to continue holding that stare or even to answer her question. Or maybe he was just confused that she hadn't run. He'd better get used to that, because she wasn't the same scared little girl he once knew.

When that cold steel gaze latched on to hers once more, he demanded, "What do you want?"

Her pulse scrambled. It was the first time she'd heard his voice in over ten years. Not since the trial when, after the summations from both sides, he'd risen from the defendant's chair and told the jury what a mistake they would be making if they found him guilty. He was innocent, he'd insisted. He had stood there, wearing that cheap suit his court-appointed attorney had probably instructed his mother to buy, and met the gaze of every person in that jury box. He'd looked young and humble and . . . terrified.

Emily had barely noticed. Her entire focus had been on seeing that he got what was coming to him.

That old familiar fury kindled inside her. The one emotion of which she seemed capable of experiencing the full range. "What do I want?" She laughed, the sound laden with bitter contempt. He didn't really want to know, but since he'd asked, she would damn sure tell him. "I want you to make a mistake. I want you to go back to prison for the rest of your worthless life." She bit down hard on her lip to prevent its blasted trembling as the rage catapulted through her. "I want you to pay for what you did until you draw your last pathetic breath."

She blinked back the burn of tears. God, she would not cry in front of him. She'd cried enough and it hadn't changed a damned thing. Heather was still dead . . . *she* was still dead.

For the first time she realized just how dead. Her life was a road that went nowhere . . . an abrupt stop. She felt nothing . . . she was nothing. Because of him.

He started to turn away but changed his mind. A muscle in his tightly clenched jaw contracted before he spoke. "Your efforts would be much better spent, *Miss Wallace,* trying to find out who else was in your room that night and whether or not it was really you they were after. Otherwise, you should do yourself a favor and stop wasting your time on me."

CHAPTER SIX

Tuesday, July 16, 7:55 A.M.

Pine Bluff's finest had cruised by Clint's place at seven that morning, but he hadn't expected to find a welcoming committee at Higgins Auto Repair Shop as well. Guess that made him a celebrity.

As he pulled into a slot in the parking lot next to the shop, he recognized the officer at the scene. Ray Hale. So the chief of police himself had come to make sure the ex-con went to work like a good, law-abiding citizen. Would the chief be following him to the bank when he cashed his paycheck? Stocked up at the Piggly Wiggly? Took a piss?

Nothing should surprise Clint at this point. Having Emily Wallace stay parked outside his house until almost midnight despite his show of force had been surprising enough.

The idea that she'd sat out there watching him had made him madder than hell. He knew what she was up to; he just hadn't realized how deeply it would get under his skin. His every move had been watched and dictated in prison. He'd had to learn to live with that constant surveillance; he didn't like putting up with it now.

Part of him had wanted to scare the hell out of her so she'd go away and leave him alone. But he couldn't do that. He needed her. So he'd stormed right up to her car with the intention of rattling her cage, of making her think twice about what she'd always believed happened that night.

And what had he done? He'd gotten caught up in looking at her. Big brown eyes and a wide, lush mouth that she had tried to hide with her long, silky hair back in high school. He'd dreamed of kissing that mouth long before he'd taken the liberty, even though she'd used it a million times to tell him to get lost.

Just hearing her voice again had damaged him somehow.

He had planned for ten stinking years what he would do and say when he had the chance, and he'd gotten that close and most of the things he'd intended to say had vanished from his tongue.

When she'd dared to get in his face to tell him off just like she used to, his gaze had ignored his objections and roamed every inch of her. The long skirt that only served to make him want to hike up the hem far enough to see those smooth thighs . . . to maybe get a glimpse of lacy panties. She had a nicely curved bottom and high, full breasts that wouldn't be disguised behind a buttoned-to-the-throat blouse.

That was the part that burned him the worst. Going into trial he'd been guilty of just one thing: lusting after Emily Wallace. That was it! And look what it had cost him.

Evidently she'd experienced a delayed flight reaction to his aggressive move. He'd seen neither hide nor hair of her this morning. He climbed out of his car and headed toward where Ray and Higgins stood talking. The conversation no doubt had to do with Clint, since both men looked less than happy. Welcome to his life.

Clint hadn't worked on a car in a hell of a long time, not

since he'd tinkered with his first heap back in high school. But he didn't mind getting his hands greasy. He had to support himself; this was as good a way to do it as any.

As he neared the front of the shop he heard the tension in the two men's voices before the clipped conversation came to an abrupt stop.

Then Clint saw the reason why. Big letters spray painted on one of the garage doors read: *Hiring killers is a sin.*

"Clint." Ray acknowledged his arrival with a nod.

Higgins glanced nervously at him and muttered, "Morning."

"What's going on?" Asking was a mere technicality, a way to enter the conversation. It didn't take a detective's shield to figure it out.

"A little vandalism. Nothing we can't handle, right, Higgins?"

The shop owner shot a look at his defaced door and then at Ray. "Sure, no problem," he said to Clint. The empathetic expression Higgins pasted on his face was not a good fit.

Life was a bitch sometimes. Even when a man tried to do the right thing.

"You know," Clint suggested in retrospect, "maybe we should forget this whole thing." He didn't need the old man's reluctant charity any more than he did Ray's. "I appreciate your offer, Mr. Higgins, but let's leave it at that."

The relief that claimed the older man's face confirmed that he desperately wanted off the hook. Ray must have had something on Higgins to prod him into going for this.

"Don't be too hasty, Clint," Ray contended. "The job is yours. Mr. Higgins has offered it to you. You can't let this nonsense put you off." He gestured to the defaced door. "If you walk away, then they've won. Besides, your parole stipulates you have to hold down a job. Might as well be this one."

Clint looked past Higgins and the chief to the others congregated inside the shop beyond one of the open overhead doors. They wouldn't welcome Clint any more than the vandals had. When he would have shifted his attention back to Ray, he recognized one of the other employees. Marvin Cook. He'd run with Troy Baker and his crew. Maybe working here would provide an opportunity for Clint to use this guy. Any connection to the friends of the woman he supposedly murdered was better than none at all.

"Maybe you're right," he said to Ray. "If Higgins is still willing."

The shop owner looked none too happy, but he stuck by his word.

"I'll get this vandalism report turned in," Ray assured him. "Let me know if you have any more trouble."

When Clint would have followed Higgins into the shop, Ray waylaid him. "Everything quiet around your place last night?"

Clint considered telling him about the truck that had run him off the road. He'd gotten a pretty good look at both the truck and the car involved, but not the drivers. Both vehicles had been older models. But what was the point in mentioning it? The people who didn't want him back here and who had the balls to take steps to show it would just have to do what they would. Having the chief of police knock on their doors wouldn't put them off. No need to mention the confrontation with Emily Wallace, either. The less said the better.

"Everything's just dandy, Chief." Clint crooked his lips into a mock smile, then turned his back on Ray and headed inside.

A few minutes later Higgins introduced Clint to the other employees. Four mechanics, all with years of experience, and one receptionist, cute in a Barbie doll sort of way.

And shop manager Marvin Cook, a hotshot back in high school, gone to seed, with his beer belly hanging over his jeans. Cook didn't let on that he remembered Clint. Knowing Clint Austin carried a stigma in this town, then and now.

Some things never changed.

5:30 *P.M.*

As the day had progressed Clint had learned that Marvin Cook was the same jerk he'd been in high school. Star quarterback for the Pine Bluff Panthers. Teacher's pet. Old Marv had been voted the guy mostly likely to succeed senior year. He'd laid claim to the all-important most valuable player trophy, much to the dismay of Granville Turner, who had expected his son, Keith, to win that treasured prize for his role as the team's tight end. Scouts from numerous universities had come to watch those two carry the team through a winning season.

Apparently Marvin's fifteen minutes of fame had come and gone in high school. Otherwise, just over a decade later he wouldn't be bossing around a handful of grease monkeys in a small-town auto repair shop.

Clint waited until the others had washed up before he headed to the big utility sink next to the parts room. He rotated first one shoulder and then the other. He hadn't worked this hard in a while. It beat the hell out of solitary confinement. The fact that none of the other employees spoke to him didn't bother him one way or the other. He'd gotten used to the silent treatment in prison. If these jokers thought they were giving him a hard time, they should think again.

"Hey, Austin."

Clint pulled off a paper towel to dry his hands and turned to face Cook. "Yeah."

"Since you're low man on the totem pole, you can clean up the shop." Cook angled his head and eyed Clint as if he expected an argument. "We like starting the day with a clean workplace."

Clint was reasonably sure they hadn't started off the day with a clean workplace since the garage had been built, but he didn't argue. He was used to taking orders. He gave a halfhearted shrug. "Whatever."

"Use the side exit when you're finished." Two steps from the door Cook hesitated and swiveled his head to send one last injustice in Clint's direction. "Oh yeah, don't forget the toilet." Cook puckered his face into one of those expressions that said he was trying hard to remember something before he added, "It's been a while since the bathroom got a cleaning, but I'm sure you can handle it considering the years of practice you probably got in prison."

Clint dropped the paper towel he'd wadded into the trash can, didn't bother responding. He'd learned the hard way that clever comebacks could cost a hell of a lot more than he wanted to pay. If negative behavior was reported to his parole officer, it would be for something more important than whether or not Clint was willing to clean a toilet.

Though there was one thing he'd waited to say until Cook was ready to call it a day. Until it was just the two of them. "Hold up, Cook."

The other man paused, one hand on the door. He looked back at Clint with a blatant mixture of disdain and impatience, maybe even a hint of apprehension. "What?"

"Wonder why the police didn't consider you a suspect during the Baker investigation? You and Heather Baker dated a few times, didn't you? What were you doing the night she was murdered?"

Cook's face went gauzy white before going bloodred. "Go fuck yourself, Austin." He slammed the door on his way out.

Clint hadn't planned to start with Marvin Cook. Hell, Clint hadn't even known he would run into Cook at his new job, but he'd certainly seized the opportunity fate had tossed his way. Too much of his life had been squandered already. He wasn't about to take for granted another minute, much less a day.

He walked to the door through which Cook had exited and watched beyond the grimy window as the pissed-off guy climbed into his truck. Within the hour word would get around that Clint Austin was asking questions. The natives would grow restless in a hurry, especially those who had something to hide.

Burning rubber, Cook spun out onto the street. Clint had to smile. It was about time someone else felt the pressure of the past. The entire investigation into Heather Baker's murder had centered around the idea that Emily Wallace was the intended victim. What if the killer had been after Heather instead? No one had even considered that scenario. Not once. It was past time someone did. And rattling Marvin Cook's cage was only the beginning.

When Clint would have turned back to the menial tasks Cook had dumped on him just because he could, his gaze snagged on another vehicle in the parking lot. Dark blue. Malibu.

Though he couldn't see the occupant, he knew it was *her*.

What do you know? She'd shown up after all. Emily Wallace had come to see him home. He hoped she was a fan of the waiting game.

This, he thought as he surveyed the shop that looked as if it hadn't been swept, much less mopped, in years, was going to take a while.

CHAPTER SEVEN

The Den
7:59 P.M.

"It just ain't right."

Troy Baker reached for his beer. It was his sixth or seventh and he hadn't even been home for supper yet. His wife would just have to bear with him. He was in the middle of a major crisis here. He hooked his heels on the footrest of his bar stool and chugged the cold brew knowing it wouldn't cool the fire in his gut. Marvin had called him, all fired up about some stupid remark Austin had made; then the fat bastard had refused to meet Troy for a beer. Asshole. Marvin wanted to stay out of this, he'd claimed. What the hell was his problem? What kind of friend backed off like that?

Fucking coward.

"Damn straight it ain't right," Larry Medford agreed as he plopped his empty bottle on the bar. "Austin should have gotten the hint when we run his ass off the road." Larry leaned on the counter, rested his head in his hand, and looked Troy in the eye. "What you think it's gonna take to send him packing?"

Troy wagged his head in frustration. "I don't know, but

whatever it is, I'm gonna make sure it gets done. God knows we can't count on the law to do this right."

The sound of pool balls breaking had Troy twisting around on his stool. "Perry, come over here, man."

Perry took his shot, sending a stripe into a corner pocket. He dropped two more before he knocked one spinning across the green only to fall short of its intended destination. He straightened away from the table and strode over to his pals, the cue stick in his hand. "You know I'm gonna have to drive you home, don't you, buddy?"

Troy didn't give a damn how he got home. He had bigger fish to fry right now. Austin was waltzing around town like he owned the place.

"We should burn Higgins out," Troy growled under his breath. "How the hell could he give that sonofabitch a job? His own daughter went to school with my sister!"

Perry shrugged. "Ray probably put the pressure on him." He gestured for his challenger not to wait before taking his turn. "You know how Ray can be. Higgins probably had a slew of parking tickets he hadn't paid." Perry slapped Troy on the back. "You're drunk, buddy; you're talking crazy."

Crazy. Yeah, right. Troy was making more sense than any damned body else in this town. As far as Ray Hale went, Troy no longer had any use for him whatsoever. It was bad enough he'd gone to see Austin in prison, but to hold his hand now that he was out . . . hell, that was just going too far. Maybe the good old chief of police was going Brokeback Mountain on him.

"I'll make him pay," Troy promised. "You know I will."

Perry nodded. "I know you will, buddy. Just not tonight, okay? I think we should lay low a while."

Perry was scared shitless that Ray would find out he'd run Austin off the road while Troy distracted Emily Wallace. Even if Austin filed charges and managed to convey a description that led the cops to Troy's pals, it would just be his word against theirs. No one was going to believe Austin over Troy. Well, maybe no one but Chief Ray Dickhead Hale.

Ray would get his if he got in the way.

"Where's Keith?" Larry asked as if he'd just noticed that another of their gang hadn't shown up.

Troy grunted. "I don't know. He's acting all weird. He gave me hell last night when he found out why I told him to park that car on the road and wait. You'd think he was on Austin's side or something."

"I don't think you have to worry about that, Troy," Perry argued. "Keith feels the same way we do; he just has a bitchier wife than the rest of us."

That got a laugh out of Troy. That damned Violet had to have been a marine drill sergeant in another life. She stayed on Keith's ass like a bad rash.

"Hell yeah," Larry endorsed. "All I can say is that woman must be part Hoover, the turbo model. Otherwise I sure as hell wouldn't put up with her bullshit."

Troy hated to burst his buddy's bubble, but he'd dated Violet Manning a couple of times before she'd gotten engaged to Keith and she'd been a major disappointment on her back and on her knees. Whatever power she held over her husband, it wasn't sex, oral or otherwise. Troy finished off his beer and gestured for the bartender to bring him another.

"Gotta take my shot." Perry sauntered back over to the pool table to drop the last of the stripes.

"I'm cuttin' you off, Baker."

Troy pointed a nasty look at the guy behind the bar. "You saying I'm drunk, Bradley?" Bradley Peters had been a bully back in school, and not much had changed. Then again, with a last name like Peters, what was a guy to do?

Bradley leaned across the bar and put his face in Troy's. "That's right; you got a problem with it?"

Troy grinned. "Hell no." He hitched his thumb toward the pool table. "No need to get your panties in a wad; Perry's giving me a ride home."

Bradley turned his junkyard dog glare from Troy to Larry. "You'd better catch a ride with Woods yourself, Medford. I don't want the chief on my back."

The chief. Ray Hale had his finger in every damned thing around this town. It hadn't been a problem until he'd come out of the closet with his secret obsession with Clint Austin. Just went to show that you couldn't really trust anybody.

Nursing his last beer, Larry leaned toward Troy and whispered, "What do you think we should do next?"

Now there was a friend a guy could count on when the chips were down. It chafed Troy's ass that Keith was wimping out the way he was. He was supposed to have loved Heather. She had sure as hell loved him.

Troy closed his eyes and tried with no luck to shut out the images from that awful night. He'd sat on the stairs watching through the railings after the doorbell rang, waking everybody up from a dead sleep. Chief Don Ledbetter had given Troy's folks the bad news. His mother had collapsed. Ledbetter's wife had stayed with Troy and his mom while his father went with the chief to the Wallaces'.

Troy had needed to know what was going on. So he'd sneaked out, barefoot and in his pajamas, and run all the way to Emily's house. The cops had been so busy trying to make heads or tails out of the crime scene that they hadn't noticed him peeking from the bedroom doorway . . . staring at his sister's motionless body and all that blood.

Emily Wallace had been rushed to the hospital. Shock or something like that. But her father had been right there in the room with the cops and Principal Call. Troy would never forget how the men in the room, including his own father and the chief, had cried.

Troy hadn't cried. Not then anyway. He'd just wanted to know where Austin was. He'd wanted to hurt Austin.

But Austin had already been taken to jail.

The county coroner took Heather away in a big, black body bag that night. It was the last time Troy had seen his sister until the funeral nearly a week later. As her coffin was lowered into the ground, he'd made a promise. Clint Austin would get what was coming to him.

Troy turned toward his friend. "I'll tell you what we do next. We make sure Austin knows we mean business."

CHAPTER EIGHT

Pine Bluff High School
Wednesday, July 17, 7:50 A.M.

Yesterday's surveillance of Austin had yielded absolutely nothing useful to Emily. The parole officer, Lee Brady, had provided her with as much information as he was allowed to give regarding the parameters of Austin's parole, but what she'd learned hadn't proved as helpful as she'd hoped.

Emily parked near the football field on school property and powered her window down to permit the meager breeze to filter into her car. The temperature was sweltering already. She'd narrowly missed running into her mother before she got away this morning. Avoiding her parents as much as possible was necessary. Leave early; stay out late. Cut way down on the friction and kept clear of the *zones*.

She could think here. This was the last place where she'd had a life and friends . . . felt safe. Plus, she wanted to talk to Principal Call. She hated, hated, hated that she couldn't put the niggling thought out of her head, but she simply couldn't. Jesse Lambert, the chairwoman of the parole board, had brought up the lack of tangible evidence used in the trial, succeeding in forcing Emily to play over and over what she remembered about that night. She knew beyond all doubt what had happened. She was there. No question about what she had witnessed. And yet some stupid part of her just wouldn't let the insensitive statements made in that hearing go. She refused to admit for a second that anything Austin had said played a part in her decision to come here this morning.

Your efforts would be much better spent, Miss Wallace, trying to find out who else was in your room that night and whether or not it was really you they were after.

Emily banished the sound of Clint Austin's voice from her head. She would not let him intrude. His suggestion was completely unfounded. Who would have wanted to hurt Heather? Austin just wanted her second-guessing herself, to get her off his back maybe.

Unfortunately, like Jesse Lambert, Austin had succeeded with the former.

While Emily waited for eight o'clock to roll around, she pulled the steno pad from her purse and fished for a pen. She considered the conditions of parole she had listed from easiest to violate all the way to the most difficult. According to Brady, more parolees than ever were being hustled back to prison for violations. That was the one thing she'd learned that had given her hope. All she had to do was be vigilant about monitoring Austin's activities and catch him in the act. Maybe her continued surveillance would goad him into making a mistake. The sooner the better.

A lot of the conditions of Austin's parole were fairly general. He was required to obey all laws, absolutely no drug or alcohol use. No travel outside Jackson County without express permission. He couldn't own any weapons. And he was supposed to sign up for counseling sessions. She didn't see the latter happening. She made a note to follow up on that one.

Her pen stilled as a dozen girls ran out onto the football field. She should have remembered that cheer practice didn't stop just because the school year ended. She and Heather had taken the field every single day all summer long. The familiar formation and chanting had Emily leaning forward in her seat, remembering the days before that night . . . when her life ended.

"Emily Wallace? Is that you?"

Her head snapped to the left so fast she was sure she'd whiplashed herself. Principal Call was just getting out of his car. Talk about zoning out. She hadn't even noticed the arrival of another vehicle.

Emily stumbled in her haste to get out and properly greet him. "Yes, sir, it's me." She righted her posture and instinctively pulled at the hem of her blouse. Just hearing his booming voice made her feel sixteen again, klutzy and worried that she would get into trouble.

He had scarcely changed at all. Big, tall, and bald and fully equipped with mind-reading capabilities.

"Good gracious, Emily, it's good to see you." Beaming, he gave her a hug. "How're your folks?"

"Fine, Mr. Call." Except for worrying about their daughter. Emily took a deep breath and prepared to ask him about that night, but he spoke first.

"Come on inside and let me show you something I'll bet you haven't seen."

Inside? The school? She couldn't do that. She only needed a moment of his time; they could talk out here.

"I'm sure you're busy, Mr. Call, and I just—"

"Nonsense. Come along."

He ushered her toward the main building even as she grappled for a reason she couldn't go. She hadn't set foot inside this school since graduation, and she'd only attended that meaningless event to make her parents happy. No one understood why Emily refused to make a speech about her dead best friend. They didn't get that all the right words had been trapped in a place Emily couldn't touch.

Five feet inside the main entrance and Emily wanted to

run. Her knees tried to buckle, but the principal's hand at her back kept her moving forward. He'd been talking nonstop, but not a word had penetrated the barrier of dread swaddling her brain and rendering the organ inaccessible.

Air rushed into her lungs when she wanted desperately to hold her breath. The smell . . . the scents found nowhere else except inside this building awakened a part of her mind that she'd shut down out of necessity long ago. Pencils and books, markers and reams of paper.

He steered her forward and, as if she had suddenly been transported back in time, the empty corridor filled with faces and sounds from the past. The rush of students late for homeroom . . . the excited chatter about the coming dance . . . the teasing, flirting, and whispered gossip.

The principal's voice dragged her back to the present. "We dedicated the senior hall to Heather."

Heather Baker Hall.

Emily managed a shaky smile even as the urge to cry knocked against her unsteady defenses. "It's great, Mr. Call. A beautiful tribute." Somehow her voice came out admirably composed.

"We wanted to keep her memory alive." Mr. Call stared at the plaque that showed Heather in her cheerleading uniform and proclaimed this wing her namesake.

"Everybody loved her," Emily murmured. "No way anyone would have wanted to hurt her . . . she didn't have any enemies."

"Not the first one," he agreed. "Heather was one of our most loved students."

Emily hadn't meant to say that out loud. Since she had, she might as well get an answer to the question she'd come here to ask. "Mr. Call?"

The principal's expectant gaze shifted to her.

"That . . . night." She moistened her lips and fought to keep her voice steady. "Did you see anyone on my street? Another car? Someone walking?" Principal Call's house had been the target that night. Hazing week. Emily's turn to lead. Another of the senior cheerleaders, her good friend Megan, had helped, along with the new freshman members of the squad. Emily had sneaked out of the house . . . left Heather in her room to cover for her in case her parents came home early.

Principal Call stroked his chin. "The police asked me that," he said, his voice sounding distant, as if he had gone back to that awful night as Emily had so many, many times. "I tried my best to recall if I'd seen anyone, but I couldn't be absolutely certain there wasn't someone lurking around the neighborhood. It all happened too fast."

"But you told the police you didn't see anyone, right?" She needed to hear him say that. Needed that confirmation. Probably the passage of time had clouded his memory. She didn't even remember him testifying at the trial and she'd thought she would never forget a moment of it. "You were called as a witness at the trial, weren't you?"

He nodded. "That's right, but it was dark, Emily. I can't be certain there was no one on the sidewalk or in one of the yards that I simply didn't see. I was too fired up at you and Megan for hitting my mailbox and then driving away so recklessly."

Emily managed a shaky smile. "I understand. I don't know if I ever told you, but I'm sorry we hit your mailbox." It was the only time she and her friends had ever gotten caught, and getting away had been instinct.

He patted Emily on the shoulder. "It was no big deal, Emily. I really just wanted to make sure you girls got home okay considering the way Megan was driving." His brow furrowed. "Are you thinking that Clint Austin had an accomplice that night?"

She should have anticipated that his curiosity would be roused by her question. "No. I . . . I just wondered." He was looking at her the way her parents did . . . entering one of those zones that spoke of sympathy or concern. She couldn't go there. She had to get out of here before the questions and advice started to flow. "I really have to go."

"You know," the principal said, his expression turning somber to match his tone, "I've wondered many times if I'd stopped at your house first instead of following Megan down the block I might have been able to help. . . . Calling the police after I heard the screams just wasn't enough." He shook his head and heaved a heart-heavy sigh. "How could anyone possibly have imagined what that boy was doing that night?" The big man shuddered visibly.

Emily wasn't sure how she resisted the impulse to run away from the moment or how she managed to reach for his hand and shake it, but somehow she did. "You couldn't have known." She cleared her throat and gestured to the plaque. "Thank you for sharing this with me."

"It was really good to see you, Emily. You'll have to be sure and attend the reunion this fall," he implored, his dark eyes suspiciously bright. "Ten years is a major milestone."

Ten years . . . a milestone all right. Just not the one he thought. He said something else, she was pretty sure she called an answer over her shoulder, but she couldn't be certain and she definitely couldn't look back.

Don't run. Walk. One foot in front of the other. She cleared the main entrance . . . had to grab on to the railing as she descended the steps and fought back the smothering panic.

"Emily!"

Her hand on the car door, she almost got in without acknowledging the person who'd called out to her. She recognized the voice . . . didn't want to do this.

"I thought that was you." The voice was closer now, practically right next to her.

She couldn't pretend not to hear.

Emily forced her lips back into a smile and turned to greet the woman who had been her coach. "Ms. Mallory, how are you?"

Justine Mallory rolled her eyes as she propped against Emily's car, delaying her escape. "Please, you're not a student anymore; call me Justine."

"Justine," Emily amended, keeping her lips bent in what had to be a sorry excuse for a smile.

Pay attention. Compliment her. Ten years and she was still as stunning, if not more so, as she had been when Emily was in high school. Blonde hair, deep blue eyes. Makeup always perfect. Long, toned legs leading up to a body to die for. Justine had to be on top of forty and still she looked amazing. The tan, the shorts, the Pine Bluff High T-shirt, all of it made her look like one of the students rather than a tenured teacher of higher math.

"You look great." The words came out a little stilted.

"So do you," Justine said, giving Emily a thorough once-over. "Where have you been keeping yourself? I've asked your parents about you from time to time. Megan, Cathy, Violet, and I were talking about you at the beauty shop just the other day."

"I've been really busy," Emily lied. She cleared her throat in an effort to force it open as she tried to think of something else to say. She should ask how the others were doing. She had cheered all through high school with those girls . . . until Heather's murder.

"So, you finally decided to take a vacation and leave the big city?"

Emily nodded. More lies. She needed a swift subject change. "How's your squad this year?"

Justine glanced toward the girls performing on the field. "They're not as good as you guys were. But they'll do." She studied Emily a moment with a critical eye. "In case I never told you, we missed you that last year."

Emily couldn't respond to that. She couldn't possibly have cheered her senior year without Heather.

Justine reached out, took hold of Emily's arm, and

squeezed. "I can't imagine how hard this must be for you." She shook her head. "His parole should have been denied."

The punch of emotions held Emily mute for several more seconds . . . long enough for Justine to keep going with things that Emily didn't want to hear.

"I shouldn't have allowed hazing week." Justine looked away a moment. "We haven't done it since that summer."

Emily braced one hand against the car in an effort to remain steady and vertical. If she'd stayed home that night . . . if Heather hadn't been in her bed. "It wasn't your fault."

"You wouldn't have sneaked out of your room and left the window unlocked. God." Justine hugged her arms around herself. "I should've put a stop to that tradition before someone got hurt."

It had been Emily's turn. The rising seniors were supposed to head up hazing week. It was tradition, like Justine said. The upcoming freshmen expected it. No one ever got hurt. Just silly pranks like rolling the assistant principal's yard.

No harm done. Until that night . . .

Her parents had ordered her to stay home with her brother. It was Ed and Carol's anniversary; they had plans. They would be home by midnight, but that would have been too late. Midnight was Justine Mallory's strictly imposed curfew. Heather had volunteered to stay at Emily's house just in case her brother woke up and needed something or her parents returned early. If they peeked in Emily's room they would see someone sleeping in her bed. All bases had been covered.

Except it hadn't been enough. . . . Emily hadn't seen disaster coming. There hadn't been any signs . . . other than that one ugly episode with Austin at the bowling alley. But that had been a whole week before. Clint Austin had waited for her outside the bowling alley. He'd teased and flirted the way he'd always done, but that time had been different.

She'd still been stinging from the way he'd kissed her a few days before and then just walked away. She'd let him have it. Called him a thug and a few other choice words. He'd lashed out at her, and everyone in the parking lot had witnessed the scene.

She shouldn't have antagonized him.

She shouldn't have left her bedroom window unlocked.

She shouldn't have let Heather stay in her place.

She should have been the one to die.

"You can't blame yourself, Emily." Justine reached out, gave her hand a quick squeeze, looked at her as if she feared Emily might be about to fly to pieces. "It wasn't your fault he went crazy. God only knows what set him off. They talked about drugs. He may not have even known what planet he was on."

But Emily did know what set him off. And they hadn't been able to prove the drug theory.

"Hey, Ms. Mallory!"

Justine turned to greet the football team jogging by in a haphazard formation. "Morning, boys."

A couple of the guys grabbed their chests dramatically at the idea that she'd even spoken. Wolf calls and flagrant gestures of adoration were showered on the school's favorite teacher as the team shuffled past like misfit military recruits in boot camp. Justine Mallory had been and, evidently, still was every high school boy's fantasy.

Justine waved off the last of the hoots and hollers. "Those boys. I swear, they never change."

"I really have to go." Emily couldn't be here any longer. "It was good seeing you again, Justine." Emily opened the car door, the panic threatening to swell again.

Justine touched Emily's shoulder. "You stay away from him, Em. You've been through enough."

Emily tensed. The breakdown had been kept a secret, but like everything else in this town, rumors got around. Folks still whispered behind their hands about her. She'd learned to hate that about Pine Bluff.

"I don't mean to scare you," Justine went on, "but he could still be dangerous. Maybe even more so now. It's not safe to get too close."

Emily introduced as much confusion as she could summon considering the realization that comment had prompted. "Why would you think I would do that?"

Had she really expected to be able to hide it? Some folks had nothing better to do. Gossip radars had likely gone up the moment she entered the city limits.

"Rumors get around." Sympathy marred Justine's remarkably unlined face. "There isn't anything you can do, you know. You need to let this go. We all do. Did you see the paper?" She visibly bristled. "They're even bringing up that nonsense about his so-called alibi. He lied then; he'll lie now . . . or worse. Stay away from him, Em."

Emily shook her head. She hadn't seen the paper. "I appreciate your concern, Justine, but I'm fine. Really." This time Emily got into the car. Her parents had the market cornered on concern for her. She didn't need any more, not even from the teacher and the principal she'd always admired.

"You let me know if you need anything."

Emily managed a wobbly "thank you" before starting the engine and backing out of the parking slot.

Waving, Justine watched her go.

Before Emily pulled out onto the street she glanced in her rearview mirror. Another woman had joined Justine. To get the latest gossip no doubt. Emily squinted to make out who she was. Haphazard ponytail, baggy clothes, a stark contrast to Justine's model-perfect appearance. The other woman looked toward Emily's car and waved. The odor of formaldehyde and mutilated frogs resurrected in her olfactory. Misty Briggs. Biology and chemistry. Batty Briggs. Emily waved back, then drove away.

The rumors were spreading.

Already all eyes were on her. Watching to see what she would do next . . . to see if she'd fall apart.

Poor Emily Wallace.

Everyone knew that Heather was dead because of *her*.

CHAPTER NINE

City Hall
11:30 A.M.

"Chief."

Ray looked up from the report on an attempted robbery at the Sack&Go last week. His secretary hovered at his door. "What's up, Mary Alice?"

"Granville Turner called. He's headed over here. Says he needs to talk to you, that it can't wait."

"Send him on in when he gets here."

Mary Alice Sullenger nodded and went back to her desk. She'd worked with Ray long enough to understand the visits he looked forward to and the ones he didn't. Though he considered Granville Turner an ally in many ways, Ray also knew firsthand what a royal pain the man could be when he got a burr under his saddle.

Ray heaved a disgusted breath and moved on to the next report. He'd worry about Granville when he got here; until then Ray had a job to do.

At least the phone was quiet for a change. Mary Alice had fielded calls all morning from concerned citizens who wanted to know the real story on Clint's release from prison.

Ray scowled at the copy of the *Pine Bluff Sentinel* lying on one corner of his desk. The picture Lassiter had taken in Brady's office was front-page news. The article read like a political debate with Troy Baker and his devastated family at one podium and Ray at the other. The whole damn mess was ridiculous, a one-sided story of Clint's upbringing. How his daddy had deserted Clint and his mother had been forced to work day and night to make ends meet, leaving him to his own devices. Every schoolyard scuffle and speeding ticket the man had ever gotten was laid out for the community to devour. If that wasn't bad enough, Lassiter had related numerous details, some he'd obviously taken from hearsay, regarding the night of Heather Baker's murder.

The entire page was dedicated to trying Clint Austin all over again. Ray had called Jacob Talbot, the other owner of the *Sentinel,* and told him how he felt about the smear campaign his paper appeared to be waging. Didn't matter one bit. Talbot's son had gone to school with Heather Baker.

Annoyed, Ray signed off on the report he'd just skimmed and reached for the next one. He could remember a time when the chief of police got a little respect around here. He wondered how Don Ledbetter would handle the situation if he were still alive and serving as chief.

Ray heard Granville Turner's arrival well before he reached the door to his office. Granville had the kind of boisterous, self-important voice that carried across a room and demanded attention.

Pushing to his feet, Ray donned a patient, welcoming demeanor. "Good to see you, Granville. How's Becky? Up and around by now, I hope." Becky was the rich old bastard's prized bluetick hound. He treated that dog better than some of his own kin. She'd had surgery recently to remove a small tumor that, thankfully, wasn't malignant.

Granville reached across the desk and pumped Ray's outstretched hand. "She's doing just fine, Chief. Thanks for asking." Without further ado, he settled into a chair.

Ray took his seat and got right to the point: "What can I do for you today, Granville?"

Mary Alice closed the door Ray's visitor had left open. She knew from past experience that a meeting with this particular citizen could get sensitive and loud.

Granville Turner was past sixty years old, with the build of an athlete. His hair had grayed into that distinguished shade that spoke of power and means rather than age. His gray eyes were clear and likely as keen as they'd been forty years ago. He was highly intelligent and filthy rich. He'd inherited well and invested better and was of the widely proclaimed opinion that he owned this town. Ray was intimately familiar with the way Granville did business, having learned fast the pecking order for keeping folks happy. Granville Turner was at the very top of that list. Whatever he wanted he generally got.

"I'd like to know what your plans are for getting Clint Austin the hell out of my town."

No mincing of words there.

"I understand your misgivings, Granville," Ray began, knowing he was wasting his breath. "But you have to understand that my hands are tied. Clint Austin served his time. Unless he breaks the law or the conditions of his parole, there isn't a thing I can do about his decision to return to Pine Bluff."

Granville Turner eased forward in his chair, his gaze narrowing. "If that boy even looks at anyone in this town crosseyed I want you to find a way to send him back to Holman. Do you hear me, Ray? You watch him like he's your goddamned reflection." Granville pointed a finger. "When I think about what that bastard could do to this town—to my son—it makes me want to tear him apart with my bare hands."

Ray chose his words carefully. "Granville, you and Keith have nothing to be concerned about. I've got the Austin situation under control. We won't have any trouble out of him."

Granville held his gaze several drama-filled seconds before rising from his chair. "All right then."

Ray joined him. If he got off this easy, he'd be tickled to death. But nothing with Granville was ever quite so easy.

"I know you possess the necessary talent to ensure this situation doesn't get out of hand." The older man's gaze locked with Ray's. "But you let that bastard cause any trouble and we'll have a serious problem. I don't want my son to suffer any more than he already has."

Ray should have been mad as hell at the man's audacity, but he and Ray had an understanding. If push came to shove, he knew the most direct route to Granville's Achilles' heel. That was something else Ray had learned early on. Always know your opponent's secrets. The right one could make all the difference.

The intercom on Ray's desk buzzed. He sat down and picked up the receiver, his head tilted to the left and his gaze still fixed on the man who'd walked out of Ray's office only to pause at his secretary's desk to chat or ask questions he more than likely had no business asking. "Yeah."

"Line one for you, Chief." Mary Alice didn't give the name of the caller, since Granville lingered at her desk.

"Thanks."

Ray stared down at the button blinking on his phone. He hoped like hell it wasn't anybody else swearing that Clint Austin had peeked in their kitchen window or stolen some tool they couldn't find in the garage. Ray blew out a burst of weary air. It was probably his wife making sure he planned to make lunch today. He'd missed more dates with her than he'd kept lately. He pressed the button and got it over with. "Ray Hale."

"I *love* the way you say that. Hmmm. So sexy."

His anger flared, but he refused to be baited. "What do you want?" He angled his head again to make sure Granville was gone.

A deep, sultry sigh intended to be sexy whispered across

the line. Ray's jaw clamped; he refused to let *her* get to him the way she'd once done so effortlessly.

"I think we have a problem, baby. I think there's a meltdown coming our way and people are gonna get burned."

A muscle started to twitch in his jaw from the hard set of his teeth. *Bitch.* "If you know what's good for you, you'll stay out of this."

"Is that a threat, Chief? You know how it turns me on when you talk rough to me."

He almost hung up, but her next words stopped him cold.

"She's close to the edge, Ray, real close. I'm afraid she's going to blow that whole shoddy investigation your department conducted wide open before she's finished."

He would not listen to any of her bullshit. "Stay away from Emily Wallace and don't call me again." He slammed the phone down.

"Chief?"

Ray's glare plowed across the room.

His secretary stood at the door looking ready to run for cover.

He reached for calm. "Yeah, Mary Alice." Damn it all to hell, he shouldn't let that woman get to him like this.

"I'm going to lunch now. You want me to forward your calls to the switchboard?"

He nodded. "Sure. I'm headed out myself."

Mary Alice flashed him a smile that didn't go anywhere near her eyes and then hurried away.

He felt like a horse's ass for allowing his secretary to see how the call had affected him. The dead last thing the folks in this town needed was something else to talk about.

CHAPTER TEN

3:00 P.M.

Clint left work a little early. Cook hadn't argued. Maybe he was impressed with the cleanup job Clint had done the evening before or maybe just didn't want to cross him. Clint would bet his left nut the guy didn't have an alibi for the night Heather Baker was murdered. Just one of many things Clint intended to learn about the good citizens of Pine Bluff.

That Emily Wallace wasn't waiting outside to follow him home surprised Clint. Since he had an appointment, one only he knew about, he was glad. If she'd followed him he would have had to lose her.

He took a moment to check his vehicle, the hood, the trunk, and then the pavement beneath it. Clear. Then he settled behind the wheel and started her up. Considering the way people felt about him around here, he'd taken certain precautions. Like stretching a strip of cheap transparent tape across the gap between his hood and the fender on each side. He'd done the same at the trunk. If either were raised, the seal of the tape would be broken. Checking the pavement beneath his car for drained fluids would let him know if a brake line had been damaged and left to leak its essential contents.

He drove, enjoying the feel of the engine's power and the wind whipping through the open windows. One neighborhood flowed into another until he slowed and made the right turn that would take him to the dead end of Red Bird Lane. The two acres of rolling green landscape with its fortresslike residence backed up to the forested land trust that surrounded the lake. Prime real estate owned by the biggest snake in the grass in the whole state, if not in the Southeast.

Six hundred and twelve Red Bird Lane, the property of Sylvester Fairgate.

Old man Fairgate was dead now. He'd died two years ago. Whatever the ailment that launched him to hell, it was no doubt prompted by the evil bastard's rotten deeds. Despite his name, fair had never been a part of Sly's way of doing business.

Sly had been a banker. Not your typical First National or City Trust. Sly Fairgate had lent money to those desperate enough to pay 200 percent interest, compounded weekly. He never carried a balance for more than thirty days. Anyone who couldn't pay in cash in that time frame paid in other ways.

An eight-foot decorative iron fence bordered the property. A couple of Dobermans paced in front of the gate and barked at Clint's Firebird. It would only take one glance for Sylvester's only son, Sidney, Psycho Sid to those who knew him, to identify who was at his gate. The red Firebird was Clint's calling card.

Sid was a different kind of bird, not cut from the same cloth as his father. Where Sly had been a balls-to-the-wall businessman, Sid preferred his games. The sadistic little prick liked nothing better than watching people squirm. Well, it was about time someone gave Sid something to squirm about.

Clint idled up to the ornate lamppost where the keypad

and speaker box hung within easy reach. If he was privy to the right code as he used to be, he would simply enter it and the gate would open, but since he wasn't he pressed the call button and waited for a response. He made sure he smiled for the camera strategically located on the massive pillar on the left side of the gate.

A full minute passed before the speaker crackled to life. "What the hell do you want?"

Psycho Sid. Clint's lips tilted in satisfaction. He would know that voice anywhere. That the man sounded on edge made Clint all the happier.

"I have a bone to pick with your daddy." Clint tapped his fingers on the steering wheel as he waited for a reaction.

Another fifteen seconds expired before, "My father is dead," vibrated from the box. The words weren't uttered like the guy cared that much that his daddy was dead. Sid sounded more pissed off at the intrusion than anything.

"I guess that means my beef is with you then." No use beating around the bush.

Another half minute or so passed before the metal scrape of the lock disengaging sounded and the gate slowly slid aside.

Clint applied just enough pressure to the accelerator to have the car roll up the paved drive. He parked in front of the house and got out, a little surprised that there was no welcoming party. Sly Fairgate had always kept at least four bodyguards on duty at any given time.

Maybe business was slow for Sid. Or maybe he was just too stupid to be afraid. Too bad for him. The kind of desperation that fueled his primary business, assuming it was the same as his daddy's, made for unstable customers.

Not that Clint gave one shit if the lowlife got himself blown away; he just preferred that it not be for a few days, since he had unfinished business with Sid and his dead daddy.

The one thing that could be counted on with men like the Fairgates was that they understood the value of information.

All sorts of information. And none, no matter how damning to themselves, would ever be taken for granted. Whatever secrets old Sly had known he'd most assuredly passed along to his evil offspring before he died. Knowledge was power. It was a rule of survival for their kind.

Clint was counting on that solid practice.

The front door opened and bodyguard number one appeared. The big guy gestured to one of the towering columns that flanked the front of the grandiose house. "Spread 'em," he ordered. He sported the traditional uniform, black suit, black tie, communication earpiece making him look a little like a Secret Service agent. Clint figured the costuming gave Fairgate a sense of importance.

Clint propped both hands against the column and spread his feet wide apart. He knew the drill. He'd watched others do it enough. The jeans, T-shirt, and sneakers he wore didn't provide for any clever places of concealment, but that didn't spare him a thorough search from his neck to his ankles.

"Let's go."

Clint straightened and walked through the front door with number one right on his heels. Two more goons waited in the entry hall. Both huge. Pumped-up bulk achieved at a gym, not lean fighting muscle culminated from basic survival.

"Mr. Fairgate is waiting for you in his office." This goon grinned, his lips curling away from his teeth the way a dog did right before he attacked. "He says you'll remember the way."

Clint walked straight to the spacious staircase in the center of the hall and started up. Sly hadn't chosen a first-floor room for his office. He preferred another layer of security between him and the outside world. He'd had the second floor renovated so that his office sat in the precise middle of the couple thousand square feet on that level. His office included his bedroom suite. The rooms where his bodyguards slept fanned out all the way around him, a barrier between him and any exterior wall.

If a threat entered the house, they would literally have to go through his bodyguards to get to him, no matter the time of day or night.

Sly had rarely left his compound. Clint doubted that his son did any differently.

More bodyguards waited on either side of the double doors that led into the office. Neither spoke as Clint walked past them. A wave of déjà vu slammed him as he surveyed the room with its posh velvet chairs facing the wide mahogany desk positioned in the very center. Sid, wearing the predictable white business suit and looking just like his daddy, sat in the same Italian leather chair his father had once occupied. Sly had always said you couldn't put an adequate value on good-quality property, but every human being on the globe, no matter how God-fearing, had his price.

Sid stared at Clint a moment with those beady black eyes, the fingers of his right hand busily twisting the ring on his left. Big, platinum, hosting a shiny rock embellished with the Fairgate family crest. Sly had worn one just like it. Thin brown hair, thinner face. Blade of a nose. The Fairgates weren't much to look at, but no one who wanted to keep breathing would risk saying so.

Sid's fingers stilled, the glare from those beady black eyes intensified. "How dare you come here like this," he rebuked. "You rise up out of that hole you were sentenced to and you think you can come to my home and threaten me. I could kill you and nobody would care. The whole fucking community would celebrate."

He was probably right about that.

"Your daddy was a lot of things, Sid, but he wasn't a coward."

Sid stood so fast his chair flew backward and banked off the credenza behind him. He rounded his desk and walked straight up to Clint. "You still a tough guy, Austin?" Sid reached beneath his tailored jacket and pulled out a big black pistol to wave. "Funny, you don't look so tough anymore.

Tell me, how did a young, pretty boy like you survive inside those prison walls with all those hard-ass motherfuckers who hadn't seen a woman in a couple of decades?"

Clint didn't let the bastard see the fury spiraling inside him. He maintained a perfectly calm exterior, even smiled. "I'm sure you're not really interested in my recent social life." He made it a point to tilt his head down to maintain eye contact with the shorter man.

"Don't waste my time, Austin. What do you want?"

Funny how no one had cared when almost eleven years of Clint's time was being stolen from him and wasted.

"I want my life back, Sid," he said bluntly. "Your daddy stole it from me and I've come to collect."

Red's most violet shade rose up Sid's neck from the collar of his white designer shirt. His closed mouth twitched two, three times before he managed to spit out the words trapped behind his clenched teeth. "Do you have a death wish, Austin?" The red darkened to the purple of rage. "You show up here and degrade the memory of my father! You must have a desperate desire to meet your Maker!"

Clint chuckled. "Get real, Sid; you hated him just as much as everybody else. I'll bet you had a party the night you buried him to celebrate your good fortune."

The muzzle of the weapon bored into Clint's ribs. "Shut up! Or I will blow your ass away where you stand."

"Go ahead." Clint nailed him with a look that let the rage and determination building inside him make an unholy appearance. "I spent ten years in that shit hole they call a prison. I've been beaten unconscious so many times I don't feel pain anymore. I've been used in ways you don't even want to imagine. So if you think the idea of being shot by a prick like you scares me, get a grip; *nothing* scares me."

The color slowly seeped from Sid's face, leaving a pallor that announced just how nervous he was. "Make your point, Austin. I have things to do."

And people to rob, Clint tacked on silently. "Your daddy

gave me a job that turned out to be my last one for him. I'm sure you recall the one."

Sid simply stared at him, without the vaguest reaction.

"He lied when the police asked him about my alibi."

Sid's mouth twitched again. "The old man was a compulsive liar, Austin; you of all people should recall that. I don't know what you expect me to do about it." His lips compressed back into that line that screamed of his impatience.

"Here's the thing, Sid." Clint leaned closer. "Your daddy fucked me big-time and I want you to make it right."

Those thin, flat lips pursed with the rage building all over again. "And if I don't . . ."

Now that was exactly what Clint had wanted the sawed-off little coward to say. "Then we have a problem."

Clint turned his back on the man and walked out of his office. Down the stairs and out the front entrance. Not one of Sid's goons attempted to stop him, and since no bullets ripped into his back, Clint had to assume he'd made his point.

He checked the Firebird before dropping behind the wheel. As he started the engine he stared up at the second floor of the Fairgate mansion. Sid would be ranting and raving about how he didn't have any protection and that no one appreciated the service he provided.

Clint roared down the drive, only slowing for the gate to open far enough for him to glide through. He barreled out onto Red Bird Lane the way he used to whenever he left the Fairgate place. Always with a new assignment to rattle somebody's cage. Sly Fairgate had never waited for a client to be late to start laying on the pressure. He firmly believed in heading off trouble before it happened. So Clint would provide the needed reminders. Occasionally he would round up a little leverage for the boss to use until the debt was paid.

That had been Clint's job that night almost eleven years ago. Take the car of a customer who failed to meet his obligations to Fairgate. Easy as taking candy from a baby. Clint had hot-wired dozens of cars. He knew the easiest way to disengage the locking mechanism in the steering column. He knew all the tricks. The car would be held hostage until the debt was paid.

The job should have been a piece of cake. Slide the Slim Jim into the door, pop the lock, do his magic inside, and drive away. Simple.

But nothing about that night had been simple.

The anger and bitterness he worked to keep in check rumbled. Clint shoved the gearshift into high, floored the accelerator, and lunged well beyond the posted speed as he exited the Pine Bluff city limits. It would take some time on the open road to work through this simmering rage and to clear his head.

For two years before that night, he'd worked for Sylvester Fairgate. Clint had done his share of customer motivation, but his primary position had been as a collector.

He'd never failed to get the job done. Not once. He'd walked a fine line with the law, but that never kept him from doing the right thing when the situation called for it.

That was his one mistake that night.

He'd gone out of his way to do the right thing, to play the hero. But he'd been left high and dry for his trouble. His boss had refused to confirm Clint's alibi, in order to protect his own fourteen-carat ass.

Now someone had to own that deceit.

CHAPTER ELEVEN

3:15 P.M.

It was a risk.

Emily chewed her lip as she studied the front door of her parents' house. It was a crying shame when a woman Emily's age was afraid of facing her own parents. Maybe not afraid. She dreaded facing them. Desperately wanted to avoid another *talk*.

But she had to go inside. She needed her cell phone charger. Her battery was almost spent. Like everyone else in the world, she couldn't survive without the damned thing.

She'd spent most of the day at the library doing research on incidents of parolees going back to prison for violations, just to reassure herself that her quest was reasonable. Focusing on that research had helped keep her mind off the whole "he might be innocent" nonsense. Clint Austin wasn't innocent. The rumors meant nothing. Principal Call hadn't seen anyone else, and neither had Emily. Only Austin.

Another warning chirp forced her out of her car. Technically, since her car was equipped with OnStar she could make an emergency call if she found herself between a rock and a hard place, but she preferred the convenience of her cell. She needed the charger. She walked deliberately to the front door. With a deep breath she turned the knob and opened it, trying hard not to make a sound. She'd had lots of practice at that the past few years.

The cool air inside made her shiver. She looked around; so far so good. Holding her breath, she eased into the hall to the right of the foyer. She was almost there.

A shout stopped her cold. Male. Her father?

More shouting. Her mother this time. Definitely coming from Emily's father's study, a fourth bedroom claimed for other purposes, just left of and across the hall from her bedroom. The door was closed. She frowned. How strange.

Dread congealed in her stomach as the arguing continued. Had her actions pushed her parents to this? Were they at each other's throats because of her?

Cringing at even the brush of fabric against her skin, she stole the rest of the way to her room and slipped inside. She narrowed the door opening to a mere inch, left it ajar just enough to peek out. Then she stood perfectly still and listened—eavesdropped, an act she'd been taught from birth was both inconsiderate and underhanded.

"There has to be something you can do!"

Her mother.

"I can try to pay him off!" Emily's father bellowed. "Maybe that's what he wants. He won't say at this point."

His tone took Emily aback. Her father never raised his voice to anyone, much less her mother.

"This was supposed to be settled," Carol insisted, much more calmly. "No matter what you offer him, what's to keep him from telling someone? You know you can't trust a Fairgate."

"Just tell me what you expect me to do, Carol!"

Fairgate? Emily couldn't fathom a reason her parents would be discussing the name Fairgate. She didn't really know the Fairgates, just the reputation, and it was all bad. Very bad.

"I have no idea," her mother snapped. "You got us into this mess, you can figure the way out."

She burst from the room. Emily jerked back.

Her father stayed behind. The silence almost tugged her out into the open and across that hall to check on him. God, she hoped this didn't have anything to do with something she had done. Or failed to do.

Fear joined the dread inside her. Austin had worked for Fairgate. Could this be about that? Surely not.

The remark Justine had made about Austin's alibi nagged at Emily. It was a lie. Old man Fairgate had sat on the witness stand and said so under oath. For a man like him the oath part probably didn't mean squat . . . nor did it mean that Austin was telling the truth. He'd lied. No question.

Her father's voice hauled her attention back to the study.

"This is Ed Wallace. Put Fairgate on the line."

The silence seemed to go on forever. Emily's pulse thumped in her ears. There had to be a mistake. She was surely missing some important piece of the conversation that would explain away the implausible portion she'd just overheard. Edward Wallace could not possibly have any dealings with a Fairgate.

"Just tell me what you want," her father demanded.

The anger in his tone startled her.

"And if I don't?"

Her heart skipped. Was that a threat he'd just issued? Her father? What the hell was going on here?

"Fine."

He slammed the phone down.

His face was a deep crimson when, like her mother, he charged from the room.

Emily grabbed her phone charger, waited until she was sure it was clear, and slunk back into the hall. She was not supposed to have heard any of that. If she left now, they might not know.

She made it to the front door. The sound of the icemaker

in the kitchen confirmed she was home free. She opened the door, stepped onto the porch—

"Emily?"

She froze, her hand still on the knob of the half-open door. Three more seconds and she might have escaped. Now her parents would know Emily had overheard their argument. She could just ask what was going on, but it didn't work that way in her family. Ed and Carol's privacy had always been sacrosanct.

"Em, is something wrong?"

Emily braced herself, produced the requisite smile, and turned to face her mother. "Hey. No, everything's fine."

"Are you just coming in?" The flash of cold suspicion in her mother's eyes settled the issue of bringing up Fairgate.

Emily nodded. "Yes. I just . . . yeah." So many lies.

Her mother's expression thawed. "Some of your friends came by this afternoon."

"Who?" Did anyone even know she was in town?

"Cathy, Megan, and Violet," Carol ticked off the names, then smiled warmly. "They were all so excited about the possibility of seeing you."

Emily moistened her lips. "I'm . . . sorry I missed them." More lies. And to her mother at that. "I just realized I left my purse in the car. I should get it." At least that was true. Emily prepared to escape once more, but Carol Wallace wasn't letting her go.

"You really should call," she urged. "Friends are important, Em."

Emily just wanted out the door before she did something rash, like ask her mother what she and Emily's father had to do with Fairgate. "I stopped by the school today."

The words just sort of popped out. Definitely a good choice, though. The idea that Emily had gone to the school seemed to relieve some of the tension in her mother's *seriously concerned* expression.

"Principal Call showed me the plaque in the senior hall,"

Emily went on. "And I talked to Ms. Mallory. I watched the squad perform a couple of routines."

Relief, sheer gratitude, and more glittered in her mother's eyes. "That's wonderful."

"I should get my purse." Emily gestured vaguely toward her car. She really wanted to go. The idea that something so simple as stopping by the school could give her mother such joy spoke volumes about just how worried Emily's parents were. "Maybe I'll try to catch the girls for dinner." Lie. Lie. Lie.

"I left Violet's number by the phone," Carol offered. "You cheered on the same squad for all those years, Em, it would be a shame not to get together."

"Don't worry; we will," Emily promised . . . just not today.

She'd actually started to close the door when her mother added, "Just so you know, I mentioned that you're having some difficulty with Clint Austin's release."

Emily counted to ten. *Don't react on impulse. Be calm. Be cool.* Her mother was only trying to help.

With far more poise than Emily would have imagined she could master, she smiled. "I appreciate that. I'm sure they're as upset by the news as I am."

Her mother nodded, regret registering along with the concern. "We all understand that it's far harder for you, Em. I think sharing your feelings with your friends would help."

"You're probably right." Whatever she wanted to hear. "See you later."

Emily closed the door behind her. She stood really still, tried to breathe away the ache in her chest.

Megan, Cathy, Violet, Heather, and Emily. The rising seniors on the squad that summer. Emily and Heather had been selected as team captains, a decision that didn't sit so well with Violet and Cathy. Both had suffered with jealousy issues. Megan pretty much went with the flow, but not the others, especially Violet. Everything had to be about her.

Emily pushed the past away and headed for her car.

She now had a more immediate issue. Were her parents in financial trouble? Why else would they have dealings with a loan shark? They would never forgive her for eavesdropping if she mentioned it.

That left only one way to find out what was going on.

3:55 P.M.

Emily steeled herself as she rolled up to the gate of the property on 612 Red Bird Lane. She'd had to ask the clerk at the Sack&Go for Fairgate's address, which would no doubt prompt more rumors. After pressing the buzzer on the speaker box, Emily waited.

Not for long. "What do you want?"

"Hello." She cleared her throat. "My name is Emily Wallace and I'd like to speak to Mr. Fairgate."

Several seconds passed with no response.

"Hello?" she repeated.

The scrape of metal dragged her attention to the gate in front of her. When it had jerked and scooted out of the way, she drove through.

Her heart climbed into her throat and stuck there in one shuddering lump as she parked in front of the massive house. She didn't know what she'd expected, but it wasn't this. She could honestly say that she'd grown up in Pine Bluff and not once had she ever seen this place. Reminded her of Graceland. Big columns. No lions, though. Ah, but he did have dogs. Two fierce-looking Dobermans alternately marched and sniffed their way around her car before marking each wheel.

Thankfully a mountain of a man lumbered from the front entrance and summoned the animals. Gifting him with a grateful smile, she opened her door, glanced around just to make sure there was nothing else to worry about before getting out. A long white limousine sat in the bend of the circular drive.

Tugging at her blouse, she closed her car door and summoned the nerve to head for the entrance. The towering door opened and another massive man gestured for her to enter. Emily walked past him and paused just inside the grand entry hall.

"Are you armed?"

She scowled at the man. "What? No."

"Lift your arms," he ordered.

Appalled but not inclined to learn the consequences of refusing, she raised her arms. He patted her down, just like in the movies. She gasped when he reached her thighs.

He glanced up. "Spread your legs."

Horrified but certain this was the only way to get past the man, she obeyed. When he'd finished, he stood. "Let's go."

Reeling at the violation, she followed him up an elegant staircase and then into a large office.

Sidney Fairgate sat behind a wide, gleaming desk. He was older than Emily by several years, but she'd seen him around at the trial. She recalled quite distinctly that he had a reputation for being as crude as he was unattractive.

"Do you need money?" he demanded, those beady eyes peering at her as if he hoped to see through her clothes.

She remembered that, too. He was known for being nasty and mean when it came to women. "No."

"Then why are you here?"

She wet her lips and took the necessary leap. "I want to know if my father is in trouble . . . financially."

Fairgate's eyebrows shot upward. "I can't discuss anyone else's business with you. What kind of man do you think I am?"

Fear sparked along her nerve endings, made standing still extremely difficult. "I just want to help."

"You can't help."

Emily blinked, startled by his indifference. "Surely there's something I can do."

A sinister smile spread across his hawklike features. "There are always things a woman can do," he said as he blatantly sized her up, "but I'm certain you wouldn't be interested."

Anger kicked up enough to make her go temporarily stupid. "Stop harassing my father."

"Or what?" Fairgate fired back.

The huge guy who'd led her here and who had waited by the door until now took a step in her direction.

Time to go. She turned her back to the pig behind the desk and started for the door.

"If you want to know your daddy's troubles, Miss Emily Wallace," Fairgate said, causing her to hesitate, "ask him to tell you the secret he's been keeping for all these years."

What kind of secret? What did he mean, all these years? Don't ask. Just go! She prepared to move toward the door once more.

"Everybody has their secrets, including your precious daddy," Fairgate taunted. "Nobody's perfect."

Anger poked at her, had her sucking up her courage and turning to face him. "There's one difference between you and my father, Mr. Fairgate." That beady, penetrating gaze probed her, but she refused to be intimidated. "My father would never keep a secret that would hurt another person. You, I am quite certain, would have no qualms doing just that."

He sneered at her. "I have secrets, Miss Wallace. Many, many secrets. And, as you say, a number of those would cause harm. Some already have."

She told herself not to be baited . . . told herself to go . . . but she couldn't walk out now without asking. Between Justine bringing it up and Emily's parents' argument and then *this* . . . she couldn't not ask.

"Like . . . ," she heard herself say, her mouth going sand-box dry, ". . . the one about Clint Austin's alibi?" Her heart stumbled as her own words, words of betrayal, ricocheted in the room.

Fairgate snickered. "I wondered how long it would take people to start asking that question now that he's out. I got one thing to say; the answer to that question is for me to know and you not to, Miss Wallace. That's the thing about secrets. You can keep them. If you have other interests regarding Mr. Austin, perhaps I can assist you with those."

Outrage unfurled, mostly at herself. "The only thing about Clint Austin that interests me, Mr. Fairgate, is making sure justice is served."

"Really." He braced his hands on his desk, leaned forward. "And here I was thinking you were interested in the truth."

She pivoted away from the amusement in those beady eyes and stamped out. Taking the stairs in a blind rush, she flew to the front door, already standing open with another of those bouncer-type guys waiting to close it behind her.

Outside, she gulped as much air as possible. *Bastard.*

She didn't care what that evil little man said, her father had to have a good reason for interacting with him. Ed Wallace wouldn't have any secrets harmful to anyone other than perhaps himself. The remark about her being interested in the truth had been designed to unnerve her. Well, Fairgate had succeeded. Damn him.

She started her car, executed a three-point turn, and barreled down the drive. She stopped for the gate, irritation pounding with every beat she waited; then she rolled out into the street.

A black Maxima parked on the other side of the street caused her to slow when she wanted to floor the accelerator and rocket away from this place. The woman behind the wheel stared at Emily, then waved.

Misty Briggs?

Emily braked automatically, powered her window down, and resuscitated one of her pretend smiles. "Hi." She could feel the new rumors forming and mutating already. She should not have come here.

Misty Briggs adjusted her clunky glasses. "Emily." She glanced at the closing gate. "Fancy meeting you here."

Emily prompted her brain to generate a plausible excuse. "I came to speak with Mr. Fairgate." No point pretending otherwise. The woman wasn't blind, just nearsighted.

"Oh." Ms. Briggs met Emily's eyes briefly, then stared in the direction of the house again as if something there kept distracting her. "Lots of people come to see him."

Okay. No need to prolong this strange reunion. Before Emily could offer a parting line, Briggs asked, "Was he there?"

Confused at first, Emily asked, "Who?"

Those huge hazel eyes, magnified further by the thick lenses, flicked to Emily's. "Fairgate."

"Oh. Yes, he was there."

"Alone?"

Stranger by the second. "You mean alone other than his apelike bodyguards?"

"Yes, that's what I mean."

"I didn't see anyone else." Sitting here having *this* discussion with her former science teacher who had clearly inhaled way too many toxic fumes was too weird. "Well, it was good to see you."

Briggs scrutinized Emily now as if she'd only just realized to whom she was speaking. "Justine mentioned that she'd spoken with you." Briggs said this as if she hadn't heard Emily's cue that she intended to go, as if she hadn't asked those odd questions about Fairgate. "She thought you seemed terribly upset about Clint Austin's release."

Emily wanted to ask what she was supposed to feel; instead she said with amazing aplomb, "I'm extremely disappointed in the parole board's judgment."

Briggs pushed at her glasses again. "You know, I almost

hate to mention this, but the subject came up in the beauty shop the other day."

Here it came. This was why Emily rarely came home and never ventured into town.

"I'm certain there's nothing to it," Misty went on. "Just a rumor."

Emily braced herself. She should just drive away and leave the woman sitting here wondering why.

"It was very disturbing, though. The rumor suggested that Austin was innocent. That his alibi was real, but he just couldn't prove it." She stared at the Fairgate house again as if God himself resided there. "I guess only *he* knows the answer to that one."

Despite having buttressed herself for the disclosure, Emily hadn't been adequately prepared. She couldn't dredge up a response. The idea that Justine had mentioned being at the beauty shop with all Emily's old friends filtered through along with Misty's remarks. Had they all been talking about Emily? About the murder?

A symphony of notes shattered the stifling silence.

"That's my phone." Briggs offered a quick smile. "Maybe I'll see you again before you go back to Birmingham."

Emily managed a choked good-bye, took her foot off the brake, and coasted away. She glanced in her rearview mirror. She'd gone through all that emotional turmoil and she still didn't know any more than she had before she'd arrived.

Except a lot of ridiculous gossip about Austin's alibi. He didn't have an alibi.

What the hell did her father have to do with any of this? Her father did not keep damaging secrets. Gossip. Rumors. That was all this was.

Secrets and lies.

None of it changed the truth.

Emily knew the truth.

CHAPTER TWELVE

"What was that all about?"

Sid snapped out of the pseudocoma he'd lapsed into and glared at *her*. "What're you moaning about?" *Goddamn bitch.* She should know better than to get into his business. He didn't even know why she was here.

She wanted something. He saw plenty he wanted. Anticipation altered his foul mood ever so slightly.

As if sensing the change, she studied him curiously. "Was that Emily Wallace?"

He pointed a threatening finger. "That is none of your fucking business." He glowered at her when what he really wanted was to fuck her brains out, but she'd never once looked at him that way. She was too high-and-mighty.

"You seem a little tense," she offered coolly.

"And why wouldn't I be?" he demanded, giving her a stare that usually had the people who dared to enter his office cowering. "It's Grand fucking Central Station around here!" First Clint Austin came shooting off his mouth, then that frigid bitch Emily Wallace. Damn straight he was tense. Ready to snap.

She hummed a note of disinterest. "Someone really should tell that man that he isn't welcome in this town anymore."

"You think that's my fucking job?" Sid snarled. It wasn't his place to straighten out his daddy's goddamn shit. But Sid did enjoy watching people thrash around like puppets on a string. There were lots of people thrashing with Austin's return.

The twat currently watching Sid folded her arms over those high, full tits, blocking his view of those firm nipples poking against the thin fabric of her dress. "So, are we doing business or what?" she challenged.

He shivered. Damn, she was powerful. He rarely met a woman who could do that to him from halfway across the room. His gaze roved over that filmy red dress, the wrap kind that tied at the waist. He imagined the wicked lingerie beneath. "That depends upon what you have to offer."

Her manicured fingers tugged at the strings of the sash, and the silky fabric swept over her shoulders and cascaded to the floor. She held out her arms, showcasing her spectacularly naked body. "What will this buy me?"

His eyes bulged, but he managed to nod, tough to do considering every muscle in his body had gone rock hard. "That could put me in a very generous mood." More so than he had anticipated, in fact.

She walked toward him, those firm, smooth thighs and the perfect tilt of her breasts making his mouth water. When she moved around his desk, she scooted onto the edge right in front of him. The idea of her bare ass on that polished mahogany sent electricity rushing through him. God, he wanted her. He'd always wanted her.

She inclined her head, causing her long silky hair to fall across one delicious tit. "You give me what I want and I'll give you this . . . *once.*"

His cock twitched. Once would be enough. "Name it."

His respiration grew ragged. He wanted to touch her. But he held back. This was business. He wouldn't do anything but look until he knew the terms.

"It's very simple." Her scent was driving him crazy. "Your father had a secret that you've been keeping for him for a very long time. You continue to keep that one secret and we'll have a deal."

He scrubbed a shaky hand over his jaw. He didn't see a problem. *What the hell?* "Which secret?"

She licked those lush, red-painted lips and then smiled. Her arms draped around his neck and drew his face close to that beautiful mouth. She whispered the words in his ear.

He should have known.

She drew back, widened her thighs enough for him to get a better view of her negotiable asset. "Do we have a deal?"

Time for him to reclaim control. He had a reputation after all. "What makes you think you can trust me to hold up my end of the bargain?" He kept his hands at his sides, no matter that his fingers itched to molest her in every imaginable fashion.

"Like I said, you've been keeping this one a very long time." Her hand settled on his fly, rubbed his thick cock. "I'm certain it'll continue to keep."

He wanted to hold out a little longer, make her beg, but— his gaze traveled over that perfect skin—that wasn't happening. What she said was true. He had kept this particular secret for a very long time. And now he intended to have some fun with it.

"Deal," he agreed. At least it was a deal until he decided differently. This bitch should know better than to trust him.

She smiled, purred like a little harmless kitten. "Excellent." She lowered his zipper, reached inside. "Just one last thing, baby." Those skilled fingers wrapped around him, made him groan. "Tell me how you want it."

CHAPTER THIRTEEN

5:10 P.M.

Emily parked across the road from Austin's house. Her antiperspirant had long since melted in the ninety-eight-degree heat. Even with every window in the car open and the shade from the maples, her clothes plastered to her skin in five minutes flat. She skimmed the list of most frequently violated parole conditions she'd made, but she couldn't seem to concentrate on that. She needed to understand what was going on with her father.

Every instinct warned that her father's business with Fairgate somehow related to Austin. That weasel Fairgate had said her father had kept his secret *all these years.* But Fairgate could be toying with her. She could be reading too much between the lines. Coupled with the rumors floating around regarding Austin's innocence, doubt as to what she thought she knew had taken far too formidable a foothold.

Fairgate was the only loan shark in town. That both Ed Wallace and Clint Austin had been involved with him wasn't such a stretch. Except for the idea that that this was her father she was talking about. He didn't do shady.

She needed answers. All these years she had focused on Heather's murder and keeping Austin behind bars. Had her parents needed her and she hadn't been there?

Her gaze settled on the house across the road. If she asked *him* for information regarding Fairgate, would he tell her what he knew? She had to be out of her mind to even consider it. But then she was desperate. The idea that her parents needed her help had shaken her from the obsession that had been her whole existence for more than a decade.

Her heart rate accelerated at the idea of getting close enough to him to carry on a conversation. She closed her eyes and blocked the sensations. All those years he'd been in prison she'd hated him . . . wanted him to die. Now he was out and she couldn't stop those damned feelings she'd thought were dead and buried. That she could still feel attracted to him made her sick with shame.

Maybe she was losing it. Her eyes popped open. Maybe her parents were right and she did need Dr. Brown.

No. It was being here, in Pine Bluff, surrounded by all those crazy rumors about Austin's innocence, getting to her. Had to be. She was doubting herself, that was all.

Austin's red Firebird appeared in her rearview mirror, roaring along the dirt road, dust flying behind it. He slowed when he neared her car, turned unhurriedly into his drive without looking in her direction, parked in his usual spot, and went inside the house.

If she worked up the nerve to ask him about Fairgate, Austin would just lie to her even if he knew the truth. She was the last person on earth he would want to help. He should be the last person she would ask for help. She had to get her head on straight and start thinking clearly.

Her brain abruptly registered Austin exiting the house.

Where was he going now? So far he'd come home each evening and stayed put, at least until she left at ten or so. He hadn't changed clothes. Same worn jeans hugging his long legs and grease-stained T-shirt stretched over his muscled torso that he'd been wearing when he got out of the car.

"What is he doing?" she muttered.

He strode right past his car and down the drive.

Toward the road . . . toward her—

Instinct had her grabbing her cell phone. She jerked it loose from the charger, her pulse reacting to an adrenaline dump as Austin crossed the road. She sat there and watched him come closer . . . something implacable and lethal in his stride. As he neared her car, the fury on his face . . . in his eyes registered. Her danger gauge abruptly kicked in full throttle. The real fear she should have felt ten seconds prior tore through the dim-witted curiosity muddling her good sense.

He stopped at her door, glared down at her with such ferocity that the oxygen stalled deep in her chest. "Get out of the car."

For an instant she couldn't find her voice. The way he looked at her . . . such anger . . . such . . . *pain.* Confusion scattered her thoughts. "Stay away or I'll call the police." Her voice shook as badly as her hands.

His jaw tightened with that fury blazing in his eyes. "Call 'em. Call right now."

He hadn't made a move to open her door or even touch her vehicle, but she couldn't be sure he wouldn't do just that any second now. He was in a rage. Was this the kind of rage he'd been in when he entered her room uninvited that night? Her mind argued with her . . . he'd looked terrified that night . . . frantic. Nothing like this.

Her fingers fumbled across the keypad. When the 911 dispatcher had finished her spiel, Emily gave her location and asked that the police be sent right away.

She closed her phone and reluctantly met his gaze once more. "The police are on the way." She meant to warn him to step back from her car, but the words got stuck in her throat.

The fury she'd seen seconds ago had dissolved into something she couldn't readily identify. A mixture of pain and . . . desperation she couldn't adequately assess.

He thrust his fingers through his hair and backed away from her car, but his eyes, hollow with grief, didn't leave hers.

A shiver rushed over her skin, prompted by a chill wind from the grave even as she sat sweating in this damned car. Some crazy part of her urged her to do something . . . to reach out to him. Before she could stop the reaction, she'd gotten out of the car. "What's wrong with you?" Her voice was small, fragile.

"Why?"

The anguish in that one syllable unsettled something lodged so deep inside her that she couldn't respond. What was happening to her?

"Why?" he repeated, fury conquering the agony. He moved in closer, trapping her against the car. "Why did you do this?"

She trembled as her senses reacted to the raw masculinity of his nearness. She told herself it was the fear that had stolen the very air from her lungs . . . but that was a lie. It was him . . . just like before when she'd dreamed of being so close to him . . . of being the one he wanted. An ache pierced her. Oh, God, how could her emotions betray her like this?

Her hands went against his chest as if that action could somehow stop this insanity. She mustered her voice: "Move."

Pushing against him was like running headlong into a mountain. His heart drummed beneath her palms . . . the contour of muscles testing the thin material of his T-shirt making her dizzy. The heat from his body, so close to her own, made her feel restless . . . afraid. She needed to run. She needed to get away from him. But she couldn't move . . . she could only stare into those haunting eyes.

The dust swirling in the distance drew her gaze toward

the spot where the road intersected the highway. A truck. Blue light throbbing on the dash.

The police.

Thank God.

The truck skidded to a stop next to her car and the driver's side door flew open.

Chief Ray Hale rounded the hood. "Get in the truck, Clint."

Austin didn't move, didn't shift that unrelenting gaze from hers. The caress of his ragged breath on her face had her quivering with something she couldn't label as fear.

"Clint," Ray repeated, "get in the truck. *Now.*"

Austin looked at Ray for the first time since his arrival. His face a hard, expressionless mask, he didn't say a word, just backed away from Emily and walked over and got into Ray's truck.

Relief made her knees weak.

"Are you all right?" Ray stood next to her now.

"Yes." Her voice quaked. "He . . ." She shrugged, at a loss for the right words. "I don't know what happened. He went in the house and he came out . . . like this."

"Do you mind," Ray's voice was gentle, "telling me what you're doing out here? My deputies have reported seeing your car a couple of times."

Austin sat completely still in the passenger seat of Ray's truck. But his eyes, that unyielding, penetrating gaze, remained on her as if she'd committed some unthinkable offense.

"Emily?"

She dragged her attention away from Austin and peered up at Ray. "I'm sorry. What did you say?"

"What're you doing out here?" That he looked more concerned than perplexed told her he thought she was just as crazy as her parents did. Her parents had probably warned him.

"I'm . . ." No use lying. He was the chief of police. He

would figure it out even if Austin didn't tell him. "I'm watching him."

Ray studied her a moment; then he nodded. "I see." He glanced at his truck and then at Austin's house. "Why don't you go on home and we'll talk later. Right now I need to find out what's going on with Clint."

Ray didn't say that he figured she had done something to antagonize Austin. He didn't have to. The innuendo was there, hanging in the tension suddenly vibrating between them.

"Thank you for coming." She looked away from Ray's prying gaze, got into her car, and started the engine, but she didn't drive away immediately. She watched until he had pulled his truck into the driveway next to Austin's car and the two of them had gotten out and gone inside the house.

Her actions on autopilot, she shut off the engine. She wasn't going anywhere until she knew what the hell had happened in there. If whatever had happened somehow violated Austin's parole, she wanted to know.

Determination charged through her and she was out of the car and marching up the driveway before her brain caught up with her emotions. She slowed as she reached Ray's truck. Technically she was trespassing.

Her heart thundering, her legs still a little wobbly, she continued toward the porch. The front door opened and Ray stepped out, stopping her cold at the bottom of the steps.

"What happened in there?"

To her surprise, the question came from her.

"Emily, you should go home now."

She shook her head, climbed those steps, and went toe-to-toe with him. "I want to know what's going on here." She had a right to know. Well, maybe she didn't, but she was taking the right. She needed answers.

Ray dragged off his hat and exhaled a heavy breath. "Somebody vandalized the house. It's chaos in there."

"What exactly do you mean by that?"

Ray glanced around as if he didn't want anyone to hear what he had to say next. "Look, Clint's out back; you can come in for a minute and see for yourself. I wouldn't even let you go in except that I need you to understand his side of this."

Before she could question his motives or argue with the idea that she could ever understand anything about Austin, Ray took her by the arm and led her inside as if she were a child and couldn't be trusted not to break something or run away.

New emotions crowded in on Emily. Curiosity. Apprehension. Then regret followed by sadness. The house looked as if it had been tossed in an effort to find valuables.

"They broke a lot of things. Tore photographs into bits. Basically made a hell of a mess."

Ray kept talking, but Emily stopped listening . . . her full attention narrowed to the damaged items scattered about the living room. Broken picture frames, the photos once protected there ripped apart. It was easy to mentally piece together the strewn parts. Clint Austin and his mother. Broken shards of something porcelain, pink and white. The shattered face of a woman with long red hair.

The screen on the small box-style television had been smashed. Furniture overturned.

". . . see anything?"

Emily pulled her attention back to Ray. "Did you say something?"

"Clint thought maybe you might have seen someone leaving his house when you arrived."

Surely he didn't think she had anything to do with this. He did . . . he'd asked her why she did this.

"There wasn't anyone here when I arrived," she said. "I'd been here maybe twenty minutes before he showed up, but I didn't get out of my car until he came out there acting crazy."

"You didn't meet anyone on the road that you recall?"

"No." She mentally replayed the drive from town. She'd

been distracted, but 18 was always deserted. To have met another vehicle would have been unusual. "I don't think so." She abruptly felt exactly like Principal Call must have that night. She couldn't answer the question with any real accuracy. Did that mean that someone other than Austin might have been in her neighborhood that night . . . in her house? Her pulse skipped, then hammered hard. *Stop it,* she ordered. She didn't need to play guessing games. She had been in the room that night.

Ray rested his hands on his hips, his hat still clutched in one. "Emily, I know how hard this has been for you."

God, she was so sick of hearing that. Before she could tell him as much, he went on. "I want you to know that I really do understand how you feel. Heather was your best friend. She died in your arms. To you, Clint must represent all that's wrong in the world. But he's done his time. He deserves the chance to get on with his life." Ray sighed. "And so do you."

The merging of anger and frustration and shock had her reeling. Shock at the idea that he would believe her capable of this kind of ugliness. Frustration at the whole world thinking she could simply get on with her life. And anger, dammit, at the suggestion that Clint Austin deserved anything. Anger at herself for waffling on the whole damned subject.

Clint Austin was guilty. He didn't deserve to breathe the same air she did. But this—she surveyed the devastation in his living room—was a disgrace, an offense against his mother and all she'd worked so hard to hang on to.

"I didn't have anything to do with this, Chief Hale," Emily said with a pointed look at the man who should know her better than that. "I can't imagine who would be low enough to do such a thing." She planted her hands on her hips just as he had. "But mainly I'm disappointed that you or anyone else in this damned town would believe for one second that Clint Austin deserves anything but a return trip to that rock he slithered out from under day before yesterday."

Her emotions got the better of her then. The confusion, the anger and frustration . . . the self-loathing. She had to pause a moment to compose herself. When Ray would have spoken, she held up a hand. "I'm not finished." He kept his mouth shut. "He's a killer; as far as I'm concerned he won't have paid for what he did until he's dead and rotting in hell. Is that plain enough for you?"

The sound of glass crunching beneath a heavy foot jerked her gaze beyond Ray's right shoulder.

Clint Austin stood in a doorway that probably led to the kitchen. He made no effort to avert his gaze when hers collided with his. She didn't know how long he'd been listening, but she had a feeling he'd heard all she had to say.

She didn't care. She meant every word. For the first time in more than a decade, denial crashed into her. She shook with the force of it.

"Emily, maybe—"

She didn't wait for Ray to finish whatever he'd started; she left. She had to get out of there. Stupidly, she cried all the way home. It made absolutely no sense. She hadn't said a damned thing that wasn't the God's truth and still the tears refused to stop.

Maybe because of what some fool had done to the memory of Austin's mother. *She* deserved better than this. That had been her home, her things. Austin ended up with her property by genetic default.

Emily parked in the driveway of her parents' home and got out. She was just tired. Tired and overreacting. Tomorrow she would figure out where she went from here. Her father's situation with Fairgate had to be top priority. Tonight she was just too mentally exhausted.

If she hadn't been so caught up in her thoughts she might have paid more attention, might have noticed the car parked at the curb and been able to prepare, but she hadn't.

She walked into the house and found her parents waiting

for her. With her parents were Heather's parents, Mr. and Mrs. Baker. All four looked at Emily with that same *deeply troubled* expression.

"Emily," her father said, "we need to talk."

Austin Place
6:15 P.M.

Clint picked up the pieces of the porcelain trinket his mother had cherished. His chest felt ready to explode. Fucking cowards. They should have taken up their beef directly with him. Doing this, he surveyed the carnage, was not right—not fair. But since when had his life been fair? The magnitude of emotions he hadn't been able to suppress all channeled into one—fury.

Someone would pay for this.

"I'll take these to a fellow I know who might be able to reconstruct them for you."

Clint glanced at Ray, resisted the impulse to lash out at him. The man was only trying to help. He'd worked diligently to gather the torn pieces of photographs into several plastic sandwich bags. The knowledge that Clint should be grateful didn't alleviate the rage quaking inside him. He placed the remnants of shattered porcelain on the mantel. He had to get out of here.

He strode out onto the porch, sucked in as much air as his cramped chest would accommodate. Emotion burned in his eyes and he closed them tight. What the hell had he been thinking, coming back here? He couldn't make these people see how wrong they were. Ray had warned him that digging around in the past wouldn't help . . . maybe he'd been right.

But how could Clint go on with his life without setting the record straight? He'd paid big-time for someone else's crime; he could live with that. His mother had gone to her grave with this ugliness hanging over her head. She'd called herself a failure. Had told Clint over and over that this wasn't his fault . . . it was hers.

That he couldn't live with.

Goddamn it! His fists clenched at his sides and it was all he could do to restrain the desire to get in his car and drive straight to Troy Baker's house . . . then Keith Turner's . . . then one by one to each of their friends'.

Ray joined him on the porch, but Clint refused to look at him. Clint just wanted the man to go. He didn't want to talk right now. He didn't even want to think. What he really wanted, considering pounding heads was not a viable option, was to get drunker than hell and escape this whole shitty reality.

But that would be a freaking violation of his parole.

"Emily didn't have anything to do with this, Clint," Ray urged. "I hope you believe that. She's just doing the only thing she can to assuage the hurt driving her. She doesn't mean any real harm."

Clint laughed out loud. Like hell she didn't mean any harm. She'd made her intentions abundantly clear. She wanted him back in Holman or dead, whichever came first.

"That's the one thing," Clint countered, "that's perfectly clear in all this." He turned to Ray, looked him dead in the eye. "I know exactly what Emily Wallace wants from me."

CHAPTER FOURTEEN

9:45 P.M.
302 Dogwood Drive

Justine finished her yoga session, turned off the DVD player, and headed for the shower. Tonight she'd selected the extended session, needing the extra relaxation benefits. This had been one hell of a week, and it was only hump day.

The squad was coming along nicely, but a couple of the girls still needed to understand who was boss. Justine Mallory did not put up with any back talk or any breaking of the rules from her girls.

Slipping off her formfitting suit, she considered her body in the mirror that spanned floor to ceiling and half the length of one wall. She liked watching herself work out. A smile tugged at her lips, then faded. It wouldn't be long now until things would start to go drastically downhill. She worked out every day, sometimes twice, but no one got to keep their good looks and firm body forever. At least not naturally, and she had no desire to deal with the surgical lines of *work*. Even lipo came with unsightly little marks.

None for her. She would just have to increase her already rigorous regimen. And then what?

She stared at her face. Not so bad for a woman approaching forty. The very best skin treatments and, most important, sunscreen, along with good genes, had ensured a minimal amount of lines. She turned her head left, then right, assessed any changes. But every year the new students arrived looking even younger. Pretty soon she'd be just another old-lady schoolteacher. She couldn't live with that. That was the very reason she had to plan better for her future. She needed long-term security. There was only one man in this town who could give her that, but the timing had to be just right.

Pushing aside the troubling thoughts, she treated herself to a long, leisurely shower. She'd no more stepped out onto the fuzzy bath mat when pounding thundered from her front door. She loathed unexpected company, and since she had no plans for the evening, whoever was at her door hadn't been invited.

"The people in this town," she muttered as she slipped on her robe and tucked her hair up out of the way. They simply didn't have any manners, much less class.

Annoyed that her routine had been disrupted, she stamped into the living room. With her wet hair twisted in a claw clip and wearing no makeup, it would take an absolute emergency for her to allow anyone to see her like this. She checked the security peephole in her door and sighed, as much from relief as frustration.

She gave the lock a twist and opened up. "Misty, what're you doing here at this hour?"

Misty pushed her glasses up the bridge of her nose and shuffled across the threshold. "I need to talk to you."

Telling Misty to go home wouldn't do any good. When she got like this the only thing Justine could do was ride it out with her. They'd talked about the incident at the beauty shop, for the good it would do. Resigned, Justine offered, "How about some tea?" Not the sweet iced kind everyone around here preferred, but a nice green tea with benefits like antioxidants.

Misty plopped onto the sofa as if she owned the place. "No thanks."

Justine closed the door and joined her. Misty knew Justine had a routine, but she simply disregarded that knowledge whenever she felt needy. "What's the problem?" Justine was spending more and more time holding Misty's hand these days. She needed to stop obsessing about the things that *might* go wrong. There was simply no purpose in it. From the moment Austin's release had been announced, Misty had been in a tizzy.

Justine wished her friend would pay a little more attention to herself instead. She could be attractive if she tried. Even after spending forty bucks at the beauty shop for a cut and style, she still stuck her hair into a ponytail. And those baggy clothes. The whole image got on Justine's last nerve.

"It's *him*," Misty said, squeezing her hands between her knees. "He won't leave."

Justine had watched Misty get like this before. She was a perpetual worrywart, and once she latched on to an idea she simply wouldn't let go. Justine couldn't say she hadn't expected this.

"Stay away from him," Justine urged, "and you'll be fine. I'm certain he won't try to bother you." The whole idea was irrational.

Misty glared at her through those Coke bottle lenses. "It's not me I'm worried about. It's *her*. It's just like before; she's following him around like a puppy."

"I see." Justine felt the first swell of significant tension. "Has something specific happened?"

"Not yet." Misty moved her shoulders in a noncommittal gesture. "But he's not going to let it go. There'll be trouble. You know what he'll do."

"You saw her following him around?"

Misty nodded. "She was at Sid's today, too. I tried discouraging her with the rumor that Austin was innocent."

Justine cringed inwardly. Misty was truly a brilliant individual. Her IQ was off the charts, but she was so dense when it came to everyday life. "Emily's never going to consider Clint Austin innocent."

"She doesn't have to think he's innocent; she just needs to leave it alone before something bad happens."

"I think," Justine said calmly, despite the suspicions now niggling at her, "that we need to just relax and talk about something else." Misty was obsessing even more than Justine had surmised.

"You saw her this morning," Misty countered, not ready to let it go. "She's not taking this well. She's . . . on the edge, just like you said." She shook her head. "I'm really worried."

Justine placed a reassuring hand on Misty's arm. "Misty, honey, I think this whole thing will settle down. Ray is taking care of everything." Ray loved this town. He wasn't about to let the past destroy all that he cared about.

Misty gave her head another of those hard shakes. "I don't think so. She's not going to stop until it's too late."

Misty had really worked herself into a state. Justine draped her arm around her friend's shoulders. "Let's forget about this whole business. Let the chief and his boys take care of it."

Justine had learned a long time ago that staying calm in most any situation was extremely valuable. She wished she could teach that lesson to Misty. Life would be so much easier for her. For everyone. Sometimes Misty's need to be protective was detrimental to both of them.

Misty leaned her head on Justine's shoulder. "You heard about the break-in at his house, didn't you?"

"I did."

"He shouldn't have come back here."

"No," Justine agreed. "He shouldn't have."

The quiet that followed was soothing. Perhaps the turbulence would pass this easily. There was just one thing, but

Justine really hated to bring up the subject again. "You weren't the one who broke into his house, were you?"

That Misty didn't immediately tense or draw away was a good sign. "Don't be silly, Justine." She laughed, poked at her glasses. "Why would I do that?"

Justine patted her hand. "See, I made you laugh."

"You did." Misty stifled a yawn. "Can I sleep here tonight? I don't want to go home."

"Sure, honey. You know you're always welcome here." Justine relaxed. "That's what friends are for."

CHAPTER FIFTEEN

Half Moon Café
Thursday, July 18, 11:59 A.M.

Emily waited before going in.

She'd had to do some major maneuvering last night to convince all involved that she was on the road to finally getting her life together. Her only recourse had been to call her old friends with her mother supervising. Today, at noon, Emily was to have lunch with Megan Lassiter, Cathy Caruthers, and Violet Manning-Turner at the Half Moon Café.

Just like old times. Except without Heather.

Emily had watched each of the others arrive. First Megan and Cathy, then, at exactly noon, Violet had made her appearance. She had probably parked down the street well ahead of time, but her intent was to make an entrance *after* everyone else had arrived. She liked being the center of attention.

Emily had stolen her thunder.

At 12:02 Emily stepped inside the door of one of Pine Bluff's historic landmarks. The cool air made her skin pebble after sitting so long in the heat outside. Not much had changed about the café. Same old dark paneled walls, tiled floor, and Coca-Cola light fixtures hanging over each booth. As unoriginal as apple pie and yet every bit as familiar and appealing.

The day's menu was written on a chalkboard hanging on the wall. Waitresses wearing starched pink uniforms scurried about delivering laden stoneware plates and refilling glasses with sweet iced tea. The smell of fresh-baked corn bread made her stomach rumble, reminding her that she hadn't eaten today. She'd stayed in the room that wasn't really hers. She'd called her office. Checked her voice mail. Checked her e-mail via her cell phone. Anything but think about Clint Austin or her father's connection to Sidney Fairgate.

She felt confused. Totally uncertain of what she could possibly do about anything, past or present. She hadn't slept well last night, kept dreaming she was back at Austin's house rummaging through all those torn photographs and trying her best to piece them together again.

She refused to feel sorry for him. And yet she did. It had to be all the silly comments about his innocence combined with the idea that someone had vandalized his house. Torn photos and broken trinkets didn't make him innocent and damn sure shouldn't garner her sympathy.

The anguish she'd seen on his face managed that all by itself.

What would Dr. Brown say? That she suffered from some bizarre form of Stockholm syndrome? Probably. Speaking of which, it was an outright miracle she hadn't found Dr. Brown sitting in her parents' living room last night.

Everyone was worried about poor Emily.

Her gaze landed on the booth where the others sat, heads together, no doubt talking about her and whether or not she would actually show and if she'd ever really recovered from the breakdown no one was supposed to know about.

The door behind Emily opened with that same jingle as when she'd arrived, signaling the entrance of another patron.

She didn't glance back, nor did her friends bother to look up from their conversation to see if it was her.

Ray Hale stopped next to her, his hat in his hand, his smile careful. "Emily."

"Ray." A new kind of tension joined the mix already churning inside her.

"You doing all right today?"

"Sure. You?"

"Can't complain." He surveyed the restaurant. "I'm here to meet my wife for lunch. Sarah Motley, you remember her, don't you? Her folks started this place, gosh, forty or so years ago."

Sarah was a year younger than her, sang in the school choir. "I remember her." Emily arranged her lips into a brittle smile. "Well, my friends are waiting."

"Just so you know," Ray said before she could get away, "a guy over in Huntsville is going to try and piece some of those photographs back together well enough to make new ones for Clint." He shrugged. "I don't know how much luck he'll have, but I'm hoping he can salvage something."

What did Ray expect her to say? That she'd dreamed of doing that herself? "I'm running late, so . . ." She gestured to where the others waited halfway across the restaurant. They had noticed her arrival anyway. Time to do something to make her parents happy. "Thanks for the update."

Another plastic smile slid into place as she made her way to the booth. All she had to do was get through the next hour. "Hey, girls."

Megan was the first to slide out and give Emily a hug. Cathy followed with somewhat less enthusiasm, then Violet of course. She had to be more dramatic about it. She hugged Emily longer and actually cried what looked like real tears.

Nothing had changed.

Once their orders had been taken, the catching up began. Emily let them talk. She didn't have much to tell anyway. Megan was still the bubbly blonde bombshell she'd been back in high school. She had married Grady Lassiter; he'd graduated a year ahead of them and after college had bought into the local newspaper. Megan and Grady had a daughter who was four, and Megan worked part-time in her father's CPA office.

Cathy was a court reporter in Huntsville. She had married Mike Caruthers. Mike had graduated with Ray Hale three years ahead of the girls. Cathy and Mike had no children. She wore her red hair, which was a near-perfect match to her husband's, in one of those short, curly dos that complemented her creamy complexion. She looked great in a jade outfit that fit like a second skin and showed enough cleavage to make Pamela Anderson envious.

"We have to do something special for the reunion. Ten years is a long time," Cathy urged as she relaxed against her seat. "You'll come, won't you, Emily?"

Megan seconded, "You have to come, Em."

Emily forced a nod. "Sure. I should be able to come."

Violet cleared her throat, drawing the attention of all seated at her table. "We have months before the reunion. Let's talk about us." She turned to Emily. "You should see my boys." She practically purred. "They're just like their father. Adorable."

Violet went on and on about her perfect husband and her perfect house. She had never worked or attended college. Her life was too busy and, of course, too perfect for her to need anything else in the way of personal gratification. She looked exactly as she had back in high school, thin, tall, and not a hair out of place. Violet had married the boy Heather had loved, Keith Turner. No matter how much time passed, Emily would always consider Keith Heather's boyfriend, but she kept that to herself, like a thousand other things.

Emily happily zoned out, barely paying attention to Megan's and Cathy's insistence that a Pilates-yoga combination was far better than yoga alone. Their husbands all appreciated that they'd kept their figures.

"Good Lord," Violet said abruptly, once more retasking the conversation back to her, "that can't be the senior necklace?"

Emily's gaze shifted to Cathy, who lifted the delicate gold chain from her throat. "I couldn't get together with all of you and *not* wear it."

"I've got mine," Megan chimed in, dangling hers from her fingertips. "Cathy called and suggested I wear it. Go, Panthers!" She turned her exuberant expression to Emily. "Do you ever wear yours, Em?"

"Mine was put away. . . ."

The look on Megan's face told Emily she didn't need to say any more.

Violet made a sound of dismissal. "I'd almost forgotten about those. I must have lost mine." She pointed a frosty look at Cathy. "And even if I could find it, no one called to suggest I wear mine today."

Cathy dismissed the jab with a wave of her hands. "You wouldn't have wanted to wear it anyway."

The sixteen-inch gold chains held two charms, a cheerleader and a megaphone. The senior cheerleaders had gotten one that year instead of the traditional charm bracelet. The necklace had seemed so important back then, marking a rite of passage and setting a new tradition. Maybe they'd all just wanted to be like Justine. Sexy and beautiful. She'd worn her necklace as proudly as any of the girls.

"So, how are things in Birmingham?" the perfect Violet inquired with a gleaming smile, her irritation at Cathy forgotten for the moment.

"Things are great," Emily lied. They would never know the difference. "I'm not married, no kids. I'm the head of my department. I live in an apartment near work." She hoped that was sufficient, because that was as good as it got.

"Your mother said you were in research," Megan enthused. "That must be really interesting."

Reports. Files. Oh yeah, very interesting. "Sometimes," Emily lied again. She was becoming very adept at lying, particularly to the people who were supposed to mean something to her.

"Isn't it funny that hardly any of us ended up doing what we thought we would back in school?"

Cathy had a valid point. Everything had changed after *that* night. They'd all taken different paths.

"That's right," Violet agreed in her perfect Bree Van De Kamp of *Desperate Housewives* style. "If I remember correctly, Cathy, you were going to be an attorney."

"And you were going to marry a rich husband," Cathy shot right back. "Looks like one of us got what we wanted. Just as well," she added. "You'd have had a hell of a time with college anyway, if your graduating GPA was any indication."

"I was going to be a journalist," Megan volunteered, cutting off the no-doubt scathing remark Violet would have launched. "I married one; does that count?"

An unexpected smile nudged at Emily's lips. Megan had always been very adept at avoiding and/or derailing trouble.

Violet turned her attention back to Emily. "You were going to medical school, weren't you, Em?"

"Medical research was as close as I got," Emily confirmed, hoping she wouldn't have to field any other prying questions.

"I have to know," Cathy said in a hushed voice. "Were you still a virgin senior year?"

That she was looking directly at Emily should have clued her in.

"I only slept with one guy before senior year," Megan confessed, ever the mediator. "Grady. We never broke up once all through high school."

"Of course she was a virgin," Violet said knowingly, totally ignoring Megan. "She was waiting for Clint Austin to sweep her off her feet."

Emily compressed her lips together and rode out the shock that radiated through her. These people were supposed to be her friends?

"A lot of girls were obsessed with him," Cathy noted without giving Emily the chance to enter the discussion. "He was damned hot. If I hadn't been so in lust with Mike, I might have fallen for him."

"He's a killer," Emily reminded, frustration expanding in her chest and loosening her tongue. How could these women, Heather's friends, say anything good about Austin? Guilt at the idea that she'd been feeling things she shouldn't for him had her wishing she'd kept her mouth shut.

Violet and Cathy shared a look.

"What?" Emily demanded, fed up with the uncomfortable direction this casual lunch had taken.

"Look." Cathy searched Emily's eyes, her own frank but concerned. "We all know what happened that night."

"That's right," Emily recapped. "We do."

"I've sat through a lot of trials since then, Em," Cathy went on, her tone uncharacteristically gentle. "There were a hell of a lot of things mishandled about Austin's case. That's all I'm saying."

That both Megan and Violet didn't speak up or argue against the point told Emily that the three had discussed the subject at length and perhaps many times.

Tension strained the muscles of her face as she fought to hold back what she really wanted to say. "I don't want to talk about Clint Austin or his trial."

"I'm sorry, Em." Cathy laid a hand on Emily's tightly clenched fist. "It was just an observation. If it makes you feel better, Mike and I don't talk about it, either. He goes ape shit every time I bring it up."

Emily was past ready for this lunch to be over.

"Did any of you hear that someone ran him off the road?" Violet announced, taking the tension to a new level. Her face beamed at the idea that she knew something the others didn't.

When had that happened? His car had been at work. Out of habit Emily had taken that route on the way here.

"Really?" Megan's eyes widened in surprise, probably at the idea that her husband hadn't written about it in the *Sentinel*.

"Mike said his house was vandalized last night," Cathy interjected, avoiding eye contact with Emily.

So much for the subject change.

"I heard about that, too," Violet confirmed. "If he were smart, he would leave town now."

Megan nodded. "It would be better for everyone."

"At the Den the other night," Cathy whispered as she leaned forward to ensure no one else overheard, "some of the guys were talking about what they'd like to do to Austin. Even knowing how closely Mike and Ray are watching the situation, I'm expecting to hear about a lynching any day now."

"What night was that?" Violet demanded, suspicious.

"Don't worry." Cathy waved her off. "Keith wasn't there."

Emily's head was spinning. Was Violet afraid of Keith cheating on her? Wasn't he supposed to be the perfect husband? And what was Cathy doing at the Den? Ten years ago the only women who dared go there were the trashy ones.

Violet cleared her throat. "Well, maybe Austin will take the hint and leave before someone has to go that far."

The food arrived, but Emily couldn't have swallowed a bite if her life had depended upon it.

"Before I forget," Violet piped up as she meticulously picked the croutons off her salad, "I thought I'd have a party on Saturday night." She looked from one to the other. "I'll invite all our friends from school and maybe Justine for old times' sake. You'll all come, right?"

And that was that. No one ever said no to Violet. Not to her face anyway. Emily felt ill about the idea already, and it was only Thursday.

CHAPTER SIXTEEN

2:00 P.M.

"I don't see why you have to be in such a hurry."

Keith Turner sat on the edge of the bed, his back to *her.* He hated the way she made him feel, cheap and dirty . . . and stupid. "I have to get back to the office." He reached for his trousers with far more enthusiasm than he'd taken them off.

"Come on," she cooed, crawling up close behind him. "Your daddy won't mind if you stay a little longer."

"I have a meeting." That was a lie, but she didn't have to know. He thrust one leg into his trousers, then the other, before standing and pulling them up.

She came up on her knees, snaked her arms around his waist, and pressed her cheek to his back. He shuddered inside, didn't dare allow her to see or feel the truth. "You were perfect," she murmured. "I should have you for dessert every day after lunch. You make me come so fast."

"I have to go." He moved out of her grasp.

She sat back down on the bed and sighed. That athletic body displayed invitingly. "Well, okay, if you really have to."

As he tugged on his shirt she adopted a look of petulance,

pouted those full red lips, and then reminded, "Don't forget next time. You promised you'd never forget."

"Right." He stepped into his shoes, ready to get the hell out of here. He'd forgotten the stupid gift he'd promised her. She always insisted on a gift. But today there had been other things on his mind. Clint Austin was back. Keith had seen him. Had gotten a long hard look at what ten years in Holman had done to the man. Even now the thought made Keith sick to his stomach. Austin had paid dearly.

After so many years Keith had thought the past was behind him. Now he knew differently. That night would never be behind him. He'd made a mistake . . . one he couldn't take back. He would never be able to forgive himself.

He'd tried to do everything right since. He'd stayed in a less than happy marriage. He'd taken care of Troy no matter what kind of trouble he got into or caused for Keith. But none of it was enough.

He had to get out of here.

"See you later, baby," she purred.

He nodded but didn't look back. He couldn't bear to look. Not with what he knew crushing in on his chest.

CHAPTER SEVENTEEN

Emily couldn't take the not knowing a minute longer. She had to find out what was going on with her parents now. Today.

She waited impatiently for them to return home from their morning walk. Shivering, she checked the thermostat, nudged it up a degree. She'd tossed and turned last night, unable to fixate on anything but Clint Austin. *Damn him.* Her parents might be in trouble and she couldn't stop obsessing about *him* and trial transcripts and rumors that couldn't possibly be true.

Her entire existence had been focused on Austin for so damned long that she'd missed the signs that her folks needed her. What kind of daughter did that make her?

The remarks Cathy and Violet had made about Emily holding out, waiting for Austin, had pushed a hot button, made her obsessively analyze last night exactly what she had done. She hadn't wanted a social life since the murder. Every day for the past ten years she'd done nothing but what she had to do. Exist. Nothing more. She felt nothing, wanted nothing.

That didn't mean she had been holding out for Austin.

Dr. Brown had had a theory about that, as usual. He'd insisted that Emily was punishing herself. Why should she have a life when Heather didn't have one? That was one time he'd probably been right.

Pacing the length of the living room again, Emily ordered her thoughts away from Austin and back on the real problem she needed to deal with right now. She didn't relish the idea of confronting her parents about Fairgate. But maybe she could help. Besides, trying to sneak around to learn the truth wasn't going to cut it. Fairgate had refused to talk and she'd found nothing in her father's study that gave any clues. Snooping in her parents' house was a new low for her. But she was desperate. Desperate enough to consider asking Clint Austin what he knew about Fairgate's dealings with her father.

A slow, swelling realization crept into her thoughts. Maybe she should do that with all the questions she had about the past. Principal Call couldn't say for certain that he hadn't seen anyone else in the neighborhood that night. Add to that the comments tossed out regarding the possibility that Austin was innocent, by her own friends no less, and she was feeling damned confused. She should demand some straight answers from all involved. Starting with Ray Hale and then maybe even Clint Austin. Why not?

First she had to deal with her father's situation. Admittedly, she couldn't seem to separate, no matter how hard she tried, the idea that her father was keeping an old secret that involved Fairgate and the fact that Clint Austin's alibi had hinged on Fairgate. There couldn't be a connection. The idea was ludicrous.

Emily perched on the edge of the sofa to wait. Why did she even go there anyway? She knew Clint was in the room that night. He'd had Heather's blood all over him. He was not innocent.

The front door opened.

Emily rocketed off the sofa.

"Hello, dear." Her mother fanned herself as she closed the door behind her. "Whew, it was hot out there this morning."

Emily's heart thumped. "Where's Dad?"

Her mother sat down in a chair in the entry hall and started to untie her walking shoes. "He had an appointment this morning. He'll be home this afternoon."

He was avoiding Emily.

Fairgate had to have told him about her visit.

"Where'd he go?" Emily stalked over to her mother, her frustration illogical, she knew. "I need to speak with him. Why would he have an appointment this morning? Is he avoiding me?"

Dammit, she hadn't meant to say that. She clamped her mouth shut at the expression that claimed her mother's face. This was new, not one of the usual four zones.

"Emily, listen to yourself. Your father had no idea you needed to speak with him." Carol slipped off her shoes and stood. "Now, what's the trouble, dear?"

Emily had seriously overreacted. But this was important. Fairgate was not the kind of man to fool around with. A new fist of fear punched her. What if her father had gone to see Fairgate?

"What's going on with Dad and Sidney Fairgate?"

The mixture of horror and disbelief in her mother's expression dissolved, turned guarded. "I don't know what you're talking about, Em. Are you sure you're all right?"

Her mother had just lied to her.

Emily stilled inside.

"Where in the world would you have heard such a thing?"

There was the crack . . . the slightest breach in her mother's always flawless poise. Uncertainty peeked beyond it.

Emily fought to control the tightening in her throat. "I heard it from you and Dad."

"Well." Her mother looked away. "You'll need to discuss

this with your father. I . . . can't help you." She picked up her shoes and walked away.

Emily smoothed her hands over her skirt, drew in an uneven breath. The silence felt so much worse than if her mother had yelled at her for eavesdropping.

She gathered her purse and keys and walked out of her parents' home. She had to think. Had to get out of here.

That was the one thing she was really good at . . . running away.

4:30 P.M.

She'd done dumb things in her life.

But what she was about to do probably made the least sense.

Emily had sought refuge in the library and spent the better part of the day making a list of all the things she didn't understand about Heather's murder and the events leading up to it. She'd labeled it appropriately: "Secrets and Lies."

The panic hadn't come after the confrontation with her mother as Emily had expected. Staying busy with the list had helped. She'd read every single newspaper article she could find in the library on that night just to refresh her memory.

None of what she thought she knew made sense any longer. The past was all scrambled so that the pieces didn't fit together the way they always had before. Fairgate and her father. Fairgate and Austin. Her friends' protecting her from what they really believed.

The one thing that remained exactly the same, despite the passage of time and changing events, was Clint Austin's insistence that he was innocent. That he had an alibi.

But that couldn't be right. Emily had played that night over and over in her head. She'd recalled the trial proceedings as best she could. God knew she hadn't been all there at the time. The most vivid moment had been Austin's testimony. At the time, she'd been appalled by his lies. Every fiber of her being had been focused on the moment when she'd found him in her bedroom. She'd blocked out all else. Had that been a mistake?

The seemingly insignificant and unconnected comments and rumors and snippets of conversation that had brought her to this place felt illogical when considered separately. But when combined, they overwhelmed her with feelings of doubt.

Was everyone else wrong?

Or was she?

Dr. Brown had suggested that she recalled that night the way she wanted to see it. But she'd never believed him. He hadn't been there; she had.

Was he wrong? Or was she?

Austin had insinuated that maybe Emily wasn't the intended victim that night . . . but Heather didn't have any enemies. Did she? There was only one aspect of Heather's life where there had ever been any friction. The theory was ridiculous, but Emily had to know for sure. She needed answers.

The sound of casual banter drew her attention back to the parking lot of Higgins Auto Repair Shop. She sat in her car and watched as the employees chatted briefly before climbing into their vehicles and preparing to leave.

Emily waited until Marvin Cook reached for the door of his truck before she got out. "Marv!" He looked up and she waved.

He met her halfway between his truck and her car. They hugged and she was keenly aware that Clint Austin had hesitated at the door of the repair shop's office.

She pulled back from Marv's embrace and smiled at her old friend. "Can we talk for a minute?"

A familiar grin spread across his face. "Your car or mine?"

"How about mine?" She gestured to her Malibu. "I've had the engine running so it'll be cooler."

"We could go for a beer."

"Maybe another time." She smiled to cover the lie. "I only have a few minutes."

Marv opened the door for her and she slid behind the wheel; then he strutted around to the passenger side. "Nice ride." He surveyed the interior. "Looks brand-new."

Her parents had pushed until Emily had traded in her old car. They'd insisted on something with OnStar since she'd been known to lock her keys in her car and to forget her cell phone.

They took overprotectiveness to a new level.

"Thanks," Emily said in answer to Marv's compliment. She needed to get to the point before he started asking her questions. But first she might as well ask what he knew about Fairgate. Marv had lived here his whole life; surely he knew something. "Marv, what do you know about Sidney Fairgate?"

His cheeks puffed, then collapsed with the breath that hissed across his lips. "You don't want to know Psycho Sid," he said, telling her nothing. "He is big-time bad news."

She braced a hand on the steering wheel and fisted the other in her lap to keep them steady. "Would you say he's the kind of man who would physically hurt someone to get what he wanted?"

Marv's gaze locked with hers. "Definitely. Em, stay away from Sid. He's frickin' nuts."

Dear God. What had her father gotten himself into?

"I had lunch with the girls yesterday," she said, propping her lips into a smile and moving on to her real reason for this impromptu conversation. She prayed Marv wouldn't see them tremble. "Cathy and Megan and Violet."

He shook his head. "I can't believe it's been ten years since you guys graduated. Twelve for me."

"Yeah." *Breathe. Keep it normal.* "Oh, I went by the school, too. I saw Justine."

"Yeah, she's still around."

Funny, the mention of Justine's name usually stirred interest in men rather than the opposite. "Misty Briggs is still around, too, I noticed."

Marv made a face. "That woman's as weird as ever."

"She is," Emily agreed with a laugh that held not a single nuance of humor. "She said the weirdest thing to me."

"Yeah?"

This was a long shot.

"Misty," Emily forged on, her voice stilted in spite of her best efforts, "told me some cockamamy story about Austin's alibi being real. That he was innocent. Isn't that the most ridiculous line of crap you've ever heard?"

"She's a fruitcake," Marv said. "Everybody knows what Austin did." He looked fully at Emily then. "Right? I mean, you were there. You of all people would know."

She nodded hesitantly.

"It's a damn shame they released him. His coming back here is making people afraid. Making them second-guess what they know is true." He studied Emily so closely that she started to feel claustrophobic. "He's not doing that to you, is he, Em? Making you second-guess the truth?"

"No," she lied. Partial lie. "It's just that . . ." She swallowed, wished her throat wasn't so dry. "You don't think Keith would have hurt Heather, do you?"

This time Marv just stared at her, seemingly stunned, before a visible guard went up. "No way. He loved her too much. Why would you ask something like that?"

She managed an awkward shrug. "I don't know . . . something's just not right."

"Nothing's right," Marv insisted. "Not with Austin walking the streets a free man."

"Yeah, that's true."

For about fifteen seconds the tension ballooned, pushing the air right out of the car.

"I guess I'll see you Saturday night?" Marv ventured finally.

Violet's party. The invitations had already been issued. Violet was on the ball as usual.

"I'm looking forward to it." Another lie. She'd lost count in the past twenty-four hours.

"Well, I'd better get going." Marv issued a halfhearted laugh. "Gotta get to the bank before closing time."

"Thanks, Marv."

He smiled at her, the expression *almost* genuine. "Remember what I said, Em. Don't let that bastard get to you."

Marvin Cook climbed out of her car, crossed to his big truck with its huge wheels, and drove away.

Emily sat there, wondering how she could suddenly feel this tug at her stomach. A tug that somehow connected the anger and hurt she felt about the past to this new, creeping sensation of doubt and confusion confounding her instincts. All this time she'd been so certain. Was it possible that she had only seen what she needed to see?

4:50 P.M.

Clint didn't hang around to see what Emily and Cook were up to. Maybe he should have, but he'd gotten pissed off watching the guy hug her and had to leave. More proof just how fucked up he was.

It was Friday. He'd gotten an advance on next week's paycheck, and, as his mama would have said, it was burning a hole in his pocket. Felt strange to have money. Felt even stranger to be pulling into the Piggly Wiggly to spend it.

Seemed the whole town had the same idea. The parking lot was jam-packed. About the only thing he'd ever taken the time to buy was clothes, the occasional gift for his mama, and beer. This would be his first time going for groceries.

Inside, after grabbing a shopping cart, he took his time moving down the first couple of aisles. He didn't remember there being so many choices. The endless possibilities left him feeling a little bewildered and a whole lot intimidated.

Now there was a hell of a note. He'd stood up to guys twice his size in prison—cold-blooded killers—and here he was flustered by the dozen or so brands of jam and jelly.

He moved on. Studied the various kinds of loaf bread on the shelves. White, wheat, white-wheat, honey-wheat. He gave up and grabbed a loaf of white. Ray had stocked Clint's shelves with canned and dried goods. Mainly all he needed was sandwich makings. Ham, bologna, cheese. And milk. Maybe some eggs and bacon.

Shoppers moved past him; those who recognized him stared briefly, then hurried on by. He didn't let on that he noticed, kept his attention focused on sifting through the available cheeses. That was a big enough problem all by itself. He played it safe and went with a block of cheddar and some sliced American.

A mother with two children in her cart moved wide around him, her horrified gaze glued to him until she'd gotten well beyond where he stood.

Now that he couldn't ignore. The idea that the woman thought her kids were in danger in his presence got to him more than it should have. He stared after her for several seconds. He didn't recognize her, but she'd definitely recognized him. But then, what had he expected? The local paper had run something about him every day since he'd gotten back to town. He refused to give Ray credit for warning him about this. He wasn't ashamed. Annoyed maybe, but not ashamed.

He picked up a jug of whole milk and placed it into his cart. The hair on the back of his neck stood on end and he hesitated before moving out of the dairy department. Slowly, he turned to find Emily watching him from the end of the canned fruits and vegetables aisle.

Those big brown eyes widened, but she didn't even flinch when he openly stared back at her. For the first time since he'd come back to Pine Bluff he wondered what she was really thinking.

Did she actually believe that following him around like this, watching him, was going to make a difference? He thought of the way she'd come into his house. He'd seen the regret on her face when she had first looked at what some asshole had done to his mother's things. But then Ray had said something that got to her and she'd gone off on a tangent about how she hoped Clint rotted in hell or some such.

He didn't believe her.

Not anymore.

He'd gotten close to her when he'd stormed out to her car that evening, ready to give her a piece of his mind. Yeah, he'd gotten damned close. Close enough to see the way the pulse fluttered at the base of her throat. To smell the softness of her skin. And to hear her breath catch at his nearness.

She could shout to high heaven just how much she hated him, but there was still something between them. Something visceral and totally beyond her or his control.

He turned away from her, picked out a pound of bacon, and headed for the checkout line.

So much for amateur psychology hour.

Bottom line, they were both completely fucked up.

He chose the checkout lane with only two customers and waited his turn. He kept his gaze on the back of the head of the woman who stood in front of him, in hopes of ignoring the whispering the other folks in line on either side had started the moment he walked up. If he even glanced at any of them they would go around telling people how he'd done or said something he hadn't. Might as well avoid any unnecessary scandal. Wouldn't want to upset the good citizens of Pine Bluff. Or provide more fodder for the paper.

Besides, he could take it. When they realized he wasn't giving up and leaving town, they'd get over it and find something else to gossip about.

When his turn to check out came, he placed the goods he'd selected on the counter and waited. Once the casher had finalized the sale with the customer in front of Clint, he expected her to move on to him . . . but she didn't.

She put out her Closed sign and walked off. Left him standing there.

Surprised, he watched her a moment thinking maybe she just needed to get some more change or something, but that wasn't the case. She didn't come back.

Annoyed but refusing to let it show, he loaded his stuff back into his cart and moved to the next line. His turn came again and he transferred his stuff to the counter and waited for the cashier to do her part.

She didn't even look at him. Just put out her Closed sign and walked away.

What the hell?

Most of the other customers were staring at him at this point. The first cashier had returned to her register and a new line had formed.

Clint exhaled his frustration, loaded his shit back into the cart, and moved on to another checkout lane.

When the Closed sign came out for the third time he'd had enough.

He abandoned his shopping cart and headed for the exit.

In a pissed-off zone that threatened his feeble hold on control, he didn't even notice Emily standing there staring at him until he'd practically bumped into her.

He should've walked around her, but he couldn't do it. Instead, he went stupid and pinned her with an icy glare. "Did you enjoy that?"

Those big brown eyes, looking uncertain or startled, held his for three seconds, then four, before she looked away.

He walked out.

Left her standing there with every customer within hearing range staring at her.

He jumped into his Firebird and roared out of the parking lot. Drove straight to the Sack&Go and purchased a twelve-pack of cheap beer. He didn't give a damn if it was a violation of his parole. Let her call Ray Hale.

Right now Clint just needed to escape his new prison.

6:00 P.M.

Troy Baker's truck sat at the curb when Emily arrived at her parents' home. He got out, slammed the door, his face dark with fury.

Mentally readying for battle, Emily emerged from her car and met the storm head-on. "Troy? What's going on?" She'd considered as an afterthought that Marv would tell Troy about their conversation; she just hadn't expected it to happen this quickly.

Troy didn't stop until he was directly in her personal space. The instinct to back up was overwhelming, but this was Heather's brother.

"You tell me!" he demanded.

"Tell you what?" Emily said carefully. She wasn't afraid of him, but the look in his eyes told her this was not going to be a pleasant encounter.

"Marv told me about the questions you were asking him," Troy snarled. "I can't believe you would even think that Austin might be innocent, much less say it out loud! Now, you tell me that Marv's wrong!"

The alcohol was heavy on Troy's breath. Another layer of tension coiled inside Emily. "I didn't say he might be innocent. I just repeated a crazy rumor."

Troy shook his head in disgust. "You know what he did. You were there. If you go taking sides with him—"

"What's going on?"

Emily's father walked toward them; her mother stood near the front door, the phone clutched in her hand. *God.* Emily hated that her parents had to see this. Just something else for them to worry about.

"Remember what I said," Troy warned, shaking a finger at her. "The best thing for you to do is stay away from Austin. I'm gonna take care of that situation personally."

Before she could respond, Troy strode back to his truck and burned rubber peeling away.

She'd hurt him. Her actions had increased the pain he felt. She hadn't meant to do that. Everything was all screwed up. But this was her confusion. Her problem. Hurting anyone else was the last thing she'd wanted to do.

When Troy had disappeared from sight, Emily turned to her father. He hadn't said anything else. Hadn't asked her if she was okay the way he usually did after something like this. Part of her understood that he was waiting for her to make the first move. The dark circles beneath his eyes and the fatigue on his face made her stomach clench with regret. She'd done this, too. But she had to know the truth.

"Is there anything you'd like to tell me about you and Fairgate?" She waited, held her breath. She desperately needed somebody to do the right thing. To just tell her the truth.

Her father shook his head and said the one word that broke her heart: "No."

Emily got into her car and left.

That battle would have to wait until she'd gotten used to the painful idea that her parents were lying to her.

What was her father hiding? What was with all these rumors about Austin's alibi and his possible innocence? None of it made sense anymore. She'd lost direction . . . lost her certainty just like Marv said.

Clint Austin couldn't be innocent, could he? She couldn't have been that wrong.

She thought of the way those people had treated him in the Piggly Wiggly and she ached. That she could feel those tender emotions for him was making her crazy. Troy hated her for even suggesting Clint's innocence, which she hadn't actually done. Marv likely thought she was nuts. Her parents had lied to her. Her friends had withheld their true feelings.

Where did she go from here? She couldn't go back, couldn't go forward.

She was trapped.

CHAPTER EIGHTEEN

Saturday, July 20, 1:03 A.M.

A sound woke her.

Emily blinked, rubbed her hands across her eyes, and looked again. The digital clock on her dash still read the same: 1:03.

Damn. She hadn't meant to fall asleep. Certainly not parked in front of Austin's house . . . but she'd had no place else to go. She doubted she was welcome at home right now. And keeping an eye on him was the only thing left she felt committed about.

She reached for the ignition, but something caused her to hesitate. The vaguest sound . . . a crackle or splintering noise . . . so soft and indistinct she wasn't sure she heard anything at all.

A frown furrowed its way across her brow. What was that smell? She inhaled deeply, analyzed the odor. Smoke . . . maybe.

In a kind of slow motion, her hand dropped away from the ignition as she turned her head toward Austin's house. The idea that maybe she was dreaming delayed her initial reaction to what her eyes saw. But then the flames flickered again, dancing beyond the front window.

Fire.

Inside the house.

Was he in there?

She looked around almost expecting to see a fire truck or the police or both . . . but the road was dark and deserted except for her. Her car door was open and she was standing in the middle of the road a second later. Didn't remember making the decision to get out. Austin's car sat in the driveway right where he'd parked after coming home.

"Jesus Christ."

Adrenaline fired through her veins like mercury rising toward the boiling point.

Clint Austin was in that house.

Emily rushed back to her car. Searched for her phone. Where the hell was it? There. Relieved, she snatched it from between the console and the seat.

She ran across the yard, bounded onto the porch. Going in through the front door was impossible.

The flames were devouring the living room like a hungry beast that hadn't been fed in a really long time. The front window had already shattered from the heat. She should have heard the window break . . . or maybe that was what had awakened her.

The crackle of the fire sent goose bumps spilling over her skin. A whoosh accompanied the flight of embers through the air.

She called 911, didn't remember closing her phone afterward or sliding it into her pocket, but somehow it was no longer in her hand.

She rushed around to the back door of his house.

Locked. She twisted the knob and pushed hard. No use. She peered through the window next to it. The fire had blocked off the doorway going from the kitchen into the living room. That route wouldn't work.

She ran to the next window on the back of the house. Closed. Locked. The room beyond was dark. She couldn't see a thing except . . . maybe a bed. Her pulse vaulted with the hysteria swiftly climbing into her throat.

Next window. Open. No screen in the way. Thank God.

It was dark. She stuck her head inside. The white linens on the bed allowed her to make out a darker lump in the middle.

"Austin!"

She braced her hands on the ledge and levered her body upward, swung one leg inside. Her blouse snagged on something. She jerked it loose and fell into the room.

"Austin!" She scrambled up, rushed to the bed. "Wake up!"

She held her breath, recognized on some level that smoke had invaded and started to burn her lungs. Would have been much worse had the bedroom door not been closed.

She shook him. He didn't grunt . . . didn't react.

She shook him harder. "Austin! Wake up, dammit!"

Where were the sirens? Shouldn't the fire trucks be here by now?

"Austin!"

He groaned . . . tried to cough.

"Wake up!" She reached to shake him again and a hand clamped around her arm. His eyes opened. He jumped up . . . staggered . . . coughed . . . but held on to her with an iron grip.

"What the hell you doing?"

"The house is on fire!" she cried, her arms and legs trembling now. "We have to get out of here." She gulped the air infused with smoke and her lungs seized, making her cough.

He hesitated as if he needed to gather his wits, as if he didn't trust her to tell him the truth.

"Hurry!" She coughed again . . . the burn in her lungs renewing her urgency.

He hauled her to the window and practically tossed her out, following right behind her. They tumbled to the ground. He jumped up and dragged her toward the barn. The fire roared and something collapsed. Emily didn't look back until they'd moved away from the danger.

The fire burst through the roof.

If she hadn't awakened him, he would be dead now. If she hadn't been parked in front of his house . . .

Someone had tried to kill him.

Her knees buckled, but his grip on her arm kept her vertical.

The reality of what she'd done hit her. She'd gone into a burning house and rescued Clint Austin from certain death.

The action hadn't resulted from conscious thought. The fire had kicked in her survival and rescue instincts. She'd reacted.

She looked up at the man beside her. The light from the flickering flames allowed her to see the shock and devastation on his face. The urge to do something . . . to reach out to him somehow was a palpable force inside her.

But there was nothing she could do.

Troy's assurance that he would take care of Austin personally echoed in her head, sent a blend of tension and fear coiling through her. Surely he wouldn't do something like this.

This was attempted murder.

Her gaze shifted back to Austin. She'd wished him dead a thousand times. She'd prayed he would rot in prison.

She'd saved his life.

3:30 A.M.

Clint felt numb.

Parts of two outer walls were about all that was left of his home. The fire was out, but the air was still filled with the smell of smoke.

Vultures from the various media outlets within a fifty-mile radius had arrived. A couple of Ray's deputies were keeping them away from the house and yard. But zoom lenses would capture more than enough.

The paramedic had wanted Clint to go to the hospital for further evaluation because of the smoke inhalation, but he had refused.

The week had caught up with him last night. The vandalism, the way the whole community treated him, all of it had come crashing down around him just like Ray warned Clint it might. But mostly it was *her*. All this time, all this pain, and she still made him want her. So he'd drunk himself as close to oblivion as a twelve-pack of cheap beer would take him, but he was stone-cold sober now.

He would be dead . . . if it hadn't been for *her*.

His gaze settled on Emily Wallace where she huddled against a squad car as Ray questioned her.

A shudder rocked through Clint.

He'd been dead to the world. Nothing would have awakened him . . . if she hadn't . . .

His eyes started to burn again. From the smoke probably.

He wasn't surprised by someone's attempt to kill him. Hell, he'd expected it. He just hadn't anticipated he'd live through it and lose every damned thing else.

He'd moved his car once the water had started to contain the fire. Hot-wiring it had been necessary, since his keys had been inside the now-destroyed house. At least he still had his car. He had no idea if there was insurance for this.

Clint scrubbed his hand over his face and wondered why the hell he even cared. Because he was a fool. He'd told himself that when and if he got out he would come back here and prove his innocence. More for his mother's sake than his own.

He'd been back five days and the only thing he'd proven was that the whole damned town hated him and believed just as deeply as ever that he was guilty.

His attention settled on the charred remains of the house that his mother had worked so hard to keep.

Maybe this was a reaction to his prods. He'd punched

Marvin Cook's buttons and he'd assuredly told all his buddies. Then Clint had gone for Sid.

Oh yeah, Clint should have seen this coming and been better prepared. He'd let the bullshit get to him instead of staying focused, and this was the result.

Whoever set this fire wanted Clint dead. Maybe the culprit thought he deserved to die because of the murder rap or maybe because someone wanted Clint silenced forever.

He knew he was innocent.

Heather Baker's real killer knew it, too.

"Clint."

Ray's voice hauled Clint from the past. The smell of smoke lingered in his lungs and the reality tore at his gut. Everything was gone.

"Clint, I have to ask you some questions now."

He turned to face the other man. Clint looked past him to the road where Emily Wallace's car still sat.

"Where's . . ." Clint swallowed in an effort to soothe the burn in his throat.

"Deputy Fitzpatrick took her to the Valley Inn. She didn't want to go home." Ray glanced at the news vans. "I guess she was afraid they would follow her. She doesn't want her parents upset. We'll see that her car gets to her later today." He turned back to Clint. "Why don't we do this in the barn?"

Suited Clint. He wasn't going to make this easy for those damned reporters. Ray contacted one of his men via his radio and ordered him to push the media to the opposite side of the road. When Clint and Ray reached the barn, he dropped into a crouch and flipped to a clean page in his notepad. He tucked his flashlight under his arm, directing its beam at the paper.

"Let's start with what time you came home last night."

Clint had no idea just how exhausted he was until he sat down on the ground and leaned against the wall. He watched the chaos around his house, the idea of what it all meant startling him all over again. He answered Ray's questions, provided any additional details he could think of, including the fact that he'd drunk himself into oblivion. Ray chose not to mention that the beer had violated a condition of Clint's parole. He could bring it up later, but right now Clint was too tired to care.

Dawn started its slow creep across the horizon. Pinks and purples streaking the dark sky as the firemen started to pack up their gear. An investigator from the fire marshal's office would be here later this morning to look for evidence.

Five days. Clint had been released less than a week and already he'd lost everything.

What the hell was he supposed to do now?

"Just one more question." Ray pushed to his feet, stretched, and made a sound that said he was about as exhausted as Clint.

Taking that as his cue, Clint got up, did some stretching of his own. Felt like he'd been sitting there for hours.

Though he'd said he had another question, Ray closed his notepad and stuffed it into his pocket. "Do you think Emily Wallace started this fire?"

Means, opportunity, and motive. It was all there. Anyone who'd sat through Clint's trial knew the necessary elements evaluated when considering a crime. Still, he and Ray were talking about Emily Wallace. They both knew she wasn't capable of anything like this. Clint studied Ray a moment, tried to assess whether he was serious or not.

Evidently taking Clint's continued silence for a mixed response, Ray went on, "I searched her car, searched the area around it. If she brought any accelerants, there's no indication. But we'll look a little closer just to be sure."

"She didn't do it."

"She didn't?" Ray kept his face clean of whatever he was thinking.

Clint had a feeling Ray was more interested in gauging his reaction to the fire than in determining if Emily Wallace had committed arson.

"I'll tell you who didn't do it," Clint said, deciding that he would just say what was on his mind. "All these good citizens who believe I killed Heather Baker and who want to see justice done."

Ray didn't interrupt.

"None of those folks are criminals." Clint knew criminals. Had spent the last ten years with the worst kind.

"So," Ray ventured, "what're you saying?"

This was the kicker. "I'm saying that whoever did this is the person who killed Heather Baker."

The silence thickened for a handful of seconds that turned into a full minute heavy with tension before Ray reacted.

"You can't know that."

Clint's gaze narrowed at the defensive tone. "I know I didn't kill her."

More of that throat-grabbing silence.

"You have to let this go, Clint. Things will only get worse if you don't. We've talked about this already. Poking around in the past is going to get you nowhere fast. Folks around here have suffered enough. It's time to move on."

Maybe it was the total lack of emotion in Ray's words or the dull, flat look in his eyes, but what he said made Clint sure of one thing. "I will find the truth. No one, not even you, is going to stop me."

Ray exhaled a blast of fatigue. "Look at what you and Emily are doing. Her folks are all torn up. The Bakers are worried sick about her. They just want her to let it go. The whole town is in an uproar, Clint. It's my job to keep the peace, to take care of the citizens of Pine Bluff, and you're both making my job damned difficult. You've got to put the past behind you and stop trying to make it right. It won't ever be right, no matter what you do, and that's the God's truth."

Clint laughed, the sound a perverse mockery of amusement. "So I'm just supposed to pretend it never happened. Just sit back and let whoever did this do it again?" He stared out at the pile of rubble that used to be his home.

"We'll get to the bottom of this," Ray promised. "We won't let anything like this happen again. You have my word."

Ray wasn't going to change his mind. That left Clint with only one option. He looked Ray square in the eye and let him in on the revelation: "I want to see the case files."

Ray choked out a laugh. "What?"

"You heard me. I want to see the files on the Heather Baker murder investigation. I have the right to request a look." He'd learned that in prison. Legally, Ray couldn't refuse. He could delay approval, but he couldn't refuse.

"And what in the hell do you hope to accomplish, Clint? Just tell me. You know there wasn't a trace of evidence to indicate anyone else was in the room. Going through those files won't help you find what you're looking for." Ray held out his hands, palms up. "And what if you did find something?" he pressed. "Something Ledbetter overlooked, which, as you know, isn't likely. Even if you could prove your innocence, you know as well as I do that the folks in this town will always see you as guilty. You can't get those years back, Clint. There's nothing you can do about any of this but live with it. Things will get better; people will forget . . . if you'll just let them."

"Sounds like you're the one worried, Ray." Clint let Ray know with a look that he was dead serious. "I want to see for myself just how badly you and your buddies screwed up. Seems to me you'd want the truth. I'm innocent; that means a murderer is still out there."

CHAPTER NINETEEN

Valley Inn
12:30 P.M.

Someone had tried to kill Clint Austin.

Emily wasn't alone in her conclusions. The headlines of the *Huntsville Times* had heralded the same.

And she had heroically, according to both the *Huntsville Times* and the *Pine Bluff Sentinel*, saved Austin's life.

Emily tossed aside the copy of the *Times* and lay back on the cool sheets of the bed. Plain old human compassion. Her actions had been instinct, nothing more. She would have done the same for anyone . . . for a dog or a cat. How many times had she told herself that already?

But it didn't change the momentum of the uncertainty mounting inside her.

She hoped the police wouldn't discover that Troy had been involved in the fire. He'd warned her that he was going to take care of Austin personally. For Troy's family's sake, she hoped he hadn't done this.

Dealing with her own unchristian thoughts about revenge after Heather's death had been a difficult aspect of facing life without her friend. But this uncertainty Emily faced now . . . was far worse.

What *if* she had been wrong?

The prospect shook her.

She had been there that night. He was there. No one else. No other suspects . . . just him.

As much as she didn't want to, she closed her eyes and allowed the memories to surface. Megan had rushed to get Emily home as soon as they'd finished leading the freshman girls through their final challenge: decorating the outside of Principal Call's house for Christmas in July, complete with lights and light-up characters like Frosty the Snowman. In her haste to leave, Megan had backed into Mr. Call's mailbox. Seconds later the principal was hot on their tail.

Knowing how much trouble Emily would be in if her parents found out, Megan had let Emily out at her house and barreled away. The principal had followed Megan's car to the other end of the block, taking the unavoidable confrontation away from Emily's house. Emily'd had only one thing on her mind. Hearing the secret Heather had to tell her. It wasn't until she'd reached her bedroom window that she'd recognized something was wrong. She'd climbed inside . . . straight into her worst nightmare.

Her heart pounded mercilessly as she recalled the instant she'd realized it was Clint in her bedroom.

She pushed the painful images away and opened her eyes to stare at the bland walls around her. The question that she had ignored at the time was why hadn't he left while he had the chance? That was the one aspect of that night that couldn't be answered logically by anything she knew or remembered. She'd told herself that the horror had just occurred. That her coming in unexpectedly had confused him, especially if he'd only just realized he'd killed the wrong girl. But looking back now, Emily had to ask herself if running had even entered his mind.

Even when she'd managed to push him away from Heather, he hadn't run.

Why was that?

And if there had been drugs involved, as some speculated, though blood tests hadn't backed it up, why hadn't he finished what he'd come there to do? Why hadn't he killed Emily? The knife had been lying on the floor right by the bed. Her parents hadn't been home yet, and several minutes had passed before the principal had heard the screams and called the police.

But Austin hadn't killed her. And he hadn't run. Why?

Had he been developing his story even then? Attempting to lend credibility to his alibi for being in the room since he'd been caught? That was what she'd told herself the days and weeks after that night. All through the trial, she'd let the momentum carry her along. Everyone thought he was guilty. There were no other suspects. There were no prints on the murder weapon, a kitchen knife that could have been purchased at any Wal-Mart or Kmart. He'd been wearing gloves. There just hadn't been anything else to believe.

A jury had weighed the evidence, no matter how meager and circumstantial, and had found him guilty.

The story should have ended there.

And, yet, it hadn't.

A knock on the door hurled her out of the past and into the present . . . there was no relief either place. How could she keep living like this?

Another knock.

"Emily?"

She sat up.

Clint Austin.

Why would he come here? How did he know she was here?

"I need to talk to you."

She scooted off the bed, even as she thought of all the reasons she shouldn't answer the door. She moved closer, angled her head for listening. "What do you want?" He could say what was on his mind and then go. She didn't need to see him . . . not right now; she was too confused . . . too vulnerable.

"I need to talk to you. I don't want to do it through this door and I'm not leaving until I've had my say."

Emily surrendered to the inevitable. She drew back the chain and opened the door.

Those intense gray eyes zeroed in on hers. "You okay?"

"No, I'm not." He should know. She prepared to shut him out. That he'd come by, that she'd answered the door, was against nature somehow.

"I drove past your house."

God, she prayed he hadn't stopped.

He lifted one broad shoulder. "Then I remembered Ray mentioning Fitzpatrick had dropped you off here."

"You found me." She didn't want to look at him any longer than necessary. And she sure didn't want to listen to his voice. She couldn't deal with all that being this close to him entailed just now. Not until she'd sorted out her feelings. "What do you want, Austin?"

He stared directly into her eyes. She should have looked away . . . but she couldn't.

"To thank you."

"Don't thank me," she said defensively. They couldn't have this conversation. "For all you know, I set that fire."

He chuckled, a rich, throaty sound that rumbled deep in his chest and sent a new kind of tension through her, one that was far too familiar. "You're right, except why would you have rescued me if you were the one to start it in the first place?"

"Temporary insanity."

"You know I didn't kill her. You were there. You know."

"I can't talk about this right now." She braced to close the door. He flattened one palm against it, keeping it open.

"I was trying to help her. I could've run, but I didn't."

"Just leave." She couldn't do this . . . not yet. She'd heard it all before . . . when he'd testified. She'd asked herself why not five minutes ago.

"Think about it, Emily," he urged before she could shut the door in his face. "That means her murderer is still out there. That's what last night was about. Someone wants me dead. You could be in real danger for helping me."

"Go! Please." Her throat closed; her stomach churned violently. *Just let him leave.*

"I'm telling the truth," he urged. "Think about it and you'll remember what really happened. I didn't kill her. You just needed someone to blame besides yourself."

She slammed the door. This time he let her.

Collapsing against it, she tried to stop his final words from echoing in her head. How could she have been wrong?

That would mean he had been the hero to the rescue he'd claimed to be. An innocent guy doing a job next door who'd heard a scream and come running. An innocent man who'd lost ten years of his life in the worst of prisons.

And just like the rest of this nightmare, that would be her fault, too.

CHAPTER TWENTY

Violet Manning-Turner was a legendary hostess. Her parties were the subject of discussions for months after the events. No one was as good at developing guest lists or creating spectacular food and drink presentations whether for a cook-out in the backyard or a black-tie sit-down dinner.

This time, however, she had made a strategic error. One she hadn't anticipated. Very unusual.

Violet surveyed the crowd gathered in her great room. Every well-dressed guest had praised Violet's grand home and the delicious hors d'oeuvres she'd made herself. The wine was the best that had ever rolled across the tongues of these people, whether they said so or not. The idea that more beer bottles than stemware floated around the room made her want to scream. But then that was to be expected in Pine Bluff; this was Alabama after all.

But it was the tension between her husband and his friends that concerned her. Troy had openly avoided Keith all evening. As had Larry and even Perry. She scanned the crowd and her gaze settled on her dear husband. This was so unfair to him. Clint Austin's return had put Keith's life in a tailspin. There didn't appear to be anything she could do to help.

Damn Heather Baker.

Violet's lips tightened as did her fingers around the bowl of her glass. Heather had had everything. She and Emily were to have been the captains of the squad senior year. Violet should have been captain from the outset. She worked harder than both of them put together, but popularity had made the decision. Justine had insisted that she had made the decision, but Violet knew.

Heather had been blessed with the honor of captain, and she'd latched on to the man Violet loved. He and Heather had broken up three times junior year. Keith had turned to Violet two of those times. Why hadn't Heather just let him go? *Selfish bitch.*

Relax. Violet took a deep breath. This was her party. She had to be a good hostess. Besides, Heather had gotten herself murdered and Violet had ended up captain anyway. And she'd gotten her man as well.

She had deserved both. She'd earned every single thing she'd attained in life. And no one, her gaze landed on Cathy Caruthers, was going to take any of it away from Violet. If Cathy's damned husband didn't work so many extra shifts, he might notice that his wife had turned unfaithful in recent years.

Putting the thought out of her mind, Violet merged into the crowd. Played the good hostess, ensuring everyone's drink was fresh and their bellies satisfied. She popped into the kitchen to check that there was still plenty of beer in the refrigerator and to remind the kitchen help to stay on top of keeping the hors d'oeuvre trays filled. The waiter was just about to make another round with the selection of wines. Excellent.

She checked her makeup in the hall mirror before returning to the great room. Her French twist looked exquisite, as did the black dress. She'd tried on a dozen dresses before selecting this one. A trip to Birmingham had been necessary to find one no one else would be wearing. At nearly one thousand dollars, no one else could have afforded it.

A muffled thumping from the hall powder room drew Violet closer to the door. Surely no one had gotten that drunk already. A chorus of "oh yeahs" and "give me all you've got," had Violet backing away from the door. Fury streaked through her. She was going to kill Cathy. That slut was having sex in her powder room!

If she made a mess in there . . .

What were obviously simultaneous climaxes rattled the painting on the wall next to where Violet stood, her jaw hanging slack in horror. She righted the picture, her lips compressed in fury, and stamped away.

How dare Cathy do this at one of *her* parties!

Three or four minutes later, Cathy, all smiles and with a fresh beer in her hand, joined the other guests. Violet's jaw dropped again when Troy Baker, still shoving his shirt into his trousers, swaggered in behind Cathy.

Another burst of outrage crashed over Violet. That no-good . . . he'd claimed the baby was sick and Patricia hadn't been able to come. Violet knew better. The two were having serious trouble. Mostly because Troy wouldn't get over the fact that the man accused of murdering his sister was out of prison now.

He was just like Emily Wallace. Both of them were obsessed with the whole Clint Austin issue. Emily hadn't even bothered to call with her regrets. The world was full of total fools, and Troy and Emily fit unerringly into that category. Violet still cringed when she allowed herself to recall the fact that she'd dated Troy once, or maybe it was twice. She'd felt sorry for him . . . and she'd needed Keith to take her a little more seriously. Her strategy had worked like a charm.

A hand waved in front of her face. Violet started, almost sloshed her wine.

Justine Mallory looked at Violet as if she had smeared her lipstick or smudged her mascara. "Are you all right, Vi?"

Violet ordered a smile into place. "Of course. I was just thinking how glad I am that so many were able to attend on such short notice."

Justine nodded. "This was a great idea." She motioned to the twenty or so people gathered in the room. "We all needed a tension breaker, and this was the perfect solution."

Violet would have agreed until a few minutes ago. She gave Cathy the evil eye. "More for some than others," Violet muttered.

"I'm surprised Emily isn't here." Justine scrutinized the guests as if looking for her.

"After her death-defying rescue of Clint Austin last night, she may have been too embarrassed."

The very idea that Emily had dashed into a burning house to rescue Clint Austin. She should have let the bastard burn and then this whole thing would finally be over.

"I heard about that." Justine sipped her wine, then said, "This whole situation is escalating. I'm afraid to think what might happen next."

Violet kept one eye on Cathy. She wasn't sure where Keith had gotten off to, but as long as she knew where Cathy was she didn't have to worry. If he was tempted, he might just stray. She felt sure he had from time to time, just as his father had done. A rich, powerful man like that had needs. But she needed Keith to be discreet as his father had been. It was the least he could do for his wife and children. Maybe he wasn't cheating on her, but there were moments lately when she saw something in his eyes or noticed that his lovemaking was off. Nothing as blatant as those times in the early years.

Why was she even thinking about that? "I agree," she said to Justine. Everything seemed to be revolving around Clint Austin these days. "I wish Ray would do something." He was here somewhere. Both he and Sarah.

"I'm sure he's doing all he can. But the uproar surrounding Austin's return is getting completely out of hand," Justine went on, her concern evident. "We need to make people like Troy see what a mistake they're making."

Violet couldn't agree more. She was all too well aware of how far over the edge the situation had pushed Troy. "Someone could get hurt."

"Not to mention," Justine pointed out, tilting her head toward Violet as if she didn't want anyone else to hear, "that all this drama is going to do nothing but keep Austin's face in the media. The next thing you know, he'll be using the moment as a platform for promoting his cause."

Violet frowned but caught herself and corrected the outward display. "Really? I'm not sure I follow."

"He had a reason for coming back here," Justine said before taking a leisurely swallow of wine. "He wants to make us pay. He wants to do that by trying to make the world believe he was innocent and that we're all guilty of railroading him. Did you see the papers this morning? The *Times* is already jumping on that bandwagon."

Violet made a sound of disbelief. "Why, that's preposterous. People know that reporters will make a story out of anything." Justine was surely making too much out of this. She couldn't know what Clint Austin was up to . . . unless someone like Ray Hale had told her. Ray knew Austin better than anyone. Justine and Ray were friends.

Justine's gaze lingered on her glass a moment but then rested heavily on Violet's. "All he has to do is dig around until he finds a single shred of real doubt to pounce on. He might not be able to change the fact that he was convicted, but he can try all of us in the media, maybe even crucify someone. All he needs is one loose end to pick at."

Uneasiness crept along the length of Violet's spine beneath the expensive silk of her dress. "I'm sure you're giving Austin far too much credit, Justine."

Justine sighed. "Maybe so, but he must think he can convince somebody, since he demanded to see the case files on Heather's murder investigation." Justine sent Violet a knowing look. "He wants to see if the police made any mistakes. If I were you," she pressed quietly, "I would make sure Keith stayed away from Troy. He's teetering on an edge that could destroy him, and anyone standing too close could go down with him."

Justine was right. Violet should find Keith. "Excuse me."

Before Violet could get away, the French doors on the far side of the room opened and Marvin Cook stalked in carrying a can of beer. God, Violet could just die. How tacky. Why couldn't he drink her bottled beer? The man had absolutely no class. He cut through the crowd and headed her way as if she'd drawn him there. Perfect.

"Hey, Marv," Justine said.

He glanced at her. "Justine."

Violet was surprised at the indifference in his tone when he said the other woman's name. Most of the men in town loved having Justine's attention even for a fleeting instant. Then Marv's gaze shifted to Violet. She hoped he hadn't brought his wife. Violet had disliked Jean Cook since she showed up at one of her Christmas parties and bragged about her new tattoo. She might be the most popular hairstylist in town, but Violet couldn't tolerate her trashy ways when the woman got a little alcohol in her.

"Violet, we have a situation."

Oh, God. "What do you mean?"

"Troy came out back mouthing off and got everybody riled up. The whole bunch is pretty drunk—"

"Get to the point, Marv," she snapped. If a single one of her rosebushes was damaged, she would have someone's hide.

"Anyway, Troy, Larry, and Perry just took off. Said they were going to finish this business with Clint Austin."

Marv's announcement combined with Justine's recent warning sent fear surging through Violet. "Where's Keith?"

"Well, that's the other thing," Marv explained, "Keith went to try to stop 'em before somebody gets hurt."

"Find Ray," Justine ordered.

Thank God. Violet was inordinately happy for Ray's attendance and for Justine's quick thinking.

Marv shook his head. "He had to take Sarah home. Left about a half hour ago."

"Call him or Mike," Violet ordered, then grabbed Justine's arm. "We have to go over there."

Justine set her glass aside. "I'll drive."

CHAPTER TWENTY-ONE

Valley Inn
10:10 P.M.

What was she missing?

Emily stared at the pages spread across the bed. She'd been juggling information and names for the past three hours. Kept her mind occupied.

You just needed someone to blame besides yourself.

She blocked Clint Austin from her head. Focused on the pages.

These were the names of all the people who had been aware of Emily's plans that night and a few others who might be somehow connected, like her father and Principal Call. Each name had two columns, "Negatives" and "Positives." The "Negatives" column, on the one hand, represented reasons that person might have had for hurting Heather or for simply being in on the plan for that night. The "Positives," on the other hand, were all the reasons that same person wouldn't possibly want to hurt Heather.

For more than ten years Emily had lived with the idea that Heather was murdered in her stead.

If Austin wasn't the killer, then the murder hadn't been about Emily. It was about Heather.

Marv, on the one hand, had gotten angry with Heather a few weeks prior because she'd gone back to Keith. Keith, on the other hand, had gotten superjealous over her dating Marv. None of which, as far as Emily could recall, had really been investigated.

The police had their murderer; why look any further?

That concept settled inside her like a block of ice.

Focus on the list.

Violet. She'd wanted to be captain of the cheerleading squad. She'd wanted Keith. Heather's death ensured the path was wide open for both.

Cathy . . . well, she was just jealous of Heather's popularity. Everyone had loved Heather the best out of their tight little group. Heather had simply been the most popular girl in the entire high school.

Megan had nothing in the "Negatives" column. Same with Principal Call.

Ed Wallace: "A secret with Fairgate." There was no reason Ed would have wanted to hurt Heather. There was only the business with Fairgate.

Fairgate. "Secrets. Lies. Protect his interests." All those things were listed in his "Negatives" column.

Justine . . . nothing.

Misty . . . weird, which didn't really count.

Austin . . . nothing. There was no reason whatsoever that he would have wanted to hurt Heather.

If Emily was not the intended victim, he had no motivation.

Why hadn't the police considered this theory? Chief Ledbetter hadn't been a fool. Ray Hale—Emily paused—maybe she should add him to her list. But why? Ray had known Heather, but he was three years older. It wasn't like they'd hung out together. Every single person who had known

Heather couldn't be a suspect. Otherwise Emily would be adding Mike Caruthers and God only knows who else.

Emily crawled around the papers and off the bed. She paced the small room. If Clint Austin wasn't the murderer . . . then Heather's killer was still out there. Just like Clint said.

That subzero sensation sank all the way to Emily's bones.

If that was the case, Clint would be a target . . . *she* would be a target. He'd said that, too.

A rap on the door nearly sent her jumping out of her skin.

She took a moment to reclaim her breath.

Maybe her father had decided to make amends. No, her parents wouldn't be out at this hour.

Clint Austin. Emily didn't want to see him again . . . yet.

She peered out the peephole in the door.

But it wasn't Clint Austin.

She drew back, gathered her courage, and opened the door, anticipation rising.

"Good evening, Miss Wallace. I'd like a moment of your time if you're not too busy."

Sidney Fairgate.

She opened her mouth to speak, but no words came out. The idea that she should be afraid crossed her mind, but no reason materialized to suspect he had anything to do with Heather's murder. But the truth was, Emily couldn't be sure.

"I can see my visit has had a profound effect. Perhaps you'll allow me to step inside so that you might hear what I have to say."

Somehow she backed up; he came inside the small room and closed the door behind him. No bodyguards. No dogs. Just him. She should be afraid. She knew this. But what she felt was hopeful. Maybe now she would know the truth about her father.

"You've changed your mind," she suggested. *Please let that be the case.* All she wanted was the truth.

"Actually, yes. I have changed my mind. A previous

negotiation failed to live up to my expectations." He smiled and those black eyes glittered. "I see this pleases you."

Her attempt to conceal the new rush of anticipation had obviously failed. "Yes." Her defenses snapped into place, a little behind the curve. "What will this cost me?" The idea that they were in a motel room alone with the bed right behind her wasn't lost on her.

"This, Miss Wallace, is for free."

Surprised, she reiterated, "No strings?"

He moved that narrow head from side to side. "None."

She moistened her lips, summoned a little extra courage. "Okay."

"Brace yourself, Miss Wallace," he said with all the pomp and circumstance of a well-rehearsed freak show. "Your father, and mine, allowed an innocent man to go to prison for murder. I won't bore you with the details. I'm sure you can learn those straight from the horse's mouth."

She started to shake. It began with a quaking deep, deep inside her and radiated outward. She wanted to demand an explanation, but she couldn't seem to summon the necessary cognitive processes.

"Have a nice evening." He turned to go, then hesitated. "I almost forgot." Those dark, toxic eyes connected with hers once more. "I heard on the scanner on the way here that there's some trouble at the Austin place. Something to do with Troy Baker and some of his friends."

Austin Place
10:40 P.M.

"I know you're out there!"

Clint stayed in the perimeter of the woods that bordered the back of his property. From his position he could see Troy Baker and some of his friends moving around in the backyard. The moonlight didn't allow for seeing their faces as well as Clint would like to, but he recognized most of the voices. They'd searched the barn and called out to him repeatedly.

There was a half dozen of them, one armed with a baseball bat. And only one of him. He was no fool. But he did have the tire iron he'd found in the barn.

This could get ugly; someone could get hurt and it wouldn't be him. But he'd end up with the blame.

No thanks. Been there, done that. He would stay put.

The whole lot had arrived drinking and hadn't let up. The only one who appeared to be sober was Keith Turner. He'd spent most of the time since they arrived trying to talk the others into going home.

Smart guy.

Clint sagged against a tree trunk. He felt sorry for Baker. Other than that, Clint was sick to death of the bullshit from these people. He couldn't even go in the goddamn Piggly Wiggly and buy food.

Every instinct told him that recent events meant he was making progress. The vandalism, his gut clenched, was about running him off. Last night had been about putting him six feet under. He'd meant what he said to Emily. She might very well be in danger as well, considering she'd saved his ass.

He was reasonably sure she wasn't going to listen to anything he said. Maybe Ray could talk some sense into her.

Like he did you, a voice he wanted to ignore nagged.

Clint straightened, tension charging through him again as Larry Medford, the guy with the bat, started toward his Firebird.

He'd figured they would get around to that. Dammit.

The initial blow shattered the windshield. Clint winced.

He had insurance but only liability, and he wasn't sure it covered vandalism. Even that was costing him a damned arm and a leg. But the insurance had been required when he got his driver's license.

Clint held himself back, remained invisible, as Medford prepared for the second swing.

The blue lights cutting through the darkness came just in time. The siren wailed to life and the baseball bat stalled in midswing.

Clint waited until the two squad cars had barreled into his driveway before he stepped out of the woods. He tossed the tire iron in the general direction of the barn.

Baker and his friends were momentarily distracted by the arrival of the cops.

"Troy, what the hell are you doing?"

Ray Hale, followed by three deputies, spread out to contain the rowdy group.

"Doing your job," Troy shouted at Ray. "That bastard needs to go back to prison!"

"Where's Clint?" Ray demanded.

"Coward's hiding," Medford said, too stupid to have dropped the bat. He held on to it as he sauntered right up to Ray. "We called his name and he was too chickenshit to come out."

"Did you want something, Medford?"

Heads swiveled in Clint's direction as he walked toward the group.

Troy lunged at him.

Clint stepped aside, narrowly escaping the impact.

"Let's go, Troy."

Ray reached for him, but he wasn't ready to go yet. He rushed Clint again. Like a linebacker coming in for the takedown, Troy's shoulder made contact with Clint's torso. They hit the ground together.

Clint shoved Troy off him and got up. The idiot scrambled to his feet and charged Clint again. He had no choice but to put Troy down.

Mike Caruthers hauled Clint off Troy. Ray and another of his men manacled the persistent little shit who would have made another dive for Clint.

"I'm gonna get you," Troy threatened. "That's a promise."

Clint stared at Troy, told himself that his sympathy was wasted on the guy. "Do something constructive, Baker," Clint suggested with enough threat in his tone to have Baker's pals backing off. "Ask some of your so-called friends about their alibis that night."

Baker tried to go at Clint again. He landed a right hook square in Baker's face.

"That's enough!" Ray glared at Troy, who was holding his bleeding nose and swearing profusely. "More than enough," Ray said to Clint.

Three more cars skidded to screeching stops on the road, drawing everybody's attention.

"Keith!"

Violet Manning-Turner rushed into the fray, Justine Mallory right on her heels.

"Are you all right?" Violet hovered around Turner. He said something to her that Clint didn't hear.

"We should all go home," Ray said. "Except the four of you." He looked at Baker, Turner, Medford, and Woods. "You fellas are coming with me."

"Ray!" Violet challenged, evidently unhappy with the chief's decision. Ray refused to back down. Justine Mallory stared at Clint for a long assessing moment before she turned and followed the others.

Clint exhaled a mighty breath. The air smelled of the charred remains of his home. His gaze lingered on the black rubble highlighted by the three-quarter moon.

He'd lost everything and the truth still felt out of reach. Like Psycho Sid said, the whole community would be happy to see Clint dead. Maybe Ray was right, Clint considered, defeat sucking at him. Maybe this whole effort was pointless. But he'd waited so long for this moment . . . he couldn't quit now.

Shouting dragged his attention back to the squad cars. Troy Baker was bellowing again. His friends backed him up, making comments of their own. Something about traitor. *"Bitch."*

Clint's blood froze.

Another car had arrived.

Emily.

Baker and his buddies were shouting at her.

Fury blasted away the chill and Clint stormed right into the middle of the ruckus.

Ray had finally gotten Baker and Woods into one of the cruisers. Turner and Medford were being hustled into the other. Not quickly enough, since Medford managed to shake loose and get right in Emily's face.

"You'll get yours, too," he warned her. "Just wait—"

Clint grabbed Medford's shoulder and jerked him around. He put one solid punch in Medford's face and the guy dropped like the bag of shit he was.

Ray restrained Clint as Medford was hauled into the squad car. "Shake it off," Ray said to Clint.

Clint yanked his arm free of Ray's grip. "Next time," he threatened, "I won't play nice."

He turned back to Emily. She hadn't moved. She stood at the edge of his yard near the end of the driveway, her arms wrapped protectively around her waist. She looked lost.

The rest of the crowd, which was bigger than Clint had realized, had to be herded back to their vehicles. Every damned one looked as if they'd come from some fancy party. Come to think of it, Baker and his friends had been dressed similarly.

Violet stopped a few feet from Emily, Justine Mallory at her side. "You should be ashamed of yourself, Emily," Violet accused. "Just look what you've done."

Justine ushered her away, toward one of the cars parked on the road. Emily stared after them; her shoulders trembled.

This was what she got for rescuing Clint last night. The ache started down low in his gut, unfamiliar and fierce. She took an unsteady step and then another. She was leaving.

"Emily." Her name came out raw. His throat was sore and swollen from the smoke last night. Couldn't be anything else.

She hesitated, glanced back at him, then walked away.

Maybe he had made a mistake coming back here. But there was no stopping the momentum now.

CHAPTER TWENTY-TWO

City Hall
11:45 P.M.

"I want the truth." Ray gave Keith and Troy equal time with his most intimidating glare. He'd had enough. He'd already questioned Larry and Perry. They didn't know anything. Just kept blustering about what they were going to do, which meant they hadn't done a damned thing.

"Why didn't you haul Austin in?" Troy demanded. "You didn't want to put him in the car with any of us? Or you just plain didn't think he did anything wrong? You're on his side in all of this, aren't you, *Ray*?"

Troy paced back and forth in the interview room like a lion on Ritalin. Ray wasn't at all sure he would get the man to calm down short of giving him overnight accommodations. He didn't want to do that. Troy had kids. It was a damned shame he wasn't thinking of them in all this.

"You trespassed on his property. He's the victim here," Ray said in answer to Troy's insolent question, "and I didn't want him kicking your ass."

Troy stuck his face in Ray's. "You think that sonofabitch

can kick my ass? No way. I'll be doing the ass kicking, by God. You should've let me do it tonight."

"You mean the way you were when we pulled Austin off you?" Ray hated to rub it in, but somebody had to wake this guy up. "Austin didn't survive ten years in prison without learning a few things. You'd better think about that before you start anything else with him."

Ray ignored the rage flashing in Troy's eyes. He'd cleaned up, but his nose was probably broken. He refused to go to the hospital. Keith, however, was almost too calm.

"Now, I'm going to ask you this one more time," Ray warned, hoping he'd get a straight answer. "Did either of you have anything to do with that fire or the vandalism? You both swore you had nothing to do with the vandalism and we found no evidence to the contrary, but I need to know. As a friend," he tacked on. "No use wasting resources looking for perps if I've got 'em right here in front of me."

Troy's mouth twisted with the words he no doubt wanted to hurl at Ray; then he relaxed visibly and spoke with amazing calm. "All right, I admit it. I busted up the bastard's shit. But I didn't start the goddamn fire. I'm just sorry as hell he didn't burn in it."

Keith rested his head in his hands. "Dammit, Troy, what the hell are you thinking?"

Ray exhaled a fraction of his frustration as he shook his head with utter exhaustion. "What about you, Keith? You have anything to do with any of this?"

"I heard about the fire on the news—"

"He's a pussy," Troy snarled. "He ain't done shit. Trust me on that. What I wanna know is," he bent down and flattened his palms on the table so he could glare directly at Ray, "are you gonna charge Austin for assault? We got plenty of witnesses. He went after Larry when your own deputies were attempting to load him into the squad car. Larry's face is in worse shape than mine. That's a parole violation."

"I figure you're even."

"What?" Troy's outrage overtook his good sense again. He reared back, his hands now clenched into fists at his sides. "You're gonna just let him get away with this shit?"

"As far as what he did to you and Medford, you were on his property. You goaded him into the incident." Ray held up a hand when Troy would have started shouting again. "We'll just call it even on the parole violation."

Before Troy could go off, Keith asked, "Even how?"

"Since you guys got away with running Clint off the road and trashing his place, he'll get by with assault. Any more questions?" Did they really think he wouldn't hear about the incident on Highway 18? Guys like Troy, good guys at heart, couldn't keep that kind of thing a secret.

"This is not over," Troy threatened.

Ray got up, opened the door. "It is over. Now go. Before I change my mind and keep you overnight." Violet was waiting to drive them both home. Ray looked each man in the eye as one then the other moved toward the door. "The law took care of the beef you have with Austin ten years ago, in case you haven't noticed. Anything you do now is only going to hurt you and your families."

Troy banged his fist against the wall before storming out. Keith glanced at Ray, his gaze steeped with regret, but he kept his thoughts to himself.

Ray'd had enough. More than enough. This had to end.

The fire at Clint's house and keeping the peace was enough on Ray's plate just now. He didn't need Troy and his buddies acting up. The past was history. Over. There was nothing anyone could do to change it. No amount of digging around in it or pilfering through files would bring back Heather Baker. And it sure as hell wouldn't give Clint his life back.

What was done, was done.

CHAPTER TWENTY-THREE

Valley Inn
Sunday, July 21, 8:00 A.M.

Emily was going to Ray with her suspicions.

Sidney Fairgate, if he could be trusted at all, had pretty much verified Clint's alibi. The revelation forced her to understand just how significant this secret her father carried was. Just how life altering.

Why would he let an innocent man go to prison?

Her father wasn't like that.

Those unpleasant moments from last night kept elbowing into her thoughts. Reminding her that her parents and everyone else she'd ever cared about around this town were disappointed in her . . . had been hurt by her actions. And would only be hurt further by what she was about to do.

But she had to do the right thing. Heather's killer was out there somewhere. If Clint Austin was innocent, and it sure looked that way, he deserved to have his name cleared. The whole community deserved the truth.

That Clint had gone after Larry Medford last night in Emily's defense had made her remember more of those feelings she didn't want to recall. The way he'd made her melt with just a look . . . before all the pain and tragedy. The way he moved, his smile, his voice, every single thing about him, had made her want him back then.

Made her want him now.

She couldn't even close her eyes without that raging fire at his house haunting her. Without seeing his face as he watched everything in his world go up in flames. He'd suffered and she was more to blame than all the others put together.

She almost didn't notice the tap on her door.

Before she even looked she knew who it wouldn't be. Not any of her friends, because she no longer had any friends. Not her parents, because they had likely disowned her.

Maybe one of her new friends, Fairgate or Austin?

Emily adjusted her blouse, smoothed her skirt, and took a breath. Might as well get it over with.

She checked the peephole. *Her father.* She drew back, wrenched the door open in one continuous action.

"Dad? Is everything all right?"

Her heart bumped her rib cage. The urge to cry came from nowhere. What if her mother was ill? What if it was Emily's fault? God, she'd already hurt them so much. The air snagged in her raw throat. What if her brother had been in an accident?

"I need to speak with you, Em."

The defeat in his voice and in his eyes, now that she looked, made her desperate to fix this whole mess somehow.

"Come in." She stepped back, to give him room to pass, then closed the door. That he carried her overnight bag registered. Was he bringing her things to her so she wouldn't have a reason to come back home?

"I thought you might need these." He set the bag on the chair by the window.

She managed a strained up-and-down motion of her head. "Thank you."

He was dressed for church, with his navy trousers and crisp

white shirt and the striped tie her mother had most certainly selected. Ed Wallace could not coordinate colors to save his soul.

"Ray called me this morning and told me what happened last night."

Emily winced inwardly. After Troy ranting at her right in their own front yard, hearing more of the same from Ray had to be hard to take. She was doing it again. Making her family miserable.

Her father gestured helplessly as if he wasn't sure how to proceed. "Between you going into that burning house and what Ray told me, your mother and I have—"

"Dad," she stopped him, "I'm really sorry—"

He put his hand on her arm to quiet her. "I need to finish this. I've put it off too long in hopes of sparing you the fresh hurt."

The anguish on his face made her want to weep for all the damage she'd done. She was certain whatever her father had done he'd only done to protect her.

"It was Homer Jenkins," he began. "He was the one who recommended Fairgate to me."

The anticipation she'd expected to feel when her father finally gave her the truth was glaringly absent. She felt cold and afraid. She wanted to ask her father to sit down, but she didn't dare move or speak for fear of somehow altering the momentum of the moment.

"I had gotten into trouble that year," he went on, his eyes distant as if he were reliving those days . . . mentally filtering through the events that had led up to his decision. "We would have lost everything. Going to Fairgate was my only option. So I took Homer's advice."

A divorced, good-hearted man of about fifty at the time, Homer Jenkins had been the neighbor on Emily's side of the house on Ivy Lane. It was his car that Clint Austin had insisted he'd been attempting to steal that night.

Emily hated that her father had to relive that awful time . . . but she had to know. This terrible secret had been buried too long.

"Fairgate lent me the money. At the time I was so glad, I didn't consider how a man like him might want his repayment." Her father's white-clad shoulders lifted and fell listlessly. "It only mattered that we could hang on to our home for a while longer.

"When it was time to repay him, the debt was four times what I had borrowed. I couldn't pay all of it . . . not even after months of unparalleled investment returns. I simply didn't have it. I went to him . . . that *day. . . .*"

Emily felt herself wilting, unsure she could hold up beneath the weight of guilt growing heavier as what Sid Fairgate had told her was corroborated. What had they done?

"I had half the money. Fairgate took it, told me what he would do if he didn't get the other half in one week." Her father stared at the floor a long, pulse-pounding moment. "One of his thugs called him to the door of his office, said it wouldn't wait. I didn't move. I was too afraid. I knew what Fairgate and his men were capable of. So I sat there. He went to the door behind me and had a conversation."

Emily braced for what came next, unsure she could bear to hear him say the words.

"I didn't see any of it," he said, his eyes urgent now, needing her to understand. "I didn't dare turn around, but I heard the exchange between him and Austin." His voice wavered. "I heard him tell Austin to take Homer's car that night."

She wanted to say something to comfort her father, but she couldn't find the words.

"After the . . . murder . . . I was so devastated I didn't even think of the conversation. Fairgate and my problems with him were the farthest things from my mind. Once the police were gone that night, he sent for me. Two of his thugs came to the house while you and your mother were at the hospital. I had been about to go there myself. Your grandparents had picked up your brother." The fleeting look he cast at Emily confirmed just how much he'd suffered with the weight of this secret.

"They took me to Fairgate and he made me an offer I couldn't refuse." He drew in a heavy breath. "He gave me back the money I'd paid him already, minus half of the original loan, and said I didn't owe him anything else. I knew then he was up to something no good. He didn't want to be dragged into the investigation. Didn't want the police nosing around in his business practices. All I had to do was keep my mouth shut about what I'd heard."

It was true. Every word. Her heart dropped into her stomach and quivered uselessly, leaving her aching all over.

Edward Wallace squared his shoulders and met what he no doubt saw in her gaze with a challenge in his own. "I refused."

Hope welled, tightened in her chest.

"I told him that he could forget it. I wasn't about to break the law for him. And then he explained how things were going to be. I would keep my mouth shut and in return not only would the remainder of my debt be dismissed, but I wouldn't have to bury my family."

Horror gripped Emily's throat, but the words burst free: "He threatened to kill us?"

"If I said a word," her father confirmed, needing her to see what he'd been up against, the desperation spelled out across his face, "he said you would be the first to die. Then James, then your mother. What was I supposed to do?"

Tears glittered in his eyes. "I told myself it wasn't such a terrible thing. Just because Austin told the truth about his reason for being next door didn't mean he was innocent of the charge against him." His eyes sought agreement from Emily's, if not forgiveness. "This doesn't mean he was innocent, Em."

But it did.

When she couldn't confirm his assertion, he looked away.

The realization that she and her father had sent an innocent man to prison changed something elemental inside her.

"There was nothing else I could do, Em. You have to know that. I've lived with this guilt . . . ," his voice caught, ". . . but I had to believe I did the right thing. . . . It was the only way to live with what I'd done."

She did know. Somehow she did.

"Daddy." She laid her hand on his sleeve, felt the familiar freshness of starched cotton. "I know you did what you had to do. Now I have to do the same."

"I'm worried about your safety, honey. Surely if Austin had been innocent the police would have figured that out. But I'll do what I should have done ten years ago; you have my word on that. Just don't expect it to change anything."

Oh, but it did. It changed everything.

CHAPTER TWENTY-FOUR

9:45 A.M.

Clint sat down with his Styrofoam cup of coffee and considered his limited options for breakfast. Doughnut or candy bar. He'd made a trip to the Sack&Go for something to fill his gut, but he hadn't spent much time on choices since folks were coming through on their way to church. He didn't want to endure the way they looked at him. He'd thought he could tolerate it, that nothing could touch him after what he'd been through at Holman, but he'd been wrong.

They could touch him, just like Ray said.

Clint swallowed a slug of coffee and banished the thoughts. He'd get through this. Giving up now was out of the question.

Moving on to the case files would put him on the right track. *Someone* was definitely getting nervous. Clint had always known that Heather had been the intended victim. He'd watched Emily too closely not to have been aware of any threat to her. He'd wanted her something fierce. Now he'd caused her to be hurt . . . again.

All those years locked in a cell Clint had lived for this opportunity.

The determined fury that usually zeroed in on Emily Wallace wouldn't stay focused on her. If he could just get her to look past his guilt, to think about the days and weeks before Heather's murder, she had to know who had it in for her best friend. Who had Heather been at odds with at the time? Who was jealous of her or would have wanted her out of the way?

There had to have been clues leading up to what happened. The way she had been murdered spoke of revenge . . . jealousy, not a mere random act. That was the very detail the DA had used against Clint.

Only it hadn't been him.

He glanced around the barn. His mother had kept his car out here, to protect it from the elements. And the old truck. He couldn't believe that old pickup was still out here. A 1964 light green Ford, a little banged up and seriously faded. He'd learned to drive in that old thing. The memory of his mother's patience made him ache with sadness. He'd lost her house . . . all her things. Now this old barn was all he had left in the way of a roof over his head. All he had left of her.

He'd gone to Wal-Mart and gotten a couple of sleeping bags. There wasn't any electricity, so lights and cooking were out unless he wanted to go the campfire route. He'd had enough smoke and fire for a while.

But there had been one unexpected turn of events. An insurance representative had dropped by on his way to church this morning and told Clint that his house was covered and temporary housing would be provided within forty-eight hours. His mother had set up automatic payments for the insurance and the taxes from her bank account. Clint hadn't even realized she had an active bank account. He doubted there was much, if any, money left. He'd have to look into that in a few days. Mainly he was just astounded that the guy from the insurance company would even bother to let him know. Maybe there were still a few good folks left. He damn sure hadn't expected to find any in this town.

The sound of a car door closing put him on alert. He set his coffee aside and stood. Probably Ray, dropping by to see if he needed anything or maybe to arrest him for beating the hell out of Baker and Medford last night.

Not Ray.

The car parked in Clint's driveway, next to the remains of his mother's house, was Emily's.

What was she doing here? The idea that she wasn't at church with her folks surprised him. She'd always gone to church before, good little girl that she was. Too good for him.

She got out of her car and looked around; the uncertainty in her movements made him want to stay in the shadows of the barn and just watch. He doubted she would come out here. She would look around the yard, take a few steps from the driveway, maybe call his name, and then she'd leave.

If he was smart, he'd let that course play out.

Evidently he wasn't so smart. He stepped out of the shadows, let her see him. Some part of him was drawn to her that way, always had been.

Her gaze collided with his and he felt that connection as surely as if he'd grabbed hold of a live wire. Clint steeled himself. Judging by the fragile expression on her face, he wasn't sure he could deal with whatever she had to say.

Even he had his limits, or so he'd learned recently.

"I need to ask you a question."

No *hello*, no *good morning*, just straight to the point. The stupid side of his brain that had deep down hoped she'd come to tell him that she'd been wrong all along sent a ripple of disappointment through him.

Clint called upon every ounce of the hard, bitter strength he'd found doing ten years in prison. "So ask." His voice was sharp and challenging. He couldn't afford to feel these crazy emotions.

"Will you tell me the whole truth about what happened that night? Don't leave anything out."

She had to be kidding. "What's the point?" That she would even ask annoyed him unreasonably.

"I need to know."

The pain in her eyes told him she wasn't playing.

He gestured to the interior of the barn behind him. "You'll want to sit down for this."

She didn't argue, just followed him into the shadows of the barn and took the seat he offered. The notion that he'd slept right where she was sitting distracted him briefly.

He couldn't sit and talk about that night. So he stood, rolled his rigid shoulders to relax them, and decided the abbreviated version was the best route to take. "Fairgate told me to take Jenkins' car for leverage. I waited until dark, dressed to fit in, and went to do my job." He pressed her with a look that showed he didn't care if she judged him. "It was what I did, and I did it well."

She nodded. "I understand."

A flare of surprise that she would admit as much caught him off guard. He looked away from her. "I heard screaming from your house and I did what I had to do." *Biggest mistake of my fucking life.* "I picked the lock on the front door and rushed through the house until I found your room. I knew which end of the house it was on, so I—"

"How did you know?"

He blinked, startled again at her reaction. "What do you mean?"

"How could you be sure about where my room was?"

The way his mouth was dehydrating forced him to lick his lips. She watched the movement and wet her own. That his entire body reacted didn't help his ability to focus here.

"I'd driven by your house a thousand times." He shrugged. Sounded mental. So what?

"Why?"

His pulse started to hammer, making it hard to catch his

breath. "Because I was stupid," he snapped, hoping to clear his head. "I wanted to get a glimpse of you." He exhaled a lungful of frustration. "I saw you and Heather climbing out that window one night." The memories were as vivid in his mind as the night he'd watched them happen. Summertime, hot like now. He would never forget the way Emily had looked in those pink shorts and tank top. "The two of you sneaked to the next block and met up with more friends. I followed you to the theater."

He'd kissed her that night. He'd been a class A jerk afterward. As tough as he was, she had been the one girl who'd scared him to death.

She stood. He barely resisted the impulse to back away when she came closer. Wariness joined the curiosity and rising tension. He didn't know what was on her mind, but he was sure it wouldn't be good for him. Nothing ever ended well for him that involved her no matter how badly he wanted it to.

"You knew where my room was, so you went there."

This had gone far enough. "You know what happened next."

"She was . . . bleeding; you . . . said you tried to help."

He jerked his head in confirmation. "I tried to help. She was . . . ," he swallowed again, but that tight feeling in his throat wasn't going away, ". . . she was trying to speak. The words were so broken and weak . . . barely a whisper. I needed to stop the bleeding, but I couldn't."

"The window was open when you came into the room?"

He shrugged. "I don't know if it was open, but it was damn sure unlocked, because you came in that way. Did you open it or was it already open?"

Emily didn't have to think about her answer. She hadn't opened the window. It had already been wide open.

On some level she'd known that was wrong. Dear God,

she'd made a terrible mistake. She fought back the emotions rising inside her so swiftly she could scarcely think.

Keep going. Get the whole story. "Why did you pick the lock on the front door?" she asked, that point suddenly poking at her. If he'd kicked the door in, his story would have been much more credible. As it was, there had been no sign of breaking and entering other than the probability that he'd entered through her unlocked bedroom window.

He looked at her funny. Even with so little light here in the barn, his every expression was stark and vivid. "Have you ever tried to kick in a steel door?"

Steel? "My front door was steel?" She just assumed it was wood.

He nodded. "So are a lot of residential exterior doors. I learned to pick locks. I could do it in seconds."

"Did you close the door when you came in?" He had to have; otherwise Principal Call wouldn't have still been trying to open it when the police arrived.

"I don't think so. I picked the lock and rushed in. I guess it could have closed behind me. I don't know."

There had to be something they'd both missed. "You didn't see anyone else or hear anything?" Whoever had done this couldn't have gotten out of the room more than a few moments before Clint came in. Maybe the killer had hidden in Emily's house and then slipped out the door after Clint came in. The killer could have closed the door . . . but would he have taken the time to lock it? Blood had been trampled all through the house by the cops and the half a dozen other people who had come into her house that night. The crime scene had been a mess. Mishandled, just like Cathy suggested. The whole case had been mishandled.

Fury streaked across Clint's face . . . the face that only moments before was twisted with agony. "You know damn well I didn't see anyone else. You sat in that goddamn courtroom every day. You've heard all this!"

She closed her eyes and fought the urge to cry. He was

right. "That was before," she said, forcing her eyes open to meet his, "before I knew you were telling the truth."

She didn't know how she managed to maintain eye contact when her whole body screamed with its own agony just looking at the desolation and fury smoldering behind six feet of sharp-edged, battle-hardened man.

"My father," she went on haltingly, "he heard Sylvester Fairgate give you that order. Fairgate threatened that if he ever told anyone he would—"

Clint held up his hand for her to stop. "I know the kind of tactics he utilized." His tone was menacing, bitter, his eyes glacial.

She managed a ragged breath. "My father said he would talk to Ray after church today. He wants to do the right thing."

"And this suddenly changes how you feel."

That Clint snarled the words at her shouldn't have surprised her, but it did. She hadn't expected his appreciation or even his understanding. Her father's refusal to risk his own family to back up Clint's alibi had cost him ten years—no, eleven years, counting the investigation and trial. He wasn't going to just say, *Thanks and let's forget the whole thing ever happened.*

"I . . . yes, it does," she admitted. "I understand that if you told the truth about that, you were probably telling the truth about the rest." Facing him this way with the rage building in his eyes was nearly more than she could handle, but she owed him that much. "Maybe you were right when you said I needed someone to blame besides myself." That she had been that selfish, that much of a coward, deeply pained her. More so than she could adequately articulate.

He took another step closer, putting his large body directly in her personal space . . . mere inches from her.

"Do you have any idea what they did to me in there?"

The words were low, guttural . . . animalistic. She should have been afraid . . . she should have run for her life, but she couldn't move.

"I'm sorry." She was. God, she was.

"The only way to survive was to learn not to feel."

She wanted to back up, to put some distance between them. She couldn't. Her entire focus was on his face. This close she could distinguish every detail. The scar was more prominent, a shade or two lighter than his skin. The years of agony and torture had carved grooves at the corners of his mouth and creased lines around his eyes. And still he was a remarkably handsome man. Gone was the smooth charm, replaced by a raw sexual energy that bordered on dangerous.

"The pain was nothing," he growled, drawing her gaze back to his. The ice blazed now with a white-hot fury that turned those gray eyes pure silver. "Blocking that wasn't so hard."

He grabbed her by the arms and shook her. She pinched her lips together to hold back the cry of fear pressing against her throat. She scolded herself for being afraid. She deserved whatever he did to her. This was her fault . . . her mistake. A mistake he'd paid dearly for.

"It was the other that killed the cocky guy you used to know."

He didn't have to elaborate . . . she knew. Dammit. She knew what they did to young guys in a place like that. Especially one as handsome as Clint.

"You had a thing for me back then." He hissed the words, his mouth only centimeters from her temple when she turned away, couldn't bear to look anymore. "No matter how you denied it publicly, you did; I know you did."

"Yes." Why lie? There had been too many lies.

"How do you like me now, Emily?" He seized her chin and forced her to look at him.

Tears crowded behind her eyes, made her feel stupid and helpless. What did she say to that? That even now, with his fingers biting brutally into her flesh, she wanted him to make her feel the way she used to? He wasn't the only one who'd lost the ability to feel.

"You're the one thing," he said with such cruelty that she flinched, "that helped me survive all those years alone in that hellhole."

Her heart shuddered at the realization that he had every reason to hate her, probably wished she were dead for what she'd done. How could she blame him?

"Every single night I told myself I would live another day just to make sure I could come back here and prove that you were wrong. To make all the people who put me there look at what they had done to me."

He didn't understand. She had suffered, but not the way he had. "Then make me pay," she urged, her voice a pitiful warble when she wanted to sound strong. "But you'll be wasting the effort. My life ended that night the same as Heather's did. . . ." She stared straight into those silver slits of fury. "The same as yours did."

She watched the battle play out on his face. He wanted her to comprehend the pain he had felt, even if it hurt her. But he wanted something else more. The realization took her breath away . . . awakened years of suppressed hunger. When his gaze dropped to her lips and his breath hitched, she knew for sure. Her whole being felt a kind of relief at the idea that this part she could make right. This was something she could do.

Slowly, knowing he would bolt at any sudden moves, she reached up and touched his face . . . touched that scar that had marred the stark beauty of it, shivered at the stubble that shadowed the lean hollows of his jaws. He flinched but didn't draw away. She tiptoed but still wasn't tall enough, so she hung her fingers on the back of his neck and pulled his head down. She pressed her lips to his. His did not yield, making her uncertain of herself, but only for a second. She kissed him until his resistance faded and his lips softened just the tiniest bit. She'd been so afraid she wouldn't know how to do this right, but his slow surrender gave her courage.

His arms went around her in a brutal hold. She didn't

fight him, no matter that fear had joined the mix of wild sensations whirling inside her. She had earned whatever punishment he chose to levy.

The fingers of one hand delved into her hair, held her head still while his mouth plundered hers. That inkling of fear vanished, gave way to the more forceful, hotter feelings of desire and need.

She wanted Clint Austin.

Maybe on some level she had always wanted him. And maybe her friends were right; maybe she had waited for him. God knew she'd never wanted anyone else . . . had never even been kissed by another man. Her body melted against his, desperate for the contact.

As if he'd suddenly come to his senses, he set her away. "Go." The single word was ragged with need, torn with uncertainty.

She had stood back and denied her feelings as a foolish young girl; she would not make the same mistake as a grown woman. "No."

Surprise flickered beyond the rage and need. His nostrils flared. As much as she wanted to make him feel again . . . this wasn't just for him. She'd waited a long time for this. A trickle of uncertainty undermined her determination. What if she did something wrong? What if the novels she'd read and instinct alone weren't enough to guide her?

Not giving herself time for any more second thoughts, she backed up a couple of steps and reached for the buttons of her blouse. This part she knew how to do. Slowly, she released each one, shrugged the fabric free, then let it drop to the ground. The longing that flashed in his eyes stoked hers to a full blaze. She kicked off her sandals, reached behind her, and lowered the zipper of her skirt. It dropped around her ankles and she stepped out of the rumpled ring it made.

She wanted him to look at her exactly this way . . . as if he could eat her alive. It was all she'd dreamed of at one time. She would listen to Heather's stories about how it was between her and Keith, and Emily would fantasize about Clint doing those same things to her. The thought of his mouth on her skin had made her shiver; it did the same now. She released the front hook of the demibra she wore and allowed it to glide down and off. Only her panties remained.

The tension visibly building in him made her unashamed of her near nakedness, gave her the courage to take a moment to simply admire the man. She liked what she was doing to him. He was breathless, that innate sexual energy humming from his powerful body. She'd been right; he was bigger than before. Those broad shoulders, bare in deference to the muggy heat this morning, had filled out with hard, lean muscle. His stomach looked equally rigid and gorgeously rippled, making her sweat, and she hadn't even touched that part of him yet. The faded jeans clung to the lean lines of his narrow hips and long legs. She looked at his crotch; he was aroused and it showed. That he studied her breasts so conscientiously made her quiver in anticipation, made her hot skin feel too tight.

When he continued to stand perfectly still, she moved toward him. He watched her, his eyes guarded as if he expected a battle. She smiled, unexpectedly thrilled at her power over him. In her mind he'd always been the one with the power. When she stood as close as possible, she inhaled deeply, loving the earthy sweet smell of his damp skin. It was so damned hot in here, but it felt so good.

She walked all the way around him, touched each scar on his back with her fingers first, then with her lips. He shuddered each time her mouth landed against his skin. The salty taste and smooth texture made her hunger for more. Made her body vibrate with need. When she came around in front of him again, the desperation in his eyes was different. It wasn't about the past . . . it was about now . . . about her.

Then she knew exactly what she wanted. To prove she could make him feel again. To prove *she* could feel again. To finally know what it was to be a woman in every sense of the word. Her fingers closed on the snap of his jeans. Her heart thumped hard, making her light-headed and clumsy. A simple button shouldn't have been so difficult to dislodge.

He touched her. *Finally.* He closed his hand over one breast. She gasped, felt the tingle in her stomach and lower, much lower. It felt so good. She renewed her efforts to open his jeans. Had to touch him *there.* She wanted to know every part of him . . . to taste and smell him . . . all of him. She was like a kid at Christmas, couldn't wait to see what came next.

Pushing her hand away from his fly, he dropped to his knees. She cried out when his mouth closed over that same breast he'd measured with urgent fingers. His mouth was equally urgent; he sucked hard. Her fingers delved into his hair, needing to encourage him. Silky, thick hair, but her senses could not stay focused on one place. The feel of his tongue on her nipple, of his lips curved around her . . . had her tingling all over. He kissed his way to the other breast, giving it the same treatment as the first. She watched, unable to take her eyes off the way he looked, the sculpted features of his face.

He clamped one arm around her waist to hold her steady against his chest, pulled her legs around him, and lowered her to the ground, coming down on top of her. The friction and weight of his chest against the damp flesh he'd tormented with his mouth had her desperate for more. His fingers tangled in her panties, ripped them from her body. She trembled, felt herself moisten in anticipation of what came next. She denied the tiny flare of fear vying for her attention.

Just when she thought the tension could go no higher, his gaze collided with hers. The tortured look she saw there made her want to cry . . . made her want to cradle him against her body, inside her body, until the pain and emptiness were gone.

She had to touch his face. He shuddered and hesitation

edged into his stark gaze. He went up on all fours, taking his weight off her, pulling away.

No way. She twisted her fingers in his hair and jerked his face down to hers. "I started this; you'll finish it."

His lips flatted with a determination of his own. *Good.* Maybe if he was pissed off, he'd do what she wanted him to.

He manacled her wrist, yanked her hand from his hair, but ensured their lips remained no more than a scarce whisper apart. "Make me," he growled.

Okay. She would. This wasn't some unfamiliar foreign language . . . this was as natural as breathing. The last of her inhibitions fled as she yanked her hand free of his hold and wrenched his fly open the rest of the way. He groaned. Using her hands and then her bare feet, she shoved the worn, soft denim over his hips. With no briefs in the way, his full erection brushed against her inner thigh. She gasped, suffered another instant of uncertainty. In spite of that trepidation, the heat of his arousal ignited a new ache, this one deep within her womb. He didn't move a muscle even as she lifted her hips in anticipation. She arched upward, rubbed against that solid erection, just barely endured the sweet fiery shock of contact without screaming from the pleasure of it. She'd never known anything could feel so wonderful.

He still didn't move . . . but it cost him. The price was etched in the stony features of his face.

She was this close to shattering into a million needy pieces at nothing more than the feel of him against her skin. She would be damned if she would fall apart alone. With a fortitude she hadn't known existed, she braced one hand on his shoulder and closed the other around his erection; longing speared through her at the feel of smooth, hot skin stretched taut over hardened muscle. For a moment or two she lost herself to exploring the size and sleekness of him. She lifted her hips again, guiding that hard tip to the spot that burned so insistently. When he didn't thrust, she did, forcing him inside, but only a mere inch. She made a sound too desperate to describe at the exquisite pressure of initial penetration, however shallow. She panted, felt herself stretching to accommodate him. She wanted more.

She clasped his shoulders more tightly, with both hands now, tried to lift her hips higher, but he shifted his own, keeping her from achieving her goal. "Just do it," she urged. "I know you want to." The charge of sensations rushing through her was too much. She needed to hurry.

He stared into her eyes, his cold as ice. "I told you I stopped feeling anything a long time ago."

"Liar." The truth was written in the harsh lines of his face, in the tension vibrating in his hard body. She squeezed that inch nestled snugly inside her.

A guttural sound ripped past his lips.

"You feel that," she challenged. His nostrils flared and something besides the fury burned in his eyes. And in that moment of distraction, she surged upward, going high on her tiptoes. She cried out at the sweet-stinging pleasure.

He caught his breath.

"I know you felt that." She tried to sound smug, but her voice quivered. Her body shuddered with the need to move . . . to feel the friction of him sliding in and out of her in that ancient rhythm that was printed on their very DNA.

He remained perfectly still. She gritted her teeth to hold steady. The muscles of her legs screamed in protest of the awkward position. But she didn't know any other way to do this, and dammit, she was winning . . . his entire body trembled violently with his efforts to hold back. That he resisted only made her more determined. God, she needed desperately to move.

"Why?" he demanded.

That single, guttural word made her heart pound harder.

She wet her lips, searched those gray eyes so cluttered with confusion and need . . . a need he wanted to deny. "Because

I want you." Her body hummed with that truth. She needed him . . . needed to feel this.

His face lined with renewed determination. "I won't do it. Not like this."

He tried to move away, but she stopped him. "This is what I want," she challenged. "If you won't do it, I will."

Then she moved. Up and down, just an inch, then two. Even that little bit felt amazing, made her muscles clench hungrily. She held on to his shoulders . . . let her body guide her. When she could bear it, she took more of him, each time losing her breath all over again. Biting her lip against the unbearable pleasure, she lowered her hips until nothing but the very tip remained inside those tight, pulsing muscles on fire for more of him. Then she surged upward again, taking as much of him as he would allow. Again. And again. Until the movements were no longer conscious . . . just instinct . . . the momentum increasing as her body rushed toward climax. Her first. She hadn't known it could be like this. She was remotely aware of his rigid hold starting to crumble. Felt his resistance faltering. But his denial no longer mattered. Her fingers dug into his shoulders . . . her body arched higher, took in more of him, when she'd thought for sure she'd reached her limit. And then she couldn't think anymore. She could only feel herself flying apart with the brilliant sensations of sheer rapture.

She collapsed on the cool dirt, breaking the contact of their bodies. For long seconds she couldn't open her eyes. When she did, the first thing she saw was him watching her melt after having come undone . . . the cost of restraint devastating his face, thawing the ice in his eyes, and revealing the uncertainty. His damp, rock-hard penis still pulsed with need against her thigh.

"You coward," she choked out between gasps for air.

The uncertainty vanished . . . replaced by a savage ferocity that stole what little oxygen she'd managed to drag into her lungs. His mouth closed over hers with punishing force. She shoved against his chest as fury exploded inside her. How dare he make her beg . . . make her practically masturbate using him and then have the nerve to kiss her so greedily like this. She shoved harder at him, used her knees to block his big body from coming down on her. But she wasn't nearly strong enough; he forced his way between her thighs.

"What's wrong?" he growled. "You waited all this time for me to pop your cherry, don't you want me to do the job right?"

Fear and hesitation nudged back into her senses. Screamed at her to get away . . . that he wanted to hurt her . . . to make her pay. She told herself she didn't care, but survival instinct kicked in and she sank her teeth into his lip.

He made a ferocious sound, jerked his mouth away from hers. He licked a trickle of blood from his bottom lip. "Afraid you'll get more than you bargained for?"

"Bastard." She tried to slap him, but he was too fast. He caught her arm, rolled her over in one fluid motion, forcing her onto her stomach before he came down on her.

"Scared yet?" he murmured against her ear. "Don't you want it this way? Don't you want to know how it felt for me?" He ground his erection against her buttocks; her body shuddered in anticipation. "You thought I was such a tough guy, but I was just a scared little girl in that fucking prison."

Emotions twisted like a hurricane inside her. He wanted to scare her; that was the point. Wasn't working. Her need and the very desire he wanted to extinguish began to build all over again. She closed her eyes . . . tried to think of the right thing to say that would somehow make up for what he'd lost . . . that would soothe that tortured part of him.

"I'm sorry," she murmured. Her breath caught as much on the words as at the feel of him rubbing . . . stroking that sensitive flesh. Her body was frantic for more of him. Something electric flowed over her skin . . . vibrated through her muscles.

"Sorry isn't enough," he snapped viciously as the head of his penis grazed the seam of her bottom more intimately, threateningly. Her body convulsed with forbidden pleasure, which he evidently took as fear, since he challenged, his voice cruel, "Say you don't want me and I'll stop right now."

He waited, held utterly still.

The feel of his weight . . . of his skin against hers made it impossible to think clearly. But there was one thing she knew with complete certainty. "I want you. All of you."

He thrust hard, fully inside her . . . not the way he'd threatened. She cried out his name as her vaginal muscles clamped around his thick girth, increasing the already unbearable friction. Yes, she wanted him. Dammit. She wanted the contrasting texture of his powerful thighs rasping against her skin . . . the deep, stretching penetration of him filling her so completely. She didn't want it to stop . . . she needed it . . . felt consumed by his strength and power.

His hand pushed between her and the dirt, fingers splayed against her belly, pulled her more tightly to him, sending an arc of sheer pleasure-pain coursing through her as he went deeper still. His lips brushed her cheek as he ground his hips into her bottom. "Had enough?"

She shook her head, tried to open wider for him. He trembled, swore at his own weakness. He straightened, settled fully on to his knees, with her bent forward in front of him. He started to move. The incredible sensation was very nearly unbearable. She urged him on with frantic, whispered pleas until he lost control. The sounds of his desperation made her want to see . . . to watch him taking her this way and losing total control. His body flexed and contracted with each withdrawal and thrust. The muscles of his abdomen gleamed with sweat . . . his powerful hands held her hips firmly . . . his eyes were closed, leaving the whisper of dark lashes against his cheeks.

The desperation fueling each move played out on his face, made her yearn to touch him there even as his movements became more urgent, almost violent . . . and then she started to come again. The climax tightening her muscles encouraged him. He roared like a beast . . . rammed harder . . . until he couldn't hold out any longer. The ferocity of their synchronized release rendered her helpless and left her shivering with the intensity of the receding sensations.

One strong arm swept around her waist and pulled her up against his chest, sending his still-throbbing erection deeper inside her and stealing her ragged breath. Sitting back on his heels with her nestled in his lap, their bodies still intimately connected . . . he pressed his face into her hair and fought to catch his breath.

"I wanted to hurt you . . . and then I just wanted you."

The regret in those softly uttered words was a stark contrast to the way he'd spoken and acted moments ago. But there was nothing to regret. He hadn't given her anything she hadn't wanted . . . hadn't asked for. The feel of his powerful muscles supporting his weight as well as her own after such extensive physical exertion made her giddy.

She'd come here to tell him that she knew the truth . . . she hadn't meant for this to happen. Or maybe she had. Maybe she'd needed it . . . needed to give herself to him this way for reasons she would still be sorting years from now.

She'd made so many mistakes already . . . what if this was just another? The warm feelings that bonded her to him so fully started to fade. She hadn't considered any consequences for her . . . or for him. Hadn't thought her intentions through. She'd put him in prison and now she did this? Her parents were right; she did need help.

"I should go." She pushed his arm away and got up. The loss of contact, the feel of him sliding out of her body, was like losing a part of herself.

She grabbed her clothes, haphazardly jerked them on. When she finally looked up again, he'd tugged on his jeans without fastening the fly, leaving that heart-stopping vee that made her foolishly want him again.

"Emily." He reached out to her, his voice low, soft.

Allowing him to touch her right now with any sort of tenderness would be her second mistake of the day.

"I . . . have to go."

She'd been wrong. He wasn't a coward. She was.

She'd wanted him to take her that way . . . brutally, almost violently, to punish her. If he'd done the worst possible to her she wouldn't have cared. She'd goaded him into being cruel.

Maybe, just maybe, if he'd really hurt her, she could have lived with what she'd done to him. Instead, he'd made her love him, and that was the most unbearable pain of all.

CHAPTER TWENTY-FIVE

125 Carriage Avenue
10:00 A.M.

He was cheating on her again.

Misty Briggs was certain of it. She couldn't prove it yet, but she sensed it. She'd watched him. His wife had rushed off to church this morning with their two sons, but he was still home. She knew he wasn't sick, not physically anyway. He was up to something.

And she intended to find out what.

Misty had tried to stop the momentum this time. She'd given plenty of warnings. But no one would listen to her. People were going to be hurt again . . . just like before. It had to stop.

His fancy car rolled out of the garage. A Jaguar. Silver. Leather interior. Cost nearly a hundred grand. Several times over what her efficient little Maxima had cost. But all that money wouldn't buy his way into heaven.

Men like Keith Turner went to hell.

She knew for sure because that was where her daddy had gone. Her mother had told her that every day of her life.

Misty, she'd said, *don't ever trust a man. Especially not a handsome one.*

So she never had.

She tried to protect the people she cared about, but sometimes it seemed like she couldn't do enough.

After sliding the gearshift into Drive, she pushed her glasses up the bridge of her nose and followed the fancy Jaguar. Maybe if she could learn who he was screwing around with on the side, she would finally understand that he was bad for her. Bad. Bad. Bad.

He'd sure been bad for Heather Baker.

Misty slowed as she passed the turn he'd taken in the quarry. Why would he go there? Didn't seem like the kind of place for a secret romantic rendezvous. But then, they could do it in that swanky car of his. She turned her car around the first chance she got and drove back to the gravel road that led deep into the limestone quarry. It was Sunday; the place was closed. But that would be all the better. No one to disturb them.

She made the turn, took her time. She didn't want to run into him or whoever he'd come there to meet. Creeping along, she decided to take the fork in the road that would lead her around to the back side of the site, the delivery entrance. The road the dump trucks used. She hoped he hadn't made that same decision. Oh well, she'd take her chances. No one really ever thought anything about her skulking around. She was plain old Batty Briggs.

They just didn't know.

She was far brighter than even her principal suspected.

She knew how to get things done when no one else could.

A large metal garage flanked this side of the excavation site. Dump trucks, backhoes, and other equipment were lined up next to the garage. The perfect place for her to hide.

She nosed up to one of the massive trucks and shut off her engine. She powered the windows down and listened.

The Jag was parked next to the office, windows up and the motor still running. She could see it clearly as she peered between the front end of one truck and the bed of another, but he'd have to be looking specifically for her to see her and then it wouldn't be easy to spot her position.

Anticipation started to hum inside her at the idea that he would get out soon. Though she didn't trust handsome men, she liked looking at them occasionally. Liked thinking about how it was when he came during sex.

She'd watched a few times. The sound of male grunting was curiously intriguing. Made her a little tingly. Keith grunted a lot when he had sex. He liked using his tongue, too. A lot of licking went on.

Her nipples hardened as she let the images play out in her head. He would start with his lover's toes. Licking and sucking, while his fingers did things to her calves and the backs of her knees. His lips formed nicely as he kissed.

But not as nice as Clint Austin's.

He had the best lips of any man Misty had ever seen.

She wondered how long it had been since Clint had had sex with a woman. She was sure he'd had plenty in prison, but none of it would have included a female, just lots of grunting and poking.

Clint Austin was strong. She'd wager it had taken at least four to hold him down.

She banished the image. She liked the kissing and licking much better. Hot, thick tongues and soft, full lips. Much, much better than the other.

Her thighs pressed together. Just thinking about it excited her. She placed a hand on her breast and squeezed. She had very nice breasts. She'd been told so many times. Justine had told her so. She would never lie to her. Misty wore her clothes loose to prevent men from staring at her breasts. They always stared if she wore form-fitting clothes.

She squeezed her breasts, felt a jolt deep inside her. Using both hands, she massaged, kneaded, enjoyed the feel of what she'd been blessed with. And why not? Better for her to enjoy them than some man.

Tighter, she squeezed, until her breath caught. Her bottom came up off the seat. She was really hot now.

The Jag hadn't moved. The motor still running.

She pushed one hand inside her shorts and touched her clitoris. "Mmmm." That felt nice. She knew how to touch a clitoris properly. With whisper-soft, feathery touches. Men were too stupid to know that. They jabbed it and pressed too hard. This, she made slow, gentle circles, was the right way.

Her legs stiffened . . . her hips started to rock ever so slightly in the seat. The need to close her eyes was almost overpowering. Couldn't do it. Had to watch him, make sure he didn't go anywhere. She came. Wave after wave of sweetness. She relaxed into the seat, licked her fingers, and sighed blissfully. Wonderful. And she hadn't needed a man at all.

The sound of wheels crushing gravel had her sitting up straighter. She frowned when Troy Baker's truck pulled up alongside the Jag. What was this? She didn't want to see Troy Baker. He was an idiot. She'd found the childish mess he'd made at Clint Austin's.

Anger blazed through her. Keith was supposed to be meeting a woman. Misty knew he was cheating. She needed to see it with her own eyes.

It was the only way to prove she was right.

CHAPTER TWENTY-SIX

10:20 A.M.

Troy was already shit-kicking mad when he finally got to the meeting place. He was pretty damned drunk, too. But not so much so that he didn't have sense enough to make sure they didn't meet out in the open in broad daylight.

Clint Austin had gone too far.

And Emily Wallace was right on his fucking heels.

What the hell was she thinking, taking up for the sonofabitch? Insinuating that he was innocent? She should've let him burn up in that damn house! Just showed how much she really cared about Heather's memory.

The bitch. Troy had no use for her anymore. *None.*

Keith climbed out of his Jag and glanced around. "What couldn't keep until after church?" He slammed the door and walked toward Troy. "This is the first time I've ever missed church with my boys. All I can say is, it better be good. I'm in enough trouble with Violet now."

Troy resisted the impulse to say, *Fuck Violet.* He had and Keith got the short end of the damned stick. Course that was before she got her wish and married Keith. And, hell, Troy'd been drunk anyway. He'd gone pretty crazy after Heather's murder. It had taken him years to get his shit back together. He'd been all right until that low-down parole board had gone and let that bastard Austin go free.

"What'd you tell her?" Troy knew for a fact Keith'd had to make up one humdinger of an excuse to get out of going to church with Violet. She had an obsession about appearances.

Keith leaned against Troy's truck. "That I puked half the night and was hungover."

Troy kicked a good-sized piece of gravel across the layer of smaller pieces that lined the ground everywhere you looked. The gravel skidded a couple of times before going over the edge into the excavation site. "You do pretty much look like shit," he said with a laugh. Violet would have a hissy if she knew Keith had left the house without shaving.

"Feel like it, too."

Keith pushed away from the truck and wandered toward the big-ass hole in the ground that provided limestone gravel for a tricounty area.

"It's time to end this, buddy," Troy said grimly.

Keith pivoted to face him, eyes slitted suspiciously. "What're you talking about?"

"Austin is just gonna keep messing with folks' heads and hanging around until people begin to think he's telling the truth, that maybe he didn't kill Heather. Hell, the newspapers are already hinting at that shit." Troy shook his head. "I can't let that happen. You heard what Violet said, the bastard's asking to see the files on the investigation? Why the hell do you suppose he would do that?"

"How should I know?" Keith flung his arms in the air, his frustration over the top. "I'm telling you, Troy, we need to let this thing go. Burning down his house . . . hell, man, that's a felony . . . could've been a murder charge. Somebody's taking some big-ass risks."

Troy scoffed. "Just not big enough or he'd be dead."

Keith got that suspicious look in his eyes again. "You said you had nothing to do with that."

"I didn't." Troy held up his hands and waved them to show they were clean. "Back off, man. He's the enemy, not me."

"Well, if not you, then who?"

"Who the fuck knows?" Troy was the one getting suspicious now. "You ain't getting like Emily Wallace, are you?"

"Emily's a good person, Troy," Keith countered, evading the question. "You know that. You and Larry were too hard on her last night."

"She's a traitor." Troy needed a beer. He wished he'd brought along more than the two six-packs he'd already consumed.

"I gotta ask you something, Troy?"

Troy swiveled his head to stare at the man who was supposed to be his best friend. "What?"

"You been binging on alcohol lately? Like before?"

"This meeting is not about me," Troy snapped. He didn't need nobody telling him how much he should drink. He got enough of that shit at home. Patricia was threatening divorce. Divorce! His whole life was falling apart and it was Austin's fault. "This is about making things right once and for all."

Keith shook his head. "I can't do this anymore, Troy. This thing with Austin is ruining all our lives. Don't you see that, man?"

"At least we have one to ruin," Troy snarled. "Heather's was taken away from her."

Keith stared at the ground a moment, his hands hanging uselessly at his sides. "I can't do it, Troy." He lifted his gaze. "I'm finished trying to make Austin pay. The law is satisfied with the time he served. We'll just have to get right with the way it is."

"Oh, I see the problem." Troy moved his head from side to side in disappointment. He stopped abruptly when the world started spinning. He blinked a couple of times, regained his balance.

"You okay, man?" Keith reached for him.

Troy snatched his arm away. "I know what your problem is. I thought about it all night. What Austin said got to you. That bullshit about asking my friends' alibis in front of all those people threw you for a loop, didn't it?"

Keith looked mad and maybe a little afraid. The anger Troy could understand . . . but the fear, what the hell did Keith have to be afraid of?

"What Austin says or thinks means nothing to me. This is about having some peace. We can't keep going like this, Troy. We have families to think of."

Troy pounded his chest. "Heather was my family."

Keith took a big breath, let it out. "You're right. And I'm sorrier than you'll ever know. But I'm out, got it?"

Maybe it was the way the alcohol suddenly kicked in or the lack of sleep, but this just didn't feel right. "Are you saying you're not gonna help me finish this? After what he did?" Troy blinked some more, tried to keep Keith in focus.

Keith met Troy's gaze and that crazy fear was still there or, hell, maybe he was imagining it.

"That's what I'm saying."

Troy's anger detonated. "What're you hiding, Keith?" He stepped closer to the man who'd been his best friend, his closest confidant, since Heather's murder. He'd been right there, helped Troy through his trouble with women and drinking. He'd gotten Troy the job at the plant his daddy owned. He'd been the best friend a man could want. But something wasn't right and it wasn't the alcohol. "What'd you do that you're not telling me?"

Keith sidestepped to go around him. "I'm going home now. I can't talk to you when you get like this."

"Hell no." Troy grabbed him by the arm and pulled him around. "You'll tell me what you're hiding. That's what you'll do."

"What are you talking about, man? You're drunk."

"I'm talking about," Troy moved in nose-to-nose, "what I see in your eyes. The fear. You're afraid. I want to know why. Don't even think about playing the Violet card. That shit won't fly."

Keith closed his eyes for a moment and dragged in another of those labored breaths. What the hell was wrong with him? Troy didn't get this. His stomach heaved. Maybe he was fucking hallucinating.

"It's my alibi. . . ."

"Your daddy said you were home in bed," Troy recalled. "What about it?"

"That wasn't exactly right."

It was Troy's turn to feel the fear. He stamped it out.

"I was with another woman."

Troy felt his gut roll and then clench. "You were cheating on Heather?"

Keith gave a reluctant nod.

"You sonofabitch." Troy took a swing at him.

Keith ducked just in time, or maybe Troy's reflexes were off. He wanted to kill Keith; that's what he wanted to do.

"You were out with another fucking girl when my sister was being murdered?"

"Yes."

"Goddamn it all to hell." Troy walked in a circle, couldn't wrap his mind around this . . . this was crazy. It had to be a mistake. He suddenly felt far too sober. "She loved you, you sick bastard!"

"Don't you see," Keith urged, "I can't keep doing this to Austin when I . . . I did what I did."

Troy looked at him, tried hard to figure his cockeyed reasoning. "You're dead right what you did was wrong, but your screwing around didn't kill my sister."

The silence that thickened between them . . . the look in Keith's eyes told Troy there was more.

"What's the rest of it?" The voice didn't even sound like

it came from him. Hollow . . . afraid . . . afraid of what he was about to hear.

Keith wouldn't look Troy in the eye anymore. "I had too much to drink. I passed out."

Troy didn't move, prayed that if there was a God in heaven he wouldn't let whatever Keith was about to say be as bad as it felt like it was going to be.

"The other woman . . . she said she woke up that night and I wasn't in the bed. Then, the next morning I was. I . . ." He looked at Troy then. "I had blood on my clothes . . . on my hands. We didn't know where it came from."

Red flashed in front of Troy's eyes. He didn't remember moving, but suddenly he had Keith pinned to the ground. Images of his sister's slashed face and throat . . . the cuts on her arms where she'd fought her attacker floated before his eyes.

"Are you telling me you killed my sister?" Troy growled, his teeth clenched, his fingers digging into Keith's throat.

Keith gagged, made a choking sound. Troy let up on his grip. He could feel Keith's heart pounding in his chest. He could smell the blood rushing through his veins. He didn't ever remember feeling this kind of rage before.

"Answer me!" he screamed, his voice echoed in the empty quarry.

"I . . . I don't know."

The bastard was crying. Troy wanted to kill him. "Damn you." Troy got up and walked off. He wrestled with the rage that had possessed him like a demon. The air sawed in and out of his lungs. This couldn't be happening.

Keith pushed to his feet, came up next to Troy, his head hung in defeat or humiliation. "I don't know what happened. I can't believe I would have hurt her . . . but I just don't know."

Troy turned his head, met Keith's gaze with fire starting to burn in his belly all over again. "Who was she? I want to talk to her. I want to know what time she woke up. Exactly what she saw or heard."

Keith looked away. "I can't tell you. If I tell you—"

Troy grabbed him by the shirtfront and shook the hell out of him. "Tell me who you were with that night or I swear to God I'll kill you, man."

Fury flashed in Keith's eyes then. "I can't tell you!"

They were on the ground again. Troy had his hands around Keith's throat. He was trying to push Troy off.

"You waited ten fucking years to tell me this." Troy squeezed harder. "You sonofabitch. You're no better than Austin."

"I'm sorry," Keith cried. "I pray every night that I didn't do it . . . but I just don't know . . . dammit . . . I just don't know."

"Then you should just fucking kill yourself and get it over with, you goddamn coward, because I'm gonna make you wish you were dead."

Troy left Keith on the ground and started for his truck.

He was finished here. He needed something a hell of a lot stronger than beer to wash down this kind of betrayal.

CHAPTER TWENTY-SEVEN

302 Dogwood Drive
Monday, July 22, 6:45 A.M.

Justine grabbed a cup of yogurt. She peeled off the foil top and stuck her finger into the rich, creamy strawberry blend. She sucked the yogurt from her finger and moaned.

Food always tasted better after a revitalizing run.

Three miles.

A hot-cold shower with a great new moisturizing wash that she absolutely adored, then some naked time to allow her skin to breathe.

She loved her naked time.

She padded barefoot into the living room and flipped the channel to the news. Draping herself across the sofa, she caught up on world events while she lapped up her yogurt.

The pounding on her front door followed by, "Justine!" reversed the relaxed state she had achieved.

What in the world had happened with Misty now?

Unreasonably annoyed, Justine plopped her yogurt cup on the end table and dropped her feet to the floor. So much for *me* time before meeting the squad at eight for practice.

She grabbed the throw from the sofa and draped it around her body.

"Justine!"

"Coming!" *Jesus, you'd think the world was coming to an end.* She strode to the door and released the locks. She and Misty had been friends since they were children. Justine hated when Misty got like this.

"What's wrong?"

Misty wore the same clothes as yesterday. Her hair had fallen from its clip and was a wild mass of windblown tangles. How could anyone so brilliant be so uncaring about her appearance?

"I . . ." She shuddered. "I just heard. Keith is dead."

The world stopped, leaving Justine stunned and unable to breathe for a time she couldn't accurately measure. "What?"

"They found his body about an hour ago."

"What happened?" Her voice was accusing, but she couldn't help that just now.

Misty flared her hands. "Don't know for sure."

Justine drew the door open wide. "Come in."

"I knew you'd want to know," Misty babbled. "I'm sure Violet is devastated."

"Yes . . . she would be." Justine's chest ached, reminding her that she needed to breathe. This couldn't be . . . not Keith.

Misty rubbed her hands up and down her arms as if she were cold. "It's terrible. Really terrible. I wanted to be here for you. I knew you'd be upset."

Justine closed her eyes to the count of three and then she ordered herself to pull it together. She had a practice to supervise in one hour. This was terrible news . . . but perhaps not totally unexpected now that she was over the initial shock and thought about it. Keith hadn't been himself since Austin's return to Pine Bluff. She would need to talk to Ray and find out if it was murder . . . or suicide.

When she felt composed once more she opened her eyes.

"Would you like some coffee?" She could use a cup for sure.

Misty nodded. "Please."

A glimpse of something red or dark brown on Misty's arm distracted Justine. "Have you hurt yourself?" She reached out, took Misty's arm, and inspected it. A nasty gash near the elbow.

"It was a stupid mistake. I fell. It's nothing."

Misty, Misty, Misty. "Did you clean it?" The answer was evident. Blood had oozed and dried.

She shrugged carelessly. "I forgot about it."

"Come on." Justine ushered Misty into the bathroom and turned on the shower. "As soon as the water's warm I want you to get in there. Wash your hair and I'll braid it for you."

She peered at Justine through her thick glasses. "You're too good to me, Justine. No one's ever been as good to me as you."

Justine ignored Misty's sentimentality and pointed at the shower. "I'll be back with coffee."

With Misty in the shower, Justine pulled on her favorite silk robe. Gold, handmade. A gift she treasured. Pushing away the pain, she went into the kitchen and made a fresh pot of coffee. Her movements felt mechanical.

Poor Violet. And the boys.

Justine braced against the counter. And Granville. He would be completely shattered. His wife was gone. He had no other children. He was all alone. This was such a tragedy. Austin should never have come back here and started this thing.

A sense of purpose filled Justine. She would see that Keith's father was well taken care of. It was the least she could do. Keith would want her to.

She took her time, sipped her coffee and resumed command of her composure. Yes. Purpose was the key. Her future might very well hinge on how she handled the aftermath of Keith's death. Granville would need someone . . . someone like her. The timing was perfect.

When the water stopped running in the shower, she poured another cup and headed to the bathroom to see to Misty's needs. She was obviously badly shaken. Justine would need to ensure her friend was calm and rational. Misty was far too easily agitated.

"Here you are." Justine walked in as Misty stepped out of the shower. She clutched the towel close to her chest. "Misty," Justine scolded. "Don't be silly. I've seen you nude before."

"But there's so much light in here."

Justine set the cup of coffee on the vanity counter and smiled. "Honey, you have nothing to be embarrassed about." She reached for the towel, tugged it from Misty's hands. "Just look at you; you're beautiful." She took Misty's hand. "Come with me."

She led Misty to her bedroom, the steaming coffee forgotten, turned on the light, and positioned her in front of the enormous mirror.

"Now look."

Droplets of water from Misty's damp hair slid down her smooth skin. Justine frowned at the claw marks on the back of Misty's other arm near her shoulder. The notion that she'd most likely gotten those scratches in a struggle twisted inside Justine. Whatever Misty had done, it was too late to do anything about it now.

"I'm ugly," Misty murmured.

Justine snapped to attention and moved up next to Misty. She pushed the other troubling thoughts aside and smiled. There would be time to sort all that out later. "Absolutely not. See how nicely shaped your breasts are." She touched one, cupped its roundness, and smiled. She swept her fingers down Misty's flat belly. "You're thin, with hips the perfect size." She dragged her fingers over the nice flare between Misty's waist and her thighs. "We've talked about this before."

"Not as beautiful as you," Misty said, looking at Justine in the mirror.

The missing glasses alone made such a difference. Misty's face was the perfect heart shape. Her eyes big and round. Justine wished she would wear her contacts. "You're every bit as beautiful as me."

"Show me." Misty turned to her, reached for the sash at her waist.

Justine didn't resist. She needed to fill this emptiness widening inside her. She didn't want to think. She needed to be touched . . . to be cherished. She could always count on Misty for that. The robe floated to the floor.

Misty touched her. Pressed her lips to Justine's skin and trailed soft kisses over her breasts as her fingers explored boldly. She ushered Justine down onto the edge of the bed. She lay back, closed her eyes as she spread her legs wide apart in invitation. Misty's palms slid up her thighs and the feel of her greedy tongue parting her most intimate folds caused Justine's fingers to fist in the covers. She arched toward the intrusion . . . wanted to feel . . . wanted to forget.

CHAPTER TWENTY-EIGHT

1:55 P.M.

Ray paused at Mary Alice's desk. "Hold my calls." Then he went into his office and closed the door.

He swallowed back a howl of misery.

Keith Turner was dead.

Violet had called Ray late last night in a tizzy to say she'd come home from church to find Keith gone and that he hadn't called or been home since. Ray had assured her that she shouldn't worry. Keith had probably gone out with some of the guys and forgotten the time. It wouldn't have been the first time he and his buddies did something so thoughtless and adolescent. Hell, Ray still forgot to call his own wife from time to time when he was caught up in a case or a report.

This morning at six the first shift reporting to work at the quarry had found Keith's body in the excavation site.

Ray had been there all morning, along with the forensic technicians from the Alabama Bureau of Investigations. Keith's body had been taken away for an autopsy. It was pretty clear what had killed him, but there were things they needed to assess. Whether or not there had been a struggle prior to his fall. Drugs, alcohol. Stuff that small-town chiefs like Ray didn't usually have to deal with.

Not since Heather Baker.

He'd just left Violet's house.

Ray sat down behind his desk and put his face in his hands. Things had been simmering toward this boil ever since Clint was released. The fight Saturday night was no surprise considering the tension eating at the whole town.

Ray had sent Mike Caruthers to pick up Clint from the repair shop and bring him in for questioning. Ray hated like hell to do it, but he didn't have an option. The whole town would consider Clint a prime suspect. Hell, any chief of police worth his salt would be a fool not to.

Except that Ray knew things that no one else did.

Troy and his buddies were being rounded up as well. Everybody at Violet's party had been talking about the tension between Troy and Keith. Usually Troy knew where Keith was at all times. Violet had said she'd called Troy last night and he claimed he had no idea what Keith was up to. Sounded damned fishy to Ray.

That was the thing. When a rich guy like Keith went missing, you worried about kidnapping and ransom. Sometimes kidnappings went wrong. But Ray knew in his gut that money had nothing to do with this. This was about the past.

Shouting outside his door jerked Ray's head up. The door flew open and Granville Turner stormed in, Mary Alice right behind him trying hard to talk him out of interrupting.

Too late.

"It's okay, Mary Alice."

She nodded, then closed the door as she left.

"There's nothing else I can tell you right now, Granville." Ray pushed to his feet, feeling immensely sorry for the man. Despite all the water that had gone under the bridge between them, and there had been plenty, Ray couldn't help the sympathy he felt.

Granville towered in front of Ray's desk. Wouldn't have

sat down had he invited him to. "You can tell me if you've hauled Clint Austin in yet. I want to know if that bastard has an alibi."

"Mike is on his way in with him right now. I'm going to question him as well as anyone else who associated with Keith on a regular basis and who might have had some idea what he was doing at the quarry."

"It's Austin," Granville said, his usual boisterous voice a dull roar. "I know it's him. I want you to get that sonofabitch, Ray; I don't care what it takes."

"I'll question him just like everybody else of interest to this case."

"You told me you would take care of this." Granville's eyes glittered with unshed tears. "That I had nothing to worry about. Now my son is dead." He shook a finger at Ray and blinked away all signs of vulnerability. "I own you, Ray Hale, lock, stock, and barrel; don't you forget it. I saw that you moved up the ranks . . . got the position of chief. You owe me."

That was truer than Ray would have liked to admit, but there were things that Ray knew, too. Things that could take Granville back down a notch or two, but not now. This was too personal and too painful for Ray to take that hard line with the man under the circumstances.

"I will find out how this happened," Ray promised, "and when I do you'll be the first to know."

"There's no way that bastard could have known. . . ."

Granville didn't have to complete the sentence. Ray knew what he meant.

"No," Ray assured him. "No one else knows." No one needed to. It was too late to right that wrong.

He'd been telling himself that for over ten years; maybe eventually he would believe it.

"I thank God his mother didn't live to endure this." Granville's voice went shaky on the last.

Ray nodded. Nothing he could say would be enough. This was the kind of tragedy no parent wanted to face. With a final warning to stay on top of this investigation, Granville left with a little less theatrics than when he'd arrived.

The intercom on Ray's desk buzzed, followed by, "Chief, Deputy Caruthers is waiting with Clint Austin in the interview room."

"I'm on my way."

2:15 P.M.

Clint had declined to have his parole officer present; he'd been advised of his rights and left to sweat in the same interview room where he'd been questioned after Heather Baker's murder. Only this time he wasn't sweating. He'd done nothing wrong, and no one could place him at the scene.

He wasn't the same man he'd been back then, either.

Right now he was a little unsure about a lot of things, but taking any grief from Pine Bluff 's finest wasn't one of them.

The smell of Emily's skin . . . images from yesterday morning flashed through his mind. She'd still been a virgin and she'd ruined herself with him . . . goaded him into taking her like that. He shouldn't have allowed it . . . but he hadn't been strong enough to walk away. He couldn't think about that. Just another line he'd crossed that would get him nowhere. Being with her that way had damaged him somehow . . . had made him powerless in a way that he didn't ever want to be again.

Not that he had to worry. She'd run away so fast his head was still swimming. She wouldn't be back. She'd been too good for him at seventeen, and she was too good for him now.

If the not knowing how it felt to touch her had been pure misery . . . the knowing and not touching her was an agony he couldn't hope to gauge.

The door opened and Ray Hale walked in with two cups of coffee. He placed one on the table in front of Clint and kept the other for himself.

He dropped into the chair opposite Clint and rubbed at his eyes as if he'd seen too much that morning.

"I need you to tell me if you know anything about Keith Turner's death." Ray took out his trusty notepad and pencil.

He didn't call it a murder. Probably waiting for the official autopsy results. "I don't know anything about it. I saw Turner Saturday night, and I haven't seen him since."

"What about Troy Baker?"

Clint shook his head. "Not since they showed up at my place drunk as skunks and acting stupid."

"I'm not going to find any evidence that you were at that quarry," Ray pressed, after jotting down a couple of notes.

"No way. I was home all day yesterday and all night." He saw the skepticism in Ray's eyes. "Until the insurance company gets the temporary trailer out there tomorrow or the next day, I'm staying in the barn."

"If you want to sleep in a bed and have a hot shower," Ray said, the hard, edgy lines of his face softening, "there's the shelter at the Methodist church . . . and that old hunting cabin you know I never use. It's pretty rustic, but there's running water and a bathroom."

Clint didn't need Ray feeling sorry for him. "I'm fine." He started to ask Ray if he took such an interest in all his suspects, but that would only piss him off.

Ray stared into his cup as if the answers he sought were bound to make an appearance. "You know." He lifted his gaze to Clint. "Most folks are going to think after the remark you made about Keith and the fight with his buddies that you were the one who killed him. It would be nice if someone could confirm your alibi. The coroner estimated the time of death between ten and eleven yesterday morning."

Ten and eleven . . . that was when he and Emily . . .

"I was at my place *alone.* Any more questions?"

Ray heaved a weary sigh. "Let me see your hands."

Clint flattened his palms on the table. "I got those skinned knuckles in the fight Saturday night. The scratches are scabbed over already. They wouldn't look like that if I'd done them yesterday."

Ray studied him a moment. He didn't have to say anything. Clint knew what he was thinking. Things in this town had gone downhill since Clint's release. People had gotten out of sorts. Lives had been disrupted. *Well, tough shit.* Clint's life had been disrupted, too. He'd lost over ten years. Like Ray himself had said, Clint had done his time. He had a right to be here the same as anyone else.

"Just stay out of the public eye as much as possible until we get a lead on this," Ray suggested. "I don't want any more trouble."

Clint pushed away from the table and stood. "You won't get any from me." He hesitated before heading for the door. "I still want to see those files, Ray. I don't know why you're putting me off."

"I'm not putting you off, Clint. Yesterday was Sunday and I've been a little busy this morning." Ray stood, looked anywhere but at Clint. "I don't know what you think you'll find. That case is over and done with. Like I told you before, there wasn't a trace of evidence to indicate anyone but you and Emily Wallace were in that room that night. Those files won't help you. It's best to move on."

"Is there something you're hiding from me, Ray? Is that the problem with me seeing the case files?" The vehemence in Clint's voice startled him. Startled Ray, too. Dammit, Clint hadn't meant to lose control like that. He'd lost too much control already. But he'd seen the guard go up in Ray's eyes. Clint knew him well enough to know when he was hiding something.

The door opened. Caruthers stuck his head inside. "Everything all right in here?"

Clint looked from the nosy deputy to his chief.

"We're good," Ray confirmed.

Caruthers closed the door, but not before he gave Clint one last hard look. That was the way things were in this town. Clint would always be the bad guy . . . even when he wasn't. But then he'd known that before he'd come back.

"Look, Clint, I'm not trying to put you off." Ray presented an understanding face that lacked any substance. "All the files ten years old or older were moved to permanent storage in the basement of the courthouse. I'll need time to find that one . . . if it wasn't damaged beyond salvaging in that water leak a couple years back. But you have my word that I'll see what I can do."

Sounded like an excuse to Clint. "You do that." Ray had no intention of allowing him anywhere near those files.

When Clint reached the door, Ray stopped him with one last question: "Any chance Emily Wallace was watching your place yesterday?"

"No." Clint started to leave it at that, but he hesitated, decided to make things perfectly clear. "I don't think she'll be coming around my place anymore."

She'd learned a hard truth. Had felt guilty. So she'd come to pay her penance. He understood that yesterday was nothing more than a pity fuck.

She wouldn't be back.

2:45 P.M.

Ray dreaded this one about as much as he had Clint's.

Getting through it was necessary.

Mike would question Larry Medford, and Fitzpatrick would handle Perry Woods.

Ray entered the interview room where Troy Baker waited for him. That was one of the perks of being chief. The jobs no one else wanted were always yours.

"Troy."

He didn't look up. Sat at the table, his head bowed as if he were praying.

Ray sat down across from him and opened his notepad. Someone had already brought Troy a cup of coffee. He hadn't touched it.

"I need some answers, Troy. Why don't you start with the last time you saw Keith," Ray suggested when Troy still didn't look up.

Troy lifted his head. One cheek was bruised and scraped. His nose was swollen; both eyes were black. "You know when I saw him last."

Ray had expected Troy to be upset. Keith had been his best friend. But where was the anger? The need for vengeance? This resignation was not typical Troy behavior.

"So you didn't see him at all after Saturday night when Violet dropped you off at home?"

Troy shook his head. "Nope."

"Where were you yesterday morning?" Ray didn't like that blank look on Troy's face. He liked Troy's lack of emotion even less. This was wrong somehow.

"Passed out in my truck in my own front yard." He met Ray's eyes again. "Ask Patricia. She came home from church and found me. I'd climbed in the truck after Violet took me home. That's where I slept it off."

That still left him with no alibi until noon yesterday. But why would Troy kill Keith? There was tension between them because of Austin. But enough to commit murder? Ray just couldn't swallow that.

"I need to see your hands, Troy."

He flattened his hands on the table. Bruised and scratched.

"Did you do all that Saturday night?"

Troy nodded. "Where else? I told you I was dead to the world after that."

"You don't know of anyone Keith was having trouble with?"

Troy shook his head. "Nobody except that bastard Austin."

Hatred glinted in those dull eyes for a beat or two before he looked away again.

"What about suicide? Was Keith having any trouble that might have made him want to end his life?" Ray couldn't see that. This was a small town. If Keith and Violet were having any real problems, he would have heard about it.

"Can't think of a thing."

Ray couldn't put his finger on the problem, but there was definitely a problem. Troy looked hungover as hell; that was true. But there was more, deeper. A defeat of some sort.

"Any more questions?" Again Troy didn't look at him.

"That's all for now."

Troy pushed out of his chair and walked to the door.

"You let me know," Ray said, "if you think of anything that might help with this investigation."

His hand on the door, Troy didn't look back. "Sure."

Ray rubbed his chin and thought about Troy's reaction for a bit. Definitely off. As badly as Troy had to be hurting, he hadn't launched a verbal attack as he usually did.

Maybe Ray would get lucky and the ABI would find some usable physical evidence at the scene.

But so far luck had been looking the other way in Pine Bluff.

CHAPTER TWENTY-NINE

3:30 P.M.

Emily was summoned to City Hall. Ray wanted her to come in and answer a few questions.

Keith was dead.

She couldn't believe it. God, Violet and the kids would be devastated.

Emily hadn't left her room since returning from Clint's place the day before. Part of her kept hoping her parents would call and invite her home. Maybe she should have taken the first step, but she hadn't. She'd tinkered with her lists some more, finally had them in shape to turn over to Ray. Outside that, she'd spent a good deal of time trying to banish the confusing episode in the barn. She couldn't say she regretted what she'd done. But she felt uncertain about herself . . . about everything.

The chief's secretary wasn't at her desk, so Emily went straight to his door and knocked.

"Come on in!"

Emily steeled herself and opened the door.

Ray pushed to his feet and offered his hand across his desk. "Thank you for coming, Emily."

She walked straight over, shook his hand, and wilted into the chair he indicated. "I can hardly believe it. I'm sure Violet is inconsolable."

Ray nodded and resumed his seat. "She's pretty torn up."

"And his father." Keith had been an only child. Granville had doted on him nonstop. The poor man would be grief stricken.

"You can imagine," Ray offered.

She could.

"That's why I called you here, Emily," he explained. "We want to be as thorough as possible."

"Of course. Anything I can do."

"You've spoken with Violet recently. Did you pick up on any trouble between them?"

What was he saying? "Surely you don't consider Violet a suspect?"

"We have to consider the spouse as well as anyone close to the victim."

Emily exhaled a weary breath. "I'm sorry. Of course you do. But, in answer to your question, I haven't been that close to anyone since . . . Heather's murder. So I'm not really the best person to ask."

"You're not aware of any encounters between Clint and Keith? I know you've been keeping a pretty close eye on Clint."

Now she understood what this was about. "Is Clint a suspect?" Dumb question. Sure he was.

"Right now most anyone who knew Keith is a suspect." Ray leaned back in his chair.

He didn't mention Heather's murder. Or Emily's father's visit.

"Do you have any reason to believe that Clint held Troy or Keith responsible for the fire?"

"No."

Ray stared at something on his desk for a long moment. Was there something more he couldn't tell her? Something that implicated Clint?

"Where were you between ten and eleven yesterday morning?"

"Is that when you think he died?"

"It's an estimate. We'll know more after the autopsy."

Evidently Clint hadn't told Ray he'd been with her. "Did you question Clint?" She was sure he had.

Ray hesitated, then said, "Yes."

"Then you should know where I was."

The confusion on his face confirmed her deduction.

"I was with Clint."

Ray's expression turned wary. "He didn't mention it."

"If the estimated time is right, Austin does have an alibi."

"He claims he was home, *alone*."

"He was home," Emily agreed, "but he wasn't alone. I was with him."

All reaction had been banished from Ray's face now. "Why would he withhold that information? Having confirmation of his alibi would be very important for Clint."

Emily moistened her lips, tried to swallow, but her throat was too dry. "Maybe to protect me; I don't know." She looked directly into Ray's eyes. "I have no reason to lie for him."

She would prefer Ray didn't ask for details. Memories, too vivid to ignore, kept filtering through her head, reminding her of what she'd done.

"This doesn't have anything to do with what your father told me yesterday, does it?" Ray eyed her closely. "If you're feeling guilty because of the information your father withheld, you shouldn't."

He did think she was lying! How could he believe that? Of course she should feel guilty. So should he! She reached for her purse. Whether it served any purpose or not, she wanted him to see what she'd come up with.

"There are things about Heather's murder that—"

"That investigation is over." He cut her off. "Closed."

"Wait." She looked up, surprised at his sharp tone. "If he's innocent—"

"We don't know that," Ray interjected.

He was the one who'd stood by Clint all these years. Had supported the parole board's decision. Why the about-face?

"What we all need to do is put this behind us," Ray explained patiently. "The past is over; we can't change it." He paused. "It's time to look to the future, Emily, not the past. We've all done too much of that already."

"You don't want to see the past set to right?" How could he not? The law was his job. "And what about the real killer? If Austin is innocent, that means the person who did it got away with murder."

"Emily, there was no evidence other than what was used to convict Clint," he said quietly but firmly. "Not a single trace. There's nothing I can do." He stood, letting her know that the conversation was over. "I appreciate you coming in, Emily. We may need to call on you again when we have a more exact time of death."

She rose, confusion making her slow to react. "Sure."

What had just happened here? She made her way out of his office and across the lobby without pausing to turn around and stare. When had Ray stopped being Clint's ally?

As the top representative of the law in this town, Ray should have jumped on the information her father had passed along. Why wasn't Ray calling Sid Fairgate in for confirmation?

Maybe it was Keith's murder.

Maybe Ray was preoccupied.

She reached the door and she had to look back. She was almost surprised when she didn't find Ray watching her go. He'd been so anxious to be rid of her.

Maybe he was preoccupied with this newest tragedy.

But that didn't explain his insistence that looking into Heather's murder was pointless. She could see him suggesting that they do so later, when Keith's death was resolved. But Ray had said there was no evidence that pointed to anyone other than Clint. In other words, why bother looking? The case was closed. End of story.

This was wrong.

Ray was ignoring the facts. She hesitated. Or maybe he was hiding a secret of his own. Every damned body else sure seemed to be.

CHAPTER THIRTY

Turner Mansion
9:30 P.M.

Justine stopped at the entrance, entered the code she knew by heart, and the massive wrought-iron gates spread open, slowly, regally, like welcoming arms. She finally had an invitation, albeit unspoken. Telepathy wasn't necessary to know Granville needed her right now.

She pressed the accelerator and rolled up the long, winding drive to the grand colonial-style mansion that still took her breath away.

This was where she belonged.

She sighed, appreciating the abundant branches of the ancient oaks and maples that shaded the lush green lawn and curving cobblestone drive. There wasn't a single home in the whole state of Alabama that even came close to being as exquisite or timelessly classic as this one.

Coming to a stop in front of the house, she got out and closed the door of her eleven-year-old Audi. It had been a long time since he'd given her that gift. Definitely time for an upgrade. He would lavish her with all the gifts she would ever require. She would never need anyone else ever again.

Only Gran. They could grow old together, but she would always be younger and more beautiful than him. She would give him exactly what he needed until death parted them.

She surveyed the beautifully landscaped property that spread out in three directions for as far as the eye could see. Rolling pastures and grazing horses covered the acres between the house and the tree-covered mountains that gently sloped downward to abut the property. This was what she'd wanted since she was just a little girl. To be rich . . . to have everything her heart desired. And now, finally, it was her turn.

No matter that she'd made Gran happy many times in the past, he'd been devoted to that snobbish wife of his. But she was out of the way now. There was nothing to stop Justine.

She climbed the steps, took a moment to touch up her favorite lipstick, Iced Cherry, and to smooth her sleek black dress; then she rang the bell. All the hired help would be gone home by now. He would be all alone.

Grieving.

He'd been a widower for six months, sufficient mourning time in Justine's opinion. Now he was faced with the most painful tragedy of his life—the loss of his son and only child.

Yes, it was her turn. Her ultimate purpose was at hand. He would see that he needed her more than ever. No more putting her off or setting her aside. Now she would take her rightful place in society.

One of the two towering doors swung inward and a disheveled Granville stood peering out at her over his askew reading glasses. "Justine?"

"I've been out of town all day." He didn't need to know that was a fabrication, that she'd actually waited, giving him plenty of time to slip deeper into his anguish. She reached for his hand and squeezed it. "I came as soon as I heard."

"My boy's really gone." His lips quivered on the frail words.

Dear Lord, he was practically a ghost of the man she knew him to be under normal circumstances.

"Gran, honey, have you eaten? You look exhausted."

Confusion lined the face that looked weary and uncertain rather than commanding and powerful.

"You shouldn't be alone." She walked in, ushering him aside. "Let's get some soup into you." She closed the door. "And a little brandy."

Perhaps the brandy first, she mused, considering his current state. She ushered him to the parlor on the left, the men's den, he liked to call it. He smoked his cigars there, kept his fine liquors and whiskeys there.

Becky's tail thumped against the floor as her master and his guest entered the room. The dog's big old soulful eyes followed their movements, but the lazy hound didn't bother getting up.

"You sit; I'll get you something to take the edge off."

Justine hurried behind the bar and selected the Raynal Brandy he liked best. As she poured a hefty serving, she kept an eye on him. He hadn't taken a seat as she'd suggested, but she saw why. There were photographs spread over every available surface.

Pictures of his poor, dead family.

Well, he'd forget about them soon enough. She would see that he forgot. She would stand beside him, hold his hand and anything else that needed holding, and when this investigation into Keith's death was over, Granville Turner would be all hers. And she would finally have the life she deserved.

She crossed back to where he stood staring at the mess he'd made with the family photo albums.

"Here, honey, drink this." She pressed the tumbler into his hand. "I'll straighten up for you. We wouldn't want any of these precious memories to be damaged."

She bent this way and that, picking up photos, stacking them neatly in the designer boxes, probably the highest-quality acid-free and photo-safe products available. But she could care less about that. What she cared about was how much of her legs showed each time she crouched down to gather a pile of photographs. Or how nice her bottom looked with the black silk pulled tight across it whenever she bent this way or that.

She'd selected this dress just for him. She knew how much he loved short black dresses that fit as tight as a smooth layer of youthful skin.

"There." She stood back and surveyed what she'd accomplished. "You ready for another, Gran?" She smiled, sugary sweet. He needed her and she wanted to be there. She'd waited a long time for this moment.

The tumbler was empty, but he wouldn't be needing another drink, she realized. His gaze had riveted to her breasts the moment she'd turned back to face him.

"Here, let me take that." She slipped the glass from his hand and set it on the coffee table. Moving closer . . . close enough for him to smell the fragrance she'd selected, his favorite, she murmured, "Is there anything else I can do for you, Gran?"

Those pale, watery eyes lifted to meet hers. "You're the only one who ever really understood what I needed."

"Of course I understand." She smoothed her hand over his stubbled jaw. He hadn't even shaved today. So unlike the Granville she knew. "You don't worry about a thing. I'll take real good care of you." She drifted down to her knees and smiled lovingly up at him.

His broad chest rose and fell rapidly as the excitement of seeing her in that submissive position coursed through his veins. Yes, she knew what he wanted, what he needed. That was her one true gift; she could please a man like no other woman could hope to. Her entire adult life she'd been blessed with the ability to induce a full erection with just a look . . . a near climax with a mere touch. Time for all that skill to pay off.

The metal-on-metal scrape of his zipper lowering, inch

by inch, echoed in the deathly quiet room. His strangled gasp encouraged her, made her all the more determined to ensure he never forgot who had taken care of him this tragic night.

By the time her fingers closed around him, he was more than ready. That she could so easily bring a man of his age to this state of arousal made her better than the little blue pill and far less dangerous to his health.

She cupped his weight, let the feel of her fingers drive him nearer to the edge. He groaned as she moved closer, close enough for him to feel her warm breath on that tender, intimate flesh that quivered and pulsed helplessly in her hands.

Justine had always tried to make the best out of every situation, good, bad, or indifferent. Always saw the glass as half-full.

Well, her glass had just filled to overflowing.

CHAPTER THIRTY-ONE

Valley Inn
10:15 P.M.

Emily's parents had called to check on her. They'd asked her to come home, but Emily wasn't ready for that yet. They had talked at length about her plans, which were actually their plans about how she should get on with her life and finally put this awful tragedy behind her now that their horrible secret was out. Surely Chief Hale would follow through.

But he wouldn't. He wanted this to go away, just like everyone else in town.

Since leaving Ray's office Emily had cried for Keith, for Violet and their boys. Emily had cried for Heather and her family, especially Troy. And Clint Austin. Finally Emily had reached that numb zone and the tears had stopped. A long hot bath had relaxed her and soothed her aching muscles. She shivered even now at the memory of how she'd gotten all those tender places.

No matter what Ray or her parents thought, Emily couldn't move on with her life until she'd found the truth for Clint's sake and for her own.

Heather's killer was out there . . . somewhere.

Could Keith's murder be connected to Heather's somehow?

Restless, Emily moved around the room. Was Ray investigating that angle?

As desperately as she wanted the truth revealed, someone else wanted it covered up. The fire was an attempt on Clint's life; there was no denying that. Was Keith's murder about shutting down this digging into the past? Had Keith known something about what really happened that night? Emily couldn't bring herself to believe that Keith would have done anything to harm Heather. But that didn't mean that he might not have known certain things. Heather had promised to tell her something important . . . had it been about Keith?

The idea that someone could be watching her right now, the same someone perhaps who had murdered Keith, had her peeking past the drapes to see if there were any new cars in the parking lot. So far there were only two other guests. Both their cars were still parked out front along with hers.

Clint had said she could be in danger. But she didn't actually know anything. She had theories, but those were irrelevant without evidence, as Ray had kindly pointed out.

As she started to draw away from the window a vehicle across the street snagged her attention. She looked again. An old green truck. Single-passenger. Goose bumps shivered across her skin. She recognized that truck from some place, but where?

Then she remembered.

Fragments of moments shared in that barn flickered, making her too warm. What was he doing here? Sure, it was possible he'd chosen that particular convenience store to patronize, even though the Sack&Go was closer for him. But the way he was parked, at the edge of the lot as far away from the store as possible—nowhere near the gas pumps or the entrance or exit to the parking lot—didn't point to a mere shopping stop.

He was watching the inn . . . watching her.

Before good sense could kick in, she'd unlocked the door

and opened it. She stood there, on the sidewalk outside her door, moths fluttering around the exterior light, and stared directly at the truck.

The engine started and the headlights came on. She put her hand up in front of her face to block the glaring lights. What was he doing now?

What if she'd been wrong? What if it wasn't him?

Her heart fluttered as the truck backed up, moved to the exit, and pulled straight across the street. Instinct shouted at her to go inside and lock the door.

She didn't.

It was him. She sensed it even before the streetlight provided the necessary illumination to verify her conclusion.

He parked the truck several doors down from where she stood. He got out, his gaze immediately colliding with hers, and started toward her. Sounds and sensations from the day before kept getting in the way of her ability to think rationally. Some part of her wanted to back away . . . but the woman that yearned for more of him refused.

"Get back in your room."

The sharply issued order shattered the distracting memories.

"What're you doing here?" she demanded, just as sharply.

"We'll talk inside."

He stopped right in front of her then, forcing the issue with his big body. She trembled. The white bathrobe suddenly felt too thin . . . too fragile a shield around her nakedness.

For three beats she argued with herself as to whether going into her room with him would be a good idea, but then an old saying of her grandmother's came to mind: *Too late to close the barn door after the cows were out.* It wasn't like he could do anything to Emily that he hadn't already. Or vice versa.

She pivoted and went back inside, her respiration growing labored with no other provocation than seeing him . . . being near him. He closed and locked the door. When his full attention landed on her once more she trembled yet again. His face was clean shaven. He'd obviously showered and changed somewhere.

"Why are you watching me?"

One corner of that sexy mouth lifted in amusement. "Turnabout is fair play. You sure as hell got in your share of watching me."

She raked her fingers through her hair and immediately felt self-conscious that it was still damp. "What're you really doing here?" *It's late*, she didn't add. *I can't trust myself alone with you.*

"Keith Turner is dead."

Pain arced through her chest. It was still so hard to believe. "I know."

"Until they find out who killed him, I'm not sure you're safe. The fire was one thing, that was about me, but this is different. This is about wiping out the possibilities. Whoever killed him may not be finished yet."

She didn't mention that she'd considered the same thing. Someone intended to end the speculation by getting rid of anyone who might know anything. "Why would you think that?" Might as well have Clint's reasoning.

He stood very still. Different from all those years before, when he'd been so confident and full of charm. She wondered if he'd learned to be very still like that in prison so as not to be noticed. The idea of what he'd endured because of her made her throat ache to say something that would adequately relate the depth of her regret.

"Are you through analyzing me?"

Her gaze snapped to his. Heat rushed up her neck and across her cheeks. "You were going to tell me why you think I might be in danger." No more getting distracted.

"I think maybe Turner knew things he never told. Whatever he knew may have gotten him killed."

"You're speculating," she countered, knowing that her own thoughts had mirrored his and were every bit as speculative.

He nodded. "Yeah. But he was her boyfriend and his alibi was shaky at best."

Emily held up her hands to stop him. "There is no way Keith hurt Heather." She'd gone down that road herself, but hearing anyone say it made it somehow worse.

"You wouldn't believe for a second that he would harm her, yet you were convinced I did."

It wasn't a question.

"I knew Keith," she offered. "I didn't know you." *Except in my dreams.*

He moved a step closer. Reached out, touched her cheek. She trembled. "Did I do that?"

"Yes." It was nothing. A small abrasion. She'd completely forgotten about it. She had other bruises and scrapes from falling out the window during the fire. And from grinding around in the dirt with him . . . none of which she intended to mention.

"I'm sorry." His hand fell away, regret registered on his face.

"It's no big deal," she argued. "I'm sure I left a few marks on you."

The intensity in his eyes escalated. "Maybe."

She shivered, wished he wouldn't look at her like that. "Why didn't you tell Ray the truth? That I was with you yesterday morning?"

"None of his business." Clint's eyes roamed over her as he spoke, a slow, measuring gaze. Her body heated everywhere his eyes touched.

She licked her lips, her mouth feeling dry and hungry. "I told him I was with you."

His gaze settled back on hers, steady, penetrating. "Why?"

The way he looked at her now made it difficult to breathe.

"Because it's the truth." He moved one more step closer. Her difficulty drawing in a breath escalated to impossible. "Because there have been enough secrets and lies in this town."

"I want you to know," he said, his voice surprisingly soft, the sound flooding her with unexpected tenderness, "that I'm clean. Every year for the past four years I've been tested because of . . . the things that happened. I wouldn't have purposely hurt you for anything."

Honestly, the concept hadn't even crossed her mind. She'd spent so many years not caring if she lived or died, the idea of protecting herself was foreign to her.

"Are you sure about that?" she countered. "The hurting-me part, I mean. I was the key witness who sent you to prison."

His gaze lingered on her mouth a moment or two before lifting back to her eyes. That moment or two was all it took to ignite a slow burn deep in her belly, a yearning that wouldn't be ignored.

"You believed you were right. You were hurting and angry. You were in shock."

"I helped ruin your life." Emotion got stuck in her throat, prodded more of those damned tears to brim against her lashes.

"Yeah." He reached for her, gently cupped her face in his hands, smoothed the pad of his thumb over her cheek. "You did. You needed someone to blame. I won't say it no longer matters, but I'm dealing with it."

"What can I do?"

He dropped his hand back to his side. "You can leave this damned town and put all this behind you."

He couldn't be serious. "And just let it go?"

"If we keep poking at this, somebody else could end up dead," he said on a heavy exhale that spoke volumes about just how weary he was.

Now she understood. He felt responsible for Keith's death. If Clint hadn't come back . . . "Keith's death wasn't your fault."

"Maybe, maybe not."

She couldn't stand it anymore. Clint stood only inches away. She needed to touch him. Her hand rested against his chest. "You don't—"

"I should go."

She'd made herself a promise—to go after what she wanted from now on. *Don't let him walk away.* She hadn't felt anything real for so long, the memory of how he could make her come alive screamed inside her, begged for more. "You shouldn't be sleeping in that old barn."

"I'll be fine."

Say it! "I don't want you to go."

Hesitation filtered into his eyes. "You sure about that?"

"I want you to . . . touch me."

Those lips she yearned to taste quirked. "I touched you." He glanced at the cheek he'd caressed.

She gave her head a little shake. "Not like that."

"Emily . . ." His gaze rested on her face. "It shouldn't have happened that way. Your first time should have—"

"Touch me," she ordered. She didn't want to hear how it should have been. She'd spent her whole adult life wallowing in regret. "Please."

The hesitation in his eyes cleared. "Show me how you want me to do it."

She took his right hand and placed it on her breast. "This is good."

He squeezed. Need keened low in her throat.

"Is that all you want?"

"No." She took his other hand and guided it to the place where her robe parted at the top of her thighs.

His fingers sifted through her pubic hair, stoking the flames already building there.

"Is that all?" His voice was gruff now.

"No."

He drew his hands away and she made a sound of protest, wanted to grab on to him . . . to make him touch her again.

"Take off your robe and lie down on the bed," he ordered instead of attempting to retreat as she'd feared he would.

She didn't hesitate. The robe hit the floor, revealing her nude body. She sat down on the edge of the mattress, scooted back to lie against the pillows.

He looked at her for a long while. Her heart pounded twice for every second. Then he reached to turn off the lamp.

"I want to see," she challenged.

He didn't argue.

He toed off his sneakers first. Then he peeled the T-shirt free of his body, revealing that muscled chest with all its reminders that he'd spent ten long years in a prison criminals weren't meant to survive. He unfastened his jeans. Her pulse rate altered significantly. The jeans slid down his long legs and he stepped out of them and shucked his socks. No briefs, just him. Ridged abdomen, narrow hips, muscled legs . . . and that thick sex that hung prominently between them.

The bed shifted with his weight as he lay down beside her. The heat of his body instantly warmed her . . . or maybe just seeing him this way had already done that. He lay on his side, his head propped in one hand. His well-muscled body exuded a kind of power that had hers humming with excitement already.

"What now?"

She tried to analyze what he was thinking. Impossible. "I don't understand."

"I'm not taking anything else from you, Emily. Whatever happens now is going to be about you taking what you want."

The idea sent power surging through her. She liked that he gave that to her.

She took him at his word and made her own choices. She pushed him onto his back and straddled him. The feel of his body beneath her was incredible. He was hard and pressed firmly between her thighs. She lifted her hips far enough to guide him where she wanted; then she slid down around him. All the way. The sensation of being filled so completely took her breath, set her on fire. He groaned savagely, his hands fisted in the pillow under his head.

She rode him until her body collapsed, sated, against his chest. His own climax had left him panting and damp with sweat. She loved the feel and smell of his clean sweat. Loved that she could make him come like that, with such intensity. He stroked her back while the rhythm of his heart lulled her toward absolute bliss.

She refused to give in to her body's need for rest. She sat up, grinding her bottom against his loins. "I want you to do what you did before." Butterflies took flight in her stomach at the memory. With him behind her, he could go deeper . . . she liked deeper. And she'd waited too long to play games or to pretend a shyness she didn't feel.

He didn't question her request. He rolled her over before he withdrew and sat back on his haunches. His solid erection glistened with their commingled fluids. Shivering, she turned onto her stomach and waited for him to take her.

"Lift your hips."

She scooted her knees beneath her, lifting her bottom into the air for his possession.

He moved against her. She moaned deeply, could hardly bear the sensation of his solid length against that part of her. Slowly, as if he wanted to be sure he did this right, he guided himself into her. That last inch or so had her charging toward climax before he'd even started to move. He held still, let her adjust to his size and the new depth. Then he did something different; he pulled her up to his chest and held her close, cupping her breasts in his hands. She moaned her pleasure, unable to tell him how awesome he was, how full and satisfied he made her feel.

Then he moved. He held her tight against him as he flexed and relaxed his hips in a slow, tightly controlled manner, his thrusts shallow but somehow mind-blowingly intense. He kissed her temple, squeezed her breasts, all the while making those small, firm moves. When she could take it no more she started to wiggle against him . . . needing more . . . needing faster. As if he understood exactly what she required, he ushered her forward, until her cheek rested against the pillow. Her entire body pulsed with the pleasure searing through her. She wanted him to make it happen before she lost her mind.

He thrust. Long, deep, hard. Faster. Until she came just as fast and just as hard. Then he slowed it down, trembling with the effort of restraint.

"Please." She wanted to feel him come undone. To feel him lose control.

He resisted . . . moved slowly, each flex of his hips a deliberate effort in discipline.

"Clint . . ." The rush of sensations started again, wave after wave, building, building . . . how could he make her come so many times?

He groaned softly.

"Hurry!"

He stopped completely, leaned down, and kissed her cheek. His breath was ragged. The damp contours of his chest branded the skin on her back. "I want to savor every second," he murmured.

Then he started those slow, steady strokes once more.

Release crashed down on her . . . took her breath completely.

Those final, exquisite ripples of tension pushed him over the edge. He pounded into his own climax, grunting savagely with the force of it.

He collapsed onto the mattress, pulling her against his chest while their bodies remained connected so completely she wondered how she had lived this long without him.

. . . *without him.*

The community—everyone she knew—considered him a

killer. Even knowing his alibi was real, her parents would never think of him as anything but dangerous.

The never-ending tragedy. Shakespeare couldn't have written a more unfortunate plot.

CHAPTER THIRTY-TWO

Tuesday, July 23, 1:30 A.M.

Emily had fallen asleep, cradled against his chest.

It still stunned Clint when he considered that this was real. She was real.

In prison he'd learned not to count on anything. As much as he wanted it to, he couldn't allow himself to hope that this connection meant anything other than the desperate need to cling to someone in all this insanity.

Allowing her continued involvement in what he knew he had to do next, her tarnished reputation with her friends might be the least of her worries.

He had confirmation of his alibi. He had the primary, the only, witness seeing that night a whole different way.

He needed to know what had happened that night. All the guessing and theories in the world wouldn't help. Emily had shown him her detailed lists, and even though much of it held merit, none of it was evidence. He needed evidence or some way to prove the investigation hadn't been properly conducted.

There was just one place he could get that information, since Ray Hale refused to talk about that night with him.

The case files.

He needed to get his hands on those files. To review the suspect/witness interviews for any details he hadn't been told. Ray claimed there was nothing to see, that he didn't have the case files in his office any longer. Then he'd offered that story about the water damage. Clint wasn't buying it.

If Ray had something to hide, and Clint wasn't saying he did, he might decide to dispose of the files before Clint got himself an attorney and forced the issue.

Clint couldn't take that chance.

Four hours ago, before he'd ended up in the parking lot across the street from the Valley Inn, he'd gathered the tools he thought he might need and decided to do what needed to be done. But as he'd passed this place he'd thought about Emily and whether or not she was actually safe, considering Turner's murder. So Clint had stopped . . . and well, he'd ended up here.

He snuggled his face into her hair and inhaled deeply. He didn't want to go . . . but he had to.

Turner's murder had made one thing crystal clear: Clint's tactic had worked. Heather's killer was nervous.

Clint wanted him.

Clint's jaw tightened. He wanted him bad.

As much as Clint would like to stay right here with Emily, he had to get this done now, before it was too late.

He carefully untangled himself from her sweet body. She mumbled something in her sleep and he held still, let her settle again, and then he managed to get out of bed without waking her. Gathering his clothes as he went, he edged into the bathroom and closed the door. He grimaced when it creaked. After dressing, he washed his face with cold water to ensure he was fully alert. He combed his fingers through his hair and stared at his reflection a moment. If he got caught . . . he would go back to prison.

It was a risk he had to take.

He opened the bathroom door slowly, hoping it wouldn't creak this time. It did. Didn't matter, he realized, when his gaze landed on Emily standing at the end of the bed, her clothes in her arms.

"Whatever you're planning," she said with a tone that told him he could forget any negotiations, "I'm going with you."

She stalked past him, went into the bathroom, and closed the door. He stood there for several moments in a kind of shock. As much as he appreciated her desire to help him, this was way too risky.

By the time he'd regrouped and come up with an argument he'd intended to shout through the door as he made his hasty exit, she emerged fully dressed and looking exactly like the next brick wall he'd be hitting.

"You're going after those files, aren't you?"

He hesitated when he should have been running, putting some distance between her and the new danger his actions could very well trigger. He shouldn't have told her about requesting to see the files. "It might not help," he countered.

"It's the only way you're going to know if the police did their job," she argued.

She was right, but that didn't give her license to get involved. "You'll only slow me down," he challenged. "This has to be done fast and with as little noise and as few mistakes as possible."

"I'm head of the files department at a major research facility. I know more about filing systems than you can imagine exists. You need me. I can evaluate the filing system and find what you're looking for in minutes. It could take you hours."

He wished she wasn't right about that. "You understand that if we're caught, this won't be just breaking and entering." He had to be out of his mind to even consider this. "The community will look at you the way they look at me."

"I understand."

Still, he stood there, hoping she'd change her mind.

She didn't.

"All right, but we do this my way. You follow my instructions without question."

She nodded. "Whatever you say."

2:45 A.M.

Pine Bluff's post–Civil War courthouse stood in the center of town, with shops, offices, and a couple of cafés fanning out around it like a square wheel. Emily had always loved this courthouse. It made her think of history and justice.

But justice didn't always show up here. Sometimes a person had to make justice happen. That was what she was doing tonight.

"You're sure he said they were stored in the courthouse basement?" She'd envisioned some run-of-the-mill storage facility. Breaking into a courthouse would go on one's permanent record . . . especially Clint's. If he was caught . . . she didn't want to think about it.

Funny, she'd wanted exactly this scenario in the beginning. She would have given anything for this opportunity to ensure he went back to prison.

She pushed the painful memories away. She had to focus. This was far too important to screw up.

"That's what he said. You can still back out."

"No way." She shook her head adamantly. "I'm in."

"Let's do it."

He grabbed a small duffel and got out of the car. She'd insisted on using her Malibu, since it was dark enough to blend in with the night. He'd left his truck several blocks away in case they needed a backup.

Emily followed his lead. They'd parked in a back alley on the east side of the courthouse. The whole world had appeared to be asleep as they drove into the heart of town. That was something one could usually count on around here.

She stayed close to Clint as they wove their way around to the front of the line of shops. Careful to stay away from the lampposts, they cut across the street and approached the courthouse on the handicapped-accessible side.

This was the part that really worried her. Considering his former profession with Sylvester Fairgate, she wasn't concerned about Clint's ability to get in, but what if there was a security system? A silent alarm could go off and they wouldn't even know it until it was too late.

When she asked as much, he said, "That's why we're not going through a door."

He found what he deemed a worthy window and then he went to work. He explained a few things about security systems: "Magnetic sensors to monitor the opening and closing of windows are costly, especially when you're talking about the whole building. Has to be a hundred windows.

"Most places use glass-break sensors. As long as we get the window open without breaking any glass we'll probably be fine."

Probably.

With the window chosen, she understood why he'd selected this side of the courthouse. The handicapped-accessible side had exterior access to the basement level, including two full-sized windows, whereas the windows leading to the basement on the other sides were small casements. Probably not even large enough to meet the current emergency egress standards.

She would never have thought of this.

He pulled a pair of gloves out of the duffel. "Here." He offered them to her. "I only have one pair; you take them."

"You," she argued. "You're the one whose prints are on file. If they find mine they won't have anything to compare them to."

He considered her reasoning, then tugged on the gloves. She liked that he listened to her. She also found it mind-boggling, since less than one week ago they had been mortal enemies.

From his duffel he removed a glass cutter along with one of those suction-cup hangy things people bought all the time to hang wreaths on windows. After licking the suction cup, which she watched avidly, he stuck it to the glass. He scored the glass and, using the suction cup, pulled the newly cut piece away from the sash, leaving a hole.

"Amazing," she muttered. Just like MacGyver.

Clint cautiously snaked his arm through the hole and unfastened the lock. The window went up and they were inside. He closed the sash and ran his fingers along the wooden edge where the two sashes met.

She leaned close so she could whisper, "What're you doing? Don't we need to hurry?"

"Checking for a sensor that would've set off an alarm when the window opened." He drew his hands away from the window and reached for his duffel bag. "We're good."

"Let's find the storeroom." She wanted this done as quickly as possible. It wasn't that she was afraid . . . okay, she was afraid. Hazing-week pranks were the closest she'd ever come to breaking the law.

The window had taken them into the property assessment office. The door leading into the basement corridor was locked but allowed for opening from the inside. Once they were in the main corridor and the door closed behind them, they would be locked out of the room.

Before permitting it to completely close and latch, she asked, "Will we be able to get back in here?" She had to assume those sensor things he worried about were on all the doors leading outside the building. Going back out the window seemed logical.

The illumination from the flashlight provided enough of a

glow without her having to aim it at his face for her to see him grin, one of those handsome, lopsided dazzlers she remembered from before . . . way before. Her heart reacted.

"You let me worry about that."

She moved away from the door, and the latch clicked into the locked position. He took the flashlight and started moving from door to door, reading the signs posted on each. When they'd reached the end of the main corridor, he took the shorter one to the right, the only other way to go. This section would lead to the bottom of the stairs that ascended to the first ground-level floor. She stayed right behind him, but she couldn't resist constantly glancing over her shoulder. If the police found her car . . . would they figure out what she and Clint were up to?

". . . has to be it."

She dragged her full attention back to Clint. The sign on the door read: Authorized Personnel Only. She had to agree. If the files were here, this was the most likely place.

"What now?"

He gave the flashlight back to her. "Hold it right there." He directed the beam on the doorknob.

She held the light steady while he retrieved a new set of tools from the duffel's exterior zipper compartment. These looked like the pointy instruments a dentist might use when cleaning and prodding at teeth. Clint crouched in front of the door. Using both hands, an instrument in each, he worked on the lock until something clicked.

He twisted the knob and the door opened. *Incredible.*

"You're pretty good, Austin."

He dropped the tools back in the bag and straightened next to her. "I hope you're referring to our other joint venture in addition to this one."

Heat flushed her face. She had started to tell him she'd have to think about that one when a sound echoed from somewhere in the main corridor. The succession of clicks and creaks that followed was unmistakable. Someone had unlocked the main exterior door on this level and opened it. A sequence of beeps warned that the security system had been disarmed.

Had to be the police.

Clint would go back to prison. This was a major violation of his parole. Not one of the dinky ones.

She couldn't let that happen.

She clicked off the light and grabbed the duffel he'd left on the floor next to the door. They stood so close together she could feel the tension roiling through his body. She grabbed his shirtfront with her free hand and pulled his face close to hers, then whispered, "Get in there and make sure the door locks behind you. Once we're gone, you get the file and get out of here. Try chronological order first, then alphabetical."

"No way I'm letting you take the rap for this."

"Do it," she urged. "How can we find the real killer if you're in prison?"

Three breath-stealing beats passed before he relented. He slipped inside the room he'd just unlocked. The barely audible rasp of leather soles on the tile floor was closer now. What should she do?

Then she knew. She dropped to her knees in front of the door behind which Clint had disappeared, turned on the flashlight, and retrieved the tools he'd been using to unlock it. She pretended to be hard at work even as the steps moved into the side corridor directly behind her.

Not looking back was one of the hardest things she'd ever done. A bright beam of light suddenly illuminated her position.

"Emily?"

Ray Hale.

She experienced some amount of relief that it wasn't a cop she didn't know. She jerked around, adopted a startled expression.

"What the hell are you doing, Emily?"

He moved nearer.

Suddenly going mute, she found herself holding her breath. "Where's Clint?"

The tools in her hands clattered to the floor as she stood. Her fingers tightened into fists to hide their trembling. "Why would Clint be with me? This is something I have to do. Heather was my best friend."

Enough illumination lit Ray's face for her to see the skepticism. "You expect me to believe you broke into this courthouse all on your own?"

She thought of all the reasons she had to be angry and she unleashed that emotion on him . . . the way she'd wanted to the last time she'd talked to him.

"You know damn well he didn't do it." She made the statement as much accusation as argument. "I want to know who killed her, Ray. If it means I have to break in here and get those files you told Clint were stored here, I'm prepared to do that."

"Where is he?"

"I'm telling you he's not here. If I'd told him about my plan he would've tried to stop me."

Ray turned all the way around, running the beam of his light over the corridor again.

She held her hands up surrender style. "Take your time; check every room if you want. He's not here. It's just me. He'd be pretty stupid to do something like this and end up back in prison."

Ray still didn't look convinced. He walked straight up to her, causing her breath to catch yet again, and tried the door behind her. The one leading to the room marked: Authorized Personnel Only. She didn't breathe again until he released the knob and stepped back.

"You know I have to take you in, Emily."

He said this with enough regret for her to believe he might even be sincere.

"Do what you have to do, Ray. I believe in what I'm doing."

"Are you sure about that?"

She stiffened, suddenly scared to death he wouldn't believe she'd gotten this far alone. Though she hadn't put anything in his "Negatives" column, who was to say he wasn't Heather's killer? That theory had fear creeping up her spine.

"Really sure," he added, "that he's innocent? I know your father confirmed his alibi, but you were so adamant in that courtroom."

A burst of anger chased away the thread of fear. She had been adamant in that courtroom . . . that was true. But now she knew better.

Clint Austin was innocent.

Why didn't his only ally believe that? He'd believed it before, hadn't he? Or had he only felt sorry for Clint? Either way, that seemed to suggest Ray wasn't a suspect.

"Let's go, Emily."

She relaxed. Apparently he believed she'd gotten in here alone. He gathered the tools she had dropped and picked up the duffel bag. She hoped there was nothing in there that would indicate it belonged to Clint.

Ray escorted her to the nearest exit.

"I'll pay for the window I damaged in the property assessment room."

When they got outside, he said, "Just to set my mind at ease, why don't you show me how you got in?"

She led him to the window and explained the process. "I used to watch reruns of *MacGyver.*" That wasn't a total lie. She'd seen a few rerun episodes. Her father had liked the show.

"This isn't a game, Emily."

"Yes, it is," she countered. "And whoever is making the rules doesn't want to be caught." The next question came out before good sense could stall it. "You're not making the rules, are you, Ray?"

CHAPTER THIRTY-THREE

City Hall
10:35 A.M.

He was going to miss lunch with his wife. He'd been remote so much of the time lately, he hated to let her down even for something as simple as lunch. There was no help for it. What he had to take care of wouldn't wait. Ray could only hope that Sarah would understand . . . eventually.

Before he left City Hall, he double-timed it up to the second floor to see to a minor bother. He'd left Emily Wallace in the holding cell for the last eight hours in hopes that the solitude and apprehension as to what would happen next might just jolt a little sense into her. She had to stop digging into the past before things got any worse. Her involvement would only give Clint additional motivation for pursuing his quest.

Ray had ordered her car picked up and brought to City Hall. No need to have it impounded. Emily sat up a little straighter as he approached the holding cell. The uncertainty in her eyes told him she wasn't feeling nearly as brave as she wanted him to believe. He'd checked on her a couple of times; once she'd even fallen asleep sitting on that hard bench. He hated like hell to do this to her, but he couldn't have folks breaking and entering county-owned property without repercussions. She needed to understand that she'd gone too far. He'd anticipated that move, but he needed it to end now. For her sake and for Clint's.

Ray unlocked the cell and opened the door. "You can pick up your things at the duty desk. You're free to go for now."

She pushed up from the bench spanning the length and width of the eight-by-twelve cell. "Why?"

Despite the unpleasant task that still lay ahead of him, he chuckled. Emily Wallace, no matter the atrocities life had thrown her way, was still far too naïve and kind for her own good. "Most folks don't ask why when given the opportunity to walk away scot-free."

Her gaze narrowed the tiniest bit with doubt. "O . . . kay."

Ray exhaled, the fatigue clawing at him. He hadn't slept in forty-eight hours. He didn't have any idea when he'd last eaten. He was tired. Mostly he was sick to death of lies and secrets and . . . murder. Hell, he was as sick of the truth as he was of the deceptions and betrayal.

Emily glanced around as if she expected someone to jump out and tell her she'd just been punked. When she'd satisfied her misgivings, she stepped out of the holding cell.

"Thank you." She met his gaze, uncertainty still holding her own hostage. "Am I being charged with anything?"

Ray shook his head. "I will send you the bill for repairing that window, though."

Hesitation slowed her, just long enough for him to recognize that there was more she wanted to say. But she didn't. She walked away.

"Just one thing," he said, instantly kicking himself for slowing her retreat. Anything else in the way of advice he offered would be too much, and yet he couldn't not warn her. When she turned back to him, he urged, "You need to be extremely careful how you proceed from here, Emily. The truth isn't always what it's cracked up to be."

She had nothing to say to that. Her spine rigid, she pivoted on her heel and strode to the duty desk. He wished he could make her see that things weren't what they seemed.

He'd learned that the hard way.

11:00 A.M.

She followed him from City Hall.

Maybe he was the one making her upset.

Misty was tired of these men having so much power. Tired. Tried. Tired.

She should have done something more about it a long time ago. But she'd thought it was over. Men were the trouble in this world. They made women feel afraid and vulnerable. They cheated on the women they were supposed to love. Started wars. All kinds of atrocities. And they thought they were better at everything.

Not so. She was the one to graduate with the highest honors in high school and from the University of Alabama. None of her male peers had been as brilliant as her. She could have been an engineer. She could have been a great scientist. But she'd chosen teaching to be close to her dearest friend.

Some women's beauty made them vulnerable to men. They got hurt. Taken for granted.

Well, Misty was tired of watching it happen. She was tired of feeling impotent.

Hale Family Hunting Cabin
11:24 A.M.

Ray couldn't remember the last time he'd come up here to hunt. Not since his daddy had died eight years ago. Ray never had cared that much for hunting, but his daddy had loved the sport. Though he had considered hunting a definite sport, Ray's old man never targeted anything he didn't intend to eat. Raymond Hale, Sr. had insisted it was the only right way to do it.

Ray had come to this secluded place since then, recently, in fact. But the visit had nothing to do with hunting. He had met her here, in this cabin that his daddy and granddaddy had built half a century before, to discuss the possibility of Clint Austin's parole. She'd been adamant that Ray had to do something to stop the process.

A smile nudged the corners of his mouth upward. He'd reveled in telling her that it was too late. Way too late. She'd just have to deal with it.

In fact, Ray had worked extra hard to ensure Clint was granted parole partly to make her life miserable. But mostly he'd done it because it was the right thing to do.

Austin had paid enough . . . more than enough.

Ray had hoped that being supportive of Clint and fighting for his freedom would relieve some of the guilt he felt, but it hadn't.

Not even a little bit.

He stared past the buildup of new dust and old pollen on the window, some part of him appreciating the gorgeous view he'd taken for granted so many times. There wasn't a better view to be found than from this cabin resting on the shoulders of the Cumberland Mountains, overlooking the verdant valley and the small, industrious town of Pine Bluff. He and his family should take the time to enjoy it more often.

If he and Sarah got past this standoff.

His wife thought he was getting too involved in Clint's problems. She didn't understand. There were things she didn't know. If Ray had his way, she would never know.

"Well, isn't this just like old times?"

Ray wheeled around to face *her*, fury instantly clenching in his gut.

"I've questioned Troy." He went straight to the point, ignored her stupid question. "He denies having anything to do with the fire."

She flicked him her usual how-dare-you glance. "And you would be telling me this for what reason?"

The move was so fast . . . so unexpected that it startled even him. He was in her face, glaring down at her feigned look of wide-eyed innocence. "Don't even fucking act like you don't know why."

"Are you threatening me, *Chief*?"

He wanted to kill her. The realization hit him so hard and furiously that he shook with the impact of it. It was the first time he'd allowed the thought to fully form in his brain. The devil himself couldn't possibly be more evil than she. She should have been the one to get murdered instead of Keith.

"Yes," Ray said frankly, with all the menace he had harbored for more than a decade. "I am threatening you."

She smiled, a purr of pure satisfaction passing over those vile red lips. "That's what I thought."

She had the nerve to flatten her palms against his chest and glide them up to his shoulders. He stiffened with revulsion.

"You know how excited I get when you act rough with me."

Narrowly suppressing the impulse to turn thought into action, he encircled her wrists and wrenched her hands away.

"You were my first mistake, my biggest mistake," he said bluntly. "I should have recognized you for what you were before someone had to die."

Her smile was patient, so sweet it made him want to vomit up the acid churning in his gut. "I'm certain you don't mean that, Ray. I remember how you loved to have me and one of your buddies . . . ," her smile turned poisonous, ". . . at the same time."

She inclined her perfectly coiffed head, totally unaware that he barely, *barely* held on to a semblance of calm. Or maybe she did know and that was part of the thrill for her. The urge to end this now was almost overwhelming.

"Tell me, Ray, was it more fun to have me on my knees in front of you or did you prefer one of your buddies like Caruthers? I'm sure there are people who would love to see that. We could call it *Cops Out of Uniform*."

His fingers were around her throat, squeezing, before he could stop the instinct. "That was your doing," he growled, his voice echoing in the room like a wild animal's.

She didn't fight him, just relaxed in his hold as if she welcomed his brutality.

Whore . . . she probably did.

He released her. She swayed . . . caught her breath.

"Do you know what happened to Keith?" The words raged out of Ray. The reality of what he had allowed to go on . . . to happen . . . ripped like a bullet through his heart.

Her eyes widened in surprise. "Of course I don't know what happened to him! Don't you have any evidence? Any suspects? Good God, Ray, what're you doing about this?"

Lies. Shift the focus to someone else. He didn't know why he even bothered to question her.

"Are you responsible for what happened at Clint Austin's home?" Every single muscle in Ray's body was rigid with the wrath he'd suppressed far too long. That she could still, despite the circumstances, arouse him made him want to tear that traitorous organ from his body.

"Don't be ridiculous." She sniffed. "Your accusations are becoming tedious, Ray."

His mouth twisted so tautly for one instant that speech proved impossible. Finally the words spewed from him. "You fooled me once. It won't happen again."

She rested her hands on her silk-clad hips. "You act as if I'm one of your suspects. I won't put up with that again."

Everything inside him . . . every cell . . . every molecule . . . went utterly still. "I will do the job right this time," he warned.

"I'm finally happy, Ray," she pleaded, her voice cajoling. "Don't try to ruin it for me."

The sound of her begging made him sick. "Final warning," he growled, barely holding on to his composure, "I'm watching."

There was no changing the past. Clint Austin had paid the price society demanded. Here and now was Ray's primary concern. There would be no more mistakes.

Satisfied that she had nothing more to say, he brushed past her. "Lock up when you leave."

Ray walked out the door without looking back, crossed the porch, and started down the steps feeling liberated for the first time in years. She was no longer going to manipulate him.

A blunt object connected with the back of his skull, and he plunged facedown in the dirt.

He tried to push himself up from the ground, but his body would not obey the commands from his brain.

Hands rolled him onto his back. His eyes refused to open . . . his arms wouldn't thrash against the threat. The pain in his skull throbbed, showering the backs of his closed lids with pinpoints of light.

Suddenly he was moving. Arms tugged at his shoulders. His heels dragged in the dirt. What the hell?

He was lifted, hefted, and shoved until his jaw flattened against fabric. His body felt crumpled in an odd position. The familiar scent nudged him. His truck? It smelled like his truck. How had he gotten into his truck? Then he remembered the hands . . . the tugging and pushing.

Why couldn't he move or open his eyes? He felt heavy.

Head trauma . . . he recognized the signs. Concussion or worse. He needed to call for help. Where was his cell phone?

Something wet dampened his shirt . . . his jeans. Was he bleeding?

His mind faded. He fought the blackness edging out his thoughts. He had to hang on! Had to fight.

Something pungent, stinging, assaulted his senses.

Gasoline? He struggled to analyze the new intrusions

against his failing senses. The sound and smell of a match lighting? Awareness was diminishing.

Focus! Don't let go!

A new odor penetrated the darkness and denial swallowing up his brain . . . something burning . . . he'd smelled it before . . . human flesh searing. . . .

He was on fire.

CHAPTER THIRTY-FOUR

CHAPTER THIRTY-FOUR

Valley Inn
1:20 P.M.

The knock finally came.

Emily jumped though she'd been anticipating it for half an hour. When she and Clint had spoken on the phone, they had agreed he would work until one so as not to draw any unnecessary suspicion.

She hurried to the door, almost opened it, but forced herself to check the peephole first.

Clint.

She slid the chain free of its catch and jerked the door open. "Hurry!" She grabbed him by the arm and yanked him inside. "I'm losing my mind!" She shut and locked the door and whipped around to face him. "Tell me what you found!"

"Do you know how hard it was to get out of there?"

Exasperation gushed out of her on a blast of air. "Tell me if you found the files!"

"First." He gestured to the bed. "Sit."

She couldn't read his eyes . . . couldn't tell if she needed to be worried. But since he appeared determined to do this his way, she did as he asked, anticipation bursting inside her.

He lowered to the mattress at her side. Even with grease staining his T-shirt and smudging his jaw, he looked good to her. Just having him next to her made her relax . . . a fraction. Beneath the smell of grease, motor oil, and hard-earned sweat, she could still smell his skin. The intimate knowledge of his body made her feel more at home than she had since . . . since before her life ended . . . that night.

"I couldn't get out of the courthouse with the entire box of case files." He held out his hands and indicated the size. "So I carefully looked through the documents until I found what I figured would help us the most. Then I put everything back just as it had been so no one would know I'd looked—unless they inventoried every single page and photo."

She shuddered at the mention of photos. But Clint had been right to be cautions. She wouldn't put inventorying those particular files past Ray.

"How did you get out?" She wanted to know what Clint had found, but she needed to know how he'd managed to escape more. The whole MacGyver concept fascinated her. Only Clint was real.

"First I had to outsmart Ray's men."

"They came in there looking for you?" *Damn.* Ray really hadn't believed she was lying. Not that she could blame him. She never had been a very good liar.

Clint nodded. "But I've had a lot of experience in making myself invisible."

She wished there were a way to even begin to make that up to him. The one thing she could do was help him solve the crime that had devastated his life. But she was doing that as much for Heather and her family . . . and herself as for anyone.

"Lucky for me, they searched the files room first. As soon as they moved on to another room, I got the hell out of there.

I barely squeezed through one of those dinky windows. Once I was outside I wasn't worried. They were still inside. I got back to my place just a couple minutes before Ray showed up to make sure I was in the barn."

A chill swept over her skin at the idea of how close he'd come to getting caught. He'd gone to work today like always. Higgins probably had orders to notify both Ray and the parole officer if Clint didn't show. Waiting until he'd gotten off work had driven her nuts!

"So where is it?" He hadn't brought anything in with him. If he said they had to go someplace else she was going to scream with frustration. He tugged the front of his T-shirt from his jeans and reached underneath. His hand reappeared with what looked like a single document folded multiple times and tucked into a sandwich bag.

"Is that it?"

He shot her a sidelong glance. "The idea was to get what wasn't consistent with anything we already knew." He tapped the small plastic bag. "This is an evidence report. I kept it taped under my dash all day. I stuck it under my shirt before coming in here just in case I was being watched."

"Good idea." She reached for the bag, but he held it away.

"Let's talk about one thing first."

Her patience thinned, but he obviously had a point to make. "Fine, but hurry."

Those intense gray eyes flashed his appreciation. "Who knew about your window? I mean, the fact that you used it for sneaking in and out at night."

Emily felt the weight of regret.

"Don't go there," he ordered. "Leave out the emotion. Concentrate. Who knew?"

She tried hard to do as he asked, but it wasn't easy. "The girls. It was kind of mine and Heather's secret, but that night the others knew because of the finagling required to get out of the house after my parents had given me strict orders to stay home with my brother."

"By 'the others' you mean the cheerleaders?"

"Not everyone, just the seniors."

"None of the guys knew?"

He meant Keith. He didn't have to say his name. "No. We didn't tell just anyone."

"You left that night, did your hazing duty, and then you came back. The window was open when it should have been closed. Do you remember anything else? Any other items outside or in the room that shouldn't have been there?"

She thought long and hard, made herself look at those painful recollections for a whole minute, then two. Her stomach roiled viciously; then she shook her head. "Nothing. I was too caught up in trying to escape Mr. Call and then to save Heather . . . in trying to get you away from her."

The ache in his eyes told Emily he remembered that part well. "I was told," he began, his eyes clearing as he moved past those details, "that the only evidence recovered from the room was the knife."

She nodded. That was right. She'd heard the same thing in the courtroom. A typical kitchen knife. No prints, nothing but Heather's blood. They'd used the fact that Clint had been wearing gloves against him. Given his alibi, the gloves made perfect sense. He had been in the middle of stealing a car to hold as hostage for a loan shark. Of course Clint had worn gloves.

"Well," Clint went on grimly, "they lied to us."

"What?" Emily had known Chief Ledbetter. He'd gone to the same church as she and her family had. "Chief Ledbetter lied? Maybe there wasn't anything else, Clint." But then he wouldn't have made the statement. She felt cold, cold and afraid of what he might be about to tell her.

"Read this." He gave her the evidence report he'd taken from the sandwich bag.

She unfolded it and started at the top, read each line carefully.

"Item: one gold necklace with attached gold cheerleading

charms. Discovered: clutched in victim's hand. Condition: broken chain, covered in blood. Disposition:" The word "LOST" had been stamped along the disposition line on top of whatever was written there. The large red letters drew Emily's eyes, past the other information.

"They lost evidence?" This was unbelievable!

"Read the disposition handwritten beneath the stamp."

The information entered on each line and within each block was handwritten. Male handwriting, she decided, peering at the small, angrily slanted words that she might have labeled simply sloppy were it not for the darkness of the ink and the deepness of the indentation made by the author. Emily angled the page and tried to read between the red letters of the single stamped word that had grabbed her attention before. "Hand carried to . . . lab for analysis . . . by Deputy . . . R . . . A . . . Y . . ."

Ray Hale.

Her breath bolted from her lungs.

"I don't believe it." The words were a scarce whisper, a thought spoken.

"The chain was broken as if it had been ripped from someone's neck," Clint clarified in case she'd missed it.

Emily tried to reason what this meant. Even as she did, her mind and body started to feel numb, as if bracing for something she didn't want to see . . . definitely didn't want to feel. She hadn't noticed anything in Heather's hand, but then she'd been distracted by the blood and the wounds.

"Does that necklace mean anything to you?"

She nodded. "All the upcoming senior cheerleaders were presented a necklace like that at the end of junior year. It was tradition."

"Do you think the one found in your room was Heather's?"

Emily's head moved from side to side of its own volition. "That's the part that startled me. It wasn't Heather's," she heard herself say as if she were far, far away in some distant place where the pain couldn't touch her. But it did. "I had

Troy get hers for me from her room the day of her funeral so she could be buried with it on."

"The funeral was closed casket," Clint countered gently.

Emily flinched. "Yes, but I was with Troy when he gave the necklace to the funeral director. Heather's was accounted for." She hauled in a big, cleansing breath. "And it wasn't broken."

"What about yours?"

Her gaze collided with his, but she knew the question wasn't accusing. "A few weeks after Heather's death my mother packed mine away with a lot of other stuff from that part of my life."

"So if the necklace wasn't Heather's and it wasn't yours, why was it in your room and logged in as evidence?"

"You know what it means." The necklace had blood on it. It was broken. Heather had been clutching it in her hand.

That couldn't be.

Lunch last week with the others barged into Emily's mind like a runaway train exploding from a tunnel. Megan had worn her necklace. . . . Cathy had worn hers. Violet hadn't. . . . *I must have lost mine.*

"This can't be right." Emily shook her head in denial. "There has to be a mistake."

"Tell me what you're thinking," Clint prodded softly. "I need to know."

She turned to him. "Megan and Cathy wore theirs at lunch the other day."

"What about Violet?"

Emily looked away, couldn't believe what she was about to say had any significance. "She said she lost hers." This was crazy. It was just a dumb necklace.

"On that list you made," Clint nudged, once more pulling her away from the emotional side of this, "you noted that Violet was jealous of Heather. That she wanted to be captain of the squad. That she wanted Keith for herself."

Emily threaded her fingers into her hair and cradled her

skull to try to ease the throbbing tension there. "That's all true. Violet is a pain in the ass, but she wouldn't hurt anyone."

Would she? Did Emily know for sure Violet wouldn't? Emily had been to a shrink enough to know that obsession could do strange things to people. She of all people knew how a single obsession could overtake one's life. Maybe Violet's obsession with having Keith all to herself had pushed her over the edge. She couldn't account for her necklace . . . she had known the window would be open and that Heather would be sitting in for Emily that night.

"This has to be wrong." Emily shot to her feet, paced the room. "Violet couldn't have been that cold." Careful calculation was required to commit a murder and get away with it. "And even if in some twisted heat-of-the-moment episode she had hurt Heather, Violet loved her husband. She wouldn't kill him. She wouldn't do that to her children . . . she couldn't."

"It's possible the two aren't related," Clint suggested.

They both knew better than that.

"Or maybe she caught him cheating on her."

Emily shrugged. "I don't know."

"Did anyone else know Heather would be in your room that night?"

"No." She thought about it another moment just to be sure. "No one."

"Did Heather have any problems with anyone in or outside school that you were aware of?"

"Everybody loved Heather. She was the most popular girl in school. Even . . ." Emily swallowed back the lump of emotion. "Even Violet seemed to adore her. She just wanted the things Heather had."

"But you said Violet seemed to worship Keith," Clint countered with a truth that couldn't be denied.

Emily sifted her memory banks, forced herself to replay images she had banished years ago.

"Keith never paid any real attention to Violet," she recalled after a bit. The memory came with a price. Keith had been the cutest guy in school, next to Clint. He'd been witty, charming, the all-around good guy and beloved athlete. The boy voted president of the class by his peers. Now he was dead. Murdered. Emily shuddered, still had difficulty accepting that he was gone. So young, and with a family.

"Wait," Clint said, drawing her attention from the painful thoughts. "We may be looking at this necklace thing with too narrow a focus. "You said it was something the senior cheerleaders received. What about the year before? There may be other people we should be considering."

"It was a new tradition. The years before us the seniors had received charm bracelets. Justine said we were special."

"Then, what do we have?"

Nothing. Even the necklace seemed so insignificant in and of itself. "We have nothing." Emily couldn't accept that, but neither was she willing to label Violet a murderer. "Violet might have lost the necklace. It's not impossible." Motive, means, opportunity. God, how did she overlook that? "I want to talk to her."

Clint stood, looked skeptical. "That could be a problem."

Violet's husband was dead. Violet despised Emily for faltering in her stand against Clint.

Emily lifted her chin in defiance of her own misgivings. "I'll just have to deal with it."

125 Carriage Avenue
2:30 P.M.

Emily wished she had called first. She'd watched cars come and go from Violet's drive for ten minutes. Most carried casseroles or a plant. Emily stood on the porch empty-handed. What could she possibly bring that Violet hadn't already received?

Emily asked God to forgive her for coming here like this with a hidden agenda. This couldn't be right. But people were dead, including Violet's husband.

Emily couldn't allow sentiment to stop her.

She pressed the doorbell and Violet's mother came to the door, her eyes red and puffy.

"Hello, Mrs. Manning."

The older woman managed a smile. "Em, it's so good of you to stop by." She opened the door wider, glanced briefly at Emily's empty hands. "Please come in."

Emily felt exactly like a traitor crossing the threshold into this home of sorrow and grief.

Mrs. Manning forced a dry sound that might have been an attempt at a laugh. "Thank God you didn't bring another casserole."

The smile that bent Emily's lips this time felt more natural. "I was feeling a little guilty that I hadn't."

The older woman pressed a hand to her chest. "Please, you're one of Violet's oldest and dearest friends. You don't need to bring anything except yourself."

She used to be one of Violet's friends. "How is she?"

The question was stupid but expected.

Mrs. Manning sighed, the effort a momentous task for her petite body. "As well as can be expected." She wrung her hands as if uncertain what to do with them since there was no casserole or plant to accept. "The children are with my husband at the park. We felt they needed a break from . . . all this."

Plants and flowers were everywhere. Emily imagined that the counters in the kitchen were loaded with casseroles that wouldn't fit into the fridge. Cookies and cakes and breads. Enough to feed an army. It was the Southern way.

"Is there anything I can do?" Another expected question.

Mrs. Manning patted Emily's arm. "Thank you, Em, but I think I have things under control for now. Why don't you come say hello to Violet? I know how excited she was to see you the other day at lunch. You'll be a ray of sunshine on this dark day."

Evidently Mrs. Manning hadn't heard about Emily's recent exploits or had decided not to hold them against her. Either way, Emily was glad for the reprieve.

She followed Violet's mother through the grand home until they reached the double doors that likely led to the master suite. Mrs. Manning rapped softly on the door. "Violet, you have company, dear."

The door opened almost immediately and Violet appeared looking her usual regal self.

"Em!" She rushed to hug Emily. "Thank you for coming." She glanced at her mother. "Would you prepare tea, Mother? Tea would be so nice."

"Certainly, dear."

"Please, don't go to any trouble," Emily offered.

"Tea will do us good." Violet tugged Emily into her room. "You're just in time, Em."

Men's suits, clearly designer and expensive, lay across the bed, four in all. Two shirts for each were draped over the jackets along with three or four ties.

"I'm just having an awful time deciding which suit he should wear." Violet turned to Emily. "Everyone will be there, you know. It's imperative that the suit is perfect. Keith wouldn't want it any other way."

They both knew it was Violet who wouldn't want it any other way. Emily watched as her friend tried different ties against the various shirts. Unlike her mother, Violet's eyes weren't red or swollen. Her black sheath looked exquisite. Her hair and makeup were . . . perfect. She chatted on and on about what an enormous task making this final selection was for her.

If Emily only looked at the surface, at this seemingly cold woman who was more worried about her dead husband's burial clothes than the fact that he was dead, she could almost imagine Violet climbing in through that bedroom window and killing the competition. Could almost see her pushing Keith over that ledge . . . for whatever reason he'd failed to meet her expectations.

But this was Violet. She'd always been this way. A perfectionist. Obsessed with appearances . . . with meeting her goals.

"I think the navy suit would be best," Emily offered, her voice too high, too shaky. "With that crisp white shirt and the tie that has that touch of red in it. Very classy."

Violet inclined her head and surveyed the selections one last time. "I think you're right." She gathered the navy suit, white shirt, and specified tie and draped them across a wing chair. "Thank you," she said to Emily. "I was leaning in that direction."

"Would you like me to help you put the others away?"

"Oh yes. You know how I like everything in its place."

Emily did know that. Together they put the fine suits away in the massive walk-in closet that was as big as Emily's entire bedroom back at her apartment in Birmingham. Violet chattered with hardly a pause for breath about all the things she and Keith used to do. Her voice remained calm and stoic.

Emily couldn't seem to find an appropriate opening to bring up the necklace. She felt exactly like a traitor.

"I called Troy and left a message that I'd like very much for him to speak at Keith's eulogy, but he hasn't returned my call." Violet said this with much confusion and disappointment. Folks, especially friends, didn't usually ignore calls from Violet Manning-Turner.

"I'm sure he will," Emily offered. Troy would be torn up pretty badly himself. He would need time to come to terms with his friend's death before he spoke with Violet.

Violet stroked the sleeve of one of the suits she'd put away. "I'll miss him." She turned to meet Emily's eyes. "I'm not sure it's hit me just yet."

Emily managed a trembling smile. "I know." And she did.

Violet's face brightened abruptly. "I'm glad you came,

Em. I felt bad about the harsh words between us. This thing with Austin has been painful for us all." Then she hugged one arm around Emily's shoulders. "Let's go see if that tea is ready."

"Vi, I was wondering—"

"Oh." Violet hesitated abruptly. "I almost forgot to tell you. I found that silly necklace." She left Emily standing in the middle of the room to go over to the ornate jewelry chest sitting atop her dresser. "I was looking for cuff links and there it was." She held up the gold necklace with its familiar charms. "I was sure it was lost."

Somehow Emily kept her smile in place until they'd had the lovely tea Violet's mother had prepared. Not the usual iced tea southerners preferred, but hot tea with sugar and lemon. Emily listened like a good friend should and then hugged Violet and offered again to help in any way needed.

Finally, when Emily could scarcely contain the mounting pressure a moment longer, she said her good-byes and left.

Clint waited for her just down the block.

She climbed into the truck and closed the door. Before he could ask, she told him, "She has her necklace. I saw it."

Clint pulled away from the curb. "How is that possible? Could she have had a duplicate made?"

"Why?" Emily looked at him. "It wasn't introduced as evidence in court. As far as we know, it wasn't really investigated at all. Probably presumed to be mine or Heather's. There was no reason for her or anyone else, even the police obviously, to think it might be relevant."

The necklace was a dead end. Where did they go from here?

"Then someone else who knew Heather had to have a necklace like that."

"No," Emily argued. "Only the . . ." She hesitated. No, that was ridiculous.

"What?" he demanded, as he slowed for the turn onto Main Street.

"Justine." Emily turned to him. "She had one."

The discordant wail of a police cruiser's siren jerked Emily's attention to the street behind them. Blue lights throbbed.

Clint checked the dash, then slowed to a stop. "I wasn't speeding. What the hell does Ray want now?"

"It's not Ray," she said after studying the man behind the wheel of the car easing up behind them at the curb.

Mike Caruthers stepped out of the official vehicle and strode to the driver's side of Clint's truck.

"Caruthers," Clint acknowledged.

"Step out of the vehicle, Austin."

Fear crowded into Emily's throat. She leaned past Clint and asked, "What's going on, Deputy Caruthers?"

He ignored her and motioned for Clint to get out.

Clint climbed out of the truck, his hands already raised in compliance with the unmistakable tension the deputy exuded.

"You'll be riding to City Hall with me for questioning. Your parole officer is waiting there."

Emily wrenched her door open and rushed around the hood. "Why are you taking him to City Hall? Where's Ray?"

Time seemed to stand still as she waited for Caruthers's response. Surely they hadn't found some evidence they thought could connect Clint to Keith's murder. She'd already told Ray that Clint had been with her.

"Are you arresting me?" Clint demanded to know.

Deputy Caruthers's head swiveled in Clint's direction. "You have the right to remain silent—"

"Don't even bother." Clint backed up a step. "I'm not going any damned where until you tell me what the hell is going on?"

It wasn't until then that Emily noticed the pale, blank look on the deputy's face. She hadn't really hung around Mike Caruthers that much back in school, but anyone could see that something was very, very wrong. Terror gripped her . . . the kind that accompanied the threat of the unknown.

He reached for the handcuffs on his utility belt. "I'm taking you in for questioning related to the murder of . . ."

Emily held her breath.

". . . Ray Hale."

CHAPTER THIRTY-FIVE

410 Oak Avenue
3:45 P.M.

Troy was scared. He slung the empty can across the kitchen and reached inside the fridge for another. The milk he shoved aside was expired. He slammed the fridge door, shook the magnets holding his little girl's artwork. His gut clenched. Goddamn it all to hell. He looked around at the empty kitchen. Dirty dishes were piled in the sink. The whole fucking place was a wreck.

Patricia had left him.

He popped the top on the beer and guzzled it down in one long, sucking swallow. He exhaled a belch and tossed the can in the corner with the last one. One can at a time just wasn't doing the job. He dived back into the fridge and grabbed a fresh six-pack and stalked off to the living room. He flopped into his recliner and popped the top on another.

The pain started to swell again and he tried his best to wash it away with more beer.

Keith was dead. And it was his fault.

"Fuck." He gulped down the rest of the beer and slung the can away. This time instead of reaching for another beer he picked up the .38 Smith & Wesson lying on the table next to his chair. He stared at its inviting black barrel. He should just blow his damn brains out and be done with it. His life was over. He'd lost his sister. He'd lost his wife and kids. He'd lost his best friend.

The man responsible for all of it was walking around free. Happy-fucking-go-lucky like nothing had ever happened. Clint Austin had come back to this town and torn it apart.

Someone had to make him pay.

Troy laughed at himself. He'd been saying that for a fucking week and he hadn't done a damned thing about it except break a few things and tear up a few damned pictures. He'd just gotten drunker and passed out.

He'd called Keith a coward when *he* was the fucking coward.

His fingers tightened on the butt of the weapon.

By God it was time he made this right. He knew one surefire way to lure Clint Austin into a trap.

Emily Wallace.

CHAPTER THIRTY-SIX

302 Dogwood Drive
4:30 P.M.

Justine was home.

Clint would be furious when he found out Emily had left the inn without him. But she couldn't wait any longer. Ray was dead. God, she couldn't believe it. How could this be happening? What were the police doing about it? Besides questioning Clint.

She had to get to the truth. She'd left Clint a note telling him where she'd gone in case he was released before she'd finished here.

The whole concept of what she was about to do felt insane. Justine had been her friend. Everyone's favorite teacher. All the cheerleaders loved her. What could she have hoped to gain by hurting Heather?

It just didn't seem logical or possible.

Then again, the missing necklace was the only other piece of evidence besides the knife. That left Emily with little choice except to follow the only clue she had.

She leaned her head back against the seat—Ray and

Keith were dead. Her chest constricted with regret. Their murders gave her all the more reason to suspect that what she and Clint were doing was not only right but also necessary. Someone was killing off every single person who might have known the truth about that night.

Someone had to do the right thing. Clint was being held for questioning, so that left her.

Emily got out of the car and walked up the sidewalk to the porch. Justine had lived in this small house since coming to Pine Bluff. She liked calling it a cottage. And it did sort of look like one with lots of architectural features and lovely fretwork. Very old world. Oodles of flowers.

Not the kind of place where a murderer lived.

Emily pressed the doorbell and waited, working hard to keep her respiration even.

The door opened and Justine appeared, her eyes red and swollen. "Emily. Did you hear the news about Ray? It's just awful."

"I did. It's terrible."

Justine's white skirt and halter blouse showed off her tan. She'd woven her blonde hair into a French braid. She looked beautiful as usual, but she also looked grief stricken. Emily should have thought of that. She'd been out of the loop so long she'd forgotten how close all of these people still were.

"You just caught me." Justine's voice was raw with emotion.

Emily mentally scrambled for the proper response. "Maybe I should come back another time." God, she didn't want to wait. She wanted to do this now!

"No. No. I was just going shopping for funeral dresses." Justine pressed a hand to her chest. "I can't believe it." With monumental effort, she drew in a breath, seemed to compose herself. "Please, come on in."

Emily went inside, briefly admired the comfortable furnishings. She remembered then that Justine had more framed photographs than anyone she knew. They were everywhere. That was Justine's hobby, she'd always said, the thing that kept her grounded.

"Would you like something to drink?" Justine asked, then sniffed and pressed a tissue to her nose.

"No, thanks." Where to start? Emily had planned this; stick with the plan. "I saw Violet this afternoon."

Justine motioned for Emily to take a seat on the sofa while she curled up in a chair. "How is she?"

"She's Violet," Emily allowed. "She won't let anyone see her pain."

"I know she must be absolutely devastated." Justine shook her head, anguish on her face. "I just can't imagine who would do such a thing. Keith was such a great guy. And Ray. My God. Everyone loved him."

Emily clasped her hands together to prevent their shaking. "It's hard to believe they're really gone."

"Did Violet say when the funeral will be held? I'm sure it's too early to know anything about Ray's."

How could Emily sit here and believe that this woman, a woman she'd known more than half her life, was a murderer?

"Depends upon the autopsy, I think." No matter what Emily wanted to believe, she had to see this through. "You know," she began, her voice sounding too chipper even to her, "while I was there Violet showed me her senior necklace. Can you believe she still has it? After all this time?" She shook her head. "I don't know what happened to mine. I guess I lost it."

Justine folded her hands in her lap, stared straight into Emily's eyes, but her gaze was blank, distant. "That's a shame."

Do it! Emily braced. "Do you still have yours?"

A tiny line formed between Justine's eyebrows. "I'm sorry, what did you say?"

"The necklace," Emily prompted, feeling horrible for pursuing the subject.

"Oh." Justine blinked. "The necklace. I haven't worn mine since Heather . . . passed away. I didn't want to risk damaging it or losing it. It's been right there in my jewelry box ever since." Regret clouded her eyes. "You girls were the first to get the necklaces. It didn't seem right to give them to anyone else after what happened. I went back to the charm bracelets after that year."

"I feel terrible about losing mine." God, she hated lying.

"Would you like me to get you another, Em?" Justine offered. "I don't mind trying. It might not be exactly the same, but it would probably be close."

This was the woman she wanted to accuse of murder?

"That . . ." Nothing in her plan about this. "That would be wonderful."

"Consider it done." Justine managed a faint smile, the effort visible. "Just give me your address in Birmingham before you go and I'll take care of it."

Banging on her front door drew Justine's attention there. She frowned as she pushed to her feet. "Excuse me, Em."

Deviation from plan. What did she do now? Emily pushed to her feet. "Could I use your bathroom?"

Justine hesitated before opening the door. "Sure. Down the hall and on the left."

Her heart thudding in warning, Emily forced her legs to move at a normal pace as she went from the living room to the hall. Three doors. One on the left, two on the right.

Shouting stopped her dead in her tracks. Both voices female. Her heart felt as if it had stopped as well. The voices turned hushed. Emily started moving again. First room on the right was a home office. The second, Justine's bedroom. The span of floor space between the bathroom and the bedroom was only about six feet. Hardly anything at all. She could do it.

Emily went into the bedroom. She glanced around, took stock of where things were. The jewelry box sat atop the dresser. She went there. Listened to ensure Justine was still engaged in conversation.

Her hands shaking, Emily opened the jewelry box. Didn't even consider that it might be one that played music until she'd opened it. She held her breath. No sound came from the box.

Thank God.

She listened again. Justine and her visitor were still talking.

Working as fast as she could, she sifted through the necklaces, bracelets, and earrings. It wasn't there.

Damn.

Then she saw the huge jewelry box that stood upright like a small dresser. Her pulse raced.

Do it.

She crossed to the jewelry box, but the array of framed photos on the bureau distracted her. Lots and lots of pictures of Justine . . . and some with Misty. One photo in particular intrigued Emily. Justine and Misty looked really young . . . grade school maybe. Emily picked up the photograph. Voices echoed in her head. Heather talking about creepy Misty Briggs. Marv saying she was weird. The memory of running into Misty outside Fairgate's house. But was any of that relevant? It felt strange, but was it important to what had happened to Heather? Not likely.

Emily replaced the framed photo and settled her attention back on the larger jewelry box. The hushed voices indicated Justine was still distracted. Emily moved across the room, opened drawer after drawer. Each one held expensive jewelry. Incredible pieces. How on earth did a teacher afford such luxury?

Last drawer, this one was the deepest. No necklace, no jewelry, period. More photos. A whole stack. The photo on top made Emily's eyes go wide. "Oh, my God." The words rushed out on a breath.

Her pulse blipping wildly, she withdrew the stack and studied the photo on top more closely. Two young men engaged in a sexual act . . . did she know those guys? The profile of the tall one with blondish hair looked vaguely familiar.

The other one had his back to the camera . . . he was on his knees.

The tempo of the conversation in the other room rose, then fell again. Emily stared at the door, told her heart to slow. She had to hurry.

She shuffled through the stack. Her fingers shook as she recognized Justine in one. A man, his face obscured by Justine's hair, was giving it to her from behind. The third person in the photo was female. Emily couldn't see her face, since she knelt in front of Justine . . . her hands on Justine's hips, her face pressed to the juncture of her thighs. The woman on her knees had long brownish hair. Misty? Emily couldn't be sure, but the hair color was right.

Okay, this was none of her business. She reached to put the stack back into the drawer and a change in the intensity of the voices jerked her attention back to the door. She had to hurry. Emily shoved the pictures into the drawer and started to turn away. Something on the floor snagged her attention. *Damn!* One of the photos. She'd dropped one.

The front door closed. The sound unmistakable.

Shit.

She snatched up the photo and hurried to the bedroom door, then across the few feet that stood between her and having to answer a hell of a lot of questions.

She eased the bathroom door closed, prayed it wouldn't creak. She flushed the toilet. Turned on the water in the sink to make it seem as if she'd been doing her business.

She needed a reason for being in here so long.

The blood pounding in her head made it difficult to think. She set the photo aside, splashed water on her face, and rubbed her eyes hard. She turned off the water, grabbed tissues from the box on the toilet tank, and prepared to rejoin her hostess.

The picture! Emily grabbed it off the counter. Shuddered at the images. She couldn't possibly know these guys.

What the hell did she do with the damned thing? If she

left it behind, Justine would most likely find it. She'd just have to take it with her. She slid it inside the waistband of her panties. Gross but necessary, since she didn't have any pockets.

Okay. Now. She took a breath and opened the door.

Justine was standing in the hall right outside.

Emily yelped.

"I'm sorry," Justine said. "I thought something was wrong."

Emily dabbed at her eyes. "I guess talking about everything . . ." She shook her head, blew her nose. "Sorry."

"Oh, Em, I understand." Justine put her arm around Emily's shoulders and escorted her back to the living room. "Would you like a brandy or something?"

Emily prayed the photo wouldn't start slipping downward. She flashed Justine a weak smile. "I should go. Let you get to your shopping." She grabbed her purse from the arm of the couch and tried her level best not to look nervous or guilty. "I hope I didn't cause you to rush away your company."

"It was nothing," Justine assured her. "A persistent salesperson." She placed her hand on Emily's arm as they walked to the front door. "I'm so glad you stopped by, Em. I'm sure I'll see you at the funerals."

"Of course," Emily promised. Her knees felt weak with relief as she crossed the threshold toward freedom.

"Emily."

Slowly, Emily turned to face Justine. "Yes?"

"Did you forget something?" Justine waited expectantly.

Emily's fingers tightened on her purse. Justine couldn't know. "Did I?"

"I need your address," Justine said. "So I can mail you a new necklace if I locate one."

"Oh. Right."

Emily gave her the address, thanked her again, and somehow managed to walk, not run, to her car. Justine waved as Emily backed out onto the street. As she drove away she passed a black car that looked vaguely familiar. Emily did a double take. Was that Misty Briggs? Too late to tell without driving past again. She damn sure wasn't driving back that way again.

Emily didn't breathe easy until she had gotten back to her room at the inn. She'd had to make a stop by the office for a key, since she'd given hers to Clint.

She took the photo from her panties, grimaced with distaste. She'd taken a hell of a risk going into Justine's bedroom.

And the pictures. Talk about disgusting. These women were teachers, for God's sake! Emily was almost sure she knew one of these two guys. She peered at the photo in her hand. But she couldn't be positive. In this one a naked, younger Justine watched two men engaged in oral sex. One had his back to the camera; the other's profile was visible. The whole setup very similar to the other photo. Again, the blondish guy in profile looked kind of familiar. Emily shook her head. Some folks were just kinkier than others, she supposed. But it was the photographing of the activity that struck her as odd.

What did she know? First thing to do was hide this photo. She couldn't prove any of this was relevant, but she wasn't taking any chances leaving it lying around. She hid the evidence of her pilfering beneath the bedside table. Her throat felt like sandpaper. She needed water. As she got to her feet, the light blinking on the telephone distracted her.

She snatched up the receiver and went through the procedure for listening to the message. If this was Clint, that could only mean things had gone worse than expected. The voice rasped in her ear and Emily's chest tightened.

"Emily, this is Troy. I need to talk to you. I'm desperate, Em. I need your help." Silence. "Please help me, Em. I'm at home all by myself."

Her fingers trembling, she dropped the receiver back in its cradle. She knew Troy was hurting. Keith had been his best friend. Ray had been Troy's friend, too.

If Troy needed her, she had to see what she could do to help. He was Heather's brother. Emily couldn't let him down. Maybe this would make up for the way he'd been hurt by her change of heart where Clint was concerned.

She wadded the old note she'd written to Clint, then hurriedly prepared another telling him where she'd gone so he wouldn't worry if he got back here before her.

As she drove to Troy's she kept replaying the way his voice had sounded. Definitely drinking heavy and definitely desperate. She hoped she wasn't too late.

First she went to the front door and tried the doorbell. She knocked a couple of times.

No answer.

He'd said he was home. His truck was here.

The possibility that he'd hurt himself had her going around to the end of the house where a garage door stood open.

She wove around the lawn mower, tricycles, and mountains of beer cans and made her way to the door that led from the garage into the house. The smell of oil, gas, and stale beer wasn't a pleasant mix. Cabinets and shelves lined every wall—all cluttered with stuff from Christmas decorations to old buckets of paint.

Rapping her knuckles sharply on the door, she shouted, "Troy! It's Emily!" She knocked again and again, pausing to listen each time. Still nothing.

She should just give up, but he'd sounded so desperate. She reached up to knock again. Pain exploded in the back of her head as she slammed face-first into the door.

She crumpled onto the cool concrete steps and the blackness closed in on her thoughts.

Her mind fought the darkness. She heard the sound of a car engine starting. Heard the rasp of rubber against concrete and brakes engaging tire tread. The smell of exhaust brushed her senses.

Wake up! She couldn't.

Open your eyes! Too heavy.

She was moving . . . sliding across the floor. She bumped something and cans rattled. Hands pulled at her, lifted her, then dropped her. Her face pressed against something soft . . . fabric?

What was happening?

A car door slammed. Then another. Movement. Music. The radio? Yes. The call letters of the station she always listened to as the deejay promised ten songs in a row. Emily inhaled, tried to analyze the smells. Her car?

Emily licked her lips. Moaned. Told herself to wake up! *Open your eyes!*

Her stomach roiled and bile rose in her throat. She swallowed it back. Had no idea how much time passed with the car moving . . . her head throbbing with pain so sharp she had to breathe shallowly to fight it. She floated in and out of awareness.

The forward momentum ceased with jarring force.

She groaned at the ache in her head.

A door slammed. The sound reverberated inside her skull, causing ripples of pain.

Silence.

Another thump . . . like the trunk closing.

Water sloshed on her clothes. Emily tried to open her eyes again . . . tried to reach up and block the splashing but couldn't make her arms move.

Not water, her mind argued, *chemical . . . gasoline?*

Her heart stumbled.

Get up!

Her body was too heavy. She couldn't move.

But the car was moving . . . rolling. Or was it?

Smoke?

She smelled smoke.

Get up!

Metal smashed; something popped as she lunged forward. She flopped into the floor.

Had she crashed?

Was there a fire? She could smell something chemical . . . something burning. Her throat convulsed. She coughed.

"Ms. Wallace? Emily?"

Was someone in the car with her?

Was she even still in the car?

Her head hurt so bad . . . her lids felt too heavy to budge. Her lungs burned. The blackness tugged at her. She needed to go there . . . escape the pain.

"Ms. Wallace, this is OnStar. Our monitors indicate that your air bags have deployed. Can you hear me, Ms. Wallace?"

Emily tried to answer the woman, but her mouth wouldn't form the words.

"Ms. Wallace, if you can hear me, don't be afraid; we're sending help. Our monitors also indicate there may be a fire in the passenger compartment; can you move, Ms. Wallace? Can you get out of the vehicle?"

Fire?

Fear detonated along Emily's nerve endings, sending a surge of lifesaving adrenaline through her veins, urging her body to react. To move.

She forced her eyes to open. Couldn't focus. Her lungs seized and her head spun. She coughed and gagged.

"Can you hear me, Ms. Wallace? I can hear you coughing . . . Ms. Wallace?"

Emily couldn't answer. Her entire focus was needed to try to make her body move . . . to reach for the door . . . she had to get out of the car. It was on fire.

CHAPTER THIRTY-SEVEN

Pine Bluff City Hall
5:00 P.M.

The interview room was becoming an all too familiar place for Clint's comfort. As usual, he'd been brought here and left alone to sweat the possibilities. This time for more than an hour. If that was what Caruthers wanted, he would be damned disappointed. The only thing on Clint's mind was the fact that there had been another murder.

Ray Hale was dead.

Anguish tore through Clint. No matter what Ray had done in the past, he was the only person in this whole god-damned town who had tried to help Clint. Not once had he shown his appreciation.

Clint grabbed back control. He couldn't let his emotions run away with him like this. He was sorry as hell that Ray was dead, but the best thing he could do for the man was find his killer. He couldn't do that in here.

Knowing that Caruthers would be watching him behind the two-way mirror on the wall, Clint sat right where they'd left him. No fidgeting, no looking around, absolute stillness. His goal was to get out of here, get to Emily, and keep her safe while finding some answers. Every time he turned around there were more questions and no answers.

The door opened. Mike Caruthers and Lee Brady, Clint's parole officer, entered the room. Brady took a seat at the table; Caruthers didn't appear inclined to sit.

"Mr. Austin," Brady began, "I would strongly advise you to have an attorney present. The questions Deputy Caruthers is about to introduce could cause you to incriminate yourself, thus violating your parole."

Clint shook his head. "I don't have anything to hide." He shifted his gaze to the deputy. "Say what's on your mind, Caruthers."

"Have you ever been to Ray's hunting cabin?"

"No. He offered it to me as a temporary place to stay after my house burned, but I declined."

"Where were you between noon and two P.M. today?"

That was easy. "At work until one. You can check with Marvin Cook and the rest of the employees at the repair shop. I left at one and drove straight to the Valley Inn. I was with Emily Wallace after that until you picked me up. The manager at the inn saw me arrive shortly after one, and Emily and I left around two to go to Violet Turner's house."

Clint wasn't sure whether it was disappointment or relief he saw in the deputy's eyes. Maybe a mixture of both.

"Can you identify these?" He placed a plastic evidence bag on the table, the contents a handful of ripped photos.

Clint studied the fragments, then said, "Torn photographs. I'd have to piece them together somewhat to be certain, but they look like some of the ones from my house. You saw the place after it was vandalized." He didn't have to remind Caruthers, but for Brady's sake he did. The memory of all his mother's damaged things squeezed his heart.

"Is there any reason Ray would have these in his possession?"

"As a favor to me, Ray took some of the pieces to a guy he thought could restore them. But I can't say whether these are any of the ones he took, not without touching them and maybe not even then."

"Once I've confirmed your alibi, you'll be free to go, but stay close to home or work. I may need to question you again. And," Caruthers glanced at Brady before proceeding and he nodded, "we're going to need to do DNA testing on any person of interest related to Keith's case."

"If you don't offer the sample voluntarily," Brady explained, "they'll get a court order. I've been made aware of the names on the list. There are several others, Mr. Austin, so don't feel singled out."

"No problem."

Caruthers turned his back and headed for the door.

Clint almost didn't ask, but he needed to know. "Can you tell me what happened?"

Caruthers hesitated but didn't look back. "We're not releasing any of the details yet. When we do, you'll read about it in the paper like everyone else."

No matter that Clint's alibi was rock solid, no way they could try to nail this on him, Caruthers didn't like him or trust him because of the past. But then, Clint had known it would be this way. There were simply some things a man couldn't live down.

Innocence would never be enough.

Valley Inn
6:15 P.M.

Clint knocked first, but when there was no answer he used the key Emily had given him and entered the room. It felt a little different, being trusted with her key. But it was only a rented room, nothing to get excited about.

"Emily?"

He checked the bathroom. No Emily.

Since her car wasn't out front, she might have decided to

spend some time with her parents, but he didn't like not knowing.

He noticed the note on the dresser then.

He swore. What the hell did she mean, meeting Baker alone?

He tossed the note back on the dresser and glanced at the clock. She'd left the time on the note. She'd been gone for an hour.

He was going over there.

410 Oak Avenue
6:40 P.M.

Baker's house was silent, but his truck was in the driveway.

Clint parked behind Baker's vehicle and got out, his senses on alert to some danger he couldn't name.

If Emily had left already, where had she gone? He supposed she could have taken a different route back to the inn.

He banged on the front door. Stabbed the doorbell a couple of times.

No answer.

Not a sound.

Well, hell. If he was going to break into the guy's house before dark, he'd better do it from the back. His lock-picking tools had been confiscated. Maybe he'd have to try kicking the door in. As long as it wasn't steel.

At the end of the house the garage door was open, so he checked there first. The garage was cluttered with junk, lawn maintenance implements and piles of beer cans. Baker was evidently starting a collection.

Steel entry door leading into the house.

Great.

Clint tried the knob, and to his surprise the door was unlocked.

Inside, the place was as dark as a tomb. Clint stayed still for half a minute and listened for any signs of life.

Nothing.

He flipped a switch in the kitchen and an overhead light flickered on. His apprehension mounting, Clint surveyed the room. Baker's wife must be on strike.

Clint moved toward the living room, then turned on a light in the short hall. Every damned blind in the house was closed tight. Baker was stretched out in his recliner apparently dead to the world. Clint watched a few seconds to make sure he was breathing. He looked like shit. Both eyes black, nose swollen.

Yep.

A .38 lay on the table by his chair. Using a dirty sock from the floor, Clint lifted the weapon and placed it on top of the entertainment cabinet out of sight and reach. Then he grabbed Baker by the shirtfront and hoisted him out of the chair. His eyes tried to open but couldn't seem to stay that way.

"Baker." Clint shook him. "Wake up, you little bastard."

Baker's eyes started that blinking, upward-roll thing.

"I said, wake up!" Clint shook him harder.

He started to struggle, mumbling nonsensical words.

Clint hauled him into the nearest bathroom and shoved him into the shower. He turned the cold water on full blast.

Baker screamed and cursed and tried to bolt.

Clint blocked his path out of the three-by-three tile cubicle. "Come alive, Baker; we need to talk."

Baker's eyes widened and fury blazed across his face. "I knew you'd come if I called her over here."

"Where is she?" Clint slammed him against the wall and held him there. He ignored the cold water.

Confusion scrunched Baker's face. "I . . . she didn't show." The fury made a reappearance. "But you're here. . . ."

Clint turned off the water and dragged Baker's ass into

the kitchen. He needed to speed up the process. He knew plenty of tricks. He'd learned them firsthand in Holman.

He plopped Baker into a chair at the kitchen table. Clint searched a couple of drawers until he found what he wanted. Baker attempted to get up, but Clint slapped a hand on his head and shoved him back down. His level of intoxication made him easy to control.

Clint sat down next to him and manacled the other man's right hand. He flatted it on the table, palm down, and held it in place with his left. "Now, tell me where she is."

"I don't have to tell you shit."

Using his free hand, Clint positioned the point of the knife's long, slender blade against Baker's hand at a strategic spot. "Tell me."

"Fuck you."

The slightest pressure and the knife pierced the skin, slid right between two bones and into the laminate tabletop beneath. Blood bloomed and slid around the wound. Baker screamed, thrashed his legs around a bit, but he didn't dare move his hand.

"Tell me where she is."

"She didn't come! I passed out. If she came by after that, she left without trying to get me up." His eyes were wild when they connected with Clint's. "I swear. I didn't see her." His voice shook.

Clint pulled the knife free but didn't release Baker's hand. The guy howled as if Clint had cut the damned thing off.

"Why did you call her?"

Troy glared at him. His eyes looking like road maps, his face red from consistent overindulgence in alcohol.

"Why?" Clint repeated as he positioned the knife again.

"Nooo!"

"Tell me," Clint urged. "This only has to hurt as much as you want it to."

"Because I wanted to get you here," Baker cried.

"Why?" The knife remained poised for the next intrusion.

"I want you to pay, you sonofabitch!"

Clint let that go. "Any other reason?"

"My life is falling apart," Baker cried. He started to sob. "My wife left me. She took my kids." His whole body shook with his anguish. "My best friend is dead and it's my fault."

Clint stilled. "Why is it your fault?"

Troy wiped his face with his free hand. "What the fuck's it to you?"

The tip of the knife pierced skin in the next spot.

Baker howled. It really wasn't that bad, but the alcohol magnified everything. This technique didn't hurt nearly as much as numerous others Clint could have used. It was the watching it happen that got to the victim.

"We had a fight!" he screamed. "He told me that he cheated on Heather that night."

Clint wasn't sure her boyfriend's cheating was relevant to her murder but pursued it anyway. "That's it?"

Baker glared at him the best a drunk could. "He was fucking another woman the night my sister was murdered."

"That's what you wanted to talk to me about?" This wasn't right.

Baker's face fell into grim defeat. "I wanted to kill you," he admitted. "You came back here and tore all our lives apart." He stared at his bloody hand, at the knife Clint still held over him. "It doesn't matter now. I've lost everything I care about." He settled his drunken gaze on Clint. "You should just cut my throat and put me out of my misery."

"You didn't kill Turner?"

Long pause.

"Why the fuck would I tell you if I did?"

The fear and uncertainty in his eyes told Clint he wasn't getting more than that.

Clint pushed out of his chair. He grabbed a clean dishcloth from one of the drawers he'd looked in before and wrapped Baker's hand.

Before leaving, Clint picked up the receiver of the kitchen

extension and punched in 911. He placed it on the counter. When no one responded a deputy would be dispatched. Baker would survive the injury to his hand, but Clint wasn't altogether sure the guy was safe from himself . . . or whoever the hell had killed Turner and Ray.

Clint wiped the knife clean and tossed it into the sink. "Sober up, Baker."

"He's dead because of me."

Clint hesitated at the door. "Who's dead because of you?"

"Keith," Baker said, his voice feeble. "I called him a coward, told him he should just kill himself and get it over with for what he'd done . . . or I'd make him wish he had."

This conversation wasn't going to make sense until Baker was sober. But something had gone down between him and Turner before he died.

Right now Clint had to find Emily.

9:00 P.M.

Clint drove around for hours with no luck. He finally returned to the inn. She hadn't come back there, either.

He'd gone by her parents' house and all of her friends', at least the ones he knew about. She wasn't anywhere.

Fear had his heart pumping double time. He was calling Caruthers. Emily wouldn't just disappear like this.

The phone's message light blinked at Clint. He snatched it up and punched the necessary buttons for retrieving the message.

"Clint . . ."

It was Emily. Her voice sounded shaky.

"I'm at the hospital. Can you come when you get this message, please? I need you."

CHAPTER THIRTY-EIGHT

Mercy Hospital
10:00 P.M.

Emily just wanted to get out of this place.

"You're sure it's okay to leave?"

She was just about to lose her patience with Clint. "Yes. That's why they released me. I'm fine."

"But you have a concussion."

"Let's go, Clint." She'd had enough trouble talking the doctor out of keeping her overnight. She had to get out of here. She and Clint were on to something and it wouldn't wait until tomorrow. Someone had attacked her in Troy's garage. She wasn't ready to believe it was Troy . . . but she had to face the fact that he might be involved.

Clint kept his arm around her waist as he gently guided her to his truck, then helped her inside.

"I don't like this," he muttered.

"I'm fine," she repeated. No thanks to whoever had tried to kill her. She shuddered. *Someone had tried to kill her.*

Clint looked at her a long moment, then closed the door. He hurried around the hood and slid behind the wheel.

"Tell me what happened?" He started the engine and backed out of the parking slot.

"Troy called." She hadn't been able to talk to Clint around all the hospital staff.

"I know that part," Clint said tightly.

"I went into the garage to try and get into the house, since he didn't answer the front door. Someone ambushed me. Drove me and my car out to Route Ten."

Clint's silence told her he was fuming.

"Thank God for OnStar." She closed her eyes and fought the emotion that tried to overwhelm her. She hated to tell Clint the rest, but considering he'd had to bring her clothes there wasn't really any way to get out of explaining what had happened to the ones she'd been wearing.

"Someone set my car on fire with me in it," she said finally. "When they pushed it into the ravine it hit a tree and the air bags deployed. The voice coming from OnStar helped me get out. . . ." She shuddered, remembered the moment when that adrenaline rush had given her the strength she needed to move.

One of the cops had told Emily that the fire had been in the front seat and had burned itself out since so much of the vehicle's interior was flame-retardant. What could have killed her, though, was if her clothes had flamed, since she'd been drenched in gasoline. For some reason, that hadn't happened. Either she was damned lucky or her would-be killer had screwed up. Emily shuddered again. "I stumbled out of the car and the next thing I knew the police and fire department were there. They're towing my car in for forensics testing."

"Sonofabitch!"

Emily closed her eyes and rode out the rest of the curse words, some of which she'd never heard before. Prison slang, she supposed.

"Feel better?" she asked when he'd finished. He shot her a look that was a definite no.

She had no idea where her purse was, but at least she had

her cell phone. She'd found it on the ground next to her car. She didn't remember grabbing it inside the car before she got out or dropping it. Since it was her phone and the last call made on it was one she'd made and she'd obscured any possible prints, the officer had agreed to let her keep it and not log it into evidence.

"Okay." Clint glanced at her, his face lined with fury. "My turn."

He told her how the interview with Deputy Caruthers went off without a hitch. Or so it seemed.

"When I got back and found your note I went to Baker's looking for you."

She tensed. "Did you find him?"

He nodded. "He was passed out in his living room."

"So," she ventured, "he wasn't likely the one who did this to me?"

Clint thought about that a moment. "I don't think so."

Emily sagged with relief. Another thought occurred to her. She moistened her dry lips. "So, did you talk to him?"

"Yeah. In fact, he was brought into the ER just as I got there to pick you up."

"You roughed him up that badly?" If Troy wasn't the one to ambush her, then he was only guilty of the same thing she had been guilty of—blaming the wrong guy for killing Heather.

"I didn't put him in the hospital," Clint assured her. "Alcohol poisoning and possibly dehydration probably did that. It'll be better if they keep him a few days. He needs to sober up and stay out of trouble until . . ." He heaved a big breath.

"Until what?" She needed him to be up-front with her.

"Until this is over. Whoever killed Ray, and maybe Keith, may have other names on their list besides yours and mine."

"But why would anyone kill Troy? He doesn't know anything about that night." Obviously someone had used Troy . . . or was watching her and had taken advantage of the opportunity.

"Maybe, maybe not," Clint countered.

After he explained what Troy said to him about his last encounter with Keith, she had to agree with Clint's assessment.

"Who would Keith have been cheating with?" She started to shake her head but remembered how much it would hurt. "I don't think it would have been Violet." She couldn't grasp the whole idea. "This is confusing. Keith and Heather seemed really happy that week or so before. . . ."

"Teenage guys can be idiots," Clint offered with a knowing glance in her direction.

She shrugged, knew he spoke from personal experience. The same could be said about teenage girls. "Maybe he was having second thoughts about their relationship." She frowned; it made her head hurt. "But he wouldn't kill Heather for that." She rubbed at her achy forehead, didn't dare touch the back of her skull. "What am I saying? He wouldn't have killed her, period. She was supposed to tell me some big secret that night after I got back. Maybe she knew he was cheating. Maybe she was going to break up with him."

"That's the thing," Clint said. "This all appears to go back to someone who wanted to hurt Heather."

"Maybe the other woman," Emily suggested, since that was the only remaining loose end she could think of at the moment. "Since Keith is dead, I guess we won't be able to find out who he was cheating with unless Troy knows and just isn't saying."

Another memory crashed into her bruised brain. "Wait. Marv . . ." She looked up at Clint. "Heather secretly dated Marvin Cook a few times just to make Keith jealous. . . ." The air in her lungs escaped on the heels of her next thought. "Marv and Keith fought over her that one time . . . no, twice. They even stopped talking for a while . . . but then Heather . . ."

Was murdered. Marvin and Keith became friends again.

"Marvin Cook had a thing with Heather Baker even after she started dating Turner?"

Emily made a wishy-washy gesture with her hands. "Not a thing. Heather used him to make Keith jealous." She hated to speak ill of her friend, but it was the truth. "We all did stuff like that back in high school. We were stupid kids."

"Then I say we see what Cook knows."

10:40 P.M.

Emily let her mind rest the fifteen minutes it took to reach Marv's place. She didn't want to form any opinions until after she'd heard what he had to say . . . if anything. She was certain he couldn't have killed Heather any more than Keith could have. But Clint was right. An open mind, objectivity, was imperative.

Clint shut his headlights off before pulling into the driveway. The double-wide trailer stood on a corner lot at the edge of the farm belonging to Marvin's daddy.

"You stay in the truck." Clint shut off the engine.

"No way." When he would have protested, she pointed out something he obviously hadn't considered. "He might actually talk to me, but we both know he's not going to talk to you. And, personally, I'd like to get this done without sending anyone to the ER."

Clint didn't argue.

The temperature had dropped just barely enough to make it bearable outside without the aid of air-conditioning, but it was still muggy. Good thing, since Clint's old truck had none, except for the windows.

He insisted on going up the steps to the deck first. She knew he wanted to protect her, and on some level she appreciated it. Right now, though, she just wanted to get some answers.

He banged on the door. Emily flinched, hoped Marv's wife wouldn't make a big fuss. What sounded like a TV game show was the only sound inside.

"Who the hell is it?" Marv bellowed through the door.

Emily put her hand on Clint's arm to restrain his response. "Marv, it's me. I need your help."

Clint ushered her back a step when the outside light came on and the doorknob turned. Good thing, too; the door flew open and banged against the exterior wall. Marvin's gaze narrowed when it landed on Clint. "What the hell do you want?" Dressed in nothing but boxers and with a beer in his hand, he glared at Emily. "Are you crazy showing up here with him, Em?"

Emily refused to let Cook make her feel like the traitor he wanted to label her. She had the truth on her side. As far as the crazy part went, yeah, maybe at one time she had been crazy. But right now she was thinking clearly for the first time in a very long time.

"We need to talk, Cook," Clint said. "We can do it without a fuss, or we can do it the hard way."

Cook pointed a finger at him. "I have to look at your fucking face every day 'cause Higgins is a fool, but I don't have to talk to you now. Get off my property!" He directed that same rage at Emily. "And you, you're—"

"Careful," Clint warned, his voice low and lethal.

A twinge of uneasiness rippled through Emily. Maybe coming here had been a bad idea. But Heather was dead. Keith and Ray were dead. There were no bad ideas when it came to attempting to solve their murders, just desperate ones.

"A witness has come forward to confirm Clint's alibi," Emily spoke up. It was past time people knew the truth. "Clint didn't kill Heather, Marv. We sent the wrong man to prison."

His eyes tapered into scornful slits. "You said he did it. You were there!"

"I was wrong," Emily admitted, her chin high, her shoulders square, in spite of the trembling his reminder set in motion. "And for your information, since you didn't bother showing up at the trial, I said he was in the room. I said he had blood on him. I couldn't say for sure he killed her, though I wanted to at the time. His attorney pointed that out repeatedly."

"I've got nothing to say," Marvin snapped, unconvinced or uncaring, maybe both.

"If you'd prefer," Clint suggested, "we could just take the information we've gathered so far to the police. After hearing it, I'm pretty sure they'll want to talk to you."

Clint was exaggerating with that, but hey, if it worked.

Marvin's face turned fire-engine red. "We'll talk right here." He stepped out onto the deck and closed the door. "I don't want Jean hearing any of this." He gave equal time with his glare, first to Clint, then to Emily.

Clint kicked off the conversation with, "The police never bothered to question you when Heather Baker was murdered."

"I wasn't her boyfriend at the time," Marvin snarled before taking a slug of his beer.

Emily wondered how she could ever have thought Marvin was cute or nice. "You dated," she reminded him, her voice sounding small after the men's deep, angry snarls.

Marvin looked at her as if he could rip off her head and spit down her throat. "A couple of times. She just used me, but then you were her best friend, so you knew that. Probably laughed about it." He folded his arms over his belly in a show of defiance.

"She did, but that didn't mean she didn't like you, Marv. Heather was young. We all were. We did stupid stuff." Talking about those days made Emily's stomach even queasier. She wished there were another way. "But nothing she did should have cost her her life."

Emily's last words seemed to take the wind out of Marvin's sails. "What do you want? Last time we talked you were accusing Keith of killing her."

"Keith is dead," she reminded Marvin.

The regret in Marvin's eyes told her she hadn't needed to

remind him. "And so's Ray," he muttered before turning up his beer can once more. "Makes you wonder who the hell's next." He didn't look at either of them as he said this.

Clint ignored his comment and took the lead again. "Was Turner cheating on Heather at the time of her murder? And why didn't the police bother to question either of you?"

Emily frowned. "The police didn't question Keith?" But that was absurd. Even though she couldn't believe he was involved in Heather's murder, logic dictated that the boyfriend would be questioned.

Clint's attention shifted briefly to Emily. "They had me. Why question anybody else?"

"Wait a minute," Marvin piped up. "You're wrong; they did question us. Anybody who knew Heather got questioned."

"And what was your alibi?" Clint pressed.

Marvin shrugged. "I was home all night."

"Who vouched for you?"

Worry etched across his face. "Nobody. . . . I told Chief Ledbetter where I was and that was the end of it."

"Then you weren't really questioned," Clint argued. "They took your word and left it at that. The parading of Heather's classmates through City Hall was for show."

Jesus. Maybe he was right. Emily vaguely recalled some of the other students saying that all they'd had to do was say what they were doing that night. No pressure. No discomfort. A mock investigation. The police hadn't been looking for a killer; they already had Clint pegged. Just like he said.

"So where were you that night?" Clint asked, pursuing the more sensitive issue.

Marvin's guard went up. "I told you, I was home."

Clint eased closer to him. "Maybe you and Turner had it out, then decided to make her pay for using the both of you, or maybe you didn't want anyone else to have her if you couldn't."

Marvin's jowls quivered with the force of his head moving from side to side in denial. "I wasn't that hung up on her.

I swear. I was pissed, yeah, but I got over it. I wouldn't have hurt Heather. No way."

"What about Violet? How did she feel about Turner sticking with Heather through thick and thin? Is that who Turner was cheating with?"

Emily wanted to deny that assertion, but she had to keep an open mind.

"Violet?" Marvin's expression went from worried to confused. "She had a thing for Keith, but he never gave her the time of day. Too fucking bossy."

"Did that make her angry?" Emily was taken aback that the question had come from her. But there it was . . . out in the open.

Marvin's gaze narrowed again. "Hell, she was your friend; you tell me."

"Watch your mouth," Clint warned.

Marvin was right. How could she do this? Emily backed off, wrapped her arms around her waist. "I can't take any more of this. Let's just go to Deputy Caruthers with this information. Let him talk to Justine about our theory and what I discovered at her house," she said to Clint, suddenly realizing that she'd forgotten to tell him about her visit to Justine's. He was going to be pissed. His gaze collided with hers and that prophecy was fulfilled.

"Wait a minute." Marvin's expression turned nervous. "Keith was my friend. Why would I hurt him? Why would I have hurt Heather? Or Ray? This is crazy! Those photos of Justine's are something else altogether. They have nothing to do with any of this."

Shock quaked through Emily. How could Marvin know about the photos? She'd meant that they should tell Deputy Caruthers about Justine's missing necklace and the fact that Ray Hale had "lost" the necklace found in Heather's hand. Surely Marvin wasn't talking about the same photos Emily had discovered.

"They might matter," she challenged, taking a shot in the

dark. And hoping like hell she'd find out what pictures *he* was talking about. Did Justine have pictures of him . . . like that?

"I think Emily's right," Clint said quietly, playing along. "We should all three go see Acting Chief Caruthers and see what he thinks."

Fear bulged Marvin's eyes. "Wait. If you want some real motivation, why don't you ask Justine these questions?"

"What does that mean?" Emily demanded as if she didn't see the connection. She didn't . . . actually.

"Violet had a major crush on Keith, sure," Marvin said with a nod as he looked from Clint to Emily. "But it was Justine who was fucking obsessed with him."

"Justine Mallory was our teacher," Emily reminded. Marvin's suggestion was ludicrous. "Ten or twelve years older than us." Recent headlines would suggest that Marvin's assertion wasn't such a ridiculous idea. As would Justine's apparently strange sex fetishes . . . but still. This was Justine. Everybody loved her. But what about the missing necklace?

Marvin exchanged a look with Clint. Emily didn't get it. What could the two of them possibly share other than species and airspace?

"Trust me," Marvin insisted, his expression manic. "She had a thing for Keith. She got all obsessed and shit with him. When she found out he was dating Heather again that last time, she went nuts. He was *all* she talked about, even when I was giving it to her—if you know what I mean," he said to Clint. "And Keith . . . ," Marvin shrugged, ". . . he was torn big-time. He liked being with Justine. Hell, who wouldn't? But I think her coming on so strong scared him."

Emily felt weak all over. Justine had been jealous of Heather? She'd been having sex with the guys? How could Emily not have known this?

"You'd better not say you got that from me," Marvin warned, his face suddenly going pale. "If she found out . . ."

"So what?" Clint argued. "What can she possibly do to

you now? If she's guilty of what you say, then she needs to face the consequences."

"You *know* she's guilty," Marvin said to Clint, then looked around as if he was afraid someone would hear. "All I can say is, it's like my daddy always told me, down here in Alabama you can raise cattle your whole life and never be called a rancher, but get caught sucking one dick and you're a queer for life." He backed toward his door. "Whatever you do, just keep my name out of it."

Clint couldn't get Emily out of there fast enough. Her head was spinning; her stomach churned.

"Is any of that possible?" she asked, knowing Marvin hadn't directed certain comments to Clint for no reason.

"I remember the year Justine Mallory started her teaching career at Pine Bluff High," he said. "All the guys thought she was beautiful. I was a freshman and damned stupid, but I wasn't blind. She was beautiful."

Emily didn't interrupt him. She was afraid if she said a word to encourage him, the truth she didn't want to hear would come spilling out faster than it already was.

"By senior year, I could see the writing on the wall. She always had her picks. A couple of guys each year, usually athletes. But nobody could prove it and the boys never said a word. I don't know how she kept them from bragging, but nobody I suspected might be involved with her ever talked.

"But I knew." He glanced at Emily. "She hit on me my senior year. I ignored her and that was the end of it. But she had it in for me after that. I barely survived her class."

Emily didn't know how to feel. They were talking fifteen years here. That meant dozens of guys. "Surely someone would've suspected something."

"I can't answer that." He braked for the first traffic light as they entered Pine Bluff proper. "All I can say is what I suspected. Maybe she stopped. Evidently there were blackmail pictures. That sure appears to be the way Justine kept

Marvin quiet." Clint held Emily's gaze. "What were you talking about when you said something about a discovery at Justine's house? Did you find the necklace?"

Oh, hell. She'd forgotten to tell him about that. He wasn't going to like it. "When I went off on that tangent about Marvin I completely forgot." She quickly told Clint what she'd seen and heard and how she hadn't found Justine's necklace where she'd said it was stored. "The pictures were really bizarre." Emily shuddered at the idea that there could be something to what Marvin had said. Definitely those could be construed as blackmail photos. "And all that expensive jewelry . . ." That part suddenly surfaced amid her worrisome thoughts ". . . How could she afford all that?"

"You went to her house," Clint said, his face stony when he glanced at her, "and took that kind of risk? What were you thinking?"

"I was desperate to find out if she had her necklace." Emily still couldn't fully absorb the scope of what they were alleging here. "It's hard to believe I was that close to her all those years and didn't suspect a thing. She was a friend to all the cheerleaders. Everybody loved her." Still did, Emily realized, recalling her recent visit to the school.

"A good enough friend to know about the open window?" Clint asked. "To know Heather would be in your bed that night?"

He braked for a light and their gazes collided again. Emily felt the earth shift beneath her. "Yes."

CHAPTER THIRTY-NINE

Turner Mansion
Midnight

Granville poured himself a brandy, downed it, then poured himself another. He repeated the process twice more before he paused to catch his breath.

He was sixty-two years old. He'd spent the past forty-odd years amassing his vast fortune. He'd worked hard to reach this place in his life. The only thing he'd ever really wanted was for his family to be happy.

There had been sacrifices, of course.

A man didn't reach this level of security without having stepped on a few toes and over a few bodies, figuratively speaking. Those times weighed on Granville's conscience. He would, in the end, answer to his Maker for those choices, but even if he had the chance, he wouldn't do a thing differently. His daddy had always preached one motto: *Do what you're big enough to do.*

As imperfect as he might be, Granville was still a damn good Christian compared to many. He'd loved his wife and she had never known about his indiscretions. He gave to his church and he gave to his community, a hefty chunk, but then, who was keeping count?

Funny thing, he realized, beyond the warm fuzziness of the alcohol finally taking hold, none of his accomplishments mattered anymore.

His son was dead.

Granville had just returned from City Hall, where he'd learned what Troy Baker had to say. Keith and Troy had met to discuss Austin. Keith had broken down and admitted to his buddy that he'd been with another woman that night. Granville had known. Ray Hale had protected Keith for more than ten years. Now both Ray and Keith were dead.

If anything Troy said could be taken for truth, Granville's boy had fallen completely apart at that damned quarry. Troy swore he'd left Keith very much alive.

Surely Keith hadn't taken his own life. Granville couldn't bear to believe that theory. The autopsy might not be able to confirm anything one way or the other unless there had been a struggle before Keith fell. And even that might not tell the tale, since Keith and Troy had fought, which might also explain the extraneous tissue found under Granville's son's nails. Granville had to face the fact that he might never know exactly what happened. He would have done anything for his son; why hadn't he come to him?

Then there was the other question that seared like acid in his gut. Three people, besides Granville, had known what really happened that night, and two of them were dead. Maybe Granville simply wanted to believe there was something wrong with that equation. It beat the hell out of the idea that his son had killed himself.

But the part that drove the idea home for Granville was the manner of Ray's death. The man had been burned to death inside his truck. The pickup was too old to have the fire-retardant materials of newer models or any other safety features that might have helped him survive. They couldn't say for sure just yet, but there appeared to have been head trauma prior to his having been doused in gasoline and lit with a match.

To Granville's knowledge Ray had no enemies who would want to hurt him in such a heinous way. The manner of death, as Caruthers pointed out, indicated a strong emotional motive. There was only one incident in Ray's career that might spawn that kind of emotion.

It would be very easy to blame Granville's son's as well as Ray's murder on Clint Austin and be done with it. If Austin had discovered the truth, he would have strong motivation, he actually had enough even without that knowledge. But he also had an alibi for both murders, leaving Granville with quite a quandary on his hands and with only one other possible candidate.

Granville had suspected his son had the occasional affair. Like the time Violet had come to him fearful that her husband was cheating after finding a gift she was certain hadn't been purchased for her. After all, Violet was not one to wear such wicked lingerie. Then there was the time before the children were born when Violet had been out of town with her folks and Keith had staggered in well after midnight, drunk and with another woman's red lipstick on his unshaven jaw. Granville had been surprised to find his son, drunk as a skunk, at his door that night. Keith had locked himself out of his own house and it had been too cold to sleep in his car, so he'd come dragging home.

Granville certainly hadn't minded the smell of whiskey on his son's breath. A man had a right to pull one now and then. It helped relieve stress, took him to the bottom so he could rise up and be whole again.

The problem was, Granville had smelled more than alcohol that night; he'd smelled *her* perfume.

At first he'd played it off, assuming she wasn't the only one who wore that particular perfume. But that combined with that bloodred shade of lipstick had nagged at him. Eventually he'd asked her and she had laughed, saying she'd helped Keith get home that night. Granville had believed her, had even thanked her for looking out for his son.

Had she been toying with Keith all this time? A more active than usual sex life was something Granville enjoyed, as had his son. Hell, there wasn't a healthy man alive who didn't need a little more than he could get at home in most instances. Unencumbered sex could be a good thing. Everyone got something they wanted. God knew he'd spent a fortune buying gifts for that woman. But could she have used that old secret to drive Keith to that edge? Granville knew her . . . knew her power. If he discovered that she had used that night to manipulate his son, she would pay.

Granville refilled his glass and brought it to his lips.

He couldn't prove any of this. All he had was his instincts. Pure speculation mostly. But there was one thing he knew after years of clawing his way to the top and then fighting ruthlessly to stay there: give a person enough rope and they would hang themselves.

"Gran, baby, where in the world have you been?" She came up behind him, pressed close to his back as she hugged her arms around his middle. "I was so worried. I missed you."

He downed the brandy in his glass and set it aside. "I needed to drive around, clear my head, after leaving City Hall."

"I'm glad you're home."

She loosened her arms so that he could turn around to face her. "Caruthers has Troy Baker in custody . . . seems he was with Keith right before he died. He thinks Keith may have jumped because of something that was bothering him. Wonder what that could have been?"

Uncertainty flashed ever so briefly in her eyes.

"I tell you," Granville went on sagely, leaving the last comment for her to stew over, "the longer Austin hangs around this town the worse things get. My son is dead because of him. He was fine until Austin showed up. His presence pushed him over that edge. I'm certain of it."

"You're right, Gran; we've got to do something. Ray apparently couldn't handle the situation. Caruthers likely won't do any better." She peered at Granville pleadingly. "Someone has to do something. Austin's ruining this town. *Your town.*"

"I don't want to talk about it anymore," he said wearily. "My son is dead; what difference does the rest make?"

She crooked her arm around his. "Let me tuck you into bed, Gran. This day has been too long."

"Did you know that Austin and that Wallace girl broke into the courthouse and pilfered through the files stored there?" he said, fertilizing those seeds of worry he'd just planted. "The man is obsessed with proving his innocence. And now he's got that crazy Wallace girl on his side."

"Let's get you to bed," Justine urged as if the idea of what Austin and Emily had done was of no concern to her.

Granville allowed her to lead him up to his bedroom. She undressed him slowly, lathing every inch of flesh she bared with kisses and caresses. She brought him to the very edge of his sanity with nothing more than those skilled hands and that carnal mouth. He let her. He was only human after all.

Slim, lithe, beautiful, with her lovely full breasts and long, shapely legs. She would try anything to pleasure him. Whatever he wanted she gave him. Like now. She swallowed him fully, drew hard on his rigid flesh, once, twice, then worked up and down with those lush red lips until he exploded so forcefully he bucked off the mattress.

She crawled naked into bed next to him. His eyes closed, but he would not sleep. He would lie here and wait for her reaction. If she went to sleep, as a part of him fully expected, all would be well—as well as could be with his son lying dead on a slab.

If she had anything to hide, she would do one of two things while she still had the cover of darkness to her advantage: run like hell to escape the coming wrath or try to cover her tracks.

Just like the Good Book said, *your deeds will always find you out*. He'd made his share of mistakes; he'd paid the price. He would find out who was responsible for his son's death. And then that person would pay dearly.

CHAPTER FORTY

Austin Place
Wednesday, July 24, 12:35 A.M.

"In the barn? That's where you want to sleep?"

"Yep."

Clint helped her out of the truck, which wasn't really necessary, but at this point she kind of liked holding his hand. And she was exhausted. Totally and completely.

"But what about that nice new trailer?" She gestured to the temporary housing that had been provided by the insurance company. They'd come and set it up without even notifying Clint. He'd been as surprised as she was when they arrived five minutes ago.

"That's where we want anyone who comes snooping around to think we are."

The heavy cloud cover didn't allow much of the moon to show through, just the occasional glimpse. Still sticky despite the cloudiness. They could definitely use some rain. If they were lucky, the ominous sky would deliver.

Clint led her deep inside the barn where it was even darker but, thankfully, cooler. He clicked on the flashlight, had her hold it, while he shook the sleeping bags to ensure no critters had crawled inside them.

"Will this work?" he asked when he'd arranged the bedding.

"Sure." A bed might have been softer, but he had a point. Out here would be safer. Considering how his house had been burned to the ground and that both Keith and Ray had been murdered, taking precautions was necessary.

"I'll be right back."

"Where're you going?" She wanted to stay close to him, but she was beat. Her head had started to ache again.

"To turn on a light inside and maybe try to make the bed look as if we're in it."

Another good idea.

Emily got comfortable and waited for him to come back. When he returned he tossed something on the ground near the sleeping bags and settled in next to her. Not as close as she would have liked. The distance, only an inch or two, felt like a yawning canyon between them. Why didn't he touch her? She needed him to hold her . . . to make her mind stop playing everything over and over.

"Don't be afraid."

His deep, reassuring voice whispering softly through the darkness made her tremble.

"I'm not afraid."

"Yes, you are."

"I'm . . . just tense." Vivid flashes of that first time they'd been together, right here in this barn, escalated that already-building tension. The cool, damp scent of earth and the vague smell of warm male flesh were drugging, and she breathed more deeply. A sudden unexpected breeze filtered in, bringing more scents and sensations. The lingering odor of charred wood . . . the chant of crickets . . . the promise of rain.

"You try to sleep; I'll keep watch. First thing in the morning we'll talk to Caruthers and start keeping an eye on Justine.

If she's involved, she's bound to be getting nervous. But tonight we rest."

She snuggled closer to him and he slipped a protective arm around her. Finally. "Do you think anyone will take us seriously? I mean, if Justine was obsessed with Keith, would she kill him? Why kill Ray?"

They had no proof of anything. Maybe Justine was having sex with some of her students, but that didn't make her a murderer. Sure, her friend Misty was weird, but that didn't make her a murderer, either. None of it connected fully. Especially the idea that Ray Hale would cover up for a murderer. Emily knew Ray. He'd been a good man. There simply was no motivation for him to protect Justine. And the idea that Justine would have killed Heather just to get to Keith was way too far-fetched. It didn't feel realistic or logical.

But then none of this did.

Clint kissed Emily's forehead. "Don't think about it, Emily," he murmured. "Get some sleep. I'll wake you every hour."

The concussion. He was right. And she was so very tired. But waking her so often meant he wouldn't get any sleep.

"We should skip Caruthers and go straight to the Alabama Bureau of Investigations," she suggested. "Or maybe the FBI." There was no way to know who they could trust at this point.

"Good idea. Now sleep. I'm not going to let anyone else hurt you."

She believed him. She was certain that as long as Clint Austin was breathing she had nothing to fear.

3:30 A.M.

Clint sat up.

Emily didn't rouse.

He heard the thud again. Some distance away from what

used to be his house. Sound carried out here, especially in the dark.

He shook Emily's shoulder, leaned close, and whispered, "Stay put. I think we have a visitor."

She sat up. Grabbed his arm when he would have gotten to his feet. "You can't go out there alone."

"You just stay put. I'll be fine." He picked up the tire iron he'd rounded up and eased to the front of the barn.

"Be careful," she whispered.

"It may just be one of Turner's or Baker's friends. If you sense there's trouble, call for help."

Clint slipped out of the barn. No point in waiting until the trouble came out here looking for them. He took his time, thankful that the clouds hadn't lifted. The breeze picked up, bringing with it the first scattered droplets of rain. Finally. Maybe it would cool things off.

And wash away some of the ugliness from the past few days.

He stayed in the shadows until he reached the well house; then he hunkered down to wait out the intruder.

At first there were only small sounds. The occasional brush of a shoe sole across gravel. Another soft thud. The sweep of footfalls across grass. Closer now.

Something sloshed.

He inclined his head and listened.

More sloshing, an occasion shuffle. His pulse reacted.

On the front side of the trailer, facing the road.

He decided to make a move. If he waited on the back side of the trailer he could nail the bastard when he rounded the corner.

Moving quickly, Clint reached the back of the trailer just in time to flatten against it as the sloshing sound came around the end. He braced for a struggle.

He frowned as a strong odor assaulted his senses.

Gasoline.

Holy hell.

He lunged away from the wall, ready to swing the tire iron. "Don't move!"

He froze. A lit match illuminated the face of the intruder. Misty Briggs.

"You come any closer and I'll drop it." Misty wagged the gas can. "I swear."

Sweat popping out across his brow, Clint dared take a step toward her. He had nothing to lose. The way she was waving that can and that match, there could be an explosion any second. "You'll die first."

"As long as you die with me, that's all that matters."

He lunged for her, driving his shoulder into her waist. The tire iron slipped from his grip. The gas can flew from her hand, splashing the remainder of its contents across his torso.

The whoosh of flames around the trailer sent heat searing after him. The match had hit its target.

Clint rolled to douse the blaze that streaked across his sleeve. Misty hung on, scratched at him like a wildcat. He rolled again, this time to escape the roar of the inferno eating at the metal walls of the trailer.

"Die!" she screamed as she fought him, tried to jab her fingers into his eyes.

Clint pinned her body with his own. He blocked the jab from her left hand with his left forearm. His right arm burned like hell from where his sleeve had caught on fire.

Screaming vile curses at him, Misty tried to buck him off. He pressed his full weight down on her.

She reached for something with her right hand. He tried to deflect with his injured arm.

Too late.

Metal connected with his skull.

A circle of flames closed in on the trailer. They needed help. Now! Emily pawed around in the dark of the barn. Where the hell was her phone?

In the truck. She'd left it in the truck.

She ran hard in that direction.

Movement in her peripheral vision caused her to stumble.

Clint and . . . *Misty*.

Misty hit him with a tire iron.

Emily altered her course.

She dived on top of Misty before she could swing her weapon again. They struggled.

Nails dug into Emily's throat. She punched at Misty's face. Fingers twisted in Emily's hair. She cried out but didn't stop pounding with her fists and kicking with her feet. She reared and twisted her torso, tried to throw Misty off.

Misty's head suddenly jerked backward.

Emily scrambled out from under her.

"Get up, you idiot!"

Justine.

"You can't let her get away," Misty wailed as she staggered to her feet. "She knows! Just like Heather did!"

"Shut up!" Clutching a gun in her hand, Justine glared at Misty.

What was Justine doing with a gun? *Oh, God*. It was true.

Emily scooted closer to Clint's motionless body, hoping the argument between the two women would keep them distracted for a moment. *Please don't let him be dead!* She reached out, felt his chest rise and fall.

Thank God.

"Get away from him!"

Emily's gaze collided with Justine's.

"Get up!" Justine aimed the gun at her.

Rage erupting inside her, Emily pushed to her feet. Her head spun and she swayed. "You killed Heather." She flung the words at Justine, her vision blurring. Emily blinked to clear it. "She trusted you . . . loved you, and you killed her."

"She knew." Justine braced her feet wide apart, like the cops on television, as if she was preparing to fire her weapon. "She was going to tell. Something had to be done."

"Don't say any more, Justine!" Misty screamed. "Just shoot her and it'll be finished."

Justine's face contorted with fury that she turned toward Misty. "If you'd done it right the first time, we wouldn't be having this discussion!"

"You can't do it; let me," Misty sneered. She held out her hand. "I'm the one who took care of all the other problems. One mistake doesn't change the fact that you need me to protect you."

"Heather was the only one who had to die," Justine snarled. "You didn't have to kill Keith. He wouldn't have told anyone. He was too afraid to tell."

"He almost told Troy," Misty argued, her voice rising with obvious frustration. "Keith was weak. He was going to screw up everything. I know it." She pounded her chest. "I'm the smart one!"

"He still loved me."

Misty laughed. "He was finished with you. That's why he spilled his guts to Heather. That's what started all of this. Or have you forgotten?"

Emily was torn between trying to make a move and listening to this insanity play out. And then her emotions made the decision for her.

"You killed Heather because you didn't want to lose Keith?"

Justine glared at Emily, her eyes ablaze with hatred. "Don't be stupid. I didn't kill anyone. Misty did it to protect me. No one can pin any of that on me." She sent a scornful glance at her friend and colleague. "Besides, it was Keith's fault Heather had to die. He told her about us. She confronted me. Snatched my necklace off my throat and had the nerve to say I didn't deserve it. After all I'd done for you girls. The bitch was going to go to the police. I would've lost my job," Justine added angrily. "Gone to jail or gotten lynched by some of the rednecks around here. All for giving a chosen few of my students the biggest thrills of their insignificant little lives."

"Heather had to die," Misty chimed in a depraved chorus. "There was no other option."

Justine glowered at her accomplice. "But you didn't get the necklace back. Ray held that over me all those years. That damned necklace kept him from buying our story that Keith was guilty, even with his blackout that night and the blood we smeared all over him and his clothes. You screwed that up, too."

"Ray was stupid, just like all the others," Misty said with a snort of derision. "Men always hurt you in the end."

"Shut up!" Justine screamed at Misty before turning her full attention back to Emily. "You shouldn't have come back, Em. Austin would have given up eventually if it hadn't been for you." She locked her elbows and adjusted her hold on the weapon. "You ruined everything."

Emily's heart stumbled as she mentally grappled for some sort of plan.

"Let me do it," Misty demanded as she sidled closer to Justine, her big eyes fixed on Emily from behind those thick lenses. "All I have to do is say how these two went crazy and I was protecting you from them." She reached for the weapon. "No one will question us. They wouldn't dare. We've got too much on them."

"No." Justine elbowed her away. "You've done enough already. You're the one who made this mess. This time I'm cleaning it up."

"You're upset," Misty insisted. "You don't know what you're doing."

"I know exactly what I'm doing," Justine argued.

Emily risked a glance in Clint's direction. He still lay on the ground seemingly unconscious, but the bunching of his biceps told her he was bracing for a move.

If he tried to stop them, Justine would shoot him.

"I said, let me have the gun," Misty commanded.

Emily had to do something first. She aimed her full attention on Justine. *She* was responsible for Heather's death. And Keith's . . . and Ray's. *She* had ruined Clint's life. And Emily's. *She* wasn't going to get away with this anymore.

Justine shoved Misty aside. "Stay out of my way. I don't need any more help from you."

When Misty protested and reached for the gun, Emily lunged at Justine, knocked her arms upward. The weapon discharged in the air, the sound deafening. They hit the ground, Justine on top. Emily's arms shook with the effort of keeping the barrel of the gun pointed away from her. Justine fought harder, tried to turn the gun toward Emily.

A shoe connected with the side of Justine's head. Her grip loosened. Emily grabbed control of the weapon as Clint shoved Justine off her. Misty, her glasses askew, was hanging on his back, her arms locked around his neck in a choke hold.

Emily scrambled to her feet, her hands shaking but closed firmly around the butt of the weapon. "Get off him," she ordered Misty, her voice wobbly.

Clint pried the crazy woman's arms free of his throat. Misty screamed and bit his ear.

"I said get off him!" Emily repeated, louder this time, but Misty wasn't listening.

Justine clambered to her feet, grabbed the tire iron, and rushed Clint.

A decade's worth of pain and suffering coalesced inside Emily in that split second. The images of Heather, Keith, and Ray flashed in front of her eyes.

The weapon fired. Emily jerked with the recoil.

Justine dropped the tire iron. She stared down at the blood bubbling from the hole in the center of her chest. Then she looked at Emily, her mouth worked as if she wanted to say something, but the words went to hell with her. She crumpled to the ground.

Misty howled in agony. She jumped off Clint and dived at Emily. Clint grabbed Misty around the waist and held her back.

The sirens wailing in the distance sent a wave of relief crashing over Emily. Help was almost here. Her head felt woozy and her knees were weak. She hadn't called them . . . had she?

"Put the weapon down, Emily," Clint urged above Misty's shrieking. "Put it down, okay?"

Emily lowered her arms to her sides as the world started to spin around her.

She'd killed Justine.

The weapon slipped from Emily's fingers, landed in the charred grass. Her gaze shifted from the gun to the woman who had been her coach . . . her teacher . . . her friend. Emily's chest rose and fell with the emotion building inside her. The tears spilled past her lashes.

She hoped that bitch burned in hell for all eternity.

Uniformed deputies rushed toward them, shouting orders.

Emily's gaze met Clint's and the corners of his lips lifted reassuringly. It might not be over, but at least they were alive.

5:20 A.M.

Night had grayed into dawn, bringing a light drizzle with it. The trailer was trashed. And cops were everywhere.

The county sheriff had dropped by to make sure backup wasn't needed. According to what Clint overheard, the arrangement had been set up by Ray a couple weeks ago. Whatever happened at Clint's place fell under the jurisdiction of Pine Bluff's finest until further notice. Paramedics had arrived and taken care of Clint's arm. It wasn't nearly as bad as it could have been.

Once she'd calmed down, Misty had given her statement, which conflicted in most every way with Clint's and Emily's. As Clint watched, the woman was settled into the back of a cruiser in preparation for transport to City Hall.

Clint had a bad feeling about how this would go down. As much as he wanted to believe that justice would prevail as long as he and Emily stood together, history wasn't on his side.

Mike Caruthers walked over to where they waited. "Clint. Emily." He looked from one to the other. "We need to go on down to City Hall and get this done."

Clint figured that might be a good idea, considering the press had arrived in force. "The sooner we get this over with, the better," he said to Emily as he put his arm around her. They were both soaked and exhausted. "You okay with this? You want to call someone first?"

As much as Justine had deserved what she'd gotten, he hated that Emily was the one who'd had to do the job. That moment would forever be indelibly etched on her psyche.

She looked up at him, her eyes sad, her expression weary. "Let's just finish this."

Caruthers escorted them toward the waiting squad cars. "My men will make sure the press doesn't follow. Clint, you'll go with Deputy Fitzpatrick, and Emily'll ride with me."

Emily looked unsure of the arrangement.

"Look, Caruthers," Clint argued. "I don't see why we can't ride together. You already have our statements. Nothing we said is going to change."

"Sorry, Clint, we have protocol on these matters."

Clint knew there was no point in arguing. He kissed Emily's forehead. "I'll see you there." Then he refused to get into the car with Fitzpatrick until Emily was settled.

Once Clint had climbed in, Fitzpatrick pulled out onto the dirt road right behind Caruthers. Clint tried to relax, but with Emily out of his reach, he couldn't. It was a short drive to

town. He had to believe in the system that had failed him
once already . . . it was all they had. No need to get himself
worked up like this, but his instincts wouldn't stop humming.

When they reached the intersection at 18, Caruthers took
a right. Clint sat up straighter.

Fitzpatrick took the left that led directly into Pine Bluff.
Clint turned around in his seat and watched Caruthers drive
off in the other direction.

"Why the hell is he going that way?"

"My orders are to take you to City Hall." Fitzpatrick met
Clint's gaze in the rearview mirror. "I'm certain Caruthers
knows what he's doing."

The vehicle carrying Emily faded out of sight . . . taking
her farther from Clint's reach.

CHAPTER FORTY-ONE

Emily didn't want to think. She kept her eyes closed and tried to block all the things Justine and Misty had said from playing over and over in her head. Now she knew what Heather had intended to tell her. About Justine. Heather was going to tell Emily and then they could have gone to the police together.

Tears scalded Emily's eyes, leaked past her clenched lids. *Damn Justine Mallory and Misty Briggs both to hell.*

Emily would see that Misty got what she deserved, too.

The car suddenly slowed and started to bump over the shoulder of the road.

Emily's eyes shot open. She sat up, looked around. Didn't immediately recognize their location.

She leaned forward. "Deputy Caruthers? Mike?"

The deputy shifted the car into park, released his seat belt, and turned sideways to look at her. "You all right, Emily?"

There was no reason to be afraid. She knew Mike Caruthers, not all that well, but he'd married one of her closest friends.

But she'd known Misty and Justine, too.

Emily blinked, stared at his profile. Recognition slammed into her . . . the blondish hair . . . he was one of the guys in the photo she'd taken from Justine's house. Emily had only seen his profile in the picture. His profile and the blond hair that wasn't quite blond. It was him. She remembered now. He'd hated his carrot top so bad, he'd tried to go blond one summer. As a freshman, she vaguely remembered making fun of him behind his back.

Mike Caruthers had been one of Justine's *boys*.

The fear pressing against Emily's throat suddenly made speech impossible. She forced her head into an up-and-down motion in response to his question. "I'm fine."

"Good." He sighed, removed his cap. "I wanted to do this myself. The others warned me against it, but I know what you've been through these past ten years. I've kept up with your folks, and Ray always said you'd paid a high price for what happened to Heather."

Emily licked her lips, wished her throat weren't so dry. "I . . . I don't understand."

"You don't have to worry. Everything will be fine now. We know Misty is lying. And we're going to take care of everything; you have my word."

Somehow she managed to squeeze two words around the constriction in her throat. "Thank you."

"You have to understand that our information was limited during the Baker investigation. Certain people had to be protected."

Keith. Caruthers meant Keith and his father. He didn't have to say so. Ray had likely confronted Justine about the necklace and she'd claimed Keith was the guilty party. There was no telling what else she and Misty had done to make Keith look guilty. Granville had no doubt paid top dollar to see that Keith was left in the clear. Clint Austin had taken the fall. He was nobody. A guy who was on thin ice with the law anyway. No big deal. Who was going to argue? Who would care enough to?

No one.

That injustice twisted in Emily's chest. Clint never had a chance.

"We'll make sure justice is carried out swiftly and fairly this time. Misty Briggs will be dead before she reaches City Hall. We won't waste the taxpayers' time or money on a trial."

Shock generated a tremor along Emily's limbs. She tried to hold still, certain she hadn't heard right. Absolutely positive she didn't want to ask him to repeat it.

"You may have forgotten, Emily, since you've lived away so long, but here in Pine Bluff we take care of our own. Misty and Justine just got out of control before we realized how much damage they'd done. Even Ray was fooled for a while. But we've got the situation under control now. We'll take care of everything. Justine's home will become a secondary crime scene, as will Misty's; whatever they're hiding, we'll find it."

Then Emily understood. "You're doing this for Ray." She tried to take comfort in that. Misty and Justine had killed Ray. His men likely wanted vengeance.

But these were officers of the law. The bizarre combination of fear and dread and even understanding churned some more, confusing Emily further. She tried to rationalize how this could be right in some capacity.

Caruthers nodded thoughtfully. "In part, you're right. We are doing this for Ray. But Mr. Granville and I spoke shortly before midnight last night. We reached an agreement about how this would be handled. He alerted me a little later to the possibility that Justine might go after you and Clint." With a heavy sigh, Caruthers added, "That's behind us now, but there are other things. Things we don't need to go into, that simply shouldn't be aired in public. We don't want any more harm done to the community and certainly not to the reputation of our fine school. It's better if we do it this way."

Her entire body quaked during the expanse of silence that followed his dissertation.

"Deputy Caruthers?"

"Yes, ma'am?"

She held her hands tightly together in an attempt to keep them still. "Why are you telling me this?"

"Well, now there's a perfectly good reason for that."

Tiny blasts of fear detonated in her veins.

"We don't want that nasty business about Ray having tampered with evidence to ever end up in the media. We know you and Clint stole that report. It really isn't that significant, since the necklace could have belonged to you or Heather or really anyone, for that matter. Unless, of course, you were to make it significant. We all feel that the best thing to do is just let all this ugliness fade into history where it belongs. We want this to end. Now."

He had just admitted to her that the Pine Bluff Police Department intended to kill a suspect and suppress evidence. Why not just do it and let her believe, along with the rest of the world, that it was whatever they decided to report to the media? There had to be more. Her palms began to sweat with the urge to try the door, but she couldn't escape, not from the backseat of an official squad car.

Clint. The idea that he could be killed just like Misty ripped through Emily. "What about Clint?"

"Oh, we'll see that he's fully exonerated," Caruthers assured her. "We don't need anyone getting restless down the line and asking questions. It's best that we all move on with our lives and put this terrible, terrible tragedy behind us once and for all. Don't you agree?"

Funny, everyone had been telling her that for ages. She met his eyes, tried her best not to allow accusation to enter hers. "Sure." Terror pounded in her ears. "You're absolutely right."

He stared at her for what felt like a whole minute. Maybe

assessing her reliability. Emily tried all in her power to look utterly unfazed and entirely agreeable.

"One last thing."

She held her breath. *Please don't let this be worse news.* "Yes?"

"I'm certain you understand that if you fail to stand by our arrangement Clint will have to pay the price."

She wasn't sure what she was expected to say to that. "I . . ." She cleared her throat but couldn't dislodge the wad of dread there ". . . I thought you said he would be exonerated."

"You can count on that," Caruthers insisted with an affirming nod, "just as long as we can count on you to keep up your end of this arrangement. I'm sure you know that these things take time. There'll be an official inquiry, perhaps questions from the ABI or even the FBI. Possibly other testimony. Once that's all settled, Clint will be free to move forward with clearing his name legally. Until then, of course, his is still a somewhat delicate situation. We wouldn't want his parole officer to get his hands on a copy of that video of Clint breaking into the courthouse—"

"Video?" What the hell was Caruthers talking about?

Caruthers smiled, the act unholy somehow. "We were pretty sure the two of you would try something foolish that night, so we took the liberty of keeping an eye on you. For insurance if we ever needed it."

. . . *if we ever needed it.* Emily had to remind herself that this was real . . . not just a nightmare. She'd known these people her whole life . . . how could this be possible?

The rest of the picture cleared for Emily; her stomach filled with dread. "If Brady sees the video, Clint goes back to Holman." And even if his name was cleared of the murder, he would have spent the intervening time back in Holman . . . he couldn't go back there. She couldn't let that happen.

"Right." Caruthers nodded. "We videoed your interview

about that, too. There's no denying it happened. We certainly wouldn't want to drag any of that up *unnecessarily*."

They had her. Had her and Clint both right where they wanted them.

Evidently her silence told Caruthers she'd reached the proper conclusion. "I'm glad you can see our dilemma. We don't want Clint to go back to prison; we just want him to move on with his life. Maybe even move to another town the way you did. Too many reminders of the past here."

Emily bit her lips together to hold back the emotions mounting inside her.

"You do your part," Caruthers assured her, "we'll do ours."

She nodded jerkily. "I understand."

"And the evidence report? Just for the sake of tidying loose ends."

"It's taped under the dash of Clint's truck."

"Very good, Emily." Caruthers settled his cap back into place. "I knew we could count on you."

Sudden inspiration awakened in Emily's fatigued mind as the events of the last twenty-four hours whipped around madly. "Just a minute, Deputy Caruthers."

He turned back to her with a questioning look.

"I'll keep your bargain because I grew up in Pine Bluff and I don't want anyone else hurt unnecessarily. And Clint will move forward with clearing his name."

"I'm certain you have a point, Emily," Caruthers suggested, his impatience showing.

"I do indeed." She looked him square in the eye. "As far as the video goes, I'll happily trade a photo of a buddy giving you a blow job for it. Sound doable?" She smiled at his stunned look. A tiny jolt of shock unsettled her just then as she realized who his buddy in the photo most likely was . . . Ray Hale. He and Mike Caruthers had been best friends forever. "Anything happens to me or Clint and, gee, the world will know your little secret." She thought of what Marv had told her. "That might be a little difficult to live down."

Fury tightened Caruthers's lips.

"I almost didn't recognize you with the blond hair," she added just to ensure there was no misunderstanding. "And, ah, don't get any ideas about doing to me what you're planning to do to Misty. That photo is my insurance, and my attorney knows just what to do with the envelope if anything happens to me." She held her breath, hoped like hell Caruthers would go for her concocted story. She didn't even have an attorney.

"I think we understand each other."

She smiled, satisfied and more relieved than she would dare let him see. "Excellent."

Caruthers checked his side mirror before executing a U-turn and heading in the direction of town. Their gazes met in the rearview mirror. She refused to show the first inkling of fear.

"I will be mighty glad," he said cordially, "to see things get back to normal in Pine Bluff."

Emily held his gaze until he looked away, but she didn't comment. When he'd settled his attention back on the road, she stared out at the passing landscape. She shivered, only then remembering that her clothes were damp from the drizzle making everything look shiny and new. *Normal.*

Pine Bluff and normal were two things that would never, ever again go together in her mind.

CHAPTER FORTY-TWO

224 Old Columbiana Road
Hoover, Alabama
Monday, September 16, 5:00 P.M.

"Clint Austin Innocent."

Emily stared at the headline of the copy of the *Pine Bluff Sentinel* her parents had mailed. She read the first few sentences even though she already knew what the article said.

> Misty Briggs was shot to death on County Road 18 on the same morning she and accomplice Justine Mallory attempted a double homicide at the residence of Clint Austin. The tragic ending gave final closure to a nightmare more than a decade in the making. . . .

The official report had said Misty tried to kick her way out through the rear window of the squad car. When the deputy driving pulled over to the side of the road so that he could better restrain the suspect, she grabbed for his weapon. The deputy had no choice but to use deadly force.

The dead had been buried and Clint's name had been cleared.

Case closed.

How could a small town harbor such depraved secrets without anyone recognizing just how ugly things had gotten? Why hadn't someone noticed?

Apparently the pictures Justine had kept of her many conquests had been powerful enough to keep men such as Mike Caruthers and Ray Hale afraid of anyone ever finding out. The only real question left in Emily's mind was how the hell had Justine gotten all those testosterone-fueled athletes to go along with her?

The fear Emily had heard in Marvin Cook's voice that night on his front deck was somehow the answer. She wasn't sure she could completely let the past go without an answer to that question. She knew how Justine had kept Keith in line, with that concocted story about him blacking out and killing Heather, but what about Ray, Mike, and all the others?

Before Emily could talk herself out of it, she'd called information and gotten the number. She entered it without hesitation and listened through the "Higgins Auto Repair Shop" spiel.

"Marvin Cook, please," she said, then waited while the call was transferred to the shop.

"Cook."

"Hey, Marv, this is Emily."

The silence on the other end of the line told her that her voice was the last thing Marvin Cook ever wanted to hear again.

"Don't worry, Marv. I just have one quick question for you." Since he didn't hang up, she went on. "How did Justine get you guys to cooperate when she made those blackmail photos? I have to know so I can maybe forgive jerks like you." She hadn't meant to let her fury make an appearance, but there it was.

"It's over, Em; let it go," he snapped.

"I'll let it go," she said, forcing a calm she didn't feel, "as soon as you tell me the truth. Last time you'll ever hear from me, I promise."

"She had a special cocktail," he said grudgingly. "A mixture of whiskey and some kind of drug. We didn't know for sure, but we figured it was like that date-rape crap. She slipped it to all of us at least once. We would have done anything she asked."

"Thanks, Marv, that's all I needed to—"

The sharp click let her know he'd hung up on her. She couldn't really blame him. He wanted to put this behind him.

Justine Mallory had been a despicable individual. How could she have looked so normal? And Misty, well, she'd simply been one of those people everyone thought was creepy, but no one suspected of harm. She'd latched on to Justine in grade school and had hung on ever since. The fear of losing Justine's unconditional love had driven Misty to murder.

The cover-up had gone deep.

Emily had the videotape of her and Clint's courthouse escapade. Caruthers had the incriminating photo. Of course, she'd kept a copy, as had he if he was half as smart as she presumed he was. Either way, it was over. The men in Pine Bluff got to keep their dirty little secret, and Clint got his life back.

Emily pushed the thoughts away. She was through with that. Moving on. Just as her parents had encouraged her to do years ago, without the therapy. In fact, she hadn't had a panic attack since . . . since that first time she and Clint made love. Sex with Clint was way better than Prozac or Xanax.

Once in a great while she let the idea that she'd fired the shot that ended Justine's life bother her, but then she remembered how many lives Justine had devastated, including her own, and she dismissed the whole concern.

Clint had moved in with her and they were both focused on the future.

Life in general was good.

"Em!"

A grin tugged at her lips and her heart skipped a beat.

Life with Clint was fantastic.

"In here!"

He burst into the room and her breath caught just as it did every morning when she woke up to find him lying in bed next to her.

"Guess what?" he said, excitement making those gray eyes glitter like silver stars. He swung his big, strong arms around her and pulled her close. "I got an A on the test."

Pride welled in her chest. "I never doubted it for a second. You're going to be the best damned paralegal in the state!" Eventually he hoped to get his law degree, but no hurry. One step at a time. He wanted to be able to counsel those in trouble, especially those in prison. He knew firsthand just how badly good advice was needed.

"We need to celebrate."

She couldn't agree more.

He kissed her. Deeply, desperately, and daringly. She wanted him to kiss her like this every day for the rest of their lives.

They'd gotten married in August and Clint had enrolled in the university with a scholarship funded fully by the State of Alabama. As soon as he finished, he would go to work full-time and Emily would go back to school and go after that medical degree she'd always planned on. Maybe not as a doctor, maybe as a nurse like her mother or a physician's assistant. Once school was behind them both, the baby making would begin. Who knew? Maybe before.

They finally had what they had both deserved more than a decade ago.

Clint deepened the kiss, dragged her down onto the bed,

and, as he undressed her, she made one more life-altering decision . . . she was never looking back again.

Some things were simply better off left in the past.

Other things—Clint dragged her panties off and kissed his way up her thighs—were best suited to the here and now.

And to tomorrow. And to the day after that. . . .

*Keep reading for an excerpt
from Debra Webb's next novel*

NAMELESS

*Coming soon
from St. Martin's Paperbacks*

CHAPTER ONE

*Thursday, September 7, 11:35 A.M.
Key West, Florida
23 hours, 25 minutes remaining . . .*

Waking up dead would have been preferable to waking up with this screaming throb inside his skull.

Ryan McBride cracked open his eyes and blinked to focus. Morning light barged into his bedroom through the slits in the blinds. "Damn." He licked his lips and swallowed back the shitty taste in his mouth.

A few seconds passed before he dared to sit up, and still he regretted the move. He reached for his half-empty pack of Marlboros and parked a cigarette in one corner of his mouth then lit it. Gratefully inhaling the noxious chemicals necessary for tolerating his continued existence, he stifled a coughing jag.

Die, you son of a bitch. Cigarettes were doing their part. The irony was if he'd given one damn about living, he'd be dead by now.

He got up, waited for the room to stop spinning before

taking a step. A muffled sigh drew his bleary gaze back to
the bed. He scratched his bare chest. Who was the redhead
tangled in his sheets? With effort he vaguely recalled picking her up at the club. Barbie or Becky. Something like that.

Maybe he'd think of her name later. Right now he had to
take a major piss. He ambled into the bathroom wishing he
hadn't consumed enough alcohol to totally erase his memory since he couldn't recall bringing anyone home—not
even himself. Just one of the many bad habits he'd acquired
since moving to the Keys. A hazard of the job. Mingling,
blending in. Then again, if he drank enough he slept like the
dead and he didn't have to worry about dreaming.

Even the thought of the dreams that haunted his sober
nights made his gut clench. His hand shook as he took another drag from his cigarette. Blocking the nightmares required the drinking that resulted in mornings like this.

Considering his downward spiral during the three years
since his career at the Bureau abruptly ended, he had decided that, in his case, FBI stood for Fucking Bad Idea. It
was a shame it had taken him ten years of active duty to realize that. Just in time to be fired by the biggest prick carrying a badge.

There were some things a man just couldn't get past.

Ryan McBride, this is your life.

What a monumental waste of air space.

More of that damned battering at his skull had him closing his eyes and trying hard to calm the assault between his
temples.

Wait a minute.

He struggled to focus enough brainpower to isolate a
source.

The pounding wasn't in his head . . . it was at his front
door.

He tossed the butt of his cigarette into the toilet then
flushed it. Moving slow to maintain his equilibrium, he followed the trail of abandoned clothing across the bedroom

and along the length of the hall. He gave up on finding his boxers but managed to locate his jeans just in time for more of that confounded banging. Dragging them on, he stumbled toward the door, wrenched it open, and glared at the person waiting on the other side.

Female.

Her perfume's subtle fragrance resuscitated his sluggish senses. The tailored navy suit, buttoned-to-the throat white blouse and rigid posture told him two things right off the bat: professional and uptight.

"Ryan McBride?"

She knew his name. That couldn't be good.

He sagged against the doorjamb, exhausted from the effort of surviving a category-IV drunk, and measured his visitor with an assessing look. Dark brown hair cinched in a French twist. Oh yeah, definitely uptight. Wide brown eyes lacking any sign of weariness or cynicism and devoid of the slightest hint of crow's feet. Young, early twenties maybe. Despite the inexperience her age gave away, her determined bearing told him she'd come prepared for battle. The idea stirred his curiosity even as he reminded himself that her appearance at his door had to mean trouble.

"Are you Ryan McBride?" she repeated firmly, drawing his full interest to her mouth.

Nice lips. Voluptuous, pillowy. Made him think of hot, raunchy sex.

"Depends on who's asking." He'd spent all that time checking her out and she hadn't once allowed her attention to stray from his eyes. Talk about discipline. Uptight *and* a control freak.

As if she'd read his mind, she squared her shoulders and drew in an impatient breath. The movement accentuated the slight bulge beneath her jacket he hadn't noticed before. On the left of her torso just above her waist.

Well, well. The lady was a cop.

What the hell else did he *not* remember about last night?

"I'm Special Agent Vivian Grace. I need to speak with you on an urgent matter. May I come inside?"

A fed. Perfect. Before he could come up with some pro-found statement that would clarify his position on what the Bureau could do with their need to talk or anything else, a sultry, feminine voice called out from behind him, "Who's at the door, baby?"

The redhead he'd left in his bed, dressed in slut-tight jeans and a hoochie-mama blouse appeared next to him. She smiled for the agent, whose disapproval was written all over her lovely, prim face.

"I can come back in half an hour," Agent Grace offered crisply.

"Don't trouble yourself, honey." The redhead leaned in and kissed his stubbled jaw. "I gotta go anyway." She dragged her French-manicured fingers down his bare chest as she backed out the door, forcing the agent to step aside. "Call me, baby."

He watched her strut off toward the yellow Mustang parked next to his aging Land Rover, purse and strappy sandals dangling from her hands. The wicked sway of her hips jogged his memory as to why he'd picked her out of the crowd last night.

Bonnie? Betty? He didn't have a clue.

McBride straightened away from the jamb. "I need a smoke." He left Grace standing at the door and went in search of his cigarettes. For about three seconds he contemplated calling Quantico and asking what the hell they meant sending some baby agent-in-training down here to harass him.

Vivian Grace couldn't be more than twenty-four, twenty-five tops. Probably hadn't even finished her in-service pro-bationary period. He flicked his lighter, sucked hard, and held the smoke deep in his lungs, mulling over what she'd said. What the hell urgent matter could the Bureau need to discuss with him? Had one of his old cases gone active again? That was doubtful. Every damned case he'd worked was closed with the perp or perps serving time or dead and the victim recovered safely.

Except one.

Pushing the memory aside, he decided there was only one way to find out why she was here. He wandered back to where he'd left her. She hadn't moved. The good little agent doing her sworn duty, braced and ready for battle.

If this was going to be complicated, he needed a little bracing of his own. "I won't be any good to either of us until I've had coffee," he warned.

She didn't object, so he headed for the kitchen. If she wanted to continue with whatever she had to say she would follow. The front door creaked closed and her heels clacked on the hardwood.

Persistent, he liked that in a woman.

He scooped the grounds into the basket, added the water and flipped the switch. The smell of fresh-brewed coffee instantly began to fill the air, signaling relief was on the way.

After a final drag, he smashed the cigarette into an ashtray and returned his attention to his uninvited guest who lingered the entire expanse of tiled floor away. "What do they want?"

"A six-year-old girl is missing and—"

"Welcome to the real world, agent," he cut her off, an abrupt blast of fury churning his gut. What the hell kind of con was the Bureau running on him? "Kids go missing every hour of every day. Your esteemed employer has an entire unit dedicated to finding them. Unless you have reason to suspect I had something to do with the abduction, I can't fathom what you want from me."

The bastards fired him, then they had the balls to come running when they hit a case that confounded their elite unit? *Three freaking years later?* And he's supposed to help them out? No. Fucking. Way.

He didn't owe the FBI squat.

Though his reaction clearly startled her, his visitor wasn't ready to give up. Her chin tilted in challenge, she ventured two steps farther into the room, in his direction. The movement momentarily lured his gaze to the shapely calves revealed by her knee-length skirt. Great legs. Probably ran five at the crack of dawn every morning. Well, she could just turn her sweet little ass right around and run back to where she'd come from. He wasn't in the mood to play whatever the hell kind of game the Bureau had in mind.

"I know your story, McBride. There isn't an agent alive who hasn't heard about the legendary Ryan McBride. That's why I've come to you."

Oh yeah, the *legend*. Another memory he'd drowned with booze.

"I hate to be the one to tell you, but that legend died three years ago, Agent Grace." He reached for a cup, looked to her for any indication she was interested. She shook her head so he filled his own and kicked back a couple slugs of the hot brew. With enough caffeine tainting his veins, he might just reach the point of caring whether or not he survived the day.

"We need your help." Outright desperation flashed in her dark eyes. "You were the best the Bureau has ever had. It's going to take you to save this little girl."

Now there was a seriously *unoriginal* line of bull. He refused to think about the child. This wasn't his case, wasn't his problem. And yet he felt the tension rising, the coiling of emotions he couldn't hope to contain threatening to strangle him. He plunked his cup down on the counter. He didn't need this shit.

"Maybe you didn't pay attention to the last chapter of my story, Agent Grace," he countered, his voice taut with a bitterness he'd tried long and hard, and evidently unsuccessfully, to bury. "They fired me. It got ugly. There's no going back."

"I read the file on your last case," she confirmed. "I'm certain you made the only decision you could based on the facts available to you. Sometimes failure is unavoidable and someone dies. That's the flip side to what we do."

He had to laugh at that. "Deep, Agent," he said, patronizing her. "Do you think that matters? Dead is dead."

"Maybe not to you, but to those of us who admire what you accomplished during your career, it matters."

"Tell that to the kid's father." He turned his back to her, braced himself against the counter and squeezed his eyes shut in a futile attempt to block the images tumbling one over the other through his head. He couldn't do *this*.

"We don't have the luxury of time, McBride." Apparently bolstered by a blast of latent courage, she moved in right beside him as she spoke. As hard as he tried not to react, he tensed. "We have less than twenty-three hours. If we don't find her before then, Alyssa Byrne will die."

Alyssa. The name reverberated through him. He banished it. Couldn't help her. He'd given the Bureau everything he had for ten years. He'd maintained a perfect record. Never failed. Except that once. And the mistake hadn't been his. When the proverbial shit had hit the fan, the Bureau had refused to take the heat. They had needed a scapegoat and he'd been it. A decade of hard work hadn't made a difference any more than his so-called legendary status. Case in point. For nearly a year afterward, he'd actually expected someone to show up and beg him to return to duty.

No one had shown up. No one had even called.

So he had found other ways to spend his time and fill the void left by the part of his life ripped away from him. He blamed the booze on his current on-again-off-again occupation, but that was just an excuse. The ugly truth was that every time an Amber Alert was issued he had turned to the one consistent thing within reach to help him forget that he wouldn't be there—distraction. With enough distraction, he could forget that he no longer made a difference.

That part of his life was over. There wasn't any going back . . . not for Agent Vivian Grace and all her hero worship . . . not for Alyssa Byrne and the people who loved her.

Truth was, even if he wanted to go back, he wasn't that man anymore. The pressure of working that kind of case was immeasurable. If he lost his focus, fucked up, someone died. If he wasn't fast enough, smart enough, someone died. He no longer had that kind of nerve, the edge it took to get the job done. The hero he used to be was long gone. Pretending otherwise would be a mistake. The kind he didn't want to make twice in one lifetime.

Nowadays he was just your plain old, garden-variety coward.

Before he sent the agent on her way, there was one thing he had to know. "Why now?" He couldn't keep the resentment out of his tone, didn't really try. "In three years the Bureau hasn't once acknowledged that I still exist. What makes this case different?"

She searched his eyes, her own still hopeful that he would change his mind. *Not going to happen.*

"The kidnapper," she explained, her voice somber, "asked for you by name. He claims he'll provide clues to facilitate the search for the girl."

That damned headache started bearing down on him again, hammering at his temples. "What kind of clues?"

"Don't know. No you, no clues." She swallowed hard, the effort visible along the length of her slender neck. "No clues, McBride, and the little girl dies."